A Hunt So Wild

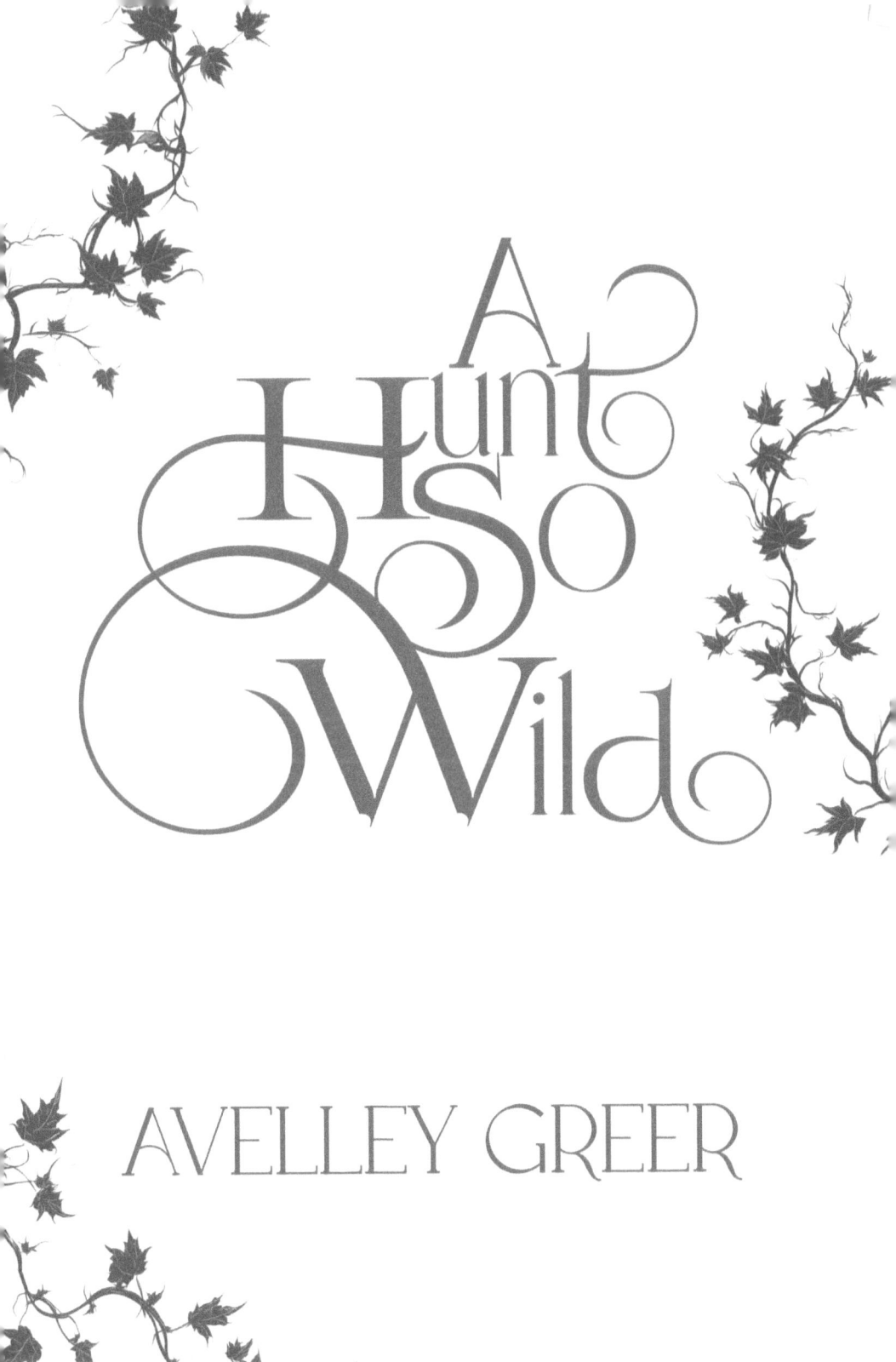

A Hunt So Wild

AVELLEY GREER

Thank you to everyone who has supported and loved my work. Special thank you to my amazing and patient editor, Stephanie, and to Mikayla, Angelina, Stacey and Miranda for being the best hype girls any author could want!

Contents

"To know the dark, go dark, go without sight, and find that the dark, too, blooms and sings, and is traveled by dark feet and dark wings."

- Wendell Berry

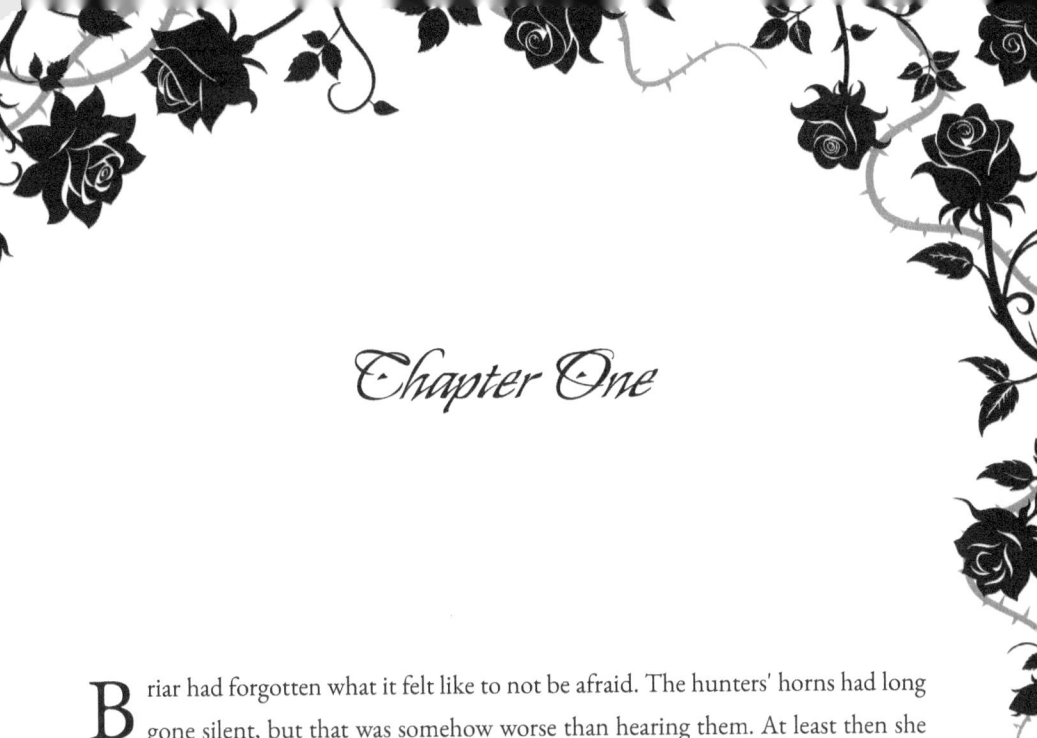

Chapter One

B riar had forgotten what it felt like to not be afraid. The hunters' horns had long
gone silent, but that was somehow worse than hearing them. At least then she
could gauge distance and knew if they were closing in.

She wasn't sure how long she'd been running, one hour? Six? It didn't matter. Time
had become meaningless, measured only in heartbeats and each gasping breath.

All she knew for certain was that she had to stop eventually, even if it was just long
enough to catch her breath and gain her bearings. The question was *where*?

Trees spread out endlessly in every direction, offering little in the way of sanctuary.

She had slowed to climb over a fallen log when something caught her ankle and
brought her crashing to the ground hard enough to drive the air from her lungs. She lay
there for a moment, cheek pressed to dead leaves, trying to remember how to breathe.

As she pushed herself up she glanced back to see what looked like hands, dozens of
them, withered and skeletal, sinking back into the earth and the soil closed over them
as if they'd never been there at all.

What the hell?

Before she could process whether what she had seen was real or a figment of her
unraveling mind, a branch creaked above her.

She looked up just in time to see it descending, moving despite there being no wind.
She threw herself sideways and the branch slammed into the ground where she'd been,
hard enough to leave an impression in the frozen earth.

More branches moved. All around her, the trees seemed to wake, their limbs reaching down with terrible intent.

Briar staggered to her feet and ran.

A branch caught her shoulder, bark rough against her skin, and she felt it tighten, trying to hold on. She wrenched free with a pained cry, felt the warmth of blood as it began to seep down her back. Another branch swept low and she ducked, felt it catch in her tangled hair. She had to stop, had to grab the branch with both hands and pull, tears streaming down her face as hair tore free at the roots.

It was then, she realized that the forest was trying to kill her.

She needed shelter. Somewhere the trees couldn't reach, where she could catch her breath and think and figure out which direction was actually away from the castle instead of in circles through this nightmare forest.

The ground began to slope upward, rocky and uneven. She used tree trunks for support when she had to, touching them as briefly as possible, always ready to jerk away if they moved.

The slope gradually turned into a proper hillside, stone pushing through the earth in gray slabs. And there, partially hidden by dead vines, a dark opening in the rock. A cave.

No trees inside a cave, no hands reaching from the earth. Just stone, dead, unchanging stone.

She stumbled toward it, hope and desperation mixing into something that made her movements clumsy. The entrance was narrow, barely wide enough for her shoulders, but she could tell by the echo that it opened into a larger space beyond. Cold air breathed out from the darkness, carrying the smell of damp stone and earth.

Briar squeezed through the opening, stone scraping against her shoulders, her torn dress catching and tearing further. The cave beyond was small, maybe ten feet across, the ceiling low enough that she could touch it if she reached up, but it was better than nothing.

Water dripped somewhere in the darkness, a steady rhythm that echoed off the walls and she pressed herself into the deepest shadows, as far from the entrance as she could get. Once she was certain she could get no deeper, her legs gave out and she slid down the wall, cold stone against her back. Every part of her hurt. Her feet were raw and bleeding, her shoulder throbbed where the branch had caught her, and her ribs ached with each shallow breath.

But she was hidden. The cave mouth showed only a small slice of gray forest beyond. If she stayed quiet, maybe the hunters would pass by. Maybe she could rest here, just for a little while, long enough to catch her breath and bind her wounds and figure out how to survive the next hour.

She closed her eyes, the warmth in her chest remaining dormant. She pressed her hand against her sternum anyway, as if she could coax it back to life through will alone. Nothing. Just hollow space where that golden thread had once lived.

She was completely alone and that terrified her more than anything the forest could throw at her.

Three days. She had to survive three days of this, of running and hiding and bleeding while the fae lords played their games. Then she'd be free. Free to leave the forest, to go back to her mother and Allegra, to—

Footsteps.

Briar's whole body went rigid. Someone was approaching the cave entrance, not even trying to mask their presence.

She pressed back against the wall, trying to become part of the shadows, barely daring to breathe. Maybe they'd pass by. Maybe they hadn't seen the entrance. Maybe—

"Well, well, we meet again, my lady."

Lord Cairn's pale face materialized from the darkness like something from nightmares, his smile all sharp edges and cruel delight. He moved with the lazy confidence of a predator who knew his prey had nowhere left to run.

"I must say, you've given us quite the chase." He remained just out of reach, savoring her fear like fine wine. "I was worried the hunt would be boring, but you've been delightfully entertaining."

The cave suddenly felt smaller, the walls pressing in. Briar's fingers scraped against stone, searching for anything—a rock, a stick, anything to defend herself with. Nothing.

"You have no idea how thrilled some of us were when Eliam finally cast you aside." His eyes gleamed in the darkness. "All that time watching him parade you around like a prize none of us could touch. And now..."

He took a step closer. Then another.

"Please." The word escaped before she could stop it.

"Say it again. Hearing you beg excites me."

He moved faster than her eyes could follow. One moment he stood watching her, the next his fingers were tangled in her disheveled hair, yanking her forward. Her legs went out from under her, stone scraping her palms as she tried to catch herself. The impact drove air from her lungs in a sharp cry.

"I've been wondering what made our Forest Lord so... protective." His grip tightened, forcing her to look up at him. "What was so special about one little human thief?"

Briar's hands clawed at his wrist, but she might as well have been fighting a statue. "You don't have to do this."

"Don't I?" His free hand lowered, fingers tracing the edge of her ruined neckline, a mockery of gentleness. "If not me, then someone else. Would you prefer Lady Sarelle? She was discussing something about fingers. Very creative, our Sarelle. She always did have a flair for the dramatic."

The warmth in Briar's chest burned suddenly, recoiling from Cairn's touch like it recognized something fundamentally wrong, causing her to flinch. The reaction seemed to amuse him.

"How fascinating. You still carry his mark, even cast out as you are." His fingers found the thorned patterns visible above her neckline. "I wonder if it still—"

A blade erupted through his chest from behind.

Cairn's expression began as surprise before quickly shifting into one of confusion. Blood bloomed across his shirt, and his grip in her hair loosened. He looked down at the weapon protruding from his ribs, its blade devouring what little light there was while leaving strange shadows in its wake.

"You always did talk too much." Thaine's voice carried that familiar dark amusement as he yanked his blade free, letting Cairn collapse.

Briar sat there too stunned to move, her heart thrumming violently in her chest. Thaine had saved her, but to what end? Had she simply gone from one predator to another? The huntsman stood over Cairn's twitching form, taking a moment to wipe his blade clean before finally addressing her.

"Hello, little mouse." His smile was all teeth. "I see you're faring well."

Before Briar could respond, more footsteps echoed from the cave mouth. multiple sets, moving fast.

"Thaine." Lady Sarelle's voice drawled as she emerged from the shadows, two other fae flanking her on either side. "How unfortunate. We invoke hunter's right. We tracked her here first."

"Did you?" Thaine didn't turn, keeping his eyes on Briar even as he addressed the newcomers. "Strange. I only see Cairn's corpse and my lord's property."

"*Former* property," Sarelle corrected, strands of silver forming between her fingers. "You heard his lordship. She has been cast out. Fair game. The Hunt's laws are clear, she belongs to whoever takes her."

"Then take her from me." Thaine finally turned, positioning himself between Briar and the others. Not protecting but claiming. "If you can."

"Three against one?" The fae on Sarelle's left laughed. "Even you aren't that good, huntsman."

"Four," another voice called from behind them. Lord Ashford stepped forward, dragging his blade across the stone, the sound setting Briar's teeth on edge. "You're not allowed to have all the fun, Sarelle."

Thaine's blade hummed, darkness spreading along its edge. "My lord gave specific instructions about the hunt. Three days. Fair chase. You're turning this into a common brawl."

"Your lord isn't here," Sarelle observed, those silver threads beginning to glow. "And accidents happen during hunts. Oh it will be such a tragedy when we tell of how the huntsman fell trying to defend prey that wasn't even his to take."

Sarelle's silver threads lashed out like whips while Ashford attacked from the side, blade singing through the air in a flash of silver. Thaine moved, not the fluid grace she'd seen before but something far more vicious. His blade carved through silver threads, deflected the sword, and opened a line across the third fae's throat in a motion too fast to follow.

But four against one? Even for Thaine the odds seemed stacked against him.

Briar retreated deeper into the cave, hands scraping along rough stone in the darkness, desperate for any way out. The sounds of battle echoed behind her—steel against something that sounded like breaking glass followed by furious snarl.

"You dare use binding magic on me?" Thaine's voice echoed around her.

The darkness around her grew denser and more suffocating. She made it only a few more paces when suddenly she was back in the Oubliette—forgotten, alone, waiting to die in the dark. Her breath came in sharp gasps, panic clawing at her chest.

Breathe, she told herself, but she couldn't get her lungs to cooperate.

Then she saw it. A single golden flower, pale and luminous, growing from bare stone.

Another bloomed beside it. Then another. A path of impossible blooms once again unfurling in the darkness, their soft light revealing a passage she wouldn't have seen otherwise.

The warmth in her chest suddenly pulled with an urgency that had her stumbling. It yanked her forward like a rope around her ribs, and she followed without thought, crawling over stone, squeezing through spaces that scraped her raw.

The flowers bloomed brighter where her blood struck earth, the warmth pulled harder, almost painful in its intensity, as if something on the other side was calling it home.

Her fingers found empty air where stone should have been. A gap barely wide enough for her shoulders. She didn't think, just pushed herself through, ignoring the way her body protested the tight space. For a terrifying moment she stuck, the rock pressing from all sides, her chest too tight to breathe—

Something exploded behind her with enough force to shake the mountain. The blast drove her forward and she tumbled out the other side, landing hard on moss damp with morning dew.

She had emerged on the far side of the hill, gasping, bleeding, but free. As much as she wanted to simply collapse and catch her breath, she knew that was impossible. The victor of the fight would come for her next. She couldn't still be here when they did.

Picking her way carefully down the rocky slope, she reached flatter ground and then she ran.

Her bare feet were numb now, which was better than the agony they'd been an hour ago. She'd stopped looking at them after seeing how much blood she was leaving with each step. The warmth in her chest had gone quiet again, that brief moment of connection in the cave feeling more like cruel mockery with each passing moment.

Without warning, her legs buckled.

Briar went down hard, catching herself on her hands before her face hit the ground. Her arms shook with the effort of holding her weight. She tried to push herself back up but her body refused.

This was it, then. This was how it ended.

She'd thought she was strong. Had survived months with Eliam, had learned to navigate court politics and cruel games. Had believed that made her capable of surviving anything.

Stupid. She was just a silly human girl who'd gotten lucky for a while. But like everything else in her life, that luck had finally abandoned her.

Her arms gave out and she collapsed fully, the ground cold against her cheek. The forest floor smelled of earth and decay and she could feel her heartbeat in her throat, too fast.

They would find her here. Maybe in an hour. Maybe less. She was too tired to care anymore. Soon it would be over and she could finally rest. Her vision had begun narrowing at the edges, darkness creeping in, when something moved beneath her.

Not the shift of an animal or the rustle of wind through leaves. Something deliberate. The roots she'd collapsed between, massive things as thick as her torso, were shifting. Growing. Curving up and around her like protective arms.

She should be terrified after the trees' earlier attempts to harm her, should have tried to drag herself away, but her body had nothing left to give.

The roots did not attempt to crush her, instead they formed a hollow around her, shielding her from view. Moss spread beneath her, thick and impossibly soft, cushioning her broken body. She could smell the green scent of new growth even in the cold air.

The forest was hiding her.

Protecting her.

But why?

The thought barely had time to form as darkness took her between one breath and the next.

Briar woke to the sensation of something crawling on her skin.

Her eyes snapped open, but she forced herself to stay still, terror ice-cold in her veins. Something soft and barely-there traced along the cuts on her arms. Multiple somethings. Moving with gentle touches that—

The *moss*. The moss was moving.

Tiny tendrils had grown over her while she slept, delicate as hair, creeping across her wounds with purpose. Where they touched, the sharp sting of her cuts had dulled to aching memory. She could feel them exploring each injury like curious fingers, leaving behind a strange coolness that numbed the worst of the pain.

A tendril brushed across a deep gash on her palm, and she watched in horrified fascination as the wound looked... smaller. Still there, still angry, but no longer gaping. No longer bleeding.

The moss had grown while she slept spreading across her legs, around her arms, gentle but present. Like being held by something that couldn't quite decide if it was helping or tasting.

A tendril touched her face, tracing the scratch Cairn's nail had left, and that was enough.

She forced herself up with a strangled cry, moss tearing away from her skin with soft, almost reluctant releases. The tendrils retreated into ordinary moss so quickly she might have imagined it, except for the faint green stains on her skin where the deepest wounds had been.

There was a soft creaking sound as the roots parted allowing her to tumbled from the hollow, biting back panic, her body protesting less than it should. Her feet still hurt, but she could stand. Her ribs still ached, but she could breathe.

Behind her, the space between the roots sank back into the earth, returning to their original positions. The moss appeared perfectly ordinary, nothing to suggest it had been anything else at all.

Then she heard it, a cascade of arguing voices, growing closer. She was reluctant to leave, to venture further into the unknown, but she couldn't stay, not with danger lurking so close.

"Thank you," she muttered, not really sure why.

Chapter Two

T he temperature began to drop as afternoon gave way to early evening and Briar moved deeper into the trees. The silence felt wrong, too heavy, as though even the forest itself was holding its breath in anticipation of what would come next.

"You've lasted longer than any of us expected."

Briar stopped short, twisting around to confront the speaker. A fae she was unfamiliar with stepped from behind a tree she could have sworn was empty shadow just a moment before. His antlers branched above his angular face, each point sharp enough to pierce, and his eyes held a hunger that made her skin crawl.

"In case you're considering it, running won't help," he continued, matching her stumbling retreat with unhurried steps. "This deep in the old forest, the trees themselves will turn you around and drive you back to me. They know the natural order of things."

She tried anyway, turning to flee, but the trees had shifted while she watched him, forming an impassable wall behind her.

"Human futility is so endearing." His voice came from directly behind her, close enough that she felt his breath roll across the nape of her neck. "You certainly know how to keep things interesting."

His hand caught her shoulder, twisting her around to face him.

"Let's see what made Eliam so—"

Briar lashed out in desperation, her nails raking across his face before conscious thought caught up to instinct. Four lines opened from cheekbone to jaw, deep enough that dark blood welled immediately, running down to drip from his chin.

He froze. His hand went to his face, fingers coming away wet. For a moment he just stared at his own blood, expression unreadable.

Then he smiled wider, something dangerous and delighted flickering in his eyes.

"Oh, you want to play?" His hand shot out, catching her wrist before she could run. He yanked her against him hard enough it left her gasping, his other arm wrapping around her waist to trap her there, arms pinned at her sides. "Let me show you how it's done properly."

She struggled, trying to twist free, but he held her easily. "Normally I'd leave a mark to match, but it'd be a shame to scar such a pretty face," he explained as his free hand caught the neckline of her dress and tore downward. The sound of ripping silk filled her ears just seconds before cold air hit her exposed skin. "This will have to do."

"No—" she gasped, but his fingers were already tracing down her throat, across her collarbone. Where his nails touched, they tore, dragging lines of fire across her skin. She felt blood well up warm against the cold.

"Beautiful," he murmured.

His grip shifted, his hand moving lower. She grit her teeth as a single clawed finger dragged across the swell of her breast, leaving a welt in its wake.

"Should I go deeper?" he murmured against her ear. "Give you something to remember me by?" The claw pressed harder, and she sobbed. "Perhaps I'll write my name. I'll take my time of course. Would you like that?"

His finger continued its path down across her chest, then back up to her shoulder, each line a promise of worse to come.

"Maybe on your back while I—"

Briar spat in his face.

The mixture of saliva and her own blood hit him across the mouth and cheek. His expression went from delighted cruelty to pure rage in an instant.

He threw her away from him in disgust and she hit the ground hard. She tried to roll, to get her hands under her, but her body wouldn't cooperate fast enough. He advanced on her, blood still dripping from the scratches on his face, his eyes promising violence.

"I was going to make it quick. But now?" He drove a sharp kick into her side that left her gasping. "Now I'm going to take my time with you. To savor every whimper, every scream until you're beg—"

The ground beneath them erupted with a sound like breaking bones.

Massive thorns, each as thick as her waist and sharp as fresh-forged steel, burst upwards with violent force. One tore through the side of her dress at the hip, and she felt its edge draw a line of fire across her skin as it passed. Another exploded up between them, missing her face by inches. The scent of disturbed earth and something else, something green and growing and wrong, filled her nostrils.

But the fae—

The thorn caught him through the middle of his torso, punching through his abdomen and emerging from his back in a spray of dark blood that steamed in the cold air. It lifted him three feet off the ground, his feet kicking uselessly, his expression shifting from rage to complete shock.

She staggered back onto her elbows, unable to tear her eyes away from the gruesome sight.

More thorns burst upward around them in a rough circle, each one three to four feet of organic spear, their surfaces smooth as glass but pulsing with faint golden veins. Another erupted precisely where she'd been standing, and only her stumble backward had saved her. Another to her right, the edge of it catching her calf as it rose, leaving a shallow gash. The pain dropped her to her knees.

"What—" he gasped, his hands scrabbling against the thorn piercing him, unable to find purchase on its unnaturally smooth surface. Dark blood ran from the corner of his mouth, staining his perfect teeth. "You're human—you can't—what IS this?"

She didn't know. The warmth in her chest had transformed into something else entirely, burning with confused fury, lashing out like a wounded animal that couldn't distinguish friend from foe. The thorns looked wrong even to her eyes, not like natural growth but like something had forced them into existence through sheer violent will. They pulsed with that golden light, almost like a heartbeat, almost like breathing.

"Get it OUT!" he snarled, his glamour failing as his control slipped. The face underneath was all sharp angles and too many teeth, beautiful in the way broken glass was beautiful. When he tried to dissolve into shadow the thorn pulsed brighter with golden light and he reformed, screaming. The sound echoed through the forest, too high to be human, too anguished to be anything but real.

She needed to be gone before more fae came to investigate.

Briar scrambled backward between the thorns, her injured leg screaming protest. Her hands found purchase on bark and stone as she pulled herself up, forcing her body to cooperate despite its desperate protests.

"Wait!" The fae's voice cracked. "You can't leave me like this—come back here! COME BACK!"

She ignored him, stumbling away from the thorns, from his screams, pushing deeper into the trees.

Blood ran steadily down her calf from where the thorn had caught her, each step leaving red prints in her wake. She couldn't keep going like this. The blood trail would lead them straight to her.

Briar stopped, leaning against a tree. She looked down at the gash, several inches long but shallow. If she didn't stop the bleeding soon, she'd leave a trail bright enough for even human eyes to follow. She needed pressure, needed a bandage, something to stem the flow.

Her eyes dropped to the dress that was barely more than rags at this point. She grabbed a hanging piece near the hem, gritting her teeth as she pulled. The fabric resisted, then gave with a sound that felt too loud in the quiet forest.

She wrapped the strip around her calf, pulling it tight enough that she had to choke back a cry. Her fingers shook as she tried to tie it, the silk slippery with blood, but she managed a knot that would hopefully hold. The bleeding slowed to a seep rather than a flow. It would have to be enough.

Pushing off from the tree, she continued forward, her gait uneven but steadier.

Briar wasn't sure how much time had passed before she heard it, the sound so faint at first she thought she was imagining it. A rushing that grew louder with each step. Water. Moving fast.

The memory rose unbidden. Some nature documentary she'd watched years ago, curled on the couch with Allegra. A mountain lion hunting deer. The prey had run through a stream and the hunter had lost the scent, circling in frustration while the deer escaped.

Water broke scent trails.

The trees opened ahead, and she saw it. Not the gentle stream she'd hoped for, but a river, swollen with recent rain. The water moved rushed by, white foam churning around rocks that jutted like broken teeth. The sound of it drowned out everything else, a constant roar that vibrated in her chest.

This was stupid. Dangerous. She'd almost died in water before, and that had been with Eliam there to save her.

Behind her, a hunting horn echoed through the trees too close for comfort.

Briar stepped to the river's edge and looked down. The bank dropped off sharply, muddy and treacherous. She could see where the current had carved away the earth, roots hanging exposed like grasping fingers. The water looked black in the shadow of the trees making it impossible to judge its depth.

Another horn answered the first, from a different direction this time.

She sat on the bank and slid down before she could reconsider. Her feet hit the water and the cold was a physical shock, stealing her breath. It rushed past her calves with force that immediately threatened her balance. The rocks beneath were slick with algae, each step she took was a gamble.

The water reached her thighs. Her knees. The current pulled at her dress, the fabric dragging, trying to sweep her downstream. She grabbed for a rock and her hand slipped, fingers scraping across stone. The makeshift bandage on her calf came loose, disappearing in the current.

She took another step and her foot came down on nothing. The bottom had dropped away and suddenly she was swimming, if the desperate flailing to keep her head above water could be called that. The current grabbed her immediately, yanking her sideways. Water filled her mouth, her nose, cold and suffocating.

I thought I explicitly stated that you are not to go near water?

Eliam's voice rose unbidden and for a split second Briar thought he might actually be speaking to her, even though that was impossible. Wasn't it? She had no time to dwell on it because if she didn't do something she *was* going to drown and she'd be damned if she died proving him right.

Her hand caught something solid. A root, thick and sturdy, jutting from the bank. She clung to it with both hands, coughing up water that burned her throat. The current tried to rip her away but she held on, her fingers aching with the strain.

With painstaking slowness, she pulled herself along the root, hand over hand, until her feet found purchase on submerged rocks. The bank here was even steeper than the other side, but she dug her fingers into it, and hauled herself up, the cold making every movement harder.

Once free of the river, she collapsed, shaking so hard her teeth rattled. Her dress clung to her like a second skin, heavy and dripping. Every part of her felt numb except where it hurt, which was everywhere. The cut on her calf had opened again, bleeding freely now without the bandage. The water would hide her scent, confuse the trail, at least for a little while.

The cold set in properly then, seeping into her bones. Her hands wouldn't stop shaking as she tried to wring water from her dress, the wet fabric sucking away what little warmth her body still produced. The air temperature, which had seemed merely uncomfortable before, now felt deadly.

As much as she wanted to rest, she knew she needed to keep moving, to get warm somehow, but her legs trembled when she tried to stand, muscles quivering from cold and exhaustion and blood loss.

Briar forced herself up anyway, one hand braced against a tree for support. She could feel hypothermia setting in, that dangerous drowsiness that whispered how nice it would be to just sit down, just rest for a moment.

She bit the inside of her cheek hard enough to taste blood, using the pain to stay focused. Keep moving. Keep going. The cold would kill her as surely as any hunter if she stopped now.

The ground began to slope downward, subtle at first, then steeper. She had to brace herself against trees to control her descent. Her feet slipped on the loose leaves and frost, each slide sending her heart racing, but she managed to catch herself.

The further she went, the worse the incline became until she was forced to turn sideways, trying to edge down more carefully, testing each foothold before committing her weight.

Her foot came down on what looked like solid ground, but the sharp edge of a hidden rock pierced through her bare sole. Pain shot up her leg and her knee gave way instantly. She pitched forward, hands grasping at nothing, and then she was rolling, tumbling down the steep incline in a chaos of leaves and stones and sky.

Her fingers caught a root—thick and gnarled, jutting from the hillside. The jolt nearly tore her arms from their sockets, but she held on, gasping, her body dangling. Below her feet, she could feel nothing but space. A hole? A fae trap? There was no way to tell how deep it went or if she would survive the fall.

The root creaked under her weight. She tried to pull herself up, but her ribs screamed in protest, and her grip was already slipping on the damp bark. She could see the earth around the root beginning to crumble, feel it starting to give.

"Please," she whispered to no one, to anyone, her fingers white-knuckled on the wood. "Please—"

The root tore free from the earth.

She fell, tumbling through darkness that felt endless. When she finally hit the bottom the impact turned the world white, then black, then white again.

"Well that was certainly dramatic."

Briar slowly turned her head, the movement making the world spin dangerously. Was she hearing things again? She blinked once, twice, three times before her vision finally cleared enough that she could make out a man illuminated by what little light managed to filter down from above.

No, not a man, not quite. He was beautiful in the way a snake was beautiful, possessing a dangerous grace even in stillness. Patches of iridescent scales shimmered with a light of their own, shifting from black to green to gold as he breathed. They were scattered across his skin like someone had painted him with pieces of midnight rainbow. His eyes, when they found hers, were distinctly inhuman—vertical pupils in irises that held too many colors to name.

Heavy chains wrapped around his torso and arms, each link as thick as her thumb. Where they pressed against his skin the flesh beneath looked wrong, darkened and seeping something too dark to be blood.

"Staring is rude," he said, his voice conversational despite his imprisoned state. "Though I suppose you're trying to figure out what I am. I'm a Drak, obviously." When she continued staring blankly, he sighed. "Dragon-kin? Fire spirit? Household pest, according to some very rude fae lords?" Another blank look. "Gods, humans really know nothing useful, do you? All that education and you can't even identify the thing dying in front of you."

Dying?

"Those chains, how..." she started, trying to push herself up. She managed to make it to her hands and knees before her ribs convinced her that was far enough.

"Oh, these?" He shifted slightly, metal scraping against stone, and even from several feet away she felt it—warmth radiating from him in waves. It called to her and she had to fight the urge to drag herself closer.

"Lord Solandis thought I'd make an amusing pet. I disagreed. Violently. With fire." He sounded almost wistful. "Did you know fae hair burns remarkably fast? Anyway, he put these on me. They are very expensive, or so I'm told. Quite painful if that matters for anything. I was being transported to his summer estate when I had a philosophical disagreement with my escorts."

Why was he telling her all of this? She managed to get into a sitting position, a numbness settling over her that should have been concerning but took the edge off the worst of the pain.

"The disagreement? I'm glad you asked. It was about whether I should kill them slowly or quickly," he clarified helpfully. "I opted for quickly—I'm not a sadist—but then I had to run while still wearing these lovely accessories. Fell into this hole two days ago? Three? Time moves strangely when iron's eating through your scales." His forked tongue flicked out, tasting the air. "You're bleeding rather badly, by the way. All over, actually. It's quite excessive."

She looked down at her leg, saw the blood had soaked through the silk and was now dripping steadily onto the leaves. When she looked back up, she realized he was still talking.

"—hunters up there will smell it soon. They're not particularly clever, but blood scent? Even idiots can follow that. I'd give you maybe ten minutes before they start circling the ravine edge." He paused, considering. "Actually, I should thank you. It might have taken me days to die from these chains. The hunters will be much quicker. Messier, probably, but definitely quicker."

"I'm sorry," she found herself saying, the words escaping before she could stop them. "I didn't mean to—"

"Oh, don't apologize. It's actually quite considerate of you." He shifted, chains scraping. "Lord Solandis wanted me to suffer for weeks. Very vindictive, that one. But a bunch of hunt-crazed fae tearing us both apart? That'll be done in minutes. Much more efficient."

A hunting horn echoed above them, closer than before. Too close.

She had to go, she had to keep moving, but... her hand went to her hair, fingers finding one of the few remaining pins. The metal felt cold against her fingertips, but then again, everything felt cold. Her fingers were stiff, clumsy, barely cooperating as she worked the pin loose. She couldn't free another creature, couldn't risk another Malus situation. But leaving him here to be torn apart by the hunters when she had even the smallest way to help seemed wrong.

"They're using a grid pattern," he observed calmly. "Smart. They'll find this ravine within, oh, five minutes? Maybe less if your blood trail is as obvious up there as it is down here."

The pin was in her hand now. Such a small thing. She wasn't freeing him, she told herself. She was just... giving him the same chance she had. To try. To possibly escape. Or not. It wouldn't be her fault either way.

"The lock's quite clever, actually," he continued, seemingly talking to himself now. "Multiple tumblers, false mechanisms. Even if someone had the right tools, it would take considerable skill to—"

Another horn, from a different direction. They were converging.

"Ah, there's the eastern group," he said with something almost like satisfaction. "They'll meet right above us. Should be quite the gathering."

She tossed the pin. It landed near his bound hands with a soft clink. He stopped mid-word, his eyes tracking from the pin to her face, that sharp attention returning.

Briar didn't wait for whatever he might say. Using the stone wall for support, she pulled herself upright and limped deeper into the ravine as fast as her damaged body would allow. Behind her, she heard the soft scrape of chains against stone as the Drak began to move, and then a low chuckle.

"Interesting," he murmured, but she was already too far away to hear whatever else he might have said.

Chapter Three

The ravine had become a maze of stone, walls rising fifteen feet on either side, sometimes opening to show darkening sky above. Briar stumbled through the narrow passages, one hand pressed against her ribs, the other trailing along the rough stone for balance. Each breath burned, shallow and insufficient. The makeshift bandage on her leg had come loose somewhere behind her, and she could feel the warm, steady seep of blood down her calf.

The sky visible between the stone walls had shifted from afternoon gold to the purple-gray of approaching evening. She'd lasted the whole day. Somehow, impossibly, she'd survived until dusk. But her body was done. Each step took conscious effort, her muscles shaking with exhaustion, threatening to give out entirely.

The passage she'd chosen narrowed, then opened into what looked like another route—no. A wall of stone rose before her, smooth and impassable. A dead end.

Her knees buckled. She caught herself against the wall, fingers finding the grooves between stones, pressing her forehead against the cold surface. The stone felt good against her fevered skin. She could rest here. Just for a moment. Just—

"Well, well." Sarelle's voice floated down from above, honeyed and amused. "I'm genuinely impressed. A whole day. No one expected you to last past noon."

Briar forced her head up. The fae woman stood at the edge of the wall above, silhouetted against the dying light. Two others stepped into view. She recognized Lord Ashford, his face still bearing marks from whatever Thaine had done to him.

"You look tired," Sarelle continued, beginning to descend as the stone itself seemed to reshape into steps beneath her feet. "All that running, all that bleeding. And for what? To die exhausted instead of fresh? Pity."

Briar's fingers scraped against stone, trying to push herself up, to run, but there was nowhere to go and her legs wouldn't cooperate anyway. She slid down the wall instead, leaving a smear of blood in her wake.

"The huntsman made such a fuss," Ashford said, following Sarelle down. "Claiming you were already his. But he's... indisposed, indefinitely if we're lucky." Something cruel flickered across his face. "Unfortunate timing."

They reached the bottom, approaching slowly, savoring her helplessness. Briar pressed back against the wall, her hand going to her throat where Eliam's marks had once blazed. Nothing. No warmth, no protection, no connection to call on.

"How should we do this?" Sarelle asked, those silver threads beginning to weave between her fingers again. "Quick would be merciful. But you did lead us on such a chase..."

A wet sound interrupted her. Like meat tearing.

Ashford's expression went from smug to confused. He looked down at the hand protruding from his chest—a hand covered in iridescent scales, holding something red and pulsing.

"You walked right past me," a voice said from behind Ashford. "ME. To chase this bleeding disaster of a human. I'm genuinely insulted."

The hand withdrew. Ashford crumpled, revealing the creature from the ravine. He looked different without the chains—taller, broader, patches of scales catching the dying light like oil on water. Blood painted his arms to the elbows. His reptilian eyes fixed on Sarelle with an expression of mild annoyance.

"A Drak," Sarelle breathed, silver threads going bright with alarm. "You're that thing Solandis was transporting—"

"That *thing*?" His voice dropped, losing its casual tone. "Now I'm offended."

Sarelle's threads lashed out, silver light cutting through the growing darkness. They should have wrapped around him, should have sliced through scale and flesh. Instead, he moved through them like smoke, if smoke could have teeth and claws. One moment he stood by Ashford's body, the next he had Sarelle by the throat, lifting her off the ground.

"You fae always think you're so superior," he said, his tone light and cordial, as though they were having tea. "But in the end you burn just like everything else."

His free hand erupted in flame. Not the orange one might expect, but white-hot, tinged with blue at the edges. Sarelle screamed, her silver threads dissolving to nothing. The third fae, Briar hadn't even seen him move, was already backing toward the stone walls.

"Run," the Drak suggested helpfully, his eyes never leaving Sarelle. "It's more fun when you run."

The fae turned and scrambled up the wall with desperate speed. The Drak watched him go, head tilted with interest, still holding Sarelle like she weighed nothing.

"Should I chase him?" he asked, and it took Briar a moment to realize he was asking *her*. "I do enjoy a good chase, but you're bleeding quite badly. More than before, actually. You really should work on not bleeding so much."

Sarelle clawed at his scaled hand, her perfect face turning purple. He glanced at her with mild annoyance.

"Oh, right. Still holding this." He opened his hand. Sarelle dropped, gasping, and tried to crawl away. He stepped on her back almost absently, pressing her flat. "What to do with this one..."

"Please," Briar whispered. She wasn't even sure who she was pleading with or for what.

He looked at her again, those reptilian eyes bright with interest. "Are you asking me to spare her? The one who was about to kill you? That seems poorly thought out, even for a human."

"I just—" Briar tried to push herself up, but her body wouldn't cooperate. "I don't want to watch—"

"Then close your eyes," he suggested reasonably.

Briar squeezed them shut, but she could still see the light through her eyelids, bright white-blue, hot enough that she felt the heat wash over her even from several feet away. Sarelle's scream cut off abruptly, replaced by a sound like logs cracking in a fireplace. The smell of burning flesh and something else, something sweetly acrid, filled the air.

Briar gagged, fighting the urge to vomit.

When she opened her eyes, Sarelle was still standing there. Or rather, the shape of her was. A perfectly formed sculpture of ash and char, holding its position for one impossible moment before the slight breeze caused it to collapse in on itself. Black flakes drifted down like snow, some still glowing at the edges.

The Drak was examining his hands, little flames still dancing between his fingers before he shook them out like someone drying their hands.

"Much cleaner than the first one," he observed with satisfaction. "Though the smell is rather unfortunate." He turned to her, and something in his expression shifted. "You're about to pass out."

She wanted to deny it, but the edges of her vision were already going dark. The last thing she saw was him moving toward her, no longer casual but quick, catching her before she hit the ground.

"Humans," she heard him mutter. "So fragile."

Then nothing.

She was back in the Star Court's garden, but everything felt wrong. The colors were muted, like looking through frosted glass, and Arion stood with his back to her, perfectly still.

"You have to be here somewhere," he said, but not to her. His voice carried that gentle determination she remembered, the voice that had promised to keep looking for answers. "The forest can't hide everything."

He turned, and she tried to call out, but no sound came. His eyes looked right through her, searching for something that wasn't there. Light gathered in his palms, that cold, beautiful radiance that had once forced Eliam's mark dormant.

The scene shifted. Now he stood at the edge of a ravine staring down into darkness.

"She fell here," someone said. "The blood trail ends."

Sian?

"Then she survived the fall." Arion's light flared brighter, illuminating the depths. "I need to—"

The dream fractured, splintering into sensations: warmth against her back, rhythmic movement, someone humming tunelessly.

Briar's eyes opened to see trees passing overhead, their branches dark against a star-filled sky. She was moving, but not under her own power. Someone was carrying her, their gait steady and unhurried. Her arms were draped over shoulders that radiated unnatural warmth, and when she turned her head slightly, she caught sight of scales glinting in the moonlight.

"—should have been more specific about direction," the Drak was saying, as if continuing a conversation. "Though I suppose precision becomes difficult when you're bleeding out."

She tried to speak, but managed only a croak.

"Conscious again." He didn't sound particularly interested. "That's three times now. You've been out about four hours. I cauterized your leg, you screamed, then went quiet. The silence was better."

The pain in her leg had changed from sharp agony to a deep, throbbing burn. She could feel bandages wrapped around it.

"Where did you—"

"The dead one had silk undergarments. Good quality." He stepped over something without breaking stride. "Shame to waste them."

"Why?" Her voice came out rough, throat raw. "Why are you helping me?"

A pause. When he spoke, his tone was matter-of-fact.

"You gave me the means to free myself. Now you're mine until the debt's paid." His grip adjusted slightly on her legs. "You belong to me now. I keep what's mine alive. Usually."

"I don't—"

"Your opinion on it doesn't matter." He sounded like he was explaining something obvious. "The debt exists. You're mine until I decide otherwise. It's simple."

She tried to process that logic and failed. "That makes no sense."

"It doesn't need to." He tilted his head slightly, listening. "The hunters are about two miles back. Moving poorly. Should I kill them all or just the loud one? He's irritating me."

"Don't kill anyone," she repeated, though her voice came out weaker than intended.

"Fine. Maiming only." He sounded mildly disappointed. "Though that really does complicate things. Dead bodies don't follow. Injured ones make noise, attract others. Very inefficient."

The forest around them had gone dark, true dark, the kind that existed only in places far from human lights. The moon filtered through branches in broken patterns, catching on his scales where they pushed through tears in his shirt, dark fabric that she suspected had been stolen from one of the dead hunters. The air tasted of pine sap and old earth, and underneath it, the metallic tang of blood. Hers, mostly, though he still carried the scent of charred flesh from Sarelle.

"Who are you?" she managed, her throat raw from screaming she didn't remember.

"You don't know? I told you. I'm a Drak."

"No, I mean... your name."

His footsteps barely disturbed the forest floor, each placement deliberate despite his casual gait. "Karse." He shifted her weight, and she felt the unnatural heat radiating from his skin, warmer than any human should be.

"I'm Briar."

"I know. You were screaming it earlier. 'Please, Briar needs to rest.' 'Briar is dying.' Very dramatic. Also you were talking in third person, which was odd."

Heat crept up her neck despite the cold night air. The movement made her aware of how she must look: dress destroyed, hair matted with blood and dirt, the carefully crafted court beauty dissolved into something feral and broken. "I was delirious."

"Obviously." Somewhere in the distance, an owl called, normal forest sounds that seemed wrong after a day of hunting horns. "You also kept reaching for something. Your chest, mostly. You kept saying something was gone. Is something missing?"

The warmth. The connection that had lived beneath her ribs for months, that golden thread that had bound her to Eliam even when she'd hated him for it. Now just hollow space, cold as winter earth. "It's... complicated."

"Most things are when fae are involved." His tone suggested complete disinterest, but she could feel his attention on her, sharp as the scales that caught moonlight along his neck. "You should sleep more. Talking is tedious and you need to heal."

"I'm not tired—"

"Yes you are. Close your eyes."

The trees around them had grown older, trunks thick enough that three people couldn't wrap their arms around them. Moss hung from branches like curtains, and the air felt heavier here, pregnant with magic that made her skin prickle. "You can't just tell me to—"

"Sleep," he said, and there was something in his voice, not quite command but absolute certainty. "I'm tired of conversation."

Against her will, her eyes grew heavy, the rhythm of his walking and the warmth at her back pulling her under...

She woke to the sensation of being lowered to the ground, bark rough against her spine as he propped her against an ancient oak. The moon had moved, painting everything in silver-blue shadows. Karse crouched beside her, and she could see the change in him—muscles coiled tight beneath skin and scales, his pupils contracted to thin lines despite the darkness. His fingers splayed against the ground, and she noticed his nails were longer than they should be, darker, more claw than human.

His head tilted, and she could see him breathing deeply, tasting the air with that forked tongue that flickered out between too-sharp teeth.

Briar heard it then, voices carried on wind that shouldn't exist, moving against the natural current of the forest.

"—blood trail leads this way." Sian's melodic tone, but worried, stressed in a way that made the words sharper. "Too much blood. If she's lost this much—"

"She's alive." Arion's voice cut through the darkness, certain as dawn. "I can feel... something. She's close."

Her heart lurched, pulse jumping in her throat. The warmth in her chest suddenly pulsed. Faint, barely there, but reaching toward Arion's voice with desperate recognition. The sensation made her gasp, her hand flying to her chest.

Karse's attention snapped to her, those reptilian eyes tracking the movement. "What's wrong with you now?"

She shook her head, struggling for a moment to breathe. His stillness transformed into something else entirely—muscles coiling, weight transferring to the balls of his feet, every line of his body ready to explode into violence.

"Three," he murmured, his voice lower now, anticipatory. The moonlight caught his eyes and they flared gold-green, reflecting light that shouldn't exist. "Water magic on one. Light on another." His lips curved, revealing teeth that had grown sharper while she watched. "Interesting."

"Karse—" she tried, but he was already flowing to his feet, moving without sound despite the carpet of dry leaves.

"Stay," he said without looking back. "This won't take long."

"Karse! Wait!"

She heard Halian's voice, closer now. "Then we should hurry before—"

The words cut off in a strangled sound, followed by the crack of wood and Sian's sharp intake of breath that preceded her magic, water gathering from moisture in the air with a sound like distant rain.

Briar forced herself up, using the tree for support. Her leg screamed protest, the cauterized wound pulling with each movement, but she pushed through it. The warmth in her chest pulsed stronger with each step toward the conflict, reaching for Arion with an intensity that made her stumble.

She broke through the trees to find chaos.

Karse had Halian pressed against an oak, one scaled hand around his throat, lifting him just enough that his feet scraped for purchase. Water whipped through the air—Sian's magic manifesting as liquid tendrils that turned to steam before they could reach Karse, the air around him shimmering with heat waves.

Arion stood between Sian and the conflict, his hands glowing with cold light that created a barrier of radiance. When Karse turned toward him, the light flared brighter, forcing him to squint and step back, but it didn't strike out, didn't attack, just... pushed.

"Let him go," Arion said, voice steady despite the tension. "We're not here to hurt anyone."

"No?" Karse tilted his head, still holding Halian. "You're tracking what's mine. Following her blood through the forest. That sounds like hunting to me."

He squeezed slightly, and Halian's face darkened. Sian pulled more water from the air, from the dew on leaves, building something larger.

"Stop!" Briar's voice cracked as she stumbled into the clearing. Her leg gave out three steps in, sending her to her knees in the leaf litter. "Karse, stop. They're—" she had to pause, gasping for breath, "—they're my friends."

Karse's attention shifted to her, though his grip didn't loosen. "You're supposed to stay where I put you."

"Please." She tried to stand again and failed. The warmth in her chest was burning now, pulling toward Arion with such force it felt like being torn in half. "They helped me before. They're not hunting—they're trying to help."

Arion moved toward her, his light dimming, but Karse's free hand erupted in white-blue flame. "Don't."

"She's injured," Arion said, keeping his hands visible, the light fading to a soft glow that illuminated rather than threatened. "Let me help her."

"She doesn't need your help. She has me." Karse's flames grew hotter, the nearby leaves beginning to curl and blacken. "I fixed her. She's mine to protect."

"Yours?" Sian's voice was sharp with disbelief. "She's not property—"

"Karse." Briar forced steel into her voice despite the pain. "Put Halian down. Now."

The Drak looked at her, really looked at her, and something shifted in his expression. Not obedience exactly, but... consideration. His fingers loosened slightly, though Halian still remained pinned.

"They were following you," he said, as if explaining something obvious. "Things that follow wounded prey usually intend to finish it."

"We were trying to find her before the other hunters did," Arion said carefully, still maintaining that soft light that pushed gently at the edges of Karse's heat. "We're not participating in the hunt. We're trying to stop it."

Karse laughed, short and sharp. "Fae helping a human? Out of kindness?" His flames grew hotter. "I've been in enough fae chains to know how that story ends."

"Not all fae—" Sian started.

"Yes, *all* fae." Karse's voice went flat. "You take what you want and dress it up in pretty words. Laws. Bargains. *Hunts.*" He looked at Briar. "They'll kill you or keep you. There's no third option with their kind."

"These ones are different," Briar managed, though the words felt weak even to her.

"Different." He considered this, fingers still loose but ready around Halian's throat. "The one with light magic keeps looking at you like you're his. The water witch is calculating how to drown me. And this one—" he squeezed slightly, making Halian wheeze, "—is trying to work his fingers to something sharp in his pocket."

Halian's hand stilled.

"See? Fae." Karse's tone carried the satisfaction of a proven point. "They can't help their nature."

The silence that followed was heavy. Finally, Karse let Halian drop. The fae collapsed to his knees, gasping, one hand pressed to his throat where dark bruises were already forming.

Sian moved to Halian's side, water still swirling around her fingers as she helped him sit up. He waved her off, one hand pressed to his throat, already assessing his own damage with the clinical detachment of a healer.

Arion took a step toward Briar.

Karse shifted immediately, placing himself directly in Arion's path. The flames around his hands dimmed but didn't extinguish, the heat still palpable in the air between them.

"She needs help," Arion said, keeping his voice level.

"She has help. Mine." Karse didn't move. "She's breathing. She's conscious. That's more than she would be if I hadn't found her."

"You cauterized her leg with fire." Arion's light flickered slightly, betraying frustration. "She needs proper healing—"

"Proper?" Karse's laugh was sharp. "Like the proper hunt your kind arranged? The proper way that Sarelle woman was going to tear her apart?"

"We're wasting time," Arion said, and there was an edge to his voice now. "Every moment we stand here arguing, more hunters are closing in. Can you not hear them?"

Briar could. Distant but unmistakable, the sound of coordinated movement through the forest. Multiple groups, calling to each other in the musical language of the courts.

She tried to push herself up from where she'd fallen, using a young birch for support. The bark felt too smooth, too cold under her palms. Her leg wouldn't hold weight properly, the cauterized wound pulling with fresh agony, but she managed to get her feet under her.

"You want to help?" Karse was saying. "Leave. Draw them off. Take your companions and make noise elsewhere."

"We're not leaving her with—"

The argument continued, but the words started blurring together. Briar took one step, then another, focusing on the space between them. If she could just get there, make them stop, make them listen—

Her leg buckled. The ground rushed up.

Karse caught her before she hit the leaves, moving without taking his eyes off Arion. One arm wrapped around her waist, pulling her against his too-warm chest, holding her upright when her legs wouldn't.

"You see?" His voice had gone quieter, more dangerous. "She can't travel. Not fast enough to matter."

That's when Halian struck.

Roots erupted from the earth, wrapping around Karse's ankles and calves in a sudden burst of growth. Not gentle vines but thick, woody bonds that locked his legs in place. Karse's attention snapped downward for one crucial second.

Sian's water came from everywhere—moisture in the air, dew from the leaves, all of it converging into a spinning vortex that engulfed them both. The water moved too fast to evaporate, constantly cycling, dousing his flames before they could fully form.

Karse's grip on Briar tightened, a snarl building in his throat, but then—

The light hit them like a physical force. Not gentle radiance but harsh, brilliant white that turned the world into nothing but glare. Briar's eyes slammed shut instinctively, but the light burned through her eyelids, disorienting, overwhelming.

She felt Karse's arms torn away from her, felt herself pulled in a different direction. Cooler hands caught her, lifted her, and she knew without seeing that it was Arion. The warmth in her chest sang at his proximity, reaching desperately.

"No—" she tried to say, but the words wouldn't come properly.

Behind them, she heard Karse roar—rage and betrayal mixed into something inhuman. The sound of steam hissing as he fought against the water, roots cracking under immense heat.

"Go!" Halian shouted. "It won't hold long!"

The forest blurred past, each jostle sending pain through her injuries. She could hear Sian and Halian behind them, their footsteps quick but controlled.

The wrongness of it twisted in her stomach. Karse had saved her, had carried her for hours, had killed for her, and they'd trapped him like an animal. But Arion's arms were steady and familiar, and the warmth in her chest pulsed with each heartbeat, settling into something almost like peace after hours of hollow cold. She hated herself for how grateful she felt, how her body relaxed into his hold despite everything.

His light magic still glowed faintly around them, creating a bubble of soft radiance in the dark forest. It felt nothing like Karse's burning heat—this was gentler, like morning sun through windows, like safety she didn't deserve after what they'd just done.

"I'm sorry," Arion murmured against her hair, and she wasn't sure if he meant for the rough handling or for leaving Karse behind. Maybe both. Maybe neither.

She wanted to tell him to go back, to free Karse, to explain that the Drak had been protecting her. But the words wouldn't come, and the shameful truth was that part of her—the exhausted, terrified, human part—was desperately glad to be in familiar arms again. The warmth spreading through her chest felt like coming home, even though home was something she'd never have again.

And further back, getting fainter but not gone, the sound of something burning. Something breaking free.

Something hunting.

Chapter Four

Behind them, terrible sounds echoed through the forest, cracking, snapping, a hissing like water thrown on forge-hot metal. Underneath it all, a low continuous sound that made the hair on Briar's arms stand up, not quite a growl, not quite a roar, but something that bypassed human understanding and went straight to primal fear.

"We need to move faster," Halian said, his voice still rough from being choked. "He's almost—"

A tree exploded into flames fifty yards behind them, the light throwing their shadows long and stark against the forest floor.

"Now would be good," Sian added tightly.

Arion shifted Briar in his arms, freeing one hand while somehow still supporting her weight. He whispered something in the old tongue, words that seemed to catch in the air and hang there, visible as soft golden mist. The forest around them grew quiet, that particular stillness that came when something ancient paid attention.

They came from between the trees as if stepping out of moonlight itself.

Three of them, moving with an ethereal grace that made no sound despite their size. They stood taller than any natural deer, their shoulders level with Arion's head. Their coats shifted between white and pearl and silver, not quite solid, as if someone had captured fog and given it form. The antlers rose like carved bone architecture, but within the tines, soft light pulsed in dawn colors of rose and gold and palest blue.

One approached Arion directly, lowering its massive head to breathe against his face. Its eyes held too much intelligence, and when it blinked, Briar saw constellations in the darkness behind its lids.

Arion grew quiet, almost reverent, speaking in low tones she couldn't understand. The formality in his posture, the careful cadence of his words. He was asking, not commanding.

The elk, though calling it that felt like calling the ocean a pond, considered. Its gaze moved to Briar, and she felt the weight of its attention, ancient and assessing. The warmth in her chest pulsed, reaching toward this creature of dawn and light.

It snorted, breath misting in the air despite the warm night, then folded its legs to kneel.

Another roar behind them, closer. The light from burning trees painted the forest orange and violent.

Arion lifted Briar onto the elk's back, the movement jarring every injury she had. The creature's coat felt like nothing she could describe—soft but insubstantial, warm but not quite there. She tried to grip with her legs but her body wouldn't cooperate, everything going loose and weak.

"Hold on," Arion said, mounting behind her. His arms came around her to take the barely-visible reins that seemed made of captured starlight. She sagged back against his chest, unable to keep herself upright any longer.

Sian and Halian mounted the other two elk, their movements quick and practiced. The creatures rose in unison, and Briar's stomach dropped at suddenly being so high. The ground seemed impossibly far below.

"Go," Arion commanded.

The elk moved.

It wasn't running, running implied normal physics, normal motion. This was something else. The forest blurred into streaks of dark and darker, trees becoming suggestions rather than solid things. The elk's gait was impossibly smooth, as if they traveled above the ground rather than on it. Wind whipped Briar's tangled hair across her face, cold enough to steal what little breath she had.

"Sleep," Arion said against her ear, his voice gentle. "You're safe now."

Chapter Four (SPLIT)

She wanted to argue, to explain about Karse, but the warmth in her chest pulsed with contentment at Arion's proximity, and her body had nothing left to give. The rhythm of the elk's movement, the solid presence of Arion behind her, the soft light emanating from the creature beneath them, it all pulled her toward unconsciousness.

The forest streamed past in ways that made no sense, trees bending away from their passage, the world becoming nothing but motion and wind and the faint chime of the elk's hooves when they struck stone. Her eyes closed without her permission, her body finally surrendering to exhaustion.

The darkness that took her was complete.

***

The sound of quiet movement stirred her from sleep. Briar's eyes opened slowly, her body feeling heavy and disconnected, as though she'd been underwater for too long. A young fae girl stood by the table near the window, setting down a fresh tray while collecting another that must have been there for hours, the fruit on it had begun to brown at the edges.

The girl's eyes widened when she noticed Briar watching. "My lady, forgive me, I didn't mean to wake you." She dipped a quick curtsy and fled before Briar could respond.

Briar knew this room. The pale wood furniture, the tapestry depicting dawn breaking over mountains, the way morning light filtered through gossamer curtains. The Star Court. Arion's home. She'd stayed here before, when everything had been different. When she'd still believed she might find a way to break her bargain with Eliam.

The smell of fresh bread and something sweet pulled her from the bed. Her feet touched the floor, expecting pain, expecting her leg to buckle. Nothing. She stood fully, waiting for the familiar agony of cracked ribs, the burn of the cauterized wound. Still nothing.

She looked down at herself, at legs that bore only faint lines where deep gashes had been. The angry burns from Karse's healing had faded to pink marks that looked weeks old, not days. Someone had dressed her in a soft nightgown, cream-colored and simple. Her skin was clean, her hair washed and braided loosely over one shoulder.

The table by the balcony held more food than she could eat in three meals. There were pastries that steamed in the cool air, fruit cut into delicate shapes, tea that smelled of honey and herbs she couldn't name. She sat, her body moving without the careful calculation of injury she'd grown accustomed to. Through the open doors, morning air drifted in, carrying the scent of the Star Court's gardens—jasmine and something else, something that only grew in places where magic lingered.

She'd barely taken her first bite when a knock came at the door.

"Come in," she said, expecting the servant girl again.

Arion entered, and for a moment she forgot to breathe. Gone were the formal robes she'd always seen him in. He wore a fitted dark green vest over a white shirt with sleeves rolled to his forearms, his usually perfect hair falling in loose curls around his face. The casual attire made him look younger, less like the Star Court's prince and more like... just Arion.

Relief flickered across his features when he saw her sitting there. "You're awake. And eating. Good."

He moved toward the balcony doors, already reaching to close them. "You shouldn't have these open, the morning air is too cold—"

"Leave them," she said. "Please. I've been inside too long."

He paused, clearly wanting to argue, then compromised by pulling a shawl from the wardrobe. It was soft gray wool, the edges decorated with tiny stars. He draped it around her shoulders with careful movements, not quite touching her but ensuring she was covered.

"You had us worried," he said quietly, settling into the chair across from her. "You've been sleeping for two days."

"Two days?" The pastry nearly fell from her hand. "But—"

"Halian healed what he could. The physical damage, most of it. Some things..." He paused, his gaze dropping to where her hand had unconsciously moved to her chest, to where the warmth pulsed weak but present in response to his proximity. "Some things can't be healed with magic. Your body was repaired, but your mind seemed to need the rest. Or perhaps it didn't want to wake."

The weight of those words settled between them. She thought of Eliam's cold dismissal, of being hunted like an animal, of Karse trapped in water and roots because he'd tried to protect her. Two days of sleep hadn't erased any of it.

"Where are Sian and Halian?" she asked, deflecting from the hollow ache beneath her ribs.

"Nearby. They wanted to check on you, but I thought you might need space first. Time to adjust."

"And Karse?" The name tasted strange on her tongue. "The Drak?"

Something shifted in Arion's expression, not quite discomfort but close. "We don't know. He didn't follow us to the Star Court, at least not yet. But Sian says..." He hesitated.

"What?"

"She says something that burns that hot doesn't give up easily." He studied her face. "He seemed to think you belonged to him."

The memory of Karse's matter-of-fact declaration rose unbidden. You're mine until the debt's paid. She wondered if he was still out there, hunting for what he considered his. The thought should have terrified her. Instead, she felt oddly guilty for leaving him trapped.

"He saved my life," she said simply. "Multiple times."

Arion nodded slowly, though something in his eyes suggested he wanted to say more. Instead, he gestured to her plate. "Eat. You need your strength. We have... much to discuss."

Briar continued eating, the food settling uneasily in her stomach despite its quality. The silence stretched between them until Arion finally spoke.

"How did you end up in the forest?" His tone was careful, gentle. "We assumed you'd escaped from Eliam somehow."

The words lodged in her throat like broken glass. She set down her cup, her hand trembling slightly. "He released me from our bargain."

Arion's eyes widened. "Released you? But why would he—"

"How did you know to look for me?" she interrupted, unable to bear that line of questioning. Not yet. Maybe not ever.

He studied her for a moment, clearly wanting to pursue the previous topic, but let it go. "I was drawn to a cave by traces of the warmth... like an echo of where you'd been. There were golden flowers growing from bare stone, already fading when I arrived. That's where we found Thaine, badly injured. He told us you were being hunted and that he had orders to protect you during the hunt, then bring you back to Eliam once it ended."

"Bring me back?" The words felt strange in her mouth.

"That's what he said. The warmth left a trail from there. It was faint, but enough to follow. When I got close enough to actually feel you, not just the echoes, that's when we found you with that Drak."

She set down her cup. "I need to speak with Thaine."

"No." The refusal was immediate. "Briar, there's no reason to put yourself through that. If Eliam released you from your bargain, then he has no claim on you. You can stay here, in the Star Court. You can be free."

Free. The word should have meant something. Instead, it just felt empty.

"I need to speak with him," she repeated.

"Why?" Arion leaned forward. "What could he possibly tell you that would be worth—"

"Please." Her voice cracked on the word. "I just... I need to know."

"Know what?"

She had no answer, none that would satisfy him anyway. How could she explain that she needed to know if Eliam regretted casting her out? If the orders to bring her back meant something or were just about reclaiming property? No, because that would mean telling Arion that she'd chosen to stay, that she had wanted to remain at Eliam's side despite everything, or perhaps because of it.

"This isn't a good idea," Arion said quietly. "He's dangerous, manipulative. Whatever he tells you will be designed to hurt you or worse."

"I know what he is." She met his eyes steadily. "But I still need to speak with him. Please, Arion."

He was quiet for a long moment, searching her face. Finally, he sighed.

"Fine. But I'm coming with you. And if he says or does anything that—"

"He won't." She didn't know why she was so certain, but she was. "When?"

"After you've finished eating. And after you've changed into something more substantial than a nightgown." He gestured to the wardrobe. "There are clothes that should fit. Take your time. Thaine isn't going anywhere."

The corridors of the Star Court were painted in soft morning light, but Briar barely noticed the beauty. Arion walked beside her, his disapproval radiating with each step.

"This is unnecessary," he said for the third time since they'd left her room. "Whatever Thaine tells you will only cause pain. He's had two days to craft whatever story will best manipulate you."

"I know what he is," Briar said, the words becoming a refrain. She'd changed into simple Star Court attire—soft gray trousers and a white tunic that felt strange after so long in torn finery. "But I need to hear what he has to say."

"You don't. You really don't." Arion stopped walking, catching her arm gently. "Briar, you're free. Why risk it?"

"Because I need to know." She pulled away, continuing down the corridor. After a moment, she heard him sigh and follow.

The room they'd given Thaine was in the guest wing, not a cell but clearly chosen for its limited exits. Two Star Court guards flanked the door, their expressions carefully neutral.

"Open it," Briar said.

The guards looked to Arion, who hesitated before nodding. One produced a key, working the lock with practiced efficiency.

The room beyond was dark, curtains drawn tight against the morning sun. Briar started forward but Arion caught her shoulder, moving in front of her.

"Let me—"

Thaine struck from the shadows beside the door, moving with the fluid violence that made him Eliam's perfect weapon. No blade this time, just hands and brutal intent, slamming Arion against the doorframe.

But Arion had been expecting it. Light flared from his palms, creating a barrier that forced Thaine back. They grappled briefly, Thaine trying to get past the light, Arion using it to keep him at bay without using physical force.

"You should have left me to die in the forest, princeling," Thaine snarled, still pushing against the barrier of light. "Would have been cleaner than whatever game you're playing."

"See?" Arion called over his shoulder to Briar, still maintaining the defensive light. "I told you this was a bad—"

"Little rabbit?"

Thaine's entire demeanor changed. The tension drained from his body so abruptly that Arion's light pushed him back a step. His dark eyes found Briar in the doorway, cataloging her from head to toe with an intensity that had nothing to do with threat.

"You're alive." The words came out oddly flat. "Whole. Walking. Not eaten or torn apart or—" He stopped, seeming to realize he was speaking aloud.

Briar stepped into the room despite Arion's sharp intake of breath. The light barrier flickered as Arion's attention split.

"I need to speak with you," she said simply.

Thaine tilted his head, that familiar predatory assessment returning. "Do you now? And here I thought you'd be halfway to the mortal realm, taking advantage of your new found freedom."

"Briar..." Arion warned.

"It's fine," she said, not looking away from Thaine. "He's not going to hurt me. Are you?"

Something akin to amusement flickered across Thaine's features. "Hurt you? My orders were quite specific about keeping you intact." He moved to the room's single chair, dropping into it with casual grace despite what must have been healing injuries. "Though I must admit, you made that remarkably difficult. Running from the one person actually trying to keep you alive during a sanctioned hunt? Not your wisest moment."

"I didn't know—"

"No, you assumed. Saw me and ran like the frightened rabbit you are." He examined his hands, voice carrying that dark humor she knew all too well. "Though I suppose I can't blame you. I don't exactly project 'helpful savior,' do I?"

"Arion," Briar said quietly, "would you wait outside?"

"Absolutely not." His response was immediate, the light still faintly glowing around his hands. "I'm not leaving you alone with—"

"Please." She finally looked at him, and something in her expression made him pause. "I need to have this conversation, and I need to have it without... Just please. Wait outside. If I need you, I'll call."

They stared at each other for a long moment. Finally, Arion's light dimmed.

"I'll be right outside the door," he said, the warning clear in his tone, both for her and for Thaine. "If I hear anything—"

"You won't." Thaine replied dismissively. "If I wanted to hurt her, princeling, I've had far better opportunities."

Arion left reluctantly, the door closing with deliberate softness behind him. The room fell into shadow again, only thin lines of sunlight through the curtains providing illumination.

"So," Thaine said after a moment. "Questions. You have them. Ask."

Briar moved to the window, not quite ready to face him directly. "Why did he send you?"

"To keep you alive during the hunt. To bring you back after." The response was matter-of-fact.

"Why?" She turned then, needing to see his face. "He cast me out. In front of everyone. Made me prey. Why would he—"

"You're asking me to explain my lord's mind?" Thaine laughed, short and sharp. "I follow orders, little rabbit. I don't interpret them."

"But it doesn't make sense. He was done with me. He crushed that circlet, severed the connection, and threw me to the hunters. Why protect what he'd already discarded?"

Thaine was quiet for a moment, and she could see him weighing his words. "My lord is... impulsive. Acts first, thinks later. Not my place to say it, but since you asked..." He shrugged.

"Impulsive." The word tasted bitter. "So I'm supposed to accept that my life gets torn apart whenever he has a tantrum? Cast out, hunted, then retrieved like nothing happened?"

"Your life is his to do with as he pleases, or did you forget? Would you prefer he'd left you to the hunt unprotected?" Thaine's voice hardened slightly. "Because that was the alternative. You lasted one day, barely. Without my intervention, without the princeling's help, you'd be a decoration in someone's hall by now."

"That's not—" She stopped, frustrated. "Why didn't he come himself? If he regrets it, why send you?"

Something shifted in Thaine's expression. He looked away, jaw tightening.

"Thaine."

"Because I stopped him." The words came out rough, forced. "He was going to come. That first night. I stopped him."

The room seemed to tilt. "You stopped him? Why?"

"Someone had to." He stood abruptly, pacing to the shadowed corner. "Malus is walking free, your doing if we're counting sins. The Forest Court is divided. Half think Eliam's gone soft, the other half are terrified. There are whispers about giving Malus his crown back, before he comes to take it himself, about Eliam being unfit to rule."

His voice was rising, anger bleeding through the careful control.

"If he'd gone after you himself, shown that kind of weakness, admitted that casting you out was a mistake..." he spun on his heel to face her. "The court would have torn him apart. So yes, I stopped him. I told him I'd bring you back quietly once the hunt ended, once things calmed—"

The door burst open. Arion stood there, light already gathering in his palms.

"Malus is free?" His voice was dangerously quiet. "When were you going to mention that detail?"

Thaine's smile was all teeth. "Wasn't my story to tell, princeling. Ask her how that particular miscreant got loose."

Arion's gaze shifted to Briar, and she felt the blood drain from her face. The weight of what she'd done crashed over her again.

"Briar?" Arion's voice gentled, but she could hear the concern beneath. "What is he talking about?"

She pressed her back against the wall, unable to meet his eyes. "When I was here, after you pulled me from the river, Ferria came to me. She told me about a prisoner in the dungeons. A human who had marks like mine, who grew golden flowers."

"Thomas," Thaine supplied darkly. "Or what Malus wanted her to think."

"She gave me a leaf that would hide me from Eliam's perception. But only if I promised not to involve you." The words came out in a rush. "I thought I was saving someone like me. Someone trapped and forgotten. I didn't know—I never imagined—"

"Ferria." Arion's voice had gone completely flat. "Ferria brought you to him."

"Your sweet little companion playing both sides," Thaine said with dark satisfaction. "How does it feel to be used?"

Arion's light flickered erratically around his hands. "She's been with us for decades. Trusted with—" He stopped, visibly struggling to process the betrayal. "You should have come to me, Briar. If she was pressuring you—"

"Oh yes," Thaine cut in, rolling his eyes. "Because the princeling here would have definitely let her risk herself for a stranger in the dungeons."

"I would have investigated—"

"You would have done nothing, and we all know it." Thaine's voice carried that casual cruelty she remembered. "Too careful, too proper. Meanwhile, Malus would have eventually freed himself anyway, just with more corpses in his wake."

"That's not—"

"Enough." Briar's voice cracked. "It's done. I freed him, and he destroyed everything. That's what matters."

Thaine studied her for a moment, then shrugged. "Well, we'll sort it out when we return. We leave at dawn, once the hunt officially ends."

"No." Arion stepped forward, positioning himself partially between them. "Briar isn't bound to Eliam anymore. She's free to choose whether she returns or not."

Thaine's expression shifted into something delighted and sharp. He looked at Briar with raised eyebrows. "Should I tell him, or would you like to?"

"What?" Arion looked between them. "What does that mean?"

"Tell him, little rabbit," Thaine said softly, savoring the moment. "Tell him about the choice you already made. Before Malus. Before the hunt. Tell him how you'd decided to stay."

"Briar?" Arion turned to her fully now, confusion clear in his features.

The room felt too small, the air too thick. Both men were staring at her—Thaine with that knowing smirk, Arion with growing bewilderment. The weight of having to explain that she'd chosen to remain with Eliam was too much.

"I can't—" She shook her head, already moving toward the door. "I can't do this."

"Briar, wait!"

She turned and fled, ignoring Arion calling after her, ignoring Thaine's low chuckle. Her bare feet slapped against the cold floor as she ran through the Star Court's corridors, not knowing where she was going, just needing to be away from questions she couldn't answer and truths she couldn't speak.

The hunt would end at dawn, and she still didn't know what choice she would make when it did.

Chapter Five

The Star Court's architecture favored light with broad windows, open archways, spaces designed to capture and hold the sun. But even here, shadows gathered. Briar found herself in one such place, an alcove between two pillars where morning light hadn't yet reached, where she could press her back against cool stone and try to make sense of the chaos in her chest.

Eliam had wanted to come for her. The knowledge sat like a coal beneath her ribs, burning in ways she couldn't name. He'd wanted to find her, but Thaine had stopped him. For politics. For appearances. For all the cold, calculated reasons that governed the Forest Court.

But he wouldn't have needed to come after her if he hadn't cast her out to begin with.

The thought circled back, inevitable as gravity. He'd thrown her to the wolves in front of the entire court. Made her prey. Watched her run.

But he wouldn't have cast her out if she hadn't freed Malus.

Another turn of the wheel. She'd released his captive brother, the monster who'd usurped his throne once before. She'd betrayed him in the most fundamental way possible.

But if he'd just given her a chance to explain—

Her fingers pressed against her temples, trying to quiet the endless spiral. If he'd listened. If she'd been honest about Thomas from the beginning. If Ferria hadn't manipulated her. If, if, if.

"There you are."

She looked up to find Arion at the alcove's entrance, relief evident in the way his shoulders dropped slightly at the sight of her. He moved closer, and the morning light caught in his pale hair, making him look like something painted rather than real.

"I'm sorry," she said automatically. "I shouldn't have run."

"You had every right to." He said, stopping just within arm's reach. His hand rose, hesitated, then gently tucked a strand of her tangled hair behind her ear. The gesture was so careful, asking permission even as he completed it.

She waited for him to ask about Thaine's revelation, about her choosing to stay with Eliam. Instead, his eyes searched hers with unexpected softness.

"Do you remember the night we danced?" His voice was quiet. "When you kissed me?"

The question hit her unexpectedly, emotion flooding through her so suddenly she could only nod, her gaze dropping to the floor between them. She remembered the music, the way he'd moved with her, the desperate hope that maybe she'd found an ally, someone who might help her escape. And then the kiss—impulsive, searching, trying to feel something other than the constant pull toward Eliam.

"I can't explain it," Arion said, his voice carrying something raw she'd never heard from him before. "In that moment, I would have done anything to protect you. To keep you from falling victim to more cruelty at Eliam's hands."

Her heart ached at the words, but not just from gratitude or affection. A small, shameful part of her wished he had. Wished he'd swept her away that night, taken the choice from her hands. Maybe then things wouldn't have gotten so complicated. Maybe then her heart wouldn't feel like it was being pulled in opposite directions, tearing down the middle.

His finger hooked gently under her chin, coaxing rather than forcing. Such a different touch than she was used to—where Eliam would have gripped her jaw, made her meet his eyes, Arion simply suggested, waited for her to choose.

She let him guide her gaze up to his.

"Whatever choices you made before," he said softly, "whatever you did in desperation to survive—none of that matters to me. You did what you had to do." His thumb brushed along her jaw, the touch feather-light. "All that matters is what you choose now, without the fear of punishment. Without coercion."

Arion watched her as he spoke, and she became aware of how intently he was studying her face, cataloging every small reaction. The weight of his attention made her pulse quicken, a flush creeping up her neck. Something shifted in his expression, a deepening of that raw quality she'd heard in his voice, mixed with what looked like wonder.

He stepped closer, closing the already small distance between them. His hand slipped from her jaw to cradle the back of her neck, fingers threading gently through her hair. The touch was warm, steady, and she could feel the slight tremor in his fingers that betrayed his own nervousness.

"I thought I'd never see you again," he murmured, his voice dropping to something more intimate. "I thought I'd lost any chance to..." He paused, his eyes dropping to her lips before meeting her gaze again. "That I'd never get another chance to show you that there's more to this realm than darkness and cruelty. That you deserve gentleness. Choice."

Briar's heart was racing now, and she knew he could probably feel her pulse where his thumb rested against the side of her neck. The warmth in her chest stirred, reaching toward him with curious recognition.

"Arion," she breathed, though she wasn't sure if it was meant to encourage or warn.

He leaned in slowly, giving her every opportunity to pull away, to refuse. His forehead rested against hers for a moment, their breaths mingling in the small space between them.

"Tell me to stop," he whispered, "and I will."

She didn't.

His lips met hers with a gentleness that made her chest ache. The warmth beneath her ribs stirred fully awake now, reaching toward him with the same recognition it showed for Eliam, perhaps softer but essentially the same. The similarity should have disturbed her more than it did.

Arion's kiss was everything Eliam's weren't—careful, sweet, asking rather than taking. His hand cupped her face like she was something precious, breakable. She could disappear into this softness, this tenderness that asked nothing of her but what she wanted to give. The Star Court prince who offered her choices instead of commands, freedom instead of chains.

I stopped him.

Thaine's words crashed through her mind, sharp as cold water. Eliam had wanted to come. Had been ready to abandon politics and appearances to find her.

She pulled back, breathless, her lips still tingling from the kiss. Arion's hand remained on her face, thumb stroking her cheek with concern.

"I'm sorry," he said immediately, though his eyes suggested he'd felt her initial response, the way she'd leaned into him before pulling away.

"No, it's not—" She pressed her fingers to her lips, trying to find words that wouldn't hurt him. "I'm just tired. Overwhelmed. Everything that's happened, everything I've learned... it's a lot to process."

Understanding flickered across his features, though she could see he wanted to say more, do more. Instead, he stepped back, giving her space.

"Of course. You should rest." He gestured toward the corridor. "May I walk you to your room?"

She nodded, grateful for the excuse to move, to not stand in this alcove where the ghost of his kiss still lingered. They walked in comfortable silence, Arion matching her pace, careful not to crowd her.

At her door, he paused. "Briar." She looked up at him, and his expression was earnest, almost urgent. "No one here would think less of you for the choices you made to survive. Whatever you decided then, whatever you decide now, you're not alone."

The words should have been comforting. Instead, they highlighted the fundamental difference between them. Arion offered absolution for survival choices, but she hadn't just been surviving at the end. She'd been choosing, wanting, staying.

She nodded, unable to trust her voice, and slipped into her room. The door closed with a soft click, and she leaned against it, eyes closed. The warmth in her chest pulsed, pulled in two directions at once, and she wondered if it was possible to be torn in half by wanting incompatible things.

Outside her window, the afternoon sun hung high, indifferent to her turmoil. Time moved steadily forward, counting down to the moment when the hunt would end and she would have to choose: the prince who offered her peace, or the cruel king who'd cast her out but haunted her still.

She moved to the bed, sitting on its edge, trying to reconcile the gentle pressure of Arion's lips with the memory of Eliam's demanding mouth. Different approaches to the same end, both wanted her, both pulled at that warmth in her chest with eerily similar resonance.

But want wasn't the same as value.

Briar rose, feeling restless, and made her way to the window, pressing her palms against the cool glass. The gardens spread below, orderly and beautiful, everything in its proper place, just as it had been the last time she was here. Nothing like the wild tangle of the Forest Court, where beauty and danger intertwined until you couldn't separate them.

Her reflection stared back at her from the glass, clean, healed, dressed in Star colors clothes. She looked like she belonged here. But looking the part and feeling it were different things entirely.

She closed her eyes and sighed. Her mind felt fractured, pulled between impossible choices. Stay in the Star Court where everything was soft edges and careful kindness. Return to the Forest Court where cruelty and passion tangled into something she still didn't fully understand.

Or leave them both behind. Find her own path.

But even as she thought it, she knew that wasn't truly an option. The warmth in her chest wouldn't let her forget either of them, and now there was Karse, somewhere out there, who had claimed her as his property.

There was no clean escape from the web she'd become tangled in.

A knock at the door interrupted her spiraling thoughts. She turned from the window, grateful for the distraction.

"Come in."

Sian entered, and Briar immediately noticed the slight sheen of moisture on her skin, the way her hair looked damp despite the afternoon warmth. The water fae's usual composure seemed frayed at the edges.

"I need your help," Sian said without preamble. "I know you're processing everything, but I have a situation and frankly, you're the only one available who won't make it worse."

Briar blinked at the unexpected directness. "What kind of situation?"

"The water sprites need to migrate to the winter pools before the upper fountains freeze, and they're being absolutely impossible this year." Sian pushed a strand of wet hair from her face. "Usually Halian helps me, but he's reinforcing the wards. Arion offered, but his light magic makes them skittish—they think he's trying to evaporate them."

Despite everything, Briar felt her lips twitch. "Water sprites?"

"Small water elementals. They inhabit the fountains and pools throughout the gardens. Every autumn, I have to coax them from the upper fountains down through the channels to the deeper pools that stay warm through winter." Sian moved to the door, clearly expecting Briar to follow. "It's tedious work. They're about as cooperative as cats, if cats were made of water and had opinions about everything."

The prospect of doing something useful, something that had nothing to do with hunts or courts or impossible choices, pulled at Briar. She found herself following Sian into the corridor.

"What do you need me to do?"

"Manage the sluice gates while I guide the water temperature. Help spot the ones hiding. Talk to the nervous ones, they respond better to voices sometimes." Sian led her through a side door into the afternoon sun. "And if we're very unlucky, help me chase down the ones that decide to make a run for it."

"They run?"

"Bounce, really. Like bubbles with attitude." Sian's expression suggested this was more annoying than amusing. "Last year, one made it all the way to the throne room before I caught it. Left puddles everywhere."

They emerged onto a terrace Briar hadn't seen before, where a series of fountains cascaded down the hillside in tiers. The water sparkled in the afternoon light, but as Briar looked closer, she saw them—tiny forms within the water, some barely visible, others catching the light like living prisms.

"There," Sian pointed to the topmost fountain. "See the ones near the lotus blooms?"

Briar leaned closer, and her breath caught. They were beautiful, translucent beings that seemed to shift between water and light, some no bigger than her thumb, others the size of her palm. One near the edge had what looked like flowing fins or fronds extending from its head, like an aquatic flower blooming in constant motion.

"They're incredible," she said softly.

"They're troublemakers," Sian corrected, but there was affection in her tone. "Watch." She held her hand over the water, and Briar felt the temperature shift, the warm surface water beginning to sink while cooler water rose from below.

Several sprites immediately darted deeper, following the warm current. But others scattered, some hiding beneath lily pads, one actually leaping out of the fountain entirely to plop into a decorative urn nearby.

"See what I mean?" Sian sighed. "This is going to take all afternoon."

Briar found herself genuinely smiling for the first time since waking. "Where do we start?"

"The first rule," Sian said, kneeling beside the topmost fountain, "is patience. Watch which direction they naturally want to go, then encourage that."

She demonstrated by creating a gentle current with her fingers, barely disturbing the surface. Several sprites followed it, their translucent bodies catching the light as they spiraled down toward the next tier. But one—a particularly small one with frond-like appendages that reminded Briar of feathered gills—kept darting behind a cluster of water lilies.

"That one's new," Sian observed. "Born this summer, probably. They're always the most skittish about their first migration."

Briar found herself drawn to the tiny sprite. It was smaller than the others, its body shifting between pale blue and crystal clear as it moved. When it peeked out from behind the lily pad, she could see large, dark spots that looked almost like eyes.

"Can I try?" she asked.

Sian gestured for her to go ahead. Briar dipped her fingers into the water slowly, careful not to create ripples. The temperature was pleasant, sun-warmed on top with cooler depths below. The hiding sprite darted deeper behind its lily pad.

"Hello, small one," Briar said softly. She kept her hand still, letting the water settle. "The others are going somewhere warm for the winter. Don't you want to go too?"

The sprite edged out slightly, those eye-like spots seeming to focus on her fingers. Its gill-fronds waved gently in the water, creating tiny currents of their own.

"There's a gate here," Sian said, moving to a bronze mechanism built into the fountain's edge. "When I open it, the water level will lower and create a current down to the next pool. Can you keep our shy friend from panicking?"

Briar kept her attention on the small sprite, watching as it ventured a bit further from its hiding spot. When Sian turned the gate mechanism, water began flowing through with a soft gurgling sound. Most of the sprites rode the current down cheerfully, some even seeming to play in the new flow.

But the small one immediately retreated, pressing itself against the fountain's wall.

"It's alright," Briar murmured, cupping her hands in the water to create a small, calm pocket. "See? Just water moving. Nothing frightening."

The sprite investigated the still water between her palms, and she carefully began moving her hands toward the flow. The sprite followed, more curious than afraid now.

When they reached the current, it hesitated, then suddenly darted through her hands and down the channel, its fronds streaming behind it like tiny banners.

"One down," Sian said with satisfaction, already moving to the next fountain. "Only about sixty more to go."

They worked their way down the terraces, each fountain presenting its own challenges. One held a cluster of sprites that had apparently decided they liked the temperature exactly as it was and refused to budge until Sian created a gradual warming gradient they couldn't resist following. Another fountain's sprites kept playing in the ornamental waterfall, riding it up and down instead of moving to the winter pools.

"How long have you been doing this?" Briar asked, helping corner a particularly evasive sprite that kept jumping between fountains.

"Since I came to the Star Court. About forty years now." Sian guided the water temperature with practiced ease, creating invisible paths the sprites instinctively followed. "They reproduce slowly, thank the gods. I know most of them by now."

Briar watched a medium-sized sprite with what looked like a crown of flowing tendrils investigate her shadow on the water. "They all look different."

"They adapt to their fountains. The ones from the rose garden pools have a pinkish tint. The ones near the meditation pools are almost perfectly clear." Sian paused at a large central fountain where three channels converged. "This is where it gets tricky. They have to choose which warm pool to winter in, and they're very particular."

The sprites began gathering at the convergence, swirling in little eddies of confusion. Some darted toward one channel, then changed their minds and tried another. The small one with the feathered gills that Briar had coaxed earlier seemed especially lost, spinning in circles.

Without thinking, Briar reached for it, and to her surprise, it swam into her cupped hands. Its body felt like cool silk against her palms, barely there but definitely present.

"The eastern pool is warmest," she told it, as if it could understand. She walked to that channel and lowered her hands into the water. The sprite hesitated, then brushed against her fingers—almost like a goodbye—before flowing away down the channel.

"You're natural at this," Sian said, but her attention was on a group of sprites that had decided to go upstream instead.

They worked until the sun began slanting low, turning the fountains to gold. By the time they reached the last terrace, Briar's sleeves were soaked to the elbows and she'd forgotten, for a while, about the choice waiting for her at dawn.

"Last one," Sian announced, approaching a small fountain tucked into an alcove. "Usually the easiest since—" She stopped, frowning. "It's empty."

Briar looked into the clear water. No sprites at all, though the fountain was otherwise pristine.

"They must have migrated early," Sian said, though she sounded puzzled. "Strange. The ones here are usually the last to go." She walked around the fountain, examining it from different angles. "Well, that's all of them then. The winter pools should be properly populated now."

She created a small whirlpool in the fountain, just to be certain, but nothing emerged from hiding.

"Thank you," Sian said, wringing water from her sleeves. "This usually takes twice as long with just me, and results in significantly more flooding."

"It was..." Briar paused, realizing she meant it, "actually enjoyable. They're beautiful creatures."

"They're just water given form and thought," Sian said, but fondly. "Simple beings with simple needs. Sometimes I envy them that." She glanced at Briar. "The sun's getting low. We should return inside. You'll want to eat something before..."

She didn't finish the sentence. She didn't need to. Before the hunt ended. Before Briar had to choose.

The peaceful afternoon of shepherding water sprites already felt distant as they walked back toward the palace, the weight of her approaching decision returning with each step. The sun cast long shadows across the courtyard, marking time she couldn't stop from passing.

Briar returned to her room, her sleeves still damp and clinging uncomfortably to her arms. The afternoon with Sian had been a welcome distraction, but now, alone again, the weight of the approaching choice settled back onto her shoulders.

She peeled off the wet tunic, draping it over a chair to dry, and moved to the wash basin to clean the fountain water from her arms. The porcelain bowl had been freshly filled, the water clear and still. She dipped her hands in, watching the ripples spread—

Something moved beneath the surface.

She jerked back, water sloshing onto the floor. There, in the center of the basin, was the small sprite from the fountains. The one with the feathered gill appendages she'd coaxed from behind the lily pad. It spun in a lazy circle, those dark eye-spots seeming to track her movement.

"How did you—" She leaned closer, studying it. The sprite drifted toward her, its translucent body catching the late afternoon light streaming through the window. "You were supposed to go to the winter pools."

The sprite's gills fluttered, creating tiny currents in the basin. It pressed itself against the side closest to her, and she could have sworn it was looking at her expectantly.

"You followed me?" The absurdity of talking to a creature made of water struck her, but the sprite responded by doing a small loop, its movements almost playful.

She reached toward the basin hesitantly. The sprite immediately swam to her fingers, brushing against them with that strange sensation of cool silk she remembered from the fountains. It wove between her fingers like a cat seeking attention, if cats were liquid and lived in wash basins.

"You can't stay here," she told it, though even as she said it, she found herself charmed by the tiny creature. "Sian will come looking for you. You need to be with the others."

The sprite released a stream of bubbles, something that looked almost like a sigh, and sank to the bottom of the basin dramatically. Its gills drooped, the whole tiny body seeming to convey dejection.

Despite everything, Briar found herself smiling. "That's very dramatic for something so small."

The sprite perked up at her voice, rising to the surface again. This time, it did something extraordinary. The water around it began to lift, forming a perfect sphere about the size of her fist. The sprite floated in the center of this bubble as it rose from the basin, hovering in the air between them.

Briar stared, captivated. The water sphere caught the light, casting tiny rainbows across the walls. The sprite swam lazy circles inside its self-made home, clearly pleased with itself.

"You can do that?" She held out her hand, and the bubble drifted over to hover above her palm. She could feel the faint coolness of it, the way it displaced the air. "That's remarkable."

The bubble descended to rest in her cupped hands. Through the water, the sprite's eye-spots seemed to study her face. Then, as suddenly as it had formed, the bubble collapsed, water running through her fingers back into the basin with a splash. The sprite swam contentedly in circles, apparently having proved its point.

A knock at the door interrupted her wonder. "Just a moment," she called, quickly pulling on a dry tunic.

She glanced back at the basin. The sprite had settled near the edge, gills waving gently. "Stay here," she whispered. "And try not to flood anything."

She opened the door to find a servant—not the young girl from this morning, but an older fae with bark-textured skin.

"Begging your pardon, my lady, but Lord Arion asks if you'll join him for the evening meal. The formal dining hall, when you're ready."

Evening already. The day had passed faster than she'd realized. "Tell him I'll be there shortly."

The servant bowed and departed. Briar closed the door and returned to the basin, where the sprite was now investigating the soap dish with apparent suspicion.

"I have to go," she told it. "But... I suppose you've already decided to stay, haven't you?"

The sprite created another bubble, smaller this time, and rose to eye level with her. Its gills fluttered in what she was beginning to recognize as its happy gesture.

"You need a name," she said, then felt foolish. Did water sprites even understand names? But the creature did a little spin in its bubble, seeming pleased by the idea. "What about... River? Too obvious. Brook? No." She studied its delicate, translucent form, the way its gill-fronds moved like aquatic flowers. "Tidal? Still too—"

The word brought back a sudden memory—tide pools along the coast, Allegra's small hand in hers, pointing excitedly at a starfish clinging to the rocks. "Frederick!" her sister had announced with absolute certainty, as if the creature had been waiting its whole life for that exact name. Everything had been Frederick to Allegra.

"Frederick," Briar said softly, the name carrying the weight of that memory.

The sprite suddenly brightened, its whole body flashing a pale blue before returning to clear, gills fluttering in what she was beginning to recognize as delight.

"Frederick it is, then," she murmured, throat tight with the reminder of everything she'd left behind, everything she'd traded to save that little girl who named starfish in tide pools.

The newly named sprite descended back into the basin with a small splash. Briar quickly changed into proper dinner attire, a gown of soft gray that seemed to float rather than fall, layers of gossamer-thin material that created an ethereal effect with every movement. A swooping neckline was both modest and tasteful with billowing sleeves that gathered at her wrists with delicate gold bands. Three more bands of gold embroidery wrapped around the bodice, drawing the eye to her waist before the skirts swept out in flowing layers that seemed to catch and hold light.

As she headed for the door, she noticed Frederick had created another bubble and was floating near her shoulder.

"You can't come to dinner," she said. The bubble drooped slightly, sinking lower in the air. "Fine. But stay hidden. If anyone asks, you're supposed to be in the winter pools."

Frederick brightened again and tucked itself behind her hair, the bubble shrinking to the size of a large marble. She could feel its cool presence against her neck, oddly comforting.

She made her way to the dining hall, trying not to think about how many hours remained until dawn, until she would have to choose between courts, between futures, between the two fae who pulled at her heart in such different ways.

At least she wasn't entirely alone. Even if her only ally was a creature made of water who'd decided she was worth following.

Chapter Six

The dining hall glowed with soft twilight colors, the Star Court's magic ensuring the light shifted gradually from gold to violet as evening deepened. The table was set for five, though the spacing felt deliberate—Thaine at one end like an after-thought, the others arranged to keep maximum distance from him while maintaining the pretense of civility.

Briar entered to find them already assembled. Arion rose immediately, pulling out the chair beside him. The gesture was smooth, practiced, but something in the way his hand lingered on the back of her chair felt proprietary.

"You look lovely," he said, his eyes taking in the gray gown with apparent approval.

She sat, aware of Frederick's cool presence against her neck, hidden beneath her hair. Across the table, Thaine lounged in his chair with the kind of casual sprawl that suggested he knew exactly how much his presence bothered everyone.

"The Star Court's colors suit you," Thaine observed, his tone neutral enough that the insult underneath—the implication of her changeability—was barely detectable. "Though I recall you looked equally at home in Forest Court green."

Arion's jaw tightened almost imperceptibly. "Briar looks well in any court's colors. Or none at all."

The last part hung in the air, carrying more weight than perhaps intended. Sian smoothly redirected, lifting her water goblet.

"The sprite migration went well today, thanks to Briar's help. We managed to relocate them all before the temperature drops tonight."

"All of them?" Halian asked, serving himself from a platter of roasted vegetables that smelled of rosemary and something distinctly fae.

"Every last one," Sian confirmed. "Briar has a natural touch with them."

"She has a natural touch with many things," Thaine said mildly, cutting into his meat with precise movements. "It's what makes her so... valuable."

The word choice wasn't lost on anyone. Arion's light flickered faintly around his fingers before he controlled it.

"Speaking of value," Halian interjected, clearly trying to manage the tension, "we should discuss the ward modifications. With the hunt ending at dawn—"

"The hunt," Thaine interrupted, looking directly at Briar for the first time. "How are you finding your last night of freedom? Assuming you're planning to embrace it."

"That's her choice to make," Arion said, his voice carrying an edge of warning.

"Of course it is." Thaine took a sip of wine. "Though choices are interesting things. Sometimes what we think is a choice is really just selecting between cages."

"Not everyone offers cages," Sian said quietly. "Some offer genuine sanctuary."

Thaine's smile was sharp. "Sanctuary. Such a pretty word for 'staying where you're put.'"

"Better than being hunted," Halian said.

"Is it?" Thaine tilted his head. "At least prey gets to run."

Briar set down her fork, the soft clink loud in the sudden silence. They all looked at her—waiting for her to speak, to choose a side in their verbal chess match. Instead, she reached for her water, taking a slow sip while they watched.

"The wards," she said finally, looking at Halian. "What modifications?"

He blinked at the redirect but adapted. "Strengthening the eastern boundaries. There have been... disturbances. Energy signatures we don't recognize."

"Someone's been testing them," Sian added. "Carefully. Professionally."

"Not my lord," Thaine said before anyone could voice the suspicion. "He has no interest in the Star Court. His focus is entirely on what was taken from him."

The weight of his gaze on Briar made his meaning clear.

"No one took me," Briar said evenly. "I was cast out."

"Temporarily." Thaine's certainty was absolute. "My lord's tempers burn hot but brief. By dawn, this will all be a memory."

"Your lord," Arion said, his hand finding Briar's on the table, covering it with his own, "has no claim here."

The possessive gesture, meant to be protective, made something in Briar's chest tighten with frustration. Everyone kept touching her, claiming her, speaking about her future as if she were a book to be placed on whatever shelf they deemed appropriate.

"The Star Court," Sian was saying, "has ancient laws of sanctuary. Once given, it cannot be revoked."

"Unless the person chooses to leave," Halian added, looking at Briar with what he probably thought was reassurance.

"Or is taken," Thaine countered. "The Forest Court has ancient laws too."

They continued debating, their voices weaving around her—laws and traditions and possibilities and threats. Arion's thumb stroked across her knuckles, a gesture meant to comfort that instead made her want to pull away. Frederick shifted against her neck, responding to her tension.

"What do you think, Briar?" Sian asked suddenly, and they all turned to her again.

What did she think? That they were discussing her like a treaty to be negotiated? That each of them had already decided what would be best for her?

Before she could formulate a response that wouldn't simply be screaming at all of them, the dining hall doors burst open.

A guard stumbled in, his face pale with something beyond fear.

"My lords," he gasped. "Someone approaches under a banner of truce. Someone who shouldn't—who can't—"

"Who?" Arion demanded, already rising, his hand still possessively on Briar's.

"We don't know. But they're using old magic. Magic that predates the courts themselves."

"The Drak," Arion said immediately, his jaw tightening. "He's come for her."

Thaine looked between them, frowning. "What Drak?"

"Karse," Sian supplied quickly. "A Drak that Briar freed during the hunt. He claims she belongs to him."

Thaine's eyebrows rose, and he looked at Briar with something between amusement and disbelief. "Of course. Because freeing one monster wasn't enough excitement for one week. Did the first one not teach you anything about the perils of misplaced compassion?"

Briar didn't respond, her chest tightening with an emotion she couldn't name. Karse had found her? Part of her felt oddly... disappointed wasn't the right word. Conflicted. He was dangerous, but he had also protected her, had carried her for hours through the forest. The thought of him fighting his way into the Star Court for her stirred something uncomfortable in her chest.

"How long?" Halian asked the guard.

"They're at the gates now."

Arion rose, moving toward the door, Briar stumbling as he pulled her with him. "We need to get you somewhere safe before—"

"My lord," the guard interrupted, his face growing paler. "They're... they're already inside. The courtyard."

"What?" Arion asked, stopping midstride. "How did they get past the wards?"

Thaine cursed under his breath. "What kind of sanctuary is this if you can't keep a single Drak out?"

"Our wards are perfectly adequate against normal threats," Arion shot back, his light flickering with irritation.

"Clearly." Thaine's tone dripped sarcasm. "Though I suppose 'adequate' is the Star Court way. My lord would have already had the intruder's head on a spike."

"Your lord," Arion said coldly, "is the reason she needs sanctuary in the first place."

"At least the Forest Court doesn't let its enemies stroll through the front door."

"Enough," Halian interrupted, already moving. "Argue after we deal with the threat."

They rushed through the corridors, Arion's light casting wild shadows as they moved. If it was Karse, would he really attack the Star Court for her? The thought should have terrified her. Instead, she found herself almost hoping—

But as they burst into the courtyard, her stomach dropped.

The copper hair hit her first—that autumn flame she'd last seen in the dungeons when he'd transformed from pitiful Thomas into something far worse. Not Karse. Malus.

He stood in the center of the courtyard as if he belonged there, examining the silver fountain with casual interest. He wore deep green trimmed with gold, and every line of him radiated power he no longer had to hide.

Her throat constricted. The compulsion he'd placed might be gone, but the memory of it lingered—that sensation of words dissolving on her tongue, the metallic taste of his magic forcing itself down her throat.

Behind him, five figures stood motionless. The sight of them made her skin crawl in ways she couldn't articulate. Antlered masks that were made up of bone or bark, tattered robes that didn't move despite the evening breeze. And beneath those masks—nothing. Just shadow where faces should be. The smell hit her then, subtle but unmistakable. Rot. Decay. The sweet-sick scent of things returning to earth.

Star Court guards lay groaning near the entrance. One clutched a shoulder bent at an impossible angle. Another's leg was wrapped in vines that seemed to be growing into his flesh. Briar's stomach turned. He'd hurt them casually, just to make his entrance.

"Ah," Malus said without turning. "There you are. I was beginning to think the Star Court's hospitality had declined." He faced them then, and his smile was exactly as she remembered—sharp, amused, dangerous. "Though I suppose letting myself in was rather rude."

Arion stepped forward, light gathering in his palms. "You're not welcome here."

"No?" Malus's eyebrows rose in mock surprise. "And here I've come all this way on legitimate business." His gaze moved over them slowly, taking inventory. It paused on Thaine, and something cold flickered in his expression. "Still breathing, huntsman? My brother always was too sentimental about his tools."

The casual dismissal of Thaine as a tool made Briar's chest tighten. Is that all any of them were to the fae lords? Implements to be used and discarded?

Finally, inevitably, Malus's attention settled on her. His smile widened, and her body remembered—the grip of his hand on her wrist, the strength that had bent iron bars, the violation of his magic forced down her throat.

"Lady Briar. Or should I say—" He paused, savoring the moment like wine. "Queen? Though I suppose the title was never quite official, was it? How awkward, to be cast out before the crown was even properly placed."

Briar felt her heart lodge itself in her throat. Queen. Beside her, she felt Arion go rigid. Sian drew in a sharp breath. When she looked she saw them staring, seeing her differently. Not just Eliam's pet or prisoner, but someone who'd been chosen for more.

The shame burned through her chest. She'd wanted it. God help her, she'd wanted to be Eliam's queen, had chosen to stay for it.

And a foolish, traitorous part of her still wanted it. Wanted to hear him whisper the words she had once resented. *You're mine.*

"What game are you playing at," Arion asked, but uncertainty threaded through his voice.

"Game? No games. If you don't believe me," Malus tilted his head, "then ask her. Ask her what my dear brother promised before his tantrum. Ask the huntsman—he knows. Don't you, Thaine?"

Arion's fingers tightened where they still grasped hers and she wasn't sure who he was angry with—Malus for his taunts, or her for what he would undoubtedly see as a betrayal.

Briar's throat closed around any possible response. How could she explain? That she'd been ready to stand beside the Forest King? That she'd chosen the darkness he offered? The words wouldn't come, trapped behind shame and grief for something that would never be.

"I'm not here to bring harm to anyone," Malus continued, as if discussing the weather. "Well, beyond those unfortunate guards, but they were rather insistent about proper channels." He straightened his cuffs with practiced ease. "I'm simply here to collect what my brother so carelessly discarded. The Hunt isn't over until dawn, after all. Her highness is still fair game." His eyes gleamed. "Laws are laws."

"The Hunt applies to the Forest Court," Halian said, but his voice shook slightly.

"The Hunt," Malus corrected, his tone edged with thinly veiled annoyance, "applies to any unclaimed prey. And since my brother publicly cast her out..." He spread his hands as if the conclusion was obvious.

The word 'prey' made her stomach turn. After everything that had happened, after surviving the forest, after Karse's protection, after thinking she might be safe, in the end she was still seen as quarry to be claimed.

"She has sanctuary here," Arion stepped partially in front of her, his light growing brighter. The protective gesture should have been comforting. Instead, it made her feel like a child being shielded, incapable of standing on her own.

"Sanctuary." Malus tested the word, amused. "From other hunters, perhaps. But I'm not exactly a hunter, am I?"

His eyes found hers again, and something knowing flickered in them. He stepped closer. "You could come willingly, you know. Spare everyone the unpleasantness." His smile sharpened. "After all, it was you who fed me. You who gave me strength when I had resigned myself to eternity in the dark." The words were almost exactly what he'd said in the dungeons, but twisted now, made public. "And I did promise I would thank you properly when the time was right."

"She's not going anywhere with you," Arion said.

"No? How fascinating that you believe your own words to be true." Malus's tone remained light, conversational. "You see, choice is an illusion given by those in positions of power. The only choice any of you have in this matter is how many of you die before I get what I want, and I will get it. So tell me, brightling, are the lives of your people worth protecting one human?"

The question hung in the air, barbed with truth. They were all doing it—Arion shielding her, Thaine expecting her to return, Malus claiming her as payment for a debt she'd never agreed to. Even now, they talked over her, about her, around her. As if her wants were secondary to their decisions.

Frederick shifted against her neck, hidden beneath her hair, responding to her rising anger. The tiny comfort of that small, chosen connection was the only thing keeping her from screaming at all of them.

"You should tend to that one," a familiar voice observed from the ruined gates. "His shoulder's completely dislocated. Probably the leg too, though that might just be the vines."

Karse strolled through the destroyed entrance, stepping over a groaning guard with the same casual indifference someone might show to fallen branches. His appearance had changed since the forest—he wore dark clothing that looked stolen from someone with better taste, and his shaggy black hair caught the dying light in ways that revealed those patches of iridescent scales along his neck and jaw.

His reptilian eyes swept the courtyard, taking in the scene with mild interest. They lingered on the Withered for a moment. "Hm, creative," he said, before his gaze settled on Malus.

"Another fae lord trying to take what isn't his." Karse's tone carried the weary annoyance of someone who'd had this conversation too many times. "You all really can't help yourselves, can you? Like magpies with opposable thumbs."

Malus's copper hair seemed to flame brighter in the growing dusk. "And what are you supposed to be?"

"The one who got here first." Karse walked past him as if he weren't surrounded by creatures of rot and decay, past Arion's defensive light, past Thaine's coiled readiness. He stopped directly in front of Briar and his fingers locking around her wrist, already turning to walk. She didn't try to pull away, too surprised to see him, but she didn't follow either. He stopped, looking back over his shoulder.

"Aren't you exhausted by all this yet?" Karse gestured vaguely at the assembled fae with his free hand. "They'll keep talking about you like furniture until dawn. You have capable legs. You should use them."

"She's not going anywhere—" Arion started.

"With you," Thaine finished, though clearly meaning something different.

Karse sighed, making no move to relinquish his hold on Briar's wrist as he turned to face them. "I really don't want to have to kill you all. It's messy, and—" He glanced at Briar, his head tilting slightly. "You look like a crier. Are you going to cry if I burn them? Because that would be tedious."

The casual way he discussed multiple murder while worrying about her emotional response made her head spin. Before she could formulate any kind of answer, Malus's patience finally snapped.

"Enough."

The quiet command came out quiet, decisive. The Withered moved as one, their stillness breaking into motion that was wrong, unnaturally fluid and far too synchronized. They spread out in a circle, antlered masks turning toward different targets. The smell of decay intensified, and where their robes brushed the ground, the grass withered and died.

"Kill the Drak," Malus said, already moving toward Briar. "Disable the others."

White-blue flame erupted from Karse's free hand, hot enough that Briar felt her skin tighten from proximity. "Finally. I was getting bored."

He pushed Briar behind him, and the others instinctively closed ranks—Arion's light flaring into a protective barrier, Thaine positioning himself at her left despite having no weapon, Sian at her right with water already gathering. For a moment, they formed a unified defense around her.

Then the Withered struck from multiple directions at once.

The formation shattered instantly. A creature lunged at Thaine, forcing him to roll away and grab a decorative spear from the wall. Another came at Sian from the side, making her pivot and lash out with water whips. Halian had to dodge backward, hands moving in complex patterns to call on what remained of the Star Court's wards.

Karse held position longest, flames roaring, but even he had to move when two Withered converged on him from opposite angles.

And through it all, Malus walked calmly toward Briar, autumn magic pooling around his fingers.

"Now then," he said, as chaos erupted around them, "we have much to discuss, you and I."

The warmth in her chest contracted so violently she gasped, responding to threats from every direction—Eliam's brother approaching with patient malice, the defenders being pulled away from her, and something else, something building that felt like thorns trying to grow from inside her bones.

She watched Arion trying to return to her, but a Withered's fingers brushed his light barrier's edge. Where they touched, the light itself seemed to rot, turning gray and crumbling like ash. He stumbled back, eyes wide with shock.

"Don't let them touch you!" Sian shouted, whipping water at another creature. The liquid struck its mask, but instead of flowing over it, the water blackened and fell as putrid sludge.

Karse laughed as he sent a torrent of white-blue flame at the Withered approaching him. The fire consumed its robes, but the thing kept coming, bones or wood or whatever else comprised its frame still moving despite being wreathed in flames.

Through it all, Malus continued his approach, steps casual.

"Such chaos," he said, stepping around Thaine as he rolled away from grasping, decay-touched fingers. "All this fuss over one human girl. You have quite a talent for garnering loyalty. Unfortunately, it won't be enough to save you."

Briar backed away, her heart hammering. The warmth in her chest pulsed erratically, responding to threats from every direction. She could see Arion still trying to reach her, but a Withered blocked his path, forcing him to retreat and avoid that terrible touch.

"There's nowhere to run," Malus continued, matching her retreat step for step. "This ends only one way."

She ducked behind the fountain, putting it between them. Malus sighed, amused, and walked around it with unhurried steps. She scrambled in the other direction, nearly colliding with Sian who was desperately trying to freeze a Withered in place.

"Briar, get inside—" Sian's words cut off as she had to dive away from reaching fingers.

"Come now, spare your friends, no one here has to die today." Malus reached towards her, palm up, as though inviting her to take his hand.

The ground beneath Briar's feet suddenly erupted.

Not just thorns this time. The stone itself cracked and split as massive vines burst through, thick as her arm and covered in golden flowers that glowed bright and blinding. They grew wild, directionless, responding to her terror rather than her will. One wrapped around a Withered's leg, and where the flowers touched the Withered, it burst into brilliant flame. Another vine caught Halian across the chest, thorns tearing through his robes as he cried out, stumbling back in surprise.

"Fascinating," Malus said, not even pausing as vines erupted around him. They seemed to bend away from him, as if recognizing a greater threat. "Your magic doesn't know friend from foe. How wonderfully destructive."

Briar staggered back, eyes sweeping the courtyard in desperation. She spotted Karse in time to watch as he incinerated his opponent, white ash drifting through the air like freshly fallen snow. She glanced back at Malus who had finally cleared the tangle of vines.

She ran towards Karse, stumbling over upturned stones and debris, and made it only a few steps before another Withered cut her off, forcing her to dodge left. The creature's fingers brushed her sleeve, and the fabric aged decades in seconds, crumbling to dust and revealing the skin beneath.

"Briar!" Arion's voice, desperate. She could see him fighting to reach her, his light burning brighter, but two Withered had converged on him now, drawn by his power.

More vines erupted, these bearing flowers that released clouds of golden pollen. Where it touched the Withered, they stumbled, their movements becoming erratic. But Thaine started coughing, eyes watering, his defense faltering.

"You're going to kill them all," Malus observed, now only feet away. "Your protectors, your admirers. Your magic responds to fear with violence. How very like my brother's power."

Her back hit the solid stone of the courtyard wall leaving her with nowhere left to run.

Malus paused, watching her for a moment with those unsettling green eyes. They looked so much like Eliam's, only more sinister. "We are going to have *so* much fun," he said as he reached for her again, his smile patient and terrible. "Don't make this more difficult than—"

A stream of water shot directly into his open mouth.

Malus choked, stumbling back, hands going to his throat. Frederick—tiny, impossible Frederick—had expanded his bubble to the size of a melon and was shooting high-pressure water with shocking accuracy. The sprite's entire body glowed with effort, more water than should have been possible pouring from his small form.

Malus coughed, retching water tinged with autumn colors, his perfect composure finally cracking. "A water sprite," he said, voice rough but steadying. "How unexpectedly clever."

Frederick, exhausted from his effort, shrank back to marble size and disappeared into Briar's hair. She could feel him trembling against her neck.

Malus straightened, autumn magic already repairing the indignity, his copper hair drying instantly. "Enough games."

Vines erupted from the ground around Briar—not golden and wild like before, but dark and twisted, reeking of decay. They reached for her with thorn-covered tendrils, moving with purposeful intent.

Without warning, Karse dropped from above, landing in a low crouch directly between them. White-blue flames erupted from both hands, incinerating the vines instantly. The air filled with the acrid smell of burning rot.

"I said, *no touching*," he said, still crouched, looking up at Malus with those reptilian eyes. "The human's mine. I thought we established this. Maybe you're just slower than most. Do you need it written down? I could burn it into your forehead if that helps."

Malus stepped back, autumn magic surging defensively. The vines around them withered instantly, the golden flowers turning to ash, even the stones cracking with sudden age. But Karse just tilted his head, flames growing hotter, scales visible along his arms where his stolen clothes had started to smoke.

Around them, the battle had stalled. The remaining Withered stood motionless, waiting for commands. Arion's light flickered with exhaustion. Thaine bled from multiple wounds where thorns had caught him.

"We can do this easy or hard," Karse said, finally standing, keeping himself firmly between Briar and Malus. "But either way, you're not taking what's mine."

Malus studied the scene: the wild vines still twitching with golden light, the scorch marks where Karse's fire had met his autumn decay, the way the magic had attacked everyone indiscriminately. Something flickered in his expression, recognition, but of what?

"How interesting," he murmured, tilting his head as he observed her. "That wasn't you at all, was it? You're as surprised as everyone else when it happens." His eyes narrowed with genuine curiosity. "Something inside you, acting on its own. Protecting you without your knowledge or control. What exactly did my brother hide in his pet?"

He took a step closer.

"Don't," Karse warned, flames dancing higher.

Malus glanced at the Drak, then at Arion approaching from the left, light gathering in his palm. Thaine had acquired another weapon and now circled in from the right. Even injured, even tired, they were converging on him.

"My my, three defenders for one human girl," Malus mused. "And something else defending her from within. Either you're all fools, or—" He paused, studying how the golden flowers pulsed with their own light. "Or my brother did something far more interesting than simply marking a human plaything."

He took a step back, and the remaining Withered moved with him, forming a protective circle.

"This has been most educational," he said, his gaze fixed on Briar with an intensity that made her skin crawl. "We're not finished. Whatever my brother hid in you, whatever he thought he was protecting—it won't stay hidden long. I'm very good at taking things apart to see how they work. Putting them back together, well, that takes time and patience but I'm sure it will be worth the effort."

The threat was somehow worse for its vagueness. Taking her was one thing, speaking of taking her apart to discover what made the magic manifest was another entirely.

Malus's smile grew contemplative. "It's a talent that runs in our family. My brother prefers to break things through force. I prefer... precision."

Karse tilted his head. "This is all *very* fascinating, but I'd like to get to the part where I burn you to cinders."

"A pity." Malus's attention never left Briar, who pressed herself harder against the wall, unable to look away from his calculating gaze. "We'll continue this another time, your *majesty*. When there are fewer interruptions."

Karse scoffed. "Don't count on it. I'm very persistent. Also violent. Persistently violent."

The sound of armored footsteps echoed from multiple corridors—Star Court reinforcements finally responding to the breach. Malus glanced toward the sound with mild irritation.

"How tedious." He stepped back into his circle of Withered. "Until next time then. Do try to keep her intact—" his eyes found Briar again, "—I'd hate for my brother's secret to be damaged before I can properly examine it."

Without another word he melted into shadow, his remaining Withered dissolving into darkness and dead leaves left to scatter on a wind that shouldn't exist. The only evidence of their presence was the destroyed gate, the wounded guards, and the lingering smell of decay.

The Star Court guards burst into the courtyard just as the last shadow faded, finding only the aftermath of violence and five exhausted defenders standing among the wreckage.

Chapter Seven

They moved with practiced efficiency, some securing the perimeter while others tended to the wounded. Their captain, a severe-looking fae with bark-textured skin, surveyed the destruction—the shattered gates, the withered vegetation, the golden vines still twitching with residual magic.

"My lord," he addressed Arion, though his eyes kept returning to Briar. "The wards are compromised. We need to—"

"Secure the grounds, tend the wounded," Arion said curtly. "We'll discuss the breach later."

Briar stood frozen against the wall, watching the organized chaos unfold. Her mind felt fractured, unable to process what had just happened. Malus had come for her. Had called her Eliam's queen in front of everyone. Had spoken of taking her apart to find what was hidden inside her. The warmth in her chest pulsed erratically, still agitated from the threat, from the violence, from the way everyone had fought over her like she was a prize to be won.

Arion crossed the courtyard to her, concern etched across his features. His light magic still flickered faintly around his hands, and she could see exhaustion in the way he moved. He'd fought for her. They all had.

"Briar," he said softly, already moving toward her. His hands went to her arms first, fingers gentle as they traced where her sleeve had crumbled to dust, checking the exposed skin. Finding no wounds there, his hands moved to her shoulders, then carefully tilted her head to examine her neck.

She stood frozen, letting him inspect her like she was made of glass. His touch was careful, clinical almost, but she could feel the tremor in his fingers. The concern in every movement. When his hands finally came up to cup her face, turning it gently to check for injuries, something twisted in her chest. She didn't deserve this tenderness, not after what she'd done, not after the chaos she'd brought to his court.

"Are you hurt?" His thumbs brushed across her cheekbones, and she had to close her eyes against the gentleness of it.

She shook her head, not trusting her voice. Frederick shifted against her neck, hidden beneath her hair, a small cool comfort against skin that felt too hot under Arion's careful attention.

"Malus says things," Arion finally said, his voice carefully neutral. "Twists words to hurt. To manipulate."

She opened her eyes to find him watching her with something desperate in his expression. He was giving her an out. A way to dismiss what Malus had said as lies, as cruelty designed to cause chaos. Part of her wanted to take it, to let him believe whatever story would make this easier.

"When he said—" Arion stopped, swallowed, started again. "The things he claimed about you and Eliam. About you being..." The word wouldn't come. He couldn't say it.

"His queen?" she finished quietly.

Pain, or maybe disappointment, flickered across Arion's face. As if by saying it aloud she'd made real what he'd been hoping would remain unspoken.

"Eliam was going to name me his consort," she continued, the words scraping her throat raw. "Before. Before everything fell apart."

Arion's expression shifted through several emotions. First surprise, followed by confusion, then something that looked like pity. "Briar... it's alright. You don't have to feel ashamed. You were trapped, doing what you had to in order to survive. Agreeing to whatever he wanted—"

"Stop." The word came out sharper than she intended. She pulled away and watched as his arms sank slowly to his sides. "Just, please, stop."

"I'm only saying you don't have to—"

"You're wrong." Her hands clenched into fists, nails digging into her palms. The warmth in her chest flared. "You think it was about survival but... I wanted to stay. I was *going* to stay."

The silence that followed felt suffocating. Arion stared at her, clearly struggling to reconcile this with whatever image he'd built of her—the trapped human, the victim needing rescue.

"I chose him," she said, her voice rising despite the shake in it. "Not because I had to. Not because I was afraid. I wanted to be his queen. I wanted—" For a moment she couldn't breathe let alone speak. She had spent days running, hoping, and it wasn't until she had to speak the words out loud that she realized just how foolish she had truly been. Eliam had only ever been honest with her, told her that it wasn't about love. She was the one who had chosen to believe otherwise. "In the end he threw me away, cast me out like I was nothing... like none of it mattered."

"Briar—" Arion reached for her again.

She jerked back, slapping his hand away. "Don't. Don't comfort me. Don't tell me it's okay or that I'm confused or that I don't know what I really wanted. I *know* what I wanted."

"And this," Thaine interjected from where he leaned against the fountain, his tone matter-of-fact, "is why we're returning to the Forest Court at dawn. My lord may have been hasty, but his claim—"

She turned on Thaine, the rage that had been simmering for days beneath the pain and grief finally boiling over. "His claim? The one he forfeited when he threw me to the wolves? What about it?" She pushed off from the wall, her exhaustion forgotten in the face of pure fury. "I'm tired of being discussed and debated and fought over like I'm not even here! Like I don't have thoughts or feelings or wants of my own."

"No one thinks—" Sain began only to stop when Briar cut her off.

"No, Sian, everyone thinks it. I'm not a prize. I'm not property. I'm not a victim to be saved or a problem to be solved. I'm a person who made a choice and had it ripped away because I made a mistake." Her voice cracked on the last word, but it was from fury, not sorrow. "And now every single one of you stands here telling me what's going to happen next, where I'm going, what's best for me."

Briar laughed, the sound sharp and bitter. "You know what? Figure it out amongst yourselves. That's what you're going to do anyway."

She pushed past Arion, who stood frozen by her outburst. Past Thaine, who for once had no sarcastic comment. Past the guards who parted automatically.

"Briar, wait—" Arion started.

"No." She didn't turn around. "I'm done being told what to do. When you've all decided my fate, you can let me know. I'll be in my room. Or wherever you've decided I should be."

She strode toward the palace entrance, Frederick still hidden in her hair, the only one who hadn't tried to claim or save or fix her. Behind her, the courtyard remained silent, five powerful beings left standing in the wreckage, none of them sure what to do with a human woman who refused to be what any of them needed her to be.

The garden terrace existed in that strange space between wild and cultivated that the Star Court favored—roses that bloomed in impossible colors but grew however they pleased, fountains whose water sang but followed no predictable pattern. Briar stood at the stone railing, gripping it hard enough that the cold bit into her palms, trying to let the familiar-unfamiliar beauty calm the storm in her chest.

It wasn't working.

"That was quite the performance."

She didn't turn. She'd felt him arrive, that particular heaviness in the air that came with his presence. Like smoke before a fire.

"Go away, Karse."

"No." He moved closer, and she could hear the lazy satisfaction in his voice. "I particularly enjoyed the part where you told them all to figure it out themselves. The princeling looked like you'd slapped him. Which you did, technically."

"I'm not in the mood for—"

"For what? Truth?" He was beside her now, leaning against the railing with casual disregard for the drop below. "You're magnificent when you're angry. All that suppressed fury finally given voice. Much better than the cowering thing you've been doing."

She turned on him, ready to unleash that fury he claimed to admire. "Cowering? I've been—"

"Letting them shuffle you around like a chess piece." His reptilian eyes caught the moonlight, reflecting it back in golds and greens. "The Forest Lord cast you out, the princeling carried you here, the huntsman plans to drag you back. Even I claimed you as mine. And you've just... accepted it all."

"I haven't accepted anything!"

"Haven't you?" He tilted his head, studying her with that unnerving intensity. "Until five minutes ago, you were letting them debate your future without you. Like a good, obedient human."

The rage that had started to cool flared white-hot again. "Don't you dare—"

"I dare whatever I want." He pushed off the railing, moving into her space with predatory grace. "That's the difference between us. I take what I want. You wait for permission that never comes."

"I don't wait for—"

"You wanted to stay with him. The Forest Lord. You chose it. But the moment he cast you out, did you fight? Did you refuse to leave? No. You ran like frightened prey."

"He would have killed me!"

"So?" Karse stepped closer, close enough that she could feel the unnatural heat radiating from his skin. "At least it would have been on your terms. Instead, you're here, letting everyone else decide whether you go back to someone who discarded you or stay with people who see you as something to protect. Never as something with teeth of its own."

"I have teeth," she snarled.

His smile was slow, appreciative. "Then use them."

Something in his tone, in the way his eyes tracked over her face, made her realize how close they were. When had he gotten so close? She could see the scales along his throat catch the light, could smell something like smoke and copper on his skin.

"You're angry," he observed, voice dropping lower. "Furious at them. At him. At yourself. Good. Anger is so much more interesting than despair."

"Stop psychoanalyzing me."

"Stop letting others do your thinking for you."

The words hit like a slap. Before she could think better of it, she shoved him. Hard. He barely moved, but his smile widened, showing teeth that were just a little too sharp.

"There she is," he murmured. "The woman who threw a hairpin at a dying creature rather than leave him to his fate. Who survived the hunt. Who just told five of the most powerful beings in this realm to fuck off."

"I didn't say—"

He kissed her.

It wasn't gentle like Arion's had been, wasn't demanding like Eliam's. It was something else entirely—hot and dangerous and tasting of smoke. For a moment, she leaned into it, into the simple fact of someone taking what they wanted without asking permission, without treating her like glass.

Then reality crashed back. She shoved him away, harder this time, and he let her. He was watching her with those inhuman eyes, a knowing tilt to his mouth.

"You kissed me back," he observed.

"You—" She was breathing hard, fury and something else making her skin feel too tight. "You can't just—"

"Can't I?" He touched his lips thoughtfully. "I wanted to. So I did. That's what making choices looks like."

"That's not—"

"You're attracted to me." It wasn't a question. "Probably because I'm the only one not trying to save you. Or maybe because I'm dangerous in ways that have nothing to do with politics or magical bonds. Either way, you want to kiss me again."

"You're delusional."

"Am I?" He moved closer again, but didn't touch. Just stood there, radiating heat and danger and absolute certainty. "Then walk away. Go back to your room like you said you would. Let them finish deciding your fate while you wait like a good little human."

The mockery in his voice made her vision red at the edges.

"Or," he continued, voice dropping to something almost intimate, "you could make a choice. One they'd never make for you. One that's entirely, destructively yours."

"You're trying to manipulate me."

"I'm trying to fuck you," he said bluntly. "But only if you choose it. I don't take anything that isn't freely given." His smile turned sharp again. "Unlike everyone else in your life."

His words hung between them, brutal in their honesty. No pretty phrases about protection or what was best for her. Just raw, simple want and the choice to act on it or not.

The fire in her chest hadn't cooled. If anything, it burned hotter, looking for something to destroy. Or someone to destroy her. Frederick trembled against her neck, then suddenly his cool presence was gone—she caught a glimpse of his tiny bubble disappearing into the nearest water feature, abandoning her to her choices.

Without giving herself time to reconsider, Briar grabbed the front of Karse's shirt and pulled him down, crushing her mouth to his with all the fury and frustration of the last few days. This kiss was nothing like the first. This time it was her claiming something, even if that something was a terrible decision.

He made a sound that fell somewhere between satisfaction and surprise, his hands coming to her waist, pulling her against him. The heat radiating off of him was almost unbearable, like standing too close to a forge, but she didn't pull back. She bit his lip, hard enough to draw blood, and tasted copper.

"Finally," he said against her mouth, "you're making a choice."

The garden terrace suddenly felt too exposed. Karse backed her against one of the stone pillars, his body caging hers, and she could feel the barely controlled violence in the way he held himself—like a predator deciding whether to play with its food or devour it whole.

"Your room or mine?" he asked his teeth grazing her throat.

"Here's fine," she gasped and felt him smile—sharp and pleased.

"The exhibitionist emerges." His hands found the laces of her dress, pulling with deliberate slowness. "How unexpected."

"They're all inside deciding my fate anyway." The bitterness in her voice made him pull back to look at her, those inhuman eyes catching every flicker of emotion across her face.

"You're using me." It wasn't an accusation, just observation.

"Yes." She met his gaze steadily, refusing to pretend otherwise.

"Good." He spun her suddenly, pressing her against the stone railing, her hands bracing against the cold surface. "At least you're honest about it."

His mouth found her throat again and she could feel scales against her skin where his shirt had come undone, the texture alien but not unpleasant. His teeth scraped against her pulse, sharp enough to threaten but not break skin.

"Tell me about him," he said suddenly, his hands sliding along her waist. "The Forest Lord. Tell me why you chose him."

"What?" She tried to turn but he held her in place, not forcefully but firmly.

"You're thinking about him anyway." His voice carried that unsettling casual tone. "Comparing us. Wondering what he'd think if he saw you now. So tell me."

The question cut through her haze of anger and want. She didn't want to think about Eliam, but Karse was right—he was there anyway, a ghost between them.

"He never asked permission," she heard herself say. "He took. But somehow... it felt like being chosen."

"And now?" Karse's hands stilled on her waist, waiting.

"Now I'm choosing to be here. With someone else who takes what they want." She pressed back against him deliberately. "Someone who won't pretend it means more than it does and make me want things I shouldn't.."

"Such a romantic." But his voice had roughened, the heat from his skin increasing until she could feel it through her dress. "Turn around."

She did, meeting those inhuman eyes. In the moonlight, she could see the scales had spread, following the line of his collarbone, down his chest where his shirt hung open. They caught the light like black opals.

"You're beautiful," she said, surprising herself with the honesty. "In a terrifying way."

"Flattery?" He tilted his head. "Unexpected."

"Truth." She traced one of the scales with her fingertip, felt him shudder beneath her touch. "You're not human. Not fae. Something else entirely."

"Does that bother you?"

"It should." She pulled him down for another kiss. "But nothing about tonight is about what should be."

His response was to lift her onto the wide stone railing, her back to the drop, only his grip keeping her stable. The height, the danger of it, should have terrified her. Instead, it felt appropriate—balanced on an edge, one wrong move from disaster.

"You're trembling," he observed, his hands steady on her waist despite the precarious position.

"It's cold." But they both knew that was a lie—his heat had turned the air around them almost tropical.

"Liar." He pulled her closer to the edge, and her hands flew to his shoulders, gripping hard. She could feel scales beneath her palms, rougher than skin but warm, almost fevered. "You're scared."

"Of falling?"

"Of jumping." His mouth found that spot where her neck met her shoulder, teeth grazing. "There's a difference."

His hand slid up her thigh, pushing fabric aside with deliberate slowness. "Let's see how close to the edge you're willing to go," he murmured against her throat.

When his fingers found her, they were impossibly hot—not quite burning but close enough that she gasped, her grip on his shoulders tightening. He made that inhuman sound again, pleased.

"Already wet," he observed with clinical detachment that somehow made it worse. "Your body's more honest than you are."

She wanted to argue, but then he shifted the temperature of his touch—hot to cool to hot again—and coherent thought scattered. The danger of their position, balanced on the edge of a killing drop, only heightened every sensation. One hand gripped the railing while the other pressed against his chest, feeling his heartbeat—too slow to be human.

"Still thinking about him?" Karse asked, sliding two fingers inside her with a twist that made her back arch.

"No." And surprisingly, it was true. There was no room for Eliam here, no space for that complicated warmth and deeper connection. This was something else entirely—raw and physical and empty of anything beyond the moment.

His laugh was dark, appreciative. "Good. I'd hate to be competing with a ghost."

He worked her with shocking skill, his thumb circling her clit while his fingers found a rhythm that had her gasping, each shift in temperature sending new shockwaves through her. When she got close to the edge, he'd slow down, pull back, leave her hanging until she was ready to scream.

"Karse—"

"Not yet." He bit down on her shoulder, not quite breaking skin. "You don't get to finish until you ask for what you really want."

"I want—"

"To feel something other than pain?" He pulled back to look at her, those reptilian eyes too knowing, his fingers still moving with torturous slowness. "

"Yes," she gasped. "God, yes, I want—I need—"

"Then take it."

She hooked her legs around his waist, digging her heels into his backside to pull him closer, while shifting forward on the railing. Her hands went to his belt, working it open with fingers that shook from more than just desire.

"Impatient," he murmured, but his breathing had roughened, and she could feel the tension in his body, muscles coiled tight beneath skin.

"You said to take what I want." She freed him, wrapping her hand around his length and finding it almost too hot to touch, with subtle ridges she hadn't expected. The texture was foreign, smooth in places, with raised patterns that felt deliberate, designed for sensation. "So I am."

She explored with curious fingers, learning where he was most sensitive, how the heat varied along his length, the way the ridges seemed to pulse slightly under her touch. He made that inhuman sound again when she stroked him base to tip, her thumb finding moisture that was hotter than it should be, almost burning against her skin.

"Careful," he warned, his voice dropping to something between human speech and dragon growl. "I'm not—"

"I know what you're not." She shifted forward on the railing, the danger making her reckless, and guided him to her entrance. The first press of him against her sensitive flesh made them both inhale sharply. The heat was intense, just shy of pain. "Stop talking."

He grunted, hands tightening around her waist, not guiding just keeping her steady as she lowered herself slowly, adjusting to the stretch and the strange texture, those subtle ridges creating friction she hadn't anticipated. He was bigger than she expected and the initial penetration burned in ways that had nothing to do with his temperature.

"Too much?" he asked, hands steadying her hips but letting her control the depth.

"No." She sank down another inch, gasping at the sensation. "Just... different."

"Different," he agreed, watching her face intently as she adjusted. "Take your time."

But she didn't want time. She wanted to stop thinking, to lose herself in sensation. She sank down further, feeling every ridge, every texture difference. The heat of him radiated outward, making her inner muscles clench and flutter around him.

"You're so tight," he groaned, his control visibly fraying. The scales on his chest seemed to shimmer more intensely, catching colors that shouldn't exist in moonlight.

She experimented with movement, lifting slightly then sinking back down, finding an angle that made them both gasp.

"That's it," he encouraged, his hands sliding up from her hips to her waist, then higher, finding the loosened laces of her dress. "Let me see you properly."

He pulled at the fabric, dragging the bodice down to pool at her waist. The night air hit her exposed skin, making her nipples immediately harden. His eyes tracked over her hungrily, taking in the marks Eliam had left—the thorned vine pattern that curved across her collarbones.

She found a rhythm that built slowly, savoring the strange new sensations. When she rolled her hips, the ridges hit different spots, creating friction that had her gripping his shoulders for stability. His hands came up to cup her breasts, thumbs brushing over sensitive peaks, the heat of his touch almost scorching against the cool night air.

His forked tongue traced the patterns on her throat, making her shiver—two points of wet heat drawing designs on her pulse point. Then he lowered his head, and she gasped when his mouth closed over her nipple. The forked tongue flicking against the sensitive peak was unlike anything she'd experienced—two distinct points of stimulation that had her arching into him.

"You're being quite vocal," he murmured against her skin, switching to the other breast. His teeth grazed carefully, followed by that maddening tongue. "Anyone walking the garden paths would hear you."

She bit her lip, trying to muffle the sounds as he shifted angles, hitting deeper.

"No, don't stop." His hand rose, his thumb gently coaxing her lip free from her teeth. "I think you want them to hear. Want them to know you're out here making your own choices." His tongue traced along her throat again. "Let the princeling hear what he's too gentle to give you. Let the huntsman know you're not waiting for dawn."

"Shut up," she gasped, but he was right, a small part of her did want them to know, wanted them to see she wasn't some fragile thing to be protected.

"Make me," he challenged, increasing his pace until her world narrowed to pure sensation—the drag of those ridges against her inner walls, the furnace heat of him spreading through her core, the rough texture of scales against the soft skin of her inner thighs.

She pulled him down for a kiss to stop his commentary, and his forked tongue slid against hers—alien and strange, the dual tips exploring her mouth in ways that made her shiver. It was like being kissed twice at once, overwhelming and intense.

When she moaned, Briar felt more than heard his satisfied rumble, the vibration traveling through his chest into hers where they pressed together.

Without warning, his hands gripped her waist and lifted—her body suddenly weightless, empty, clenching on nothing. The loss made her whimper before she could stop herself. "Needy," he murmured before he spun her like she weighed nothing, and then she was facing the drop, her palms hitting stone that felt frigid against her overheated skin. The rough texture of the railing bit into her hipbones as he pressed her forward, and her heart lurched at the sight of the ground so far below.

"Better view," he said, his boot nudging her feet apart, forcing her stance wider. The position made her back arch, changing the angle completely. "And better access."

When he entered her again from behind, the penetration was devastatingly deep and the cry that tore from her throat was embarrassingly loud, echoing off the garden walls below. His fingers tangled in her hair, not cruel but insistent, pulling until her neck arched back, changing the angle again so each thrust ground against something that made her legs shake.

"Look down," he commanded, his other hand firm on her hip, controlling the pace now. "Do you think you'd fall if your hands slipped?"

The vertigo hit immediately—the garden path a ribbon of silver thirty feet below, the carefully manicured hedges looking like children's toys. If she fell... Her fingers went white-knuckled on the stone, arms trembling from more than exertion.

The danger of it, the complete recklessness, somehow made everything more intense. Each thrust pushed her forward slightly, the stone railing pressing hard into her thighs, her breasts swaying over the drop. The cool night air kissed her heated skin, making her hyperaware of every exposed inch. She could feel his scales catching against her inner thighs with each movement, leaving what would probably be faint scratches. The contrast of textures, of rough scales and smooth skin, the burning heat and cold stone, overwhelmed her senses.

"Someone's coming," he said casually, and she could hear dark amusement in his voice. "Guard patrol. Lower garden path."

Her entire body went rigid. She could hear it too, the measured footsteps on gravel, the quiet murmur of conversation drifting up. If they looked up, if they saw... The shame should have cooled her ardor, but instead it made everything sharper, more urgent.

He leaned over her, his chest pressing against her back, scales rough. His breath was hot against her ear when he whispered, "Should we stop?" But he didn't slow his pace—if anything, he went deeper, grinding against her in a way that made her bite her lip hard enough to taste blood.

"No," she gasped, beyond caring about consequences, about tomorrow, about anything but this moment of choosing chaos. "Don't stop."

"Such a rebel tonight." His hand slipped around her hip, fingers finding where they were joined. She could feel him touching himself as he entered her, then his fingers moved higher, finding her swollen clit. The heat of his touch there was almost too much, that controlled dragon-fire temperature that bordered on pain. "Let them look, let them see you choosing the monster over the prince."

The footsteps grew closer, boots on gravel clear in the night air. She could make out words now. The guards were discussing shift changes and patrol routes. Her body tensed, caught between paralyzing fear of discovery and the building pressure his fingers created. Every nerve felt exposed, raw. She was so close and he knew it. His fingers worked faster, circling with devastating precision while his thrusts became deliberately harder, forcing her to grip the railing tighter while fighting to keep from crying out. The stone bit into her palms, probably leaving marks she'd see tomorrow. She could feel her climax building, inevitable as gravity.

"Sir Fyren said Prince Arion wants increased patrols," one guard said, voice carrying clearly through the darkness. They must be directly below now, she didn't dare look down.

"After that attack earlier? No surprise," the other responded.

Karse chose that moment to thrust particularly deep, snapping his hips forward while pressing hard on her clit, and the combination nearly undid her. She bit down on her own hand, tasting blood, to muffle the cry that wanted to escape. Her whole body shook with the effort of staying silent. Against her back, she felt his chest vibrate with silent laughter, *the absolute bastard.*

"Did you hear something?" The first guard stopped, gravel crunching as he turned.

Briar's heart hammered so hard she was sure they must hear it. One sound, one whimper, and they'd be discovered. The Prince's rescued human bent over a railing being thoroughly debauched by a Drak...

"Probably just wind," the second guard said.

They moved on, their footsteps and voices fading down the garden path, but the close call combined with Karse's relentless fingers had pushed her past the point of return. She crested, the orgasm crashing over her with unexpected force. Her inner walls clenched around him in waves, her legs trembling so badly that only his grip and the railing kept her upright. She buried her face in her arm to muffle the cry that escaped. Every nerve felt raw, oversensitized, the pleasure almost painful in its intensity.

"Such pretty sounds for just wind," Karse thrusted through her climax, drawing it out until she was whimpering from overstimulation. Then his rhythm faltered, becoming erratic. His hands gripped her hips hard enough that she'd have fingerprint bruises tomorrow, pulling her back against him as he buried himself deep and followed her over the edge. The growl that rumbled from his chest vibrated through her back—inhuman, primal, purely dragon.

For a moment, they stayed frozen like that, both breathing hard. Then the reality of what she'd just done crashed over her like cold water.

"Get off me," she said, voice rough.

He pulled back immediately, no comment, no mockery. She felt him withdraw, heard the rustle of clothing being adjusted. Her own hands shook as she pushed herself up from the railing, trying to fix her ruined dress into something resembling decent. The fabric was torn in places, wrinkled beyond repair, and she could feel the wetness of his release beginning to slide down her inner thigh.

Chapter Eight

Briar's room was dark when she finally made it back, having avoided the main corridors and anyone who might ask questions about her torn dress or wild hair. She closed the door and leaned against it, finally alone.

The silence was deafening.

She moved mechanically to the bathing chamber, fingers fumbling with what remained of the dress's fastenings. The fabric pooled at her feet, ruined beyond repair. In the mirror, she caught sight of herself and immediately looked away. She didn't want to see what she'd become—or what she'd always been.

The water was almost too hot when she sank into the tub, but she welcomed the burn. It matched the rawness between her legs, the ache in her hips where bruises were already forming in the shape of fingers. She scrubbed at her skin, trying to wash away the scent of smoke and copper, but it seemed to cling.

A soft splash made her look up. Frederick emerged from the water pitcher on the side table, his tiny form creating a bubble that floated over to hover near the tub's edge. His gill-fronds drooped slightly, those dark eye-spots fixed on her with concern.

"I'm fine," she told him, though they both knew it was a lie.

He settled on the tub's edge, occasionally reaching out a translucent appendage to touch the water, as if testing her mood through the liquid. The gesture was so gentle, so without judgment, that her throat tightened.

She sank deeper into the water, letting it cover her shoulders, her neck, stopping just below her jaw. The warmth in her chest, that constant reminder of connection, pulsed weakly. Not reaching for Arion, who was probably somewhere in the palace worrying about her. Not reaching for Karse, who had already dismissed her from his thoughts.

It reached, as it always did, in the direction of the Forest Court.

The realization hit her with crushing clarity. After everything, after being cast out, hunted, nearly killed, treated like property, her traitorous heart still ached for Eliam. She could still feel the phantom pressure of his hands on her skin, different from the bruises Karse had left. Could still remember the way he'd looked at her that last morning, bringing her tea with purple flowers, his fingers gentle in her hair.

She pressed her palms against her eyes, but it didn't stop the tears from coming. Silent, hot, mixing with the bath water. She'd thought—what? That sleeping with someone else would burn him out of her system? That choosing destruction would somehow free her from wanting someone who'd thrown her away?

"I'm such a fool," she whispered to Frederick, who floated closer, his bubble pressing gently against her arm.

The worst part was knowing it didn't matter. Whether she went back to the Forest Court at dawn or stayed in the Star Court, whether she ran into the mortal realm or let Malus take her apart—none of it would change the fundamental truth that she'd fallen in love with someone incapable of loving her back.

Karse had been right about one thing. She'd used him to break something. But it hadn't been her attachment to Eliam or her pain or her helplessness. She'd just broken herself a little more.

Eventually, the water cooled. She forced herself to get out, to dry off, to put on a clean nightgown. Her body moved automatically through the motions while her mind stayed trapped in that circular path—wanting Eliam, hating that she wanted him, knowing it would destroy her, wanting him anyway.

Frederick followed her to the bed, his bubble settling on the pillow beside her. She curled on her side, one hand unconsciously going to her chest where the warmth pulsed its endless, futile reaching.

Dawn would come in a few hours. She would have to choose. Did she return to someone who had discarded her, or stay with people who would never understand why part of her would always be looking back toward the forest, toward the thorns, toward the beautiful, terrible fae lord who had marked her in ways that went deeper than skin?

"What's wrong with me?" she asked Frederick, who made a soft chiming sound and pressed his cool bubble against her cheek.

She knew the answer, though. She'd fallen in love with her captor, chosen to stay with someone who saw her as possession rather than person, and even after everything, even after tonight's desperate attempt to feel something else, she still wanted him.

The tears came again, quieter this time, and she let them. Tomorrow she would have to be strong, would have to make choices, would have to pretend she hadn't shattered something inside herself tonight.

But for now, in the dark with only a tiny water sprite for comfort, she could admit the truth—she was hopelessly, foolishly, destructively in love with Eliam, and no amount of rebellion or rage or other men would change that.

The warmth in her chest pulsed once, strong and yearning, as if agreeing with her realization. She pressed her hand against it, feeling the echo of connection that would never fully fade, and waited for dawn.

A soft knock pulled her from the edge of sleep. The sound was tentative, barely louder than the settling of old wood in the walls. She lay still against sheets, unsure if she'd imagined it.

"Briar?" Arion's voice, muffled by thick oak.

She didn't answer. Her throat still ached from crying, raw and swollen, and the bruises on her hips throbbed with each heartbeat, a reminder of what she'd done, of the choices she'd made in anger that now felt hollow. She sat up, the blanket falling away, and shivered. The room held that particular chill that came before morning, when night had leached all warmth from stone and air.

The silence stretched and her heartbeat seemed too loud in the quiet.

"You're probably asleep," he continued. "You may not even... I don't know if you're listening." His voice was different than she'd ever heard it, as if it had been stripped of its usual confidence, raw at the edges. "I should have said this earlier. Before everything went... I'm not good at this, at saying what I mean when it matters."

Briar pushed the blankets aside against her better judgement and slipped from the bed. Her toes curled when they hit the floor. It felt like ice against her bare feet. It should have been enough to drive her back beneath the blankets, but the warmth in her chest had stirred, reaching toward his voice through the door.

"When I kissed you that night, during the dance, it was so impulsive, I—" His voice caught. "I felt something I couldn't explain. The whole world shifted. Everything suddenly made sense and no sense at all, and then you were gone, back to him, and I haven't stopped thinking..."

She moved closer, her palm finding the smooth wood of the door. Through it, she could almost feel his presence, the gentle light that always seemed to surround him.

"I know you said you chose him, that... you wanted to stay with Eliam, but I keep thinking if I'd been stronger, if I'd fought for you then instead of letting you go back—" Another pause. Briar let her forehead fall to rest against the door. Her mind spinning with the possibilities. What if he *had* fought? What then? Malus might still be locked away in Eliam's dungeons, but the Star Court would have been destroyed. If Briar had to choose again knowing the end result, she didn't think she would change her decision.

"What I mean is... damn it, none of this is coming out right."

Her fingers found the door handle, the metal cool and solid.

"I know you're angry. You have every right to be. We've all been making decisions about your life, treating you as if your thoughts don't matter. But they do and when you stood in that courtyard and told us all exactly what you thought, I saw you. Really saw you. The woman who kissed me back, who survived everything this cruel world could throw at her,,."

The handle turned slightly under her palm. One full turn and she could open it, could face him, could apologize for not being the person he needed her to be, she could—

A hand clamped over her mouth from behind followed by an arm locking around her waist, pulling her back against a solid chest.

"Not a sound," Thaine breathed in her ear. "He comes through that door playing hero, I put a blade through his righteous heart. Nod if you understand."

The threat froze her more effectively than any restraint. She nodded, the movement small and defeated.

"I should go," Arion said at last, unaware of the violence waiting just beyond. "I'm sorry if I disturbed you... you need rest. I just... wanted you to know that whatever you decide, you don't have to justify it. Not to me, not to anyone. You'll always have an ally in the Star Court. Goodnight, Briar."

Briar tensed and Thaine's arm tightened. There was a moment of silence and then footsteps retreating down the corridor. The sound of them leaving made something in her chest constrict—relief that he was safe, grief that another choice was being taken from her.

"How touching," Thaine murmured, already dragging her backward toward the terrace. "The noble prince pining through doors, it's so very pathetic."

Briar twisted, trying to break free, but his arm squeezed tighter making breathing difficult.

"Did you enjoy that little confession? Must be confusing, wanting them both." His tone was light, lace with amusement at her plight. "Though after what you did with the Drak tonight, I'd say you're handling the confusion creatively."

Heat flooded her face, shame and anger mixing until she couldn't separate them. He knew about Karse. She shouldn't have been surprised, he'd probably followed her, heard it all. The very thought of Thaine lurking in the shadows, watching—it made her sick to her stomach.

The terrace doors stood open, cold air flowing in and carrying the scent of dew and night-blooming jasmine. How long had Thaine been planning this? The breeze raised goosebumps along her arms, her nightgown too thin for the early morning's bite.

"Did you think it would help?" His tone stayed conversational as he maneuvered her toward the railing, though she could hear exhaustion threading through it. "Fucking something like that to forget about my lord? I'm curious about the logic. I wonder how he'll react when—"

That's when Frederick struck.

Water erupted from the decorative fountain to their right, not a gentle stream but a concentrated blast that caught Thaine full in the face. The water was ice-cold and he cursed in the old tongue, sputtering. His grip loosened just enough—

Briar wrenched free, staggered a few steps before she regained her footing and ran for the door. Her fingers grasped the handle and pulled.

The door didn't budge.

She looked and saw that vines had grown through the mechanism, around the frame, through the very wood itself. They were fresh, still green and supple, smelling of sap and earth.

When had he—

Pain exploded against her temple, sharp and bright. The world tilted sideways, the floor rushing up to meet her. Her knees hit stone, the impact jarring through already-bruised flesh. Thaine caught her before she could fall completely and hefted her over his shoulder.

Everything spun, nausea rising in her throat. She caught pieces through the growing haze—the terrace railing passing beneath them as he vaulted over, her stomach lurching at the drop. The garden rushed up, twenty feet that should have broken bones, but he landed in a crouch that barely jarred her. The impact still drove what little air remained from her lungs.

They moved through shadows while her vision swam, the world going gray at the edges. The scent of crushed mint assaulted her senses where his boots found an herb garden. Voices nearby, guards discussing increased patrols, their words floating just out of reach. She tried to call out but her mouth wouldn't work properly, her tongue thick and useless. The sound that emerged was barely a whimper, lost in the pre-dawn darkness.

The guards passed without stopping, their footsteps fading on gravel paths. Thaine kept moving, each step jarring her aching head, sending new waves of pain through her skull. She caught glimpses of water following as Frederick darted between fountains and puddles, his tiny form bright with distress, before the gray at the edges of her vision swallowed everything whole.

Pain split through her skull before she even opened her eyes. The world swayed in a way that had nothing to do with movement and everything to do with the throbbing above her temple. Her stomach churned, bile rising in her throat. She swallowed it down and forced her eyes open.

Trees passed overhead in a steady rhythm, their branches creating a canopy that filtered sunlight into broken patterns. She was moving, but not walking. Beneath her, around her, vines and roots formed a living cradle that rolled forward in waves. The plants erupted from the earth ahead, carried her forward, then sank back into the soil behind in an endless cycle. Bars of twisted wood rose on either side, curving overhead but never quite meeting—a cage that reformed itself with each surge forward.

Her wrists were bound in front of her with rope that smelled of sap and something bitter. A cloak covered her—Thaine's, judging by the scent of forest and steel—but her nightgown beneath offered little protection against the morning chill that seeped through the gaps in her moving prison.

She tested the ropes carefully, working her wrists in small circles. The bonds were tight but not cruel, professional rather than vindictive. Her feet pressed against the lattice of roots beneath her, feeling for weakness, for any gap that might—

"I wouldn't," Thaine said from ahead, not bothering to turn around. He walked with the steady pace of someone who had miles to go and no reason to hurry. "Those roots will take whatever pushes through them. You might get your body out, but your foot would stay behind."

To prove his point, a smaller vine near her ankle tightened briefly, not enough to hurt but enough to demonstrate how quickly the plants could constrict.

Briar pulled her feet back, fury replacing her methodical testing. "You kidnapped me."

"I retrieved you." His tone carried no particular emotion, as if they were discussing weather. "The hunt ended. You belong to the Forest Court."

"I belong to no one." The words came out rough, her throat still raw from whatever he'd hit her with. "You had no right—"

"I had every right." He still didn't turn, navigating the forest path with unconscious ease. "My lord wants you back. That's all the right I need."

"Your lord cast me out." She shifted, trying to find a position that didn't make her head spin. "Made me prey. Let them hunt me like an animal."

"Yes." Simple agreement, no attempt to soften it. "And now he wants you back."

"And that's enough for you? His whims, his tantrums, his—"

"Yes." Thaine stepped over a fallen log without breaking stride, the vine conveyance following, lifting slightly to clear the obstacle. "I serve the Forest Court. Not his moods, not his reasons, not whatever complicated thing you two have between you. I serve."

The motion of climbing over the log made her stomach lurch. She pressed her bound hands against her mouth, willing herself not to be sick. The last thing she needed was to vomit while trapped in a moving cage with nowhere to escape the smell.

"Are you going to tell him?" The question escaped before she could stop it.

That made him stop. He turned, finally, and she could see the bruises still shadowing his jaw, the healing cuts from his fight with the Withered. His dark eyes studied her curiously.

"Tell him what?"

Heat flooded her face but she forced herself to hold his gaze. "About Karse."

He tilted his head, considering. The morning light caught the edges of his dark hair, showing threads of silver she hadn't noticed before. How old was Thaine really? How long had he served the Forest Court, done Eliam's bidding without question?

"You mean am I going to tell my lord that you fucked a Drak on a balcony while the Star Court slept?" His tone remained conversational, but she saw something flicker in his expression.

The crude summary made her stomach turn for different reasons. She looked away, unable to hold his gaze.

"He cast you aside," Thaine said, and his voice carried an odd note. Not sympathy exactly, but understanding. He paused, stepping closer to her moving prison. "I understand why you did it. The Drak was there, willing, and you wanted to feel something other than pain."

She looked up, startled by the accuracy of his assessment.

"I'll make you a deal," he continued. "You don't mention my... extended stay as the Star Court's prisoner, and I don't mention your evening activities. My lord doesn't need to know that his best hunter spent three days failing to retrieve one human woman, and he doesn't need to know what that woman did when she thought she was free."

"You're protecting your reputation."

"Obviously." He turned back to the path ahead, starting to walk again. The vines resumed their wave-like motion, carrying her forward. "I have no interest in being seen as incompetent. You have no interest in Eliam knowing about the Drak. We both benefit from selective silence."

The pragmatism of it, the casual way he reduced her pain and rebellion to a simple transaction, should have made her angrier. Instead, she found herself oddly grateful for his lack of judgment. He understood what she'd done and why, without trying to excuse it or condemn it.

"He's not well," Thaine said suddenly, still walking ahead. "Since you've been gone."

Something in her chest tightened—the warmth responding to even this distant mention of Eliam. "What do you mean?"

"Volatile. More than usual. The court walks carefully around him, never knowing what might set him off. That first morning a servant brought him morning tea with the wrong flowers—not purple, but white. He destroyed half the morning room before I could calm him."

Purple flowers. Her memory supplied the image immediately. Eliam bringing her tea and breakfast, the delicate bloom decorating the tray, his fingers gentle in her hair. The warmth in her chest pulsed, reaching eastward with painful intensity.

"The strange thing is," Thaine continued, navigating them around a massive oak, "he couldn't explain why the purple flowers matter. Just kept insisting they're wrong. That everything's wrong. That's when I had to stop him from leaving to go after you."

Frederick chose that moment to appear, his tiny form rising from a puddle beside the path. He kept pace with her moving cage, his bubble throwing tiny rainbows in the morning sun. Thaine glanced at the sprite but didn't comment.

"And then there's you," Thaine said. "Growing thorns that attack anyone near you. Creating flowers that burn. Magic that responds to threats without your control..." He stopped again, turning to face her fully. "How long has this been happening?"

Briar hesitated. How much did she tell him?

"It started when I first arrived," Briar said at last, watching Frederick maintain his position beside her moving cage. "The golden flowers that grew in the Oubliette, leading me out when I was drowning in the dark. I thought I was hallucinating at first, but they were real. Eliam saw them too."

Thaine's pace slowed slightly. "Flowers in the Oubliette. That should have been impossible. Nothing grows there."

"Since he cast me out, it's gotten worse, or stronger, I don't know..." She closed her eyes, temple still throbbing dully, and pressed her bound hands against her chest where the warmth pulsed. "It feels like something else is acting through me, protecting me whether I want it or not."

"Has it always responded to—"

The air around them grew unexpectedly warmer.

"You."

The word came from above them, dripping with fury that made the air itself feel sharp. Karse dropped from the canopy, landing in a crouch that cracked the earth beneath him. He rose slowly, and Briar's breath caught.

His human form was slipping. Scales covered most of his visible skin now, black and green and gold shifting with each movement. His eyes had gone completely reptilian, the pupils contracted to slits despite the forest shade. When he smiled, his teeth were far too sharp and numerous for any human mouth.

"You took her. Again." Each word came out with visible heat, the air shimmering around him. "I'm getting very tired of people taking what's mine."

Thaine glanced at Briar with exasperation clear in his expression. "Next time you find something dangerous trapped and dying, perhaps consider that it was trapped for a reason before you decide to set it free?"

"She's not yours," Thaine continued, hand already on his blade. "She belongs to the Forest Court."

"She belongs to me." Karse's fingers lengthened, scales spreading down to form claws. "I claimed her. She accepted the claim when she—"

"Don't," Briar said sharply, heat flooding her face.

Karse's attention shifted to her, taking in the vine cage, the bound wrists, the cloak covering her nightgown. His expression darkened further, if that was possible.

"He caged you." Not a question. The temperature rose another degree with each word. "After I specifically said no one touches what's mine."

"This doesn't concern you, Drak," Thaine said. "Walk away while you can."

Karse laughed, the sound more growl than mirth. "Walk away? I'm going to burn you down to bone, use the ash to make glass, then shatter it into pieces so small even the wind won't remember you existed."

White-blue flame erupted from both his hands. Thaine dove aside as fire engulfed where he'd been standing, leaves igniting instantly. The heat washed over Briar's cage, and she felt the vines begin to smoke.

"Stop!" She pulled against her bonds, the rope burning her wrists. "Karse, stop! You're going to—"

Thaine's blade sang as he drew it, the steel gleaming with an edge that looked wrong, too sharp for normal metal. He rolled to his feet and struck in one motion, but Karse moved like water, scales deflecting the blade with a sound like striking stone.

"Is that all?" Karse grabbed the blade bare-handed, scales protecting his palm. "The famous huntsman of the Forest Court, reduced to waving sharp metal?"

Thaine smiled grimly and whistled—three short notes.

The forest responded. Roots erupted from the earth, wrapping around Karse's legs, his arms, trying to bind him. For a moment they held, then burst into flame so hot they turned to ash instantly.

"Predictable," Karse said, advancing on Thaine. "You fae and your nature magic. As if wood could hold fire."

The vines of Briar's cage were definitely burning now, smoke rising thick and choking. She kicked at the weakening bars, ignoring how they scraped her legs. One gave way, then another. She tumbled out, still bound at the wrists, coughing from the smoke.

Neither man noticed her escape. They were fully engaged now, Thaine's blade dancing through patterns that should have filleted anyone normal, Karse moving through the attacks like they were choreographed, leaving burning footprints with each step.

"Stop!" Briar shouted again, struggling to her feet. "Both of you, just—"

Movement in her peripheral vision made her freeze.

High in the trees, pale shapes perched on branches. At first she thought they were enormous birds, white-feathered and still. Then one tilted its head, and she saw the almost-human face beneath wild white hair. Their wings flexed, not feathered but membranous, like a bat's but white as fresh snow. Their bodies were wrong, elongated and too thin, wrapped in tight clothing or perhaps just their own pale skin.

More appeared, silent as snowfall, surrounding the burning clearing where Thaine and Karse fought.

"In the sky!" she called. "There's something—"

One of the creatures dropped.

It plummeted straight down, talons extended, moving faster than gravity alone could account for. Briar threw herself sideways, her bound hands making the movement clumsy. Talons raked the ground where she'd been, leaving gouges in the earth.

The creature's face turned to her, beautiful in the way winter was beautiful—stark and deadly. Its mouth opened, revealing rows of needle teeth.

"Warm one," it said, voice like wind through ice. "Lord waits. Lord wants."

Another dropped behind her. "Bring the warm one."

"Not yours!" A third landed between her and where Thaine and Karse had finally noticed the new threat. This one was larger, its wings spanning fifteen feet. "Mountain claims. Mountain takes."

Karse's fire roared toward it, but the creature launched itself upward, the flames passing beneath. Two more dove at him from different angles, forcing him to defend rather than attack.

Thaine's blade sang as he struck at another, but they moved like wind itself—there one moment, gone the next. "Harpies," he snarled. "Mountain Court creatures. Malachar's pets."

Malachar.

Every muscle locked with remembered terror. The way his hand had felt on her throat, the cold touch of his ice as it bled across her skin while he'd discussed what he planned to do to her. She could still smell his breath, feel the bruises he'd left, hear his promise that he'd finish what he'd started.

And now his creatures were here. For her.

"Pets?" The large one laughed, the sound like breaking icicles. "Allies. Hunters. Take warm one to ice lord. He waits. He promises feast."

Her legs wouldn't work properly, terror making her clumsy. She tried to run but tangled in the remnants of burned vines, going down hard. Her palms scraped against earth that had gone cold—too cold for the forest, as if winter itself was reaching for her through Malachar's creatures.

Talons seized her shoulders.

Not the large one but a smaller harpy that had circled behind while the others fought. Its grip pierced through the cloak and nightgown, sharp points finding flesh. She screamed as it lifted, her weight tearing the wounds wider. Not just from pain but from the knowledge of where they were taking her. To him. To whatever revenge he'd planned while nursing his ruined eye.

Thaine's vines shot toward her, but the harpy carrying her twisted, using Briar's body as a shield. The vines recoiled rather than risk hitting her.

The smaller harpy struggled with her weight, wings beating frantically. They rose slowly, too slowly. Briar twisted despite the agony in her shoulders, trying to break free.

The harpy shrieked and released her.

She fell ten feet, hitting the ground hard enough to drive all breath from her lungs. Through tears of pain, she saw Frederick clinging to the harpy's face, his water form forcing itself into the creature's nose and mouth.

"Brave sprite," the large harpy said, almost approving. Then its talons found Briar's shoulders—deeper than the first, meant to hold. "But small. Not enough."

This time the ascent was swift and sure. She caught glimpses of the battle below. Karse was wreathed in flame, multiple harpies keeping him earthbound despite their burns and Thaine was entangled in a fighting retreat, his blade barely keeping them at bay.

The forest canopy rushed past, branches whipping at her legs. More harpies joined them in the air, surrounding her bearer, their broken speech a chorus.

"Ice lord waits."

"Warm one comes."

"Mountain claims."

"Feast promised."

The forest fell away beneath them as they flew north. The temperature plummeted with each wingbeat, her thin nightgown useless against the cold. Blood ran warm down her back where the talons gripped, the only heat she could feel.

Through blurring vision, she saw Frederick's tiny bubble struggling to keep pace, jumping from cloud to cloud with desperate determination.

The mountains rose before them, white-capped and forbidding. At their highest peak, a tower of ice caught the setting sun, and even from this distance, she could see a figure on its balcony.

Malachar.

Chapter Nine

The harpy released her without warning.

Briar fell the last six feet, her shoulder hitting the ice-slicked stone of the balcony first. The impact sent lightning through the talon wounds, fresh blood seeping through the cloak. She rolled, gasping, her bound wrists making it impossible to catch herself properly. The stone was so cold it burned through the thin nightgown, stealing what little warmth she had left.

She looked up to see a polished boot inches from her face.

Memory and terror crashed over her simultaneously—his hand tangling in her hair, yanking her head back. The cold invasion of his kiss, tongue forcing past her lips while she couldn't move, couldn't fight. The frost spreading from his touch, claiming over Eliam's marks.

She scrambled backward, ignoring the screaming pain in her shoulders, her palms sliding on ice that coated everything. The balcony stretched behind her, twenty feet of carved stone and decorative railings with a deadly drop beyond. No doors. No stairs. No escape except through the archway where he stood, blocking it completely.

"Lady Briar." Malachar's voice carried the same cultured tone she remembered, smooth and satisfied. "What an unexpected pleasure."

He looked different than her nightmares had painted him. An ornate patch covered his ruined eye, the metal worked to look like frozen tears or perhaps ice crystals, beautiful in its craftsmanship. The remaining eye studied her with an intensity that made her skin crawl. He wore white and pale blue, every inch the Winter Lord in his domain, and when he smiled at her, she wanted to vomit.

"Stay away from me." The words came out cracked, her throat raw from screaming during the flight.

"Such hostility." He stepped forward, unhurried, and she retreated further back until her spine hit the balcony railing. The cold of it shocked through the wet fabric. "And after I've gone to such trouble to ensure your safe arrival."

Safe. She might have laughed if she hadn't been so cold.

"Though I must say," he continued, moving closer with deliberate steps that echoed off the stone, "you look somewhat worse for wear. My allies were clearly... overly enthusiastic in their retrieval."

He crouched just out of her reach, or what would have been her reach if her hands weren't bound. This close, she could see the frost that gathered in his platinum hair, the unnatural paleness of his skin, and the way his remaining eye tracked over her slowly, cataloging damage.

"Shoulder wounds need tending. Wrists are bleeding. And you're shivering." He tilted his head, and she saw something shift in his expression, a flicker of something like anticipation. "We can't have you catching your death before Lord Malus arrives to collect his gift."

Gift? The word made her stomach turn. "I'm not—"

"Oh, but you are." He stood smoothly, looking down at her with that satisfied smile. "My dear friend specifically requested that I retrieve you. Hold you safely until he completes his business in the Forest Court. Three days, he said. Perhaps four." The smile widened. "So much time for us to become reacquainted."

Three days. Three days of this, of him, of whatever revenge he'd planned while nursing his ruined eye. The warmth in her chest contracted painfully, recoiling from him, from this place, from the wrongness that saturated everything here. It made her feel sick, dizzy, like her body was rejecting the very air.

"Come now." He extended a hand toward her, palm up in mock courtesy. "Let's get you inside before you freeze. I've had rooms prepared, warm clothing, and a healer for those unfortunate wounds." His eye glinted. "I am more than just the monster you seem to think I am."

Briar pressed harder against the railing, the drop behind her almost preferable to taking his hand. But the cold was already making her fingers numb, her body shaking so hard her teeth chattered. The blood loss was making everything fuzzy at the edges.

"I can have the harpies carry you inside instead," he offered, his tone suggesting he might enjoy it. "Though they're less gentle than I am. As you've discovered."

Through the archway behind him, she could see warmth shimmering in the air like a haze. Beyond there were fireplaces and furs and walls that would block the killing wind. In the end, her body betrayed her, leaning toward him even as her mind screamed warnings.

"There we are." His satisfaction was palpable as she forced herself to her feet, ignoring his hand and using the railing for support. "Such a practical creature when properly motivated."

He turned, walking through the archway without looking back, completely confident she would follow. And she did, because the alternative was freezing to death on his balcony, and she needed to survive long enough for—

For what? For someone to rescue her? Karse and Thaine had been fighting harpies when she'd been taken. The Forest Court didn't know where she was. The Star Court thought she'd left with Thaine.

No one was coming.

The thought nearly brought her to her knees, but she forced herself forward, each step leaving bloody footprints on the pristine floor. At least inside she might find something, a weapon, an exit, anything.

Malachar led her through corridors of ice and stone, past windows that showed nothing but white peaks and more impossible drops. Her wet nightgown clung to her, and she could feel his eye on her, watching.

"Your rooms," he said finally, opening a door to reveal a space that took her breath away despite her terror.

The chamber was vast, dominated by soaring gothic windows that reached nearly to the vaulted ceiling. The glass was frosted at the edges but clear in the center, revealing a view of snow-covered peaks and endless sky. Ornate columns framed each window, carved with patterns that looked like frozen waterfalls or perhaps climbing ice.

A fire crackled in an elaborate hearth carved from what appeared to be a single piece of pale marble, the mantle decorated with crystal formations that caught and threw back the firelight. The bed was massive, its frame made of dark wood that contrasted with the pale stone walls. White and silver furs were piled so high she could barely see the elaborately carved headboard beneath them. Pillows in shades of ice blue and pearl were arranged against it, soft as clouds.

To one side, a smaller arched alcove held a copper bathing tub that steamed gently, the scent of winter herbs—pine, mint, something sharp and clean—drifting from the water. Candles clustered on every surface, their warm light fighting back the cold that pressed against the windows. A wardrobe of the same dark wood as the bed stood open, revealing gowns in white and silver and palest blue, all of them far too fine for a prisoner.

The floor was covered in thick rugs that looked like fresh snow had been woven into patterns, soft under her bare feet. A low couch upholstered in white velvet sat near the windows, positioned to take in the terrifying beauty of the view. Beside it, white flowers she didn't recognize filled crystal vases, their petals so pale they seemed to glow in the firelight.

It was a room for a cherished guest, not a captive. The luxury of it made her skin crawl.

"I'll send a healer shortly. And food. You must be hungry after your journey."

He stood in the doorway, blocking her exit again, studying her with that single eye while the ornate patch caught the candlelight.

"Three days, Lady Briar. Do try to make them pleasant for both of us."

The door closed, and she heard the lock turn. Heavy. Final.

She collapsed beside the fire, pulling her knees to her chest, trying to stop shaking. The room was beautiful, warm, everything her frozen body craved. But it was still a cage, just one lined with velvet and fur instead of iron bars.

Three days. Three days of Malachar's games, his revenge, his satisfaction at having her exactly where he wanted her.

The warmth in her chest pulsed weakly, pulling toward the south, toward forests and thorns and safety that might as well have been on the moon.

Time lost meaning as she sat there, watching flames dance over logs that never seemed to burn down. The fire's warmth barely penetrated the cold that had settled into her bones—not from the mountain air but from the knowledge of where she was, who held her.

A knock broke through her numbness. Before she could respond, the door opened to admit a procession of servants.

First came an elderly woman with bark-brown skin and knowing eyes, carrying a leather satchel that smelled of herbs and something metallic. Behind her, two younger fae balanced trays of food—breads that steamed despite the journey from the kitchens, soups that smelled of root vegetables and winter herbs, fruits she didn't recognize preserved in what looked like ice but didn't melt.

More servants followed, these carrying linens and a copper basin that matched the tub in the alcove. They moved with practiced efficiency, not meeting her eyes, filling the basin with steaming water that smelled of pine and something medicinal.

"My lady," the healer said, her voice neither kind nor unkind, simply professional. "Lord Malachar has instructed me to tend your wounds."

Briar didn't move from her position by the fire. "I'm fine."

"You're bleeding through that cloak." The healer set down her bag, movements brisk. "The talons of mountain harpies carry a mild venom. Not fatal, but it prevents proper clotting. If untreated, you'll continue bleeding until you're too weak to stand."

As if to prove her point, a wave of dizziness swept through Briar. She'd attributed it to exhaustion, fear, the cold. But now that the healer mentioned it, she could feel the steady seep of warmth down her back.

"The bath is ready, my lady," one of the younger servants said. This one did meet her eyes briefly—a flash of something that resembled sympathy before her expression smoothed back to neutrality. "We'll need to clean the wounds before the healer can work."

They waited, clearly expecting her to comply. The alternative was bleeding out slowly on Malachar's floor, which would only give him satisfaction. Survival meant accepting their help, even if it came on his orders.

She forced herself to stand, legs unsteady. The servants moved immediately, one steadying her elbow, another beginning to work at the cloak's fastenings. Their hands were impersonal but gentle as they peeled away the blood-stiffened fabric. She heard a soft intake of breath when they revealed her back.

"Three punctures on each shoulder," the healer noted, clinical in her assessment. "Deep but clean. The venom's kept them from closing. We'll need to draw it out first."

They guided her to the alcove where the copper tub waited and the servants worked with mechanical efficiency, removing the ruined nightgown, their faces carefully blank at the bruises on her hips that had nothing to do with harpies.

The water burned when she sank into it, every cut and scrape announcing itself. The healer added something to the bath that turned it pale green and made the wounds sting worse before the pain began to numb. Blood clouded the water, more than seemed possible.

"The venom's breaking down," the healer explained, working some kind of paste into the punctures. It smelled sharp, medicinal, and made her skin tingle. "This will draw out the rest."

While the healer worked, other servants laid out clothing on the bed. Not one dress but several, as if she had a choice in what cage she wore. The gowns were beautiful enough to make her chest ache—one in white so pure it seemed to glow, embroidered with silver thread in patterns that looked like frost on windows. Another in the palest blue, like winter sky just after dawn, with billowing sleeves that gathered at the wrists with pearl clasps. A third in deeper blue-gray, the color of storm clouds over snow, with white fur trim at the neckline and hem.

All of them were designed to cover more than anything she'd worn at Eliam's court. All of them were meant to make her look like she belonged here, in Malachar's domain.

"This will scar," the healer said, finishing her work with bandages that seemed to adhere to skin without wrapping. "But you'll live. The venom's neutralized."

They helped her from the bath, wrapping her in soft towels that smelled of lavender and something else, something that made the warmth in her chest recoil slightly. Magic of some kind, woven into the very fabric. Mountain Court magic that her body recognized as foreign, wrong.

"Which gown, my lady?" The servant who'd shown that flash of sympathy held up the white one.

"I don't care." The words came out flat.

They chose the pale blue, perhaps thinking it most appropriate for day wear. Their hands dressed her like a doll, layer after layer—chemise, corset that they mercifully didn't tighten too much given her injuries, the gown itself with its impossible softness. They braided her hair in a style she didn't recognize, weaving white ribbons through it that caught the light like fresh snow.

When they finished, she looked in the mirror they held up and saw a stranger. A winter lady, pale and ethereal, nothing of the forest left on her. Nothing of Eliam's marks visible beneath the high neckline. Even the warmth in her chest seemed muted, struggling against the wrongness of everything she wore.

"Lord Malachar wishes you to know he'll visit this evening," the sympathy-servant said quietly as the others gathered their things. "To ensure you're... settling in comfortably."

The words sent ice through her veins that had nothing to do with winter magic.

They left the food, the fire still crackling, everything arranged as if she were an honored guest. But the door still locked behind them. The windows, she'd already checked, were sealed with magic that made her fingers burn when she touched the latches.

Three days, he'd said. Three days of this mockery of hospitality before Malus came to claim his "gift."

She sat back down by the fire, finding what little solace she could in its warmth, and wondered if Karse and Thaine were even still alive. If anyone knew where she was.

If it mattered either way.

The hours stretched, marked only by the slow crawl of shadows across the floor. The food grew cold on its trays, untouched. Briar couldn't bring herself to eat anything he'd provided, her stomach twisted too tight with dread.

The sky beyond the windows had long since grown dark when the lock turned with a soft click. Briar held her breath, hoping, praying, that it was a servant come to check on her.

It wasn't.

Malachar entered without waiting for permission, closing the door behind him with deliberate care. He'd changed from his earlier clothing into something darker, midnight blue that made his platinum hair seem to glow in the firelight. The ornate eye patch caught the light as he turned to study her.

"I hope you're finding your stay satisfactory?" His voice carried that same cultured tone, as if this were a social call. "I see you haven't eaten. That won't do at all."

He moved further into the room, gliding casually past where she was sitting to pause at the window and gaze out at the darkening sky. "Beautiful evening. The storms that come through these mountains at night are quite spectacular."

She watched him warily, not trusting his casual demeanor.

"Nothing to say?" He turned towards her, their eyes meeting from across the room. "You were far more talkative the last time we met."

The reference to that night, to what he'd tried to do, made her grip the chair arms tighter.

"Oh, how thoughtless of me. I brought you something," he said, producing a box from his jacket. It was made of carved wood, beautiful and intricate. He set it on the small table between them, then stepped back. "A gift. To commemorate your stay."

"I don't want anything from you."

"No? Not even curious?" He settled into the chair across from her, the fire between them. "Your Forest Lord enjoyed giving you gifts, didn't he? That dress you wore to dinner—exquisite work. Though I notice you're no longer wearing his marks so proudly."

Her hand went unconsciously to her throat, where the high neckline hid Eliam's thorns.

"Ah, they're still there then." His satisfaction was evident. "How loyal. Even after he threw you away. No matter, you're here now and I am not so foolish as to let you slip away."

"Open the gift," he said, his tone shifting from conversational to commanding.

She didn't move.

He sighed, standing with fluid grace. "Very well."

He crossed to the table and opened the box himself, revealing what lay inside. It was a collar. Silver, delicate, decorated with etched patterns that looked like frost spreading across metal. Beautiful enough to be a necklace if not for the unmistakable latch, the way it was clearly meant to close around a throat and stay there.

"No." She stood, backing toward the door.

"Where do you think you're going?" He didn't move, just watched her with amusement. "The door is locked. The windows are sealed. There's nowhere to run."

She tried the door handle anyway, pulling at it uselessly.

"This can be civilized," he said, lifting the collar from its box. "You can sit, let me put this on, and we can continue our evening. Or..." He let the threat hang.

"I won't wear it."

"Won't you?" He moved toward her slowly, collar in hand. "You have such limited options here."

She darted left, trying to get around him to the fireplace where there were tools, weapons. He cut her off easily, herding her toward the corner.

"This game grows tiresome," he said.

When he lunged, she was ready, dropping and rolling beneath his grasp. But he was fae, faster than human reflexes could match. His hand caught her braid, yanking her back. She cried out, hands going to her hair.

"Such spirit," he murmured, using the grip to force her to her knees. "Let's see how long that lasts."

She fought him, clawing at his hands, trying to twist away. But he was stronger than she could hope to match. He forced her head back, exposing her throat, and she felt the cold metal settle against her skin.

The moment it clicked shut, something changed.

The fight drained out of her, siphoned away like water through a drain. Her raised fist fell, the strength in her arms evaporating. The fury that had been burning in her chest dimmed to an ember, leaving her gasping.

"There we are." He released her hair, stepping back to admire his work. "Much better."

She raised shaking hands to the collar, fingers finding the latch. It wouldn't budge, sealed by magic or mechanism she couldn't determine. The metal was ice-cold against her throat, pressing against the marks Eliam had left.

"What did you—"

"It's quite ingenious, really." He produced a length of pale blue ribbon from his pocket, threaded with tiny silver bells that chimed softly. "The more you fight, the more it takes. Your defiance, your anger, your will to resist—it feeds on all of it."

He knelt in front of her, threading the ribbon through a loop in the collar she hadn't noticed. The bells chimed with every movement, delicate and musical and horrible.

"Eventually," he continued, tying the ribbon in an elaborate bow, "you'll learn not to fight at all. It's so much easier to simply... comply."

The warmth in her chest recoiled from the collar's magic, shrinking deeper inside her. She felt disconnected from it, like trying to reach something through thick glass.

"We're going for a walk." He stood, holding the end of the ribbon like a leash. "You can walk beside me with dignity, or I can drag you. Your choice."

She tried to summon anger at the mockery of choice, but the collar pulled it away before it could fully form, leaving her feeling hollow and strange. When she tried to stand on her own, her legs shook from the energy drain.

"I see you need a moment to adjust." His satisfaction was palpable. "The first drain is always the most dramatic. You'll learn to manage it. Or not."

He waited while she struggled to her feet, the bells chiming with every movement. The sound would announce her presence wherever they went, ensuring everyone looked, everyone saw what she'd become.

"Come." He tugged the ribbon gently. "I have something to show you. Some new additions to my collection you might find... interesting."

The way he said it made dread pool in her stomach. She followed on unsteady legs, the bells singing her humiliation with every step, the collar a weight around her throat that had nothing to do with its physical presence.

Whatever he wanted to show her, she knew it would be another cruelty, another turn of the knife. But the collar had taken her ability to properly resist, leaving her hollow and compliant, exactly as he'd intended.

Chapter Ten

The corridors grew colder as they descended, ice forming naturally on the stone walls. Malachar led her through passages that seemed carved from the mountain itself, the ribbon taut between them, bells chiming with each unsteady step. Her legs still shook from the collar's drain, though she'd stopped actively fighting it. Each time anger rose, it siphoned it away, leaving her feeling hollow.

"The dungeons here are quite different from your Forest Lord's," Malachar said conversationally, as if they were taking a pleasant tour. "We don't need oubliettes or iron bars. The mountain itself serves as prison. The cold does what chains cannot."

They passed cells carved directly into rock, most empty, some containing shapes she didn't want to examine too closely. Frost covered everything, and her breath misted in the air despite the warm gown.

"Here we are." He stopped before a larger cell, gesturing with theatrical pleasure. "My newest acquisitions."

At first, she couldn't process what she was seeing. Thaine sat against the far wall, frost in his dark hair, his hunting leathers inadequate against the cold. Beside him—practically on top of him—was Karse, pressed close enough that it should have been comical except for how wrong the Drak looked. His scales had dulled from their usual iridescent black-green to something gray and lifeless. His reptilian eyes were half-closed, and she could see him shivering—actually shivering—his body unable to maintain its usual furnace heat.

"Briar." Thaine's voice came out rough as he struggled to his feet. His gaze went immediately to the collar, the ribbon, the bells that sang with her slightest movement. Something dark crossed his expression. "What did you—"

"Careful," Malachar warned pleasantly. "Your words might have consequences you don't intend."

Karse tried to rise but stumbled, catching himself against the bars. The metal was so cold it steamed against his palms, and he jerked back with a hiss. "You put a leash on her." His words came out slurred, wrong. "Like an animal."

"Like the gift she is," Malachar corrected. "For Lord Malus, who should arrive in two day's time. He's tending to business at the Forest Court."

The casual mention of Malus caused Briar's stomach to twist. She stepped toward the cell, but Malachar held the ribbon firm, keeping her just out of reach.

"Are you hurt?" she asked, looking between them. It pained her to see them injured and suffering because of her.

"We're magnificent," Karse said, though his legs barely held him. "Your mountain lord's rock monsters were very welcoming. Didn't even break all our bones."

"Stone golems," Thaine clarified, his attention still fixed on her collar. "Ancient magic. We crossed the border and they rose from the mountain itself." He shifted, and she saw him wince. Broken ribs, probably. "The cold's killing him," he said bluntly, indicating Karse. "Draks aren't meant for this climate."

"No, they're not," Malachar agreed cheerfully. "Rather like keeping a tropical bird in a blizzard. Fascinating to watch them slowly freeze."

Anger flared in Briar's chest, but the collar drank it immediately, leaving her gasping. The bells chimed as she swayed.

"What is that thing doing to her?" Thaine demanded, moving to the bars.

"Teaching her the value of compliance." Malachar wound the ribbon around his hand, drawing her closer to him and further from the cell. She had no choice but to comply. "Every time she fights, resists, even thinks about defying me, it feeds. Eventually, she'll learn it's easier to simply... accept."

"Coward," Karse managed with a grimace. "Can't even break her yourself. Need jewelry to do it."

Malachar's remaining eye glinted with amusement. "Says the creature who claimed her as property. At least I'm honest about what she is—a prize to be displayed, a gift to be given."

How did Malachar know that? Just how long had he been watching them? Watching her?

"She's not—" Thaine started.

"Not what? Not property? Not a possession?" Malachar laughed, the sound echoing off stone. "Then why are you here, huntsman? To retrieve your lord's lost toy? She arrived to me with her hands bound. My harpies are smart, but that was your doing." He tilted his head, studying Thaine with interest. "Tell me, when you found her, was your first thought her wellbeing? Or your master's orders?"

Thaine's jaw clenched, but he didn't answer.

"And you," Malachar turned to Karse. "Claiming life debts, declaring ownership. You're no different. We all want to possess her, control her, use her for our own ends." He stroked a hand down Briar's hair, making her skin crawl. "I'm simply the most honest about it."

"When I get out," Karse said, each word deliberate despite his weakness, "I'm going to burn you so slowly you'll beg to die like your eye did."

The temperature in the corridor plummeted so fast ice crackled across the walls. Malachar's pleasant demeanor vanished, replaced with something ancient and terrible.

"My eye," he said softly. "Yes. Let's discuss that."

Briar let out a startled gasp when he yanked the ribbon and pulled against him, one arm encircling her waist to keep her still. "Your Forest Lord took my eye defending her. Such a noble gesture. Shall I tell you how it felt? The thorn piercing through, the sensation of it dying in the socket?"

His hand came up to trace the edge of his ornate patch. "I learned something from the experience. Perspective. A new way of seeing." He looked directly at Thaine. "For instance, I can see your heat signature, huntsman. How it spikes when you look at her collar. How it flares when she stumbles. You care. How unfortunate for you."

"If you hurt her—" Thaine started.

"Hurt her? I've been nothing but civilized. Fed her, clothed her, tended her wounds." Malachar's smile was sharp as winter. "But you... you knocked her unconscious. Kidnapped her from her bed. Dragged her through the forest in a cage of vines. Who's really hurt her more?"

The words hit their mark. Briar saw Thaine's expression shift. Was that guilt? She didn't think the huntsman was capable.

"But you raise an interesting point about hurt," Malachar continued. "About balance. I lost an eye because of her. Perhaps someone else should lose one too. For symmetry."

The words hung in the air, their meaning clear. Briar tried to pull away, but Malachar held her fast, and when she fought, the collar drained more energy, leaving her knees weak.

"Don't," she whispered.

"Don't?" Malachar's tone was mock surprise. "But he's so eager to threaten me. To speak of what he'll do when he's free. Perhaps he needs a lesson in consequences."

He produced a thin blade from his coat, the metal so cold it seemed to smoke in the air. "Choose."

"What?" Briar's voice came out cracked.

"Choose which eye he loses. Left or right. You have ten seconds, or I take both."

"You sick bastard—" Thaine started.

"Five seconds."

Briar's chest constricted. The collar sensed her panic, her desperate need to fight, and began draining harder. Her vision grayed at the edges.

"Time's up."

Malachar moved faster than Briar's eyes could track. One moment he stood beside her, the next he was at the cell bars. His hand shot through, grabbing Thaine's hair, slamming his head against the frozen metal. Thaine grunted but didn't cry out, even as Malachar brought the blade up.

"Wait!" Briar tried to surge forward, but the collar's drain dropped her to her knees. "Please—"

"Too late."

But it wasn't Malachar who moved. Karse, despite his weakness, lunged forward and grabbed Malachar's wrist through the bars. For a moment, heat flared, not his usual dragon fire, but enough to make Malachar jerk back with a hiss.

The blade fell, clattering on stone.

"Touch him," Karse said, swaying but standing, "and I'll burn through this cold if it kills me. And it will be worth it to watch you melt."

For a moment, they all stood frozen. Briar was certain they would both suffer for Karse's intervention. Instead Malachar laughed, stepping back from the cell, flexing his burned wrist.

"Such loyalty among thieves and monsters." He picked up his blade, sliding it back into his coat. "Very well. The huntsman keeps his eyes. For now." He looked down at Briar, still on her knees, the collar having drained her attempt at intervention. "But you've learned something, haven't you? Your defiance has costs. And others will pay them."

He tugged the ribbon and it was the sight of Thaine and Karse broken and beaten that finally forced her to stand on shaking legs. "Come. Lord Malus will want a full report on his gifts. All of them."

As he led her away, she looked back once. Karse had collapsed again, whatever reserve of heat he'd summoned gone. Thaine was checking him, his own injury forgotten. They were trying to survive, to protect each other despite being natural enemies.

And she was leaving them there to freeze, too weak from her own imprisonment to even protest.

The bells chimed with each step, a musical mockery of her helplessness, echoing through the frozen dungeons long after she'd gone.

Malachar guided her back through the frozen corridors, the ribbon taut between them, her legs barely managing each step. When they reached her room, he guided her inside with mock courtesy, finally releasing the ribbon.

"You should eat," he said, gesturing to the cold trays. "If you don't, I'll have no reason to feed your companions. The Drak is already halfway to frozen. Without food, he won't last another day."

She turned to face him, trying to summon defiance, but the collar sensed it and pulled, leaving her gripping the back of a chair for support.

"There's that fight again." He moved closer, close enough that she could smell winter on his clothes, see the faint burn marks on his wrist where Karse had grabbed him. "The collar will train you out of that eventually. Though I do hope you retain some spirit for when I visit you later."

Her stomach dropped. "When—"

"Oh, I couldn't say. Tonight? Tomorrow? An hour from now?" His remaining eye studied her with satisfaction. "We have unfinished business, you and I. From that night in your Forest Lord's castle. But this time, you'll be so much more... accommodating."

He traced a finger along the collar, making the bells chime softly. "No thorns to save you. No Forest Lord bursting through doorways. Just you and I, and all the time in the world to explore what made him so possessive."

She wanted to pull away, to fight, but even the thought of it made the collar activate, a steady drain that left her trembling.

"Eat," he commanded, moving toward the door. "Keep your strength up. You'll need it."

The lock clicked behind him with finality.

Briar stood frozen for a moment, her mind racing through possibilities that all led nowhere. The windows were sealed, the door locked, the collar ensuring she couldn't even properly rage against her imprisonment. She moved toward the fireplace, needing its warmth, when she heard it—the faintest sound, like rain on glass.

She turned toward the wash basin and gasped.

Frederick floated in the water, but barely. His usually translucent body had gone nearly opaque, a sickly white color that reminded her of frozen milk. The delicate gill-fronds that normally waved gracefully were stiff, crystallized at the edges. His tiny form listed to one side, the bubble he usually maintained completely absent.

"Frederick!" She ran to the basin, plunging her hands into water that felt far too cold. His body was like ice against her palms as she scooped him up. "No, no, no—"

She rushed to the fireplace, water dripping through her fingers. The copper tub was too far, but there—a ceramic bowl on the side table. She grabbed it, setting it on the hearthstone closest to the flames. The water from the basin was barely enough to cover him when she poured it in, his tiny form settling at the bottom, unmoving.

"Please," she whispered, adding more water from the pitcher by her bedside. It wasn't enough—barely two inches, and Frederick lay at the bottom like a piece of clouded glass. She grabbed the water from the washing pitcher, not caring that it was scented with lavender, and added it until he was properly submerged. "You followed me all this way. You can't—"

Nothing. No movement, no response. The crystallized edges of his gill-fronds were spreading, the ice claiming more of his translucent body with each second. She could see it happening—watch him dying—and her hands shook as she positioned the bowl on the hearthstone.

Too close to the flame and she'd boil him. Too far and he'd finish freezing. She adjusted it twice, three times, finally settling on a spot where the heat radiated gently.

"Frederick, please." Her voice cracked. She touched the water with one finger, and his body was so cold it hurt. Nothing like the cool silk sensation she knew. This was the cold of death, of things that would never move again.

The opacity wasn't fading. If anything, it seemed to be spreading, his entire form going that horrible milk-white color. She watched, counting heartbeats, counting breaths, waiting for something, anything.

Twenty heartbeats. Fifty. A hundred.

Nothing.

"No." The word came out as a sob. She pressed both hands against the bowl, as if she could will her own warmth into the water. "You're all I have left. You can't leave me here alone. Please, Frederick, please—"

The collar sensed her desperation, her rage at the unfairness of it, and began to drain. But she didn't care. Let it take everything if Frederick was gone. This tiny sprite who'd chosen to follow her through horror after horror, who'd attacked Malus to protect her, who'd tried to save her from the harpies despite being so small against their size.

"I'm sorry," she whispered, tears falling into the bowl, rippling the surface. "I'm so sorry I brought you here. You should have stayed in the fountains where it was safe, where it was warm. This is my fault, all of it is my fault—"

Was that movement, or just the water settling?

She leaned closer, barely breathing. There, the tiniest shift in one gill-frond. So small she might have imagined it.

"Frederick?"

Another twitch, barely visible. Then the opacity at the edges began to recede, not quickly, not dramatically, but present. Definite. The ice was releasing him so slowly she had to stare to be certain it was happening at all.

She didn't move, didn't breathe too hard, terrified that any disturbance might stop this fragile revival. The white cloudiness retreated toward his center with agonizing slowness. One gill-frond lifted slightly, fell back. Then another.

It took so long she lost track of time, watching each microscopic improvement. The water in the bowl warmed degree by degree, and with each increase, a little more of Frederick returned. The opacity faded from white to gray to merely clouded. His eye-spots, which had been invisible beneath the frozen surface, began to show through.

When he finally moved, truly moved, not just twitched, rising just slightly from the bottom of the bowl, she let out a sob of relief. Frederick was alive. Barely, weakly, but alive.

A bubble had formed, no bigger than a pearl and trembling with the effort it took to maintain. He rose another inch, those dark eye-spots focusing on her face with what seemed like tremendous effort.

"You ridiculous, loyal thing," she said softly, one finger gently touching the water's surface. "This place is killing you and you still came."

Frederick's response was to strengthen his bubble slightly, though she could see it cost him. He pressed against her finger, the closest thing to comfort he could offer.

Rocking back on her heels, she caught sight of her reflection in the water and frowned.

The collar glittered, the light from the fire playing on its polished surface. Her hands rose to touch it, the metal seamless except for where the latch lay flush against her throat. No keyhole, no obvious mechanism.

"I need to get this off," she said to Frederick, who watched from his bowl with what she imagined was concern. She tried prying at it with her fingernails but the metal might as well have been part of her skin. The collar remained perfectly fitted to her throat, the ribbon still threaded through it, bells silent only when she was perfectly still.

When frustration rose, the collar responded immediately, that horrible draining sensation that left her gasping. Even thinking about removing it triggered the response, as if it could sense intent as well as emotion.

"He's going to come back," she whispered, the truth of it settling over her. "Tonight, tomorrow, I don't know when. And this thing will keep me from fighting him."

Frederick created a small spout of water, his version of anger, but even that small display exhausted him. He sank back into the bowl, bubble shrinking.

Briar looked at the trays of food. Her stomach rebelled at the thought, but if she didn't eat, Thaine and Karse would starve. She forced herself to take a piece of bread, though it tasted of nothing and sat heavy in her stomach.

Outside the sealed windows, night had fully fallen. Somewhere below, Karse was freezing in a cell while Thaine tried to keep them both alive. She pulled the bowl with Frederick closer, his small presence the only comfort in the beautiful prison of her room.

Consciousness returned slowly, warmth on one side from dying embers, cold seeping through from everywhere else. Briar's neck ached from sleeping propped against the chair, and her dress was wrinkled beyond repair. Something was wrong—the quality of light, the sense of being observed.

She opened her eyes to find three servants standing near the door, trays balanced in their hands. They'd entered while she slept, silent as shadows. Behind them, Malachar stood in the doorway, today wearing deep burgundy that made his white hair seem to glow.

"Good morning." His tone carried that same false pleasantry. "Though it's nearly noon. You've slept half the day away."

She straightened, wincing at the protest from her stiff muscles. Frederick's bowl was still beside her, and she could see him floating weakly, bubble barely maintained. One of the servants—a young man with bark-textured skin—moved toward it.

"I'll clear this—"

"No." She grabbed the bowl, water sloshing dangerously. Frederick sank to the bottom, trying to hide.

Malachar's interest sharpened immediately. He raised a hand, and the servant stepped back.

"What have we here?" He moved into the room with predatory curiosity. "Something precious, clearly."

She held the bowl against her chest, but he was already close enough to see. His remaining eye studied Frederick with genuine surprise.

"A water sprite. In my domain." He laughed softly. "It must be suffering terribly in this cold. How did it even survive the journey?"

"Leave him alone."

"Him?" His amusement deepened. "You've named it. Of course you have." He gestured to the servants, who began setting out breakfast on the small table. "Bring the bowl. And yourself. You're going to eat."

It wasn't a request. She stood on unsteady legs, Frederick's bowl clutched carefully. Malachar had already seated himself, pouring tea from a silver pot that steamed in the cold air.

"Sit."

She set Frederick's bowl on the table's edge, as far from Malachar as possible, then took the only other chair. The food spread between them looked beautiful—pastries dusted with sugar that sparkled like snow, eggs prepared with herbs she didn't recognize, meat that smelled rich and wrong somehow.

"You didn't eat yesterday. Not properly." He selected a pastry, setting it on the plate in front of her. "That ends now."

"I'm not—"

"Hungry? No, I imagine not. But you'll eat anyway." He leaned back, studying her appearance with critical assessment. "You look terrible. Hair unwashed, dress ruined, sleeping on floors like an animal. Is this how the Forest Court taught you to present yourself?"

Heat crept up her neck, but when anger tried to rise, the collar drained it. She picked up the pastry with trembling fingers.

"Smaller bites," he instructed. "You're not a starving peasant."

The pastry tasted of nothing. She chewed mechanically while he watched, occasionally correcting her posture, the angle of her wrists, the way she held her cup. Each correction came with subtle threats—mentions of Karse's deteriorating condition, Thaine's frostbite spreading, how much colder the dungeons could become.

"Better." He pushed another plate toward her. "The sprite is watching you."

She glanced at Frederick, who had indeed risen slightly in his bowl, eye-spots focused on her. Worried, even in his weakened state.

"Touching, really. Such loyalty from something so insignificant." Malachar's finger traced the rim of his teacup. "I could freeze that bowl solid in an instant. Would it shatter, do you think? Or simply... stop?"

Her hand stilled on her fork.

"Eat," he commanded softly. "And I'll leave it alone."

She ate. Every bite felt like surrender, but Frederick floated there, vulnerable and trusting, and she couldn't risk him. Malachar watched her consume everything he selected, occasionally reaching across to adjust her hair, to straighten her collar where the bells had tangled. Each touch made her skin crawl, made the warmth in her chest contract with revulsion.

"There's going to be a dinner tomorrow night," he said finally, when the plates were empty. "Lord Malus will arrive by evening. You'll sit beside him, of course, as his gift, but I want you presentable."

He gestured to one of the servants, who brought forward a gown draped over her arms. It was exquisite—white as fresh snow with silver embroidery that looked like frost patterns. The neckline was high, with a collar of white fur that would hide both Eliam's marks and the silver collar completely.

"You'll wear this. Your hair will be properly styled. You'll sit quietly while we discuss the division of the Forest Court." He stood, moving around the table to stand behind her chair. His hands settled on her shoulders, thumbs pressing against the collar. "And if you behave—truly behave—perhaps I'll allow the sprite to stay in a warmer bowl during dinner."

The casual cruelty of using Frederick as leverage made her vision blur with frustrated tears. The collar sensed her rage and fed on it, leaving her gasping.

"Oh, and one more thing." His hands slid from her shoulders to her throat, fingers tracing the collar through her hair. "I've cleared my afternoon schedule. I thought we might... continue getting reacquainted. After all, we have so much time to make up for."

The promise in his voice made her stomach turn. He pressed a kiss to the top of her head—possessive, mocking—then straightened.

"Bathe. Fix your hair. Try to look less like something dragged from the dungeons." He moved toward the door, pausing to look back. "I'll return after lunch. Be ready."

The door locked behind him, leaving her shaking at the table. Frederick had pressed himself against the side of the bowl closest to her, offering what comfort he could. She touched the water gently, feeling his cool presence respond.

"I don't know how to stop him," she whispered. "The collar won't let me fight. And if I try, he'll hurt you. Or them."

Frederick's bubble strengthened marginally, a tiny show of defiance that probably cost him greatly. But it was something. Even here, even dying slowly in the cold, he was still fighting in his small way.

She looked at the beautiful dress that would hide all evidence of who she really belonged to, then at the locked door Malachar would return through in just a few hours. The warmth in her chest pulsed weakly, reaching south toward forests and thorns, toward a lord who didn't even know where she was.

Chapter Eleven

The late afternoon light slanted through the windows, painting long shadows across the floor. Briar sat at the vanity, her reflection showing someone she barely recognized. The servants had dressed her like a doll—efficient hands fastening the silver buttons, adjusting the fit, styling her hair into something elegant and unfamiliar. She'd stood passive through it all because fighting would only drain her, and she needed whatever strength she could preserve.

The dress was deep blue, almost black, fitted perfectly to her frame. Which disturbed her more than if it hadn't fit at all. How long had Malachar been planning this? How many measurements taken while she slept?

Frederick floated more actively in his bowl, now positioned on the vanity where she could see him. She'd added the remaining hot water from the tea service after the servants left, and the warmth had revived him considerably. His bubble was nearly normal size, and he'd even managed a few small spouts of water when she'd whispered to him—his version of conversation.

The lock turned.

Malachar entered without announcement, closing the door with deliberate care. His eye swept over her, taking in the styled hair, the proper dress, the straight posture.

"Much better." He moved into the room with the confidence of ownership. "You clean up remarkably well when you apply yourself."

She said nothing, watching him in the mirror as he approached. The collar sat heavy against her throat, hidden beneath lace but ever-present.

"Stand. Let me see you properly."

She rose, turning to face him. He circled her slowly, occasionally adjusting something—a fold of fabric, an escaped strand of hair. Each touch was light but lingering, claiming territory.

"Tomorrow's dinner will be significant," he said, stopping in front of her. "The formal transfer of ownership, so to speak. Malus is quite eager to receive his gift."

"I'm not—"

"Not what? Not property?" He smiled, reaching out to trace the line of the collar through the fabric. "This says otherwise. As does the mark beneath it. As does your presence here."

His fingers moved from the collar to her jaw, tilting her face up. "You've been passed from keeper to keeper. The Forest Lord, the Star Prince, that Drak creature. Now me and soon Malus. At what point will you accept what you are?"

The truth of it sat heavy in her stomach. She *had* been passed between them, each claiming ownership in their own way. The collar sensed her despair and fed lightly, just enough to keep her docile.

"Nothing to say?" His thumb traced her lower lip. "You were more spirited that night in the Forest Court. Before your protector arrived."

The reminder of that night, of what he'd tried to do, made the warmth in her chest contract with terror. He felt her tense and smiled.

"Yes, you remember. The way you struggled, bit my hand. Drew blood." He held up his hand, showing faint scars from her teeth. "I kept these. A memento."

He moved closer, backing her against the vanity. The mirror was cold against her back.

"Shall we continue where we left off? No interruptions this time. No Forest Lord bursting through shadows." His hands settled on her waist, holding her in place. "Just you and I, finishing what we started."

"Don't." The word came out weak, the collar already draining the defiance from it.

"Don't?" He leaned closer, his breath cold against her cheek. "But we have such history, you and I. That kiss we shared—do you remember the taste of winter?"

One hand moved to her hair, pulling pins free until it tumbled down her back. "Better. You look less severe this way."

She tried to turn her face away, but he caught her chin, forcing her to meet his eye. The patch gleamed in the afternoon light, and she wondered if he could see her elevated temperature, the fear radiating from her skin.

"I can see your heart racing," he confirmed, as if reading her thoughts. "The heat blooming across your skin. Fascinating, really. Your body's responses are so... honest."

His lips brushed her jaw and made her stomach turn. The warmth in her chest recoiled, pulling away from his touch, trying to retreat somewhere safe that didn't exist.

"Stop." She pushed against his chest, but the collar immediately activated, draining the strength from her arms.

"Still fighting." He caught her wrists easily, pressing them against the mirror on either side of her. "The collar will train you out of that eventually. But for now..."

He kissed her.

It was like that first time—cold, invasive, and wrong. His tongue forced past her lips, bringing winter into her mouth. The taste of frost and something metallic made her try to pull back, but she was trapped between him and the vanity.

The warmth in her chest thrashed, desperate and wild. It pushed against the collar's suppression, fighting to respond to the threat. She could feel it building, something beyond the collar's ability to drain—not her anger but the magic itself, acting independently.

Malachar pulled back, studying her face. "You taste different than before. Sweeter. Fear, perhaps? Or resignation?"

His hands released her wrists to travel down her arms, over her ribs, settling at her waist again. "Let's see what else has changed."

He turned her roughly to face the mirror, pressing against her back. "Watch," he commanded, his reflection meeting her eyes over her shoulder. "I want you to see yourself surrender."

One hand moved to the buttons at her back, working the first one free. Then the second. She could see his fingers in the mirror, pale against the dark fabric, methodical in their violation. The dress loosened, and his hand slipped inside, fingers ice-cold against her spine.

"Your skin is so warm," he murmured against her throat, watching her face in the glass. "Like touching summer itself."

Another button. Another. The dress gaped open, and he pushed it off one shoulder, revealing the chemise beneath. His mouth found the exposed skin, teeth scraping lightly, and she watched herself flinch in the mirror—watched him smile at her reaction.

"The collar is working beautifully," he observed, his hand sliding around to her stomach, pulling her back against him. "You want to fight, I can see it in your eyes, but you simply... can't."

The warmth in her chest thrashed wildly, pushing against the collar's suppression. Not her emotion but something deeper, older, protective. She felt it gathering, coalescing, fighting to break through.

His other hand came up to her throat, fingers tracing the collar through the remaining fabric. Then lower, over her collarbones, pushing the dress off her other shoulder. It pooled at her elbows, trapping her arms.

"Perfect," he said, turning her chin to force her to keep watching. "Look at yourself. Is this what the Forest Lord saw? This mixture of fear and—"

The warmth surged.

It pushed through the collar's suppression like water breaking through a dam. Building into something she couldn't control, power gathering in her chest, behind her ribs, spreading outward.

Then the flowers began to bloom.

The first one rose from the floorboards by the vanity's leg, pale petals unfurling like a hand opening. Then another pushed through near the door, and another by the window. They were beautiful—white tinged with the faintest gold at the edges, their centers glowing softly in the afternoon light.

Malachar paused, his hands still on her shoulders, holding the dress that trapped her arms. "What is this?"

"I don't—" But she did. Memory supplied the image suddenly: Eliam in his garden at dusk, pointing out flowers that only opened as day turned to night. Dusk Blooms, he'd called them, though he'd warned her never to smell them directly. "They defend themselves with dreams," he'd said. "One breath and you'll sleep where you stand."

More of the flowers bloomed, pushing up through cracks in the stone, spreading across the floor in a slowly expanding circle. Malachar's fascination overcame his caution.

"Extraordinary." He didn't release her, but his attention had shifted to the display as his hand moved to her throat, turning her face toward him. "Can you control it? Make them stop?"

"I don't know how—"

"No, of course you don't." His grip tightened slightly. "Pure instinct, pure protection. How beautifully primitive."

The flowers continued blooming, their petals fully open now, trembling slightly though there was no breeze. She could see golden dust beginning to form in their centers, gathering like tiny storms.

"They're quite lovely," he said, returning his attention to her partially exposed form in the mirror. "Harmless things. Though I suppose even rabbits try to run when cornered."

His mouth returned to her shoulder, teeth grazing skin. "Where were we?"

The golden dust swirled deeper in the flowers' centers. She recognized the signs, they were about to release. Eliam's warning echoed in her memory: "Hold your breath if you're ever near them when they spread their pollen."

She inhaled deeply just as the flowers erupted.

Golden clouds burst from every bloom simultaneously, filling the air with shimmering dust that caught the afternoon light like suspended gold. Malachar, mid-sentence about her warmth, took a full breath of it directly.

The effect was instantaneous.

His eye rolled back, showing white. His grip on her shoulders went slack, then his knees buckled. He dropped like a puppet with cut strings, hitting the floor with a heavy thud that shook the vanity.

But she'd breathed some too—just a small amount before holding her breath, but enough. The room tilted strangely. Her limbs felt heavy, disconnected. The collar, sensing her attempt to flee, began draining what little strength remained.

Frederick. She had to get Frederick.

She stumbled forward, pulling her arms free of the dress, hiking the skirts up to keep from tripping. The bowl. There—on the vanity where she'd left it. Her fingers felt thick and clumsy as she grabbed it, water sloshing. Frederick bobbed anxiously, his bubble expanding and contracting with distress.

The door. She needed the door.

But the golden pollen hung everywhere, a beautiful glittering cloud she had to move through. Each step required conscious thought. Lift foot. Put down. Balance. The collar pulled at her energy, interpreting her escape as defiance, making her knees weak.

She made it to the door, fumbling with the handle. Locked. Of course it was locked.

Malachar groaned behind her, already fighting the pollen's effect. His body was fae, stronger than human. He wouldn't stay unconscious long.

The keys. He had to have keys.

She stumbled back to his prone form, dropping to her knees beside him, Frederick's bowl clutched in one hand while the other searched his pockets. The pollen was settling now, coating every surface in fine golden dust. She tried not to breathe, but her lungs burned for air.

There—a ring of keys in his inner pocket. Her fingers were barely working, the combination of pollen and collar making everything feel distant and strange. She grabbed them, stumbling back to the door.

Five keys on the ring. Her hands shook so badly she could barely get the first one to the lock. It scraped against the metal, missing the keyhole entirely. Finally in. Didn't turn.

The second key went in but jammed halfway. Wrong one. Behind her, Malachar groaned, his body shifting on the floor.

"Come on, come on—" The third key. Her vision was blurring, the edges going dark. The key slipped from her numb fingers, the whole ring clattering to the floor.

She dropped to her knees, Frederick's bowl hitting the ground hard, water sloshing out. The sprite swirled in distress as she frantically felt for the keys with fingers that barely responded. There—cold metal against her palm.

Back to standing took everything she had. The room spun violently. The third key again, hands shaking so badly it took three tries to find the keyhole. It slid in. Turned.

The lock clicked open.

She practically fell into the corridor, gasping for clean air. But that was a mistake. The deep breath made the pollen in her lungs activate more fully. The world swam, edges going soft.

"No, no, no—" She pressed one hand against the wall for support, Frederick's bowl in the other. The water sprite was agitated, creating tiny spouts that wet her hand.

Which way? She couldn't remember which way led to the stairs. The collar continued its steady drain, punishing her for running. Combined with the pollen, she could barely stand.

Behind her, she heard movement from the room. Malachar waking. Fighting through the sleep.

She picked a direction and ran—or tried to. It was more of a stumbling lurch, bouncing off walls, Frederick's bowl sloshing dangerously. The corridors all looked the same. Ice-touched stone, frozen windows, endless doors that could hide anything.

Footsteps behind her. Unsteady but gaining.

"Briar." Malachar's voice, thick with the pollen but conscious. Angry. "The collar will bring you back. You know this."

She turned a corner and found stairs. Down was the only option—down toward the dungeons, toward Karse and Thaine. Her legs barely managed the steps. Twice she almost dropped Frederick. The collar's drain was constant now, feeding on her desperate need to escape.

The golden dust clung to her hair, her dress, leaving a trail anyone could follow. Her vision kept trying to narrow, to fade into the welcoming darkness of sleep. But Malachar was behind her, and if he caught her now, after what she'd done—

She kept moving, deeper into the frozen heart of the mountain, clutching Frederick's bowl like the lifeline it was.

The stone steps descended into darkness, each one requiring her full concentration. Hold the wall. Move foot. Don't drop Frederick. The collar pulled steadily at her strength, interpreting every movement away from her room as defiance. The pollen made everything feel like she was moving through honey.

She missed a step near the bottom, her knee cracking against stone. Frederick's bowl flew from her hands, water arcing through the air as it clattered across the floor. She heard it rolling, the tinny sound echoing off frozen walls, but couldn't see where it had gone in the dim light.

"No—" She crawled forward on hands and knees, feeling for the bowl, for Frederick, for anything. The floor was ice-cold, numbing her fingers instantly.

Light ahead. The soft glow from the occupied cell. She crawled toward it, dress dragging through the frost that coated everything. Her body wanted so desperately to sleep, to just lay down on the frozen stone and let the darkness take her.

"Briar?" Thaine's voice, sharp with alarm.

She reached the bars, fingers wrapping around them for support. The metal burned with cold, but she couldn't let go. Through blurring vision, she saw them—Thaine pressed against the bars, Karse behind him barely conscious, his scales now almost completely gray.

"What did he—what happened to you?" Thaine's hands covered hers through the bars.

She tried to speak but her tongue wouldn't work properly. The words came out slurred, incomprehensible. The keyring slipped from her numb grasp, hitting the floor with a metallic clatter.

"Dusk Blooms," She managed to get the words out, though they sounded wrong, thick. "The flowers. Made him sleep, but I breathed some..."

Footsteps on the stairs, slow and deliberate.

"No." She tried to stand, to run, but her legs wouldn't respond. The collar had taken too much, the pollen clouded everything. She could only kneel there, clinging to the bars, as Malachar descended into view.

His hair was disheveled, golden pollen still dusting his shoulders. His eye blazed with rage that made the temperature drop another degree.

"Clever little thing," he said, voice deadly soft. He moved closer, and she tried to crawl backward but her body wouldn't obey. "Do you have any idea what you've done? The disrespect you've shown?"

He grabbed her arm, hauling her upright. Her legs trembled, refusing to hold her. She was conscious but barely, everything swimming in and out of focus.

"Look at you. Can't even stand." He pressed her against the bars, his body caging hers. "All that effort to escape and you ran straight to them. As if they could help you. As if anyone could."

His hand tangled in her hair, yanking her head back. A whimper escaped her and she heard Karse curse. "Maybe you wanted them to see? Wanted to show them how well you're learning to surrender?"

Then he kissed her, hard and punishing, right there in front of them. She couldn't fight, couldn't even turn away, the collar and pollen having stripped her of everything but consciousness. He made sure it lasted, made sure they watched, his mouth cold and invasive against hers.

When he pulled back, she saw Thaine's hands white-knuckled on the bars and Karse trying to rise.

"Remember this," Malachar said to them, though his eye stayed on her. "This is what defiance brings. This is what happens when you forget who holds the power here."

He scooped her into his arms, her head lolled against his shoulder, the world spinning. From this angle, she could see Frederick's bowl overturned near the wall, the puddle of water spreading. Frederick himself, just a glimpse of translucent form in the water, trying to maintain cohesion.

No.

Tears burned at the corners of her eyes.

"Enjoy the rest of your evening," he told Thaine and Karse. "Tomorrow, Lord Malus arrives, and you'll all understand what true ownership means."

He carried her from the dungeon, her vision fading in and out. The last thing she saw was Thaine dropping to his knees by the bars, his hand stretching through, reaching for something on the floor.

The journey back to her room passed in fragments—cold corridors, stairs that made her stomach lurch,

"Such trouble you've caused," he said against her hair. "But we'll correct that. Tomorrow you'll kneel beside Malus's chair and thank him for his mercy. You'll wear the gown I chose and speak only when spoken to."

Another turn, another hallway, each looking identical through her blurred vision. The collar pulled steadily at what little strength remained, interpreting even her unconscious resistance as defiance.

"The Drak will be dead by morning," Malachar continued. "The cold is killing him by degrees. Your huntsman might last longer, but even fae blood freezes eventually."

She tried to speak, to protest, but her tongue wouldn't obey. Only a soft sound escaped, wordless and weak.

"Yes, you're upset about that," he observed, shouldering open a door she recognized even through her haze—her prison room. "Perhaps if you'd simply accepted your situation, they wouldn't be suffering. Their pain is your selfishness made manifest."

He dropped her on the bed without gentleness, then stood back. He watched her for a moment and then began removing his jacket, folding it with deliberate care over the chair. The message was clear in every unhurried movement.

There was no escape.

He unbuttoned his cuffs while watching her watch him, taking his time with each small button. When he rolled the sleeves up, she could see old scars marking his forearms, thin white lines that looked like frost patterns against his pale skin.

"You're fighting it," he observed as he moved closer to the bed. "Good. It makes breaking you more fun."

She managed to pull herself higher against the headboard, but there was nowhere left to retreat. The pollen was wearing off and she could feel clarity returning, but the collar compensated for her increased resistance by draining harder.

His hand reached for her ankle and his fingers closed around it like a shackle. His thumb found the hollow beneath the bone and pressed lightly, just enough to make his possession clear.

"Still so warm," he murmured while his touch traveled upward to her calf. "Even now, even here in my domain, you burn with summer heat."

She tried to pull away but he held firm, bringing his other hand to rest on her knee with deliberate slowness. The touch was light but promised so much worse.

"I can feel your pulse racing here," he said, his fingers tracing the inside of her knee before moving higher to her thigh. "Your body tells such honest stories, even when your mouth lies. What else is it going to tell me?"

The fire went out and with it the temperature began to plummet.

This wasn't Malachar's winter cold. This was the chill of deep forest shadow, of places where sunlight never reached, of roots that grew down into the earth's bones.

"I thought losing an eye would have taught you not to touch what's mine."

The voice came from everywhere and nowhere. Malachar's hand released her ankle as he spun toward the shadows gathering in the corner, shadows that shouldn't have existed with afternoon light still coming through the windows.

"But apparently," Eliam stepped from the darkness like he was built from it, and he was wrong, all wrong, too tall and crowned with antlers that weren't quite there, "you need a more thorough lesson."

Chapter Twelve

At the sound of Eliam's voice, the warmth in Briar's chest exploded outward, reaching for him with desperate intensity. It pulled toward him so hard she gasped, and the collar interpreted this as the ultimate defiance. She let out a whimper as it began draining her very essence at a rate that bordered on agony.

"Eliam." Malachar's voice stayed controlled, though his hand had gone to his blade. "You're outside your territory. You are in my lands now, you have no authority here."

"Authority?" Eliam tilted his head, the fire in his eyes burning hotter. "You have her in your bed. You have your hands on her. And you speak to me of boundaries?"

Malachar raised his hand and ice coalesced from the air itself, forming a blade as long as his forearm, its edge gleaming. "She was given to me. A gift for my assistance in necessary changes."

"Given? She was stolen." Eliam moved further into the room, and darkness followed him, eating the afternoon light from the windows.

Briar tried to speak, but the drain was too intense. She could feel it pulling her life away in steady draws, the warmth's desperate reach toward Eliam only making it worse. Her fingers were going numb, her breath coming in shorter gasps.

Malachar struck first, his blade cutting through the air where Eliam had been. But Eliam dissolved into the shadows, reforming behind him, thorns erupting from his hands. One clipped Malachar's shoulder, tearing through his shirt and drawing blood that steamed in the cold air.

"You've gone soft in your forest," Malachar snarled, twisting to face him. Ice spread from his feet across the floor, racing toward Eliam. "Forgotten how to fight without your trees."

They collided in the center of the room, ice meeting shadow, winter against forest. Malachar's blade shrieked against Eliam's thorns, both drawing blood, neither gaining clear advantage. They were matched, two Great Lords at the height of their fury, and the room itself groaned under the pressure of their power.

But Briar was dying.

She could feel it, the collar draining faster than her body could sustain. The warmth, desperate after so long, kept pulling toward Eliam, and the collar kept punishing her for it, a vicious cycle that was shutting her body down. Her heartbeat stuttered and slowed.

Eliam felt it too, his attention flickering to her for just an instant. It was enough. Malachar's blade found his side, sliding between ribs with a wet sound that made Eliam grunt. But instead of pulling back, Eliam grabbed the blade with his bare hand, holding it in place while more thorns erupted from his other palm, driving straight through Malachar's chest.

The Winter Lord gasped, blood bubbling from his lips. Eliam twisted the thorns deeper, his face terrible in its fury.

"You should have kept to your mountain halls, Malachar," Eliam sneered, preparing to drive the thorns deeper.

"Wait," Malachar choked out, his eye finding Briar. "The collar she wears. Only I can remove it."

Eliam's hand stilled but didn't withdraw. "Lies."

"Look at her," Malachar managed, blood running down his chin. "It's killing her, it's tied to my magic, my life. If I die, it becomes permanent. She'll be dead in minutes."

Eliam's gaze snapped to Briar, and she saw his expression change as he truly looked at her. She knew what he was seeing—her lips blue from lack of oxygen, her body barely moving with breath, the frost spreading from the collar as it consumed her. She tried to reach for him but her hand wouldn't lift.

"Remove it," Eliam demanded, twisting the thorns again.

"Remove your thorns first," Malachar countered, though speaking clearly cost him.

They stood frozen for a moment, locked in mutual destruction while Briar's breathing grew shallower. She could feel herself fading, sliding toward darkness that had nothing to do with Eliam's shadows. The warmth in her chest was growing quieter, pulling less strongly, as if it too was dying.

Eliam withdrew his thorns with a vicious twist that made Malachar scream. The Winter Lord collapsed to his knees, one hand pressed to the hole in his chest.

"Get up," Eliam said, his voice quiet.

Malachar grit his teeth and stumbled towards the bed.

"If you've deceived me," Eliam said, shadows coiling around him like living things, "I will take you apart piece by piece and scatter those pieces across every realm."

Malachar reached Briar with shaking hands, his blood dripping onto the white sheets. His fingers found the collar and he spoke words in the old tongue. The collar grew colder, then burning hot, then simply fell away, clattering to the floor in two pieces.

The relief was instant and overwhelming. The drain stopped, the warmth in her chest settled, and she could breathe again. Deep, gasping breaths that hurt but proved she was alive.

Eliam gathered her into his arms, pulling her far from Malachar's reach. She collapsed against his chest, her fingers clutching at his shirt with what little strength had returned. He was solid and real and here, when she'd thought no one would come.

"You found me," she whispered against his shoulder, and she felt him tense at how broken her voice sounded.

"You're surprised?" he replied. "I'll always come for what belongs to me."

"I don't.... you threw me out," she reminded him, and she felt his arms tighten around her.

She pulled back just enough to look at his face, seeing the terrible fae features softening as he looked at her. The antlers were fading, his height returning to something more human, though his eyes still held that green fire.

"I... may have acted rashly..." his hand rose to brush hair from her face, his fingers tangling briefly in the loose strands.

Briar felt her heart skip in her chest. It wasn't an apology, but then she didn't expect one. It was, however, acknowledgement.

"Take me home," she said. "Please."

He said nothing as he lifted her gently, cradling her against his chest as he turned toward the window. She saw the movement over his shoulder—Malachar pushing himself up with one hand while the other drew a thin blade from his belt.

"Eliam—!"

The warning came too late. Malachar drove the ice blade into Eliam's shoulder, the frozen weapon sliding deep between muscle and bone. Eliam grunted, nearly dropping her as he staggered. He reached back and ripped the blade free, ice shards breaking off in the wound as blood immediately soaked through his shirt, but Malachar was already forming another weapon from winter air.

"Did you think I'd just let you—"

The vase shattered against Malachar's skull with a deafening crash. The Winter Lord's eye rolled back and he collapsed forward, the blade falling from nerveless fingers. Behind him stood Thaine, holding the remains of the vase's base, looking deeply satisfied. Karse leaned against the doorframe beside him, Frederick's bowl clutched carefully in his scaled hands.

A shriek echoed from somewhere high above—then another, and another.

"The wards," Thaine said, moving deeper into the room. "Your magic must have triggered the mountain's defenses."

Eliam carried her to the shattered window, and she could see the first white shapes descending from the peaks beyond. They were still distant but closing fast. Blood ran freely down his arm, and when he began speaking in the old tongue, his voice caught on the third word. The shadows outside the window gathered but wouldn't hold, dissipating like smoke each time they started to solidify.

The shrieking grew louder. Closer.

"Eliam," she said urgently, her hand finding his uninjured shoulder. The warmth in her chest reached for him instinctively, recognizing his magic and trying to help.

He started the incantation again, and this time she felt her warmth flowing into him, mixing with his forest magic. The shadows responded, thickening, but the moth was only half-formed when Thaine's voice cut through from the doorway.

"They're here!"

A harpy slammed into the tower somewhere above, its shriek making the stones vibrate. Then another impact, and another. They were landing on the tower itself, looking for ways in.

The moth was still forming, its wings translucent and wavering. The raven beside it was barely more than a shadow with eyes. Eliam's voice grew more strained with each word of the summoning, fresh blood soaking through his shirt where the ice shards were melting, cutting deeper.

A harpy's face appeared at the window above them, upside down, teeth bared in a horrible grin. It started to squeeze through but Karse sent a weak jet of flame at it, driving it back with a shriek.

"Jump," Eliam commanded, though the moth's wings were still solidifying. "Now."

They had no choice. Briar could hear claws on stone, wings battering against windows throughout the tower. Eliam lifted her onto the half-formed moth and pulled himself up behind her just as its wings became solid enough to hold them. Thaine literally threw Karse onto the raven, causing Frederick's bowl to slosh dangerously, before leaping up himself.

The moth fell more than flew at first, its wings still gaining substance as they plummeted along the tower's side. A harpy dove after them, talons extended, only to strike through wings that were still partially shadow. The creature's confusion bought them seconds as the moth's form finally solidified completely, catching air just before they hit the mountain's slope.

Behind them, the tower erupted with white bodies, harpies pouring from every window in pursuit.

The moth's wings beat frantically, still gaining strength as they rose. Briar could feel Eliam's breath harsh against her neck, his arm around her waist trembling from blood loss and effort. The raven beside them cawed in distress, struggling with the weight of two riders while still partially shadow.

A harpy slammed into them from above, talons raking across the moth's wing. The creature screamed—a sound Briar hadn't known moths could make—and spiraled sideways. She gripped the soft fur desperately as they tumbled through air, Eliam's arm the only thing keeping her from falling.

More harpies converged from all directions. The smaller ravens materialized to intercept, but there were too many. A harpy's talons caught Thaine's shoulder, tearing through leather before Karse managed to burn its face. Their raven lurched, losing altitude.

The moth recovered, diving toward the treeline, but the harpies formed a wall of white bodies and membranous wings between them and safety. Eliam spoke through gritted teeth, and the moth suddenly folded its wings completely, plummeting like a stone. They fell past the startled harpies, Briar's stomach in her throat, the ground rushing up—

The moth's wings snapped open just above the canopy. They crashed through the upper branches, leaves and twigs whipping past. Behind them, the harpies followed, shrieking their fury.

But the moment they entered the forest's domain, everything changed.

The trees moved. Not gently, not slowly, but with violent purpose. Branches that had bent to let the moth pass suddenly became spears, piercing through harpy wings. Roots erupted from the earth, coiling around ankles and throats. A harpy that dove too low was caught between two trunks that slammed together, cutting off its shriek instantly.

The forest was hunting.

An oak's branches wrapped around a harpy mid-flight, pulling it into the trunk where the bark split open like a mouth and swallowed it whole. Vines dropped from above, forming nooses that snapped necks with efficient brutality. The very air under the canopy became thick, hostile to the mountain creatures, choking them with pollen and sap.

The moth wove between the carnage, following paths that opened just for them. Beside them, the raven carrying Thaine and Karse navigated the chaos, both mounts knowing exactly where the forest would strike next. Behind them, harpy shrieks turned from hunting cries to sounds of terror and pain.

One harpy, faster than the rest, managed to avoid the trees and lunged for Briar. Its talons were inches from her when a branch as thick as her waist swept it from the air, slamming it into a trunk with a wet crack that meant it would never fly again.

The pursuit ended as suddenly as it began. The remaining harpies fled back toward the mountains, leaving their dead tangled in branches and buried in bark. The forest settled slowly, branches returning to normal positions, roots sinking back into earth. But Briar could still feel the watchfulness, the readiness to kill anything that threatened their lord.

They flew in silence after that, deeper into the forest where the trees grew ancient and the air tasted of old magic. When the moth finally descended into the grove, setting down on soft moss, Briar could still hear the occasional distant shriek of a harpy discovering that one of its companions had been taken by the trees.

The forest had welcomed them home with blood, and she wasn't sure if that should comfort or terrify her.

The grove was quiet except for normal forest sounds—no shrieking harpies, no sound of pursuit. Just the whisper of wind through leaves and the distant call of a normal, properly-sized owl. They were safe, for the moment, but Briar could feel the weight of everything that had just happened settling over them.

Eliam hadn't moved from where he'd slumped against an oak trunk, his hand pressed to his shoulder where blood still seeped between his fingers. The ice blade had left more than just a wound—she could see frost spreading slowly from the injury, white tendrils creeping across his skin.

"Let me see," Thaine said, crouching beside him with professional efficiency.

Eliam removed his hand reluctantly, revealing the deep puncture wound. Ice crystals glinted within it, and more concerning was the second wound lower down where Malachar's blade had found the space between his ribs during their fight. Both wounds wept blood steadily, and the flesh around them had gone gray-white with cold.

"Ice magic," Thaine stated the obvious. "It's preventing the wounds from closing. You need to burn it out or it'll reach your heart."

Eliam nodded, his jaw clenched as he placed his palm over the shoulder wound. Green light flickered weakly, forest magic trying to purge winter's touch. The ice fought back, and Eliam made a sound of pain through gritted teeth as the two magics warred in his flesh.

The frost receded slightly but didn't disappear. He tried again, and this time Briar saw him sway, exhaustion written across his features. The shadow walking, the summoning, the fight—it had all taken its toll, and now this healing was draining what little remained.

Frederick, who had been quiet in his bowl on the ground beside Karse, suddenly became agitated. The sprite swirled in tight circles, creating a tiny waterspout that splashed over the rim.

"What's wrong with it?" Karse asked, his voice still rough from the cold he'd endured.

Frederick's response was to flow completely out of his bowl, something Briar had rarely seen him do. He formed a tiny rivulet on the forest floor, moving with determined purpose toward the trees.

"Frederick?" Briar struggled to her feet, concerned. The sprite had been so weak in the mountain, and now he was expending energy he couldn't spare.

The rivulet of water reached the base of a moss-covered boulder and began flowing up it, defying gravity in the way only magical water could. At the top, Frederick reformed into his sprite shape and began gesturing frantically back the way he'd come.

"I think he wants us to follow," Briar said.

"We don't have time for—" Thaine began, but Eliam cut him off with a raised hand.

"The sprite's found something." Eliam pushed himself to his feet with visible effort, fresh blood seeping through his shirt. "Water knows water. We follow."

Frederick led them through the trees, staying visible as a ribbon of water that gleamed in the moonlight. The path wound between ancient oaks and over moss-covered stones, and gradually Briar became aware of a change in the air. It grew warmer, heavier, carrying a faint mineral scent.

They heard it before they saw it—the soft bubbling of water over stone. Frederick disappeared over a small rise, and when they crested it, Briar saw what he'd found.

The hot spring was nestled in a natural depression, surrounded by smooth stones worn by centuries of mineral-rich water. Steam rose from its surface in gentle wisps, and the water itself was crystal clear despite the late hour, somehow luminous from within. Frederick was already there, floating in the shallows where the temperature was bearable for him, his form more solid and healthy-looking than she'd seen since they'd left the Star Court.

"Clever sprite," Thaine admitted, then looked at Eliam. "The heat might help draw out the ice magic."

Eliam was already moving toward the spring, though his steps were unsteady. He sat heavily on one of the smooth stones at the edge, working to remove his blood-soaked shirt with trembling fingers. The movement pulled at both wounds, making him hiss through his teeth.

"You two keep watch," Briar said to Thaine and Karse. "Please."

Thaine looked like he might argue, but something in her expression stopped him. He nodded once and moved back toward the trees, taking position where he could watch the approaches. Karse followed more slowly, still recovering from his imprisonment but understanding the need for privacy.

Briar approached Eliam carefully, kneeling beside him on the stones. Up close, she could see how bad the wounds really were. The ice had spread further while they walked, creating patterns like frozen veins beneath his skin.

"You need to get in the water," she said softly. "The heat will help."

"I know." But he didn't move immediately, just sat there breathing carefully, gathering strength.

She helped him with his boots, her fingers working the laces when his own couldn't manage the task. The simple domesticity of it, after everything that had happened, made her chest tight with emotion she couldn't name.

When she finished with his boots, he stood slowly and began working at the fastenings of his trousers. His movements were stiff, pained, and she could see him struggling with the simple task. Without thinking, she reached to help, then stopped, her hands hovering uncertainly.

"I can manage," he said, but his fingers fumbled at the ties, slick with blood from his wounds.

She helped anyway, keeping her touch clinical, practical. This was about healing, about necessity. When he finally stepped into the spring, the sound that escaped him was part relief, part agony as the hot water hit the ice-infected wounds.

He sank down until the water reached his chest, bracing himself against the smooth stones at the spring's edge. The mineral-rich water turned pink around him as it worked to clean the blood from his injuries. She could see the ice magic fighting the heat, steam rising where the two forces met.

Briar hesitated at the edge, still fully dressed in the gown from Malachar's castle. It was ruined anyway—blood-stained, torn, smelling of fear and mountain cold. And Eliam needed help. The wounds on his back, where the ice blade had entered, he couldn't reach properly himself.

She unlaced the dress with efficient movements, letting it fall to pool at her feet. The shift beneath was thin, already damp with sweat and blood—his and hers. She kept it on as she slipped into the water, the heat a shock after the cold of recent days.

The mineral-rich water reached just below her ribs, the thin shift clinging to her skin, transparent now but she couldn't bring herself to care. Eliam's breathing had gone shallow, controlled—the way it did when he was fighting not to show pain.

Steam rose between them, carrying the scent of earth and stone and something green that belonged to him despite the blood. The ice crystals in his wounds fought the spring's heat, creating wisps of vapor where opposing magics met. She moved behind him, careful not to disturb the water too much, and sucked in a breath at what she saw.

The entry wound was worse from this angle. The ice had spread in veins across his shoulder blade, the skin around it that terrible gray-white of frostbite. Lower, where

Malachar's blade had found the gap between ribs, blood still seeped steadily, refusing to clot.

"This is going to hurt," she warned, though they both knew it already hurt, would continue hurting until the ice magic was purged or killed him.

"Do it." His voice came out rough, tired in a way she'd never heard from him.

She cupped water in her palms, letting it heat her skin before pouring it directly over the shoulder wound. His whole body tensed, muscles locking beneath her touch, but he made no sound. The ice hissed, fighting the heat, and she saw one crystal actually crack and fall away, leaving raw flesh behind.

Again. Cup the water, pour it over the wound. Watch the ice fight and slowly, slowly lose. The warmth in her chest pulsed with each repetition, reaching toward him, wanting to help but not knowing how. She could feel it pressing against the boundaries of her ribs, desperate to flow into him the way it had during the summoning.

"Why did you come for me?" The question escaped before she could stop it, her hands still working, still pouring heated water over wounds that should never have been earned in her defense.

His head turned slightly, not enough to see her but enough to acknowledge the question. "You know why."

"I don't." Another pour of water, another hiss of dying ice. "You cast me out. Made me prey. You were done with me."

"I was angry." The admission came grudgingly, pulled from him like thorns from flesh. "You freed my brother. You betrayed—"

"I made a mistake." Her voice cracked. "I thought I was saving someone like me, someone human and trapped and forgotten. I never meant—"

"I know." Two words, soft enough she almost missed them over the bubble of the spring.

The ice in his shoulder wound had receded to a few stubborn crystals embedded deep. She worked at them carefully, using her fingers now to direct the heated water precisely where it needed to go. Each touch made the warmth in her chest pulse harder, reaching through her hands toward him.

"Karse claimed me," she said, needing him to know though not sure why. "Said I belonged to him because I freed him from chains."

Eliam's laugh was dark, unamused. "The Drak can claim whatever he wishes. It doesn't make it true."

Would now be the moment to tell him what else had happened with Karse? The thought of confessing that desperate coupling on the Star Court's terrace made her stomach turn. Not from shame exactly, but from the knowledge of how it would hurt him—and more confusingly, the certainty that it would hurt him, despite everything.

"The collar," she said instead, her fingers finding the marks it had left on her throat, already bruising dark. "Malachar's collar. It fed on defiance, on anger, on any attempt to fight. It was killing me just for wanting to reach you."

His hand rose from the water, fingers covering hers where they pressed against her throat. The touch was gentle, careful of the bruising, but she felt him trembling—whether from pain or rage, she couldn't tell.

"He'll never touch you again," Eliam said, and there was something final in it, a promise written in blood and thorns.

The last of the ice cracked away from his shoulder wound. The flesh beneath was raw, angry, but no longer infected with winter magic. She moved her attention to the lower wound, the one still seeping steadily.

"This one's deeper," she observed, seeing how the ice had worked its way between his ribs, dangerously close to vital organs.

"I'm aware." His hand dropped back to brace against the stone, and she saw his knuckles go white with the grip.

The warmth in her chest suddenly surged, pushing outward so forcefully she gasped. It wanted out, wanted to flow into him, wanted to heal what winter had broken. Without thinking, she pressed her palm flat against the wound.

The warmth poured through her hand into his flesh like liquid sunlight.

Chapter Thirteen

The moment her palm made contact, the warmth erupted from her chest like a dam breaking. Not the gentle flow she'd expected but a torrent, golden and burning and alive. It poured through her hand into his wound with such force that they both cried out—him from the shock of it, her from the sensation of something essential being pulled from her core.

"Briar—" He tried to turn, to pull away, but she pressed harder, her other hand coming up to his uninjured shoulder to hold him in place.

"Don't move." The words came out strained. She could feel it working—the warmth flooding through damaged tissue, meeting the ice magic with violence that made the water around them bubble. "It needs to finish."

The ice fought back, winter magic recognizing its antithesis. Where the two forces met, steam rose thick enough to obscure them both. She felt each crystal of ice like a splinter in her own flesh, felt them crack and dissolve under the onslaught of whatever lived in her chest. The warmth wasn't gentle—it burned through Malachar's magic with savage purpose, reclaiming territory that had been taken.

Eliam's breathing had gone ragged. She could feel his heartbeat through her palm, too fast, struggling with the invasion of foreign magic even if it was trying to heal. His skin grew fever-hot where her hand touched, the temperature spreading outward in visible waves.

"What are you?" The question came out rough, wondering.

She didn't know. The warmth had never acted like this before—so directed, so violent in its protection. It recognized him, reached for him always, but this was different.

This was the warmth turning into something with teeth, devouring the ice magic like a starved thing finally fed.

The wound beneath her palm began to close. She could feel it happening—flesh knitting together from the inside out, ribs realigning, the puncture sealing itself with unnatural speed. The ice magic gave one last surge of resistance, spreading frost across the water's surface, then shattered completely under the warmth's assault.

The healing moved to his shoulder without her directing it, the warmth flowing through his body to find every trace of winter's touch. It burned through the frostbite, restored circulation to damaged tissue, sealed the ragged puncture with the same savage efficiency.

Golden flowers began blooming in the water around them.

They rose from nothing, materializing on the surface like memories made solid—small, delicate things with petals that caught the moonlight. Not sunset tears this time but something else, something she'd never seen before. They floated in expanding circles, releasing a faint perfume that smelled of summer afternoons and honey.

"Briar." Eliam's voice held warning now. He'd turned enough to see her face, and whatever he found there made him reach back, his hand covering hers where it still pressed against his now-healed shoulder. "That's enough."

But the warmth wasn't listening to her anymore. It poured out faster, seeking hurts that went deeper than flesh—exhaustion, old wounds that hadn't healed properly, the constant drain of maintaining his power. It wanted to fix everything, make him whole, make him hers in a way that terrified her with its intensity.

Her vision started to gray at the edges. The warmth was taking too much, pulling from reserves she didn't have after days of torture and starvation. She felt herself listing forward, her forehead coming to rest against his back.

"Stop," she whispered, though she wasn't sure if she was talking to the warmth or herself.

Eliam twisted in the water, his arms coming around her just as her legs gave out. He pulled her against his chest, one hand tangling in her wet hair, the other pressing flat against her chest where the warmth originated.

"Look at me." Command threaded through his words, the kind that had once compelled obedience through their bargain. Now it just focused her attention and drew her gaze to his. "You need to pull it back. The magic. Call it home."

"I don't know how—"

"Yes, you do." His hand pressed harder against her chest, and she felt him push his own magic through the touch—not fighting the warmth but guiding it, showing it the way back. "It's yours. It answers to you."

The warmth resisted, wanting to continue its work, to pour everything she was into him until there was nothing left to give. But slowly, reluctantly, it began to recede. The golden flow thinned, then stopped, settling back beneath her ribs.

The flowers on the water began to dissolve, petals scattering into golden dust that sank beneath the surface.

She was shaking. Her whole body trembled with exhaustion, and only Eliam's arms kept her from sliding under the water. He adjusted his grip, pulling her more firmly against him, and she became suddenly aware of their position—her shift transparent, his skin bare against hers, the mineral water hot around them.

"Your wounds," she managed, needing something practical to focus on.

"Healed." He showed her his shoulder, the skin perfect and unmarked where the puncture had been. "Whatever that was, it worked."

Whatever that was, because neither of them knew what had just happened, what the warmth truly was or why it acted with such violent protection when he was threatened.

"You came for me," she said, the words soft against his collarbone. The truth of it, the impossibility of it, kept circling back.

"Yes."

"Why?" She pulled back enough to see his face, needing the answer.

His hand came up to cup her jaw, thumb tracing the bruises the collar had left on her throat. For a moment, she thought he might actually answer, might finally say the words that would explain the contradiction of casting her out then coming to save her.

Instead, he kissed her.

For one desperate moment, she let herself sink into it. His mouth moved against hers with an intensity that made her breath catch, and the warmth in her chest responded instantly, reaching for him with recognition that went bone-deep. Her fingers curled against his chest, feeling his heartbeat, and for that brief moment nothing else existed—not the hunt, not the betrayal, not the days of terror.

Then reality crept back in.

She pulled away, not violently but firmly, turning her head so his lips met her cheek instead of her mouth.

"I can't," she whispered.

His hand tightened on her waist, not releasing her. "Briar—"

"Please. Don't." She pressed against his chest, needing distance, and air, to think past the pull of the warmth that wanted to ignore everything else.

"I came for you." His voice was low.

"I know." She pushed harder, and this time he let her create space between them, though his hands remained on her. "I know you did, and I'm grateful, but—"

"But?" Something sharp entered his tone.

"But none of this would have happened if you hadn't cast me out like a spoiled child throwing a tantrum." The words burst out before she could stop them. "You sentenced me to death, Eliam. You're the reason Malachar had the opportunity to take me in the first place!"

His hands dropped from her waist. "I protected you. I sent Thaine—"

"You protected me?" She laughed, the sound bitter and raw. "You threw me to your court like meat to dogs and act like sending your huntsman to watch makes it better? That's not protection, that's—" She searched for the word. "That's you trying to have it both ways. Punish me but keep your conscience clean."

"You freed Malus." His voice had gone cold, that familiar mask sliding into place. "You went behind my back and released the one being who could destroy everything. Did you expect me to simply overlook that?"

"Yes! No. I—I expected you to listen!" Her voice rose. "I expected you to ask me what happened instead of immediately assuming the worst. I thought you—" She stopped, swallowing hard. "I thought I mattered enough for at least a conversation before you sentenced me to die."

"You betrayed me." The words were flat, final.

"I thought he was human!" She was shouting now, not caring if Thaine and Karse could hear. "I thought he was an innocent prisoner, someone like me who was trapped and suffering. When I learned the truth, I couldn't even tell you. I tried everything to break the compulsion. I—"

"You should have been more careful."

"And you should have been less cruel!" She shoved at his chest with both hands, and this time he didn't just let her. This time he grabbed her wrists. "I made a mistake. One mistake. And your reaction was to let your entire court hunt me for sport. How is that justice? How is that anything but you lashing out because your pride was wounded?"

"My pride?" His grip tightened on her wrists, his voice dropping to something dangerous. "You freed the one person capable of taking my throne, destroying my court, killing everyone under my protection. This wasn't about pride. This was about consequences."

"Consequences?" She wrenched one hand free. "The consequence for helping someone who used *me* should be death? That's not a consequence, Eliam. That's revenge."

"What would you have me do?" He released her other wrist, water sloshing as he gestured sharply. "Smile and pat your head? Tell you it was fine that you handed my worst enemy his freedom? There had to be punishment—"

"Yes, but not that!" Her voice cracked. "You could have imprisoned me. You could have turned me into a tree. You could have done a thousand things that weren't sending me out to be torn apart by your court."

Silence fell between them, both breathing hard.

"You're right." The words came out quiet, almost lost beneath the gentle lap of water. She blinked. "What?"

"You're right." He wouldn't look at her. "The punishment was... disproportionate. I was angry, and I reacted without—" He stopped, exhaling sharply through his nose. "I should have listened and given you a chance to explain before I passed judgement."

The admission was unexpected and Briar felt her anger waver, confusion rushing in to fill the space.

"Then why?" she asked, the fight draining from her voice. "Why did you do it?"

He was quiet for a long moment, his hands curling into fists beneath the water. When he finally spoke, the words came slowly, like each one had to be dragged from somewhere deep.

"Because you terrified me."

She stared at him. "I... what?"

"You." He finally met her eyes, and there was something raw in his expression. "What you make me feel. What you make me want. I've ruled for centuries, Briar. I've made alliances, waged wars, outlasted enemies who had centuries more experience than you have years of life. And none of them, not one, has ever made me as vulnerable as you do without even trying."

"I don't understand."

"I know." A bitter smile crossed his face. "Neither did I. But when Malus revealed what you'd done, when he exposed how you'd deceived me—even if you didn't mean to—all I could think was that I'd been weak. That caring about you had made me blind. That if I didn't cut you out completely, you would be the thing that destroyed me."

He turned away. "So I threw you to the hunt because having you gone felt safer than admitting that I—" He stopped. "That you had power over me I've never given anyone."

Briar felt her heart squeeze, the warmth pulsing with an emotion she couldn't name. The fight had gone out of her completely now, replaced by something far more complicated. He'd hurt her. Deeply. Possibly irreparably. But hearing him admit this—that he'd acted from fear rather than just cruelty—changed something.

It didn't fix it, but it changed it.

"I had decided to stay," she said quietly. "I went down one last time to tell Thomas that I would speak to you on his behalf, to get him released... but I wasn't going to leave. I was going to stay with you because I wanted to."

His head turned sharply toward her. "What?"

"I chose you." The words hurt to say. "And you never knew, because you threw me away before I could tell you."

The expression on his face was difficult to read—regret, certainly, but also something that looked almost like pain. "Briar." He moved toward her, then stopped himself. "If I could undo it—"

"But you can't." She wrapped her arms around herself. "You can't undo the hunt. You can't erase what I went through."

"No. I can't." He looked at her with an expression she'd never seen before—helplessness. "All I can do is tell you that I was wrong. That I let fear dictate my actions when I should have been stronger. That I failed you in every way that mattered."

The anger had faded to something duller now—an ache rather than a burn. She was exhausted, wrung out from healing him and fighting him and feeling too much all at once.

"We should get back," she said finally. "The others are waiting."

He nodded slowly, making no move to touch her again. "Can you walk?"

"I'll manage."

She waded toward the spring's edge and as she pulled herself onto the rocks, she noticed his cloak lying folded where he had left it before entering the spring. She moved past it, reaching for the hem of her shift instead, wringing out what water she could.

A moment later, warmth settled across her shoulders.

She stilled as the cloak's weight draped around her, Eliam's hands adjusting it briefly before falling away. He stepped back immediately, giving her space, saying nothing.

She pulled the fabric tighter around herself, not looking at him.

They emerged from the steam-shrouded grove to find Thaine and Karse in tense silence near the tree line. Karse sat propped against an oak, his scales still dulled but looking marginally better than in Malachar's dungeons. The huntsman himself stood apart, arms crossed, his expression unreadable in the moonlight.

Both men's gazes tracked to them immediately. Thaine's eyes lingered on Eliam's shoulder, where the puncture wound had been. He said nothing, but his expression shifted slightly—surprise, perhaps recognition of what the absence of injury meant.

Frederick chose that moment to flow toward his bowl, creating a small indignant splash as he settled in, as if scolding them all for the delay.

"Malus," Thaine said after a moment. "It won't be long before finds out his plan with Malachar failed. He'll come looking."

Eliam moved past them, already shifting into the cold efficiency she recognized from court. "Then we don't have much time to prepare. Drak, can you fight?"

Karse pushed himself more upright, trying for his usual casual arrogance. "It's Karse. I can burn things. Whether I'll survive it is another question."

"The cold damaged him more than he's admitting," Thaine said bluntly. "His core temperature is still too low. Dragon fire in his state might kill him."

"Might," Karse emphasized. "I've survived worse odds."

"No, it's not worth the risk," Briar said quietly, studying the gray tinge to his scales, the way he trembled despite trying to hide it. "The cold got too deep."

Surprise flickered across his face. "Your concern is touching, but unnecessary."

"My concern," she said, moving closer, "is practical. We need everyone capable if we're going to survive what's coming."

She knelt beside Karse, ignoring the way both him and Eliam went still. The warmth in her chest, still humming from the spring, pulsed with recognition of damage.

"What are you doing?" Karse's voice had lost its casual edge.

"Being practical." She placed her hand on his chest, feeling the scales beneath her palm. They were too cold, barely warmer than the surrounding air. "Stay still."

"Briar—" Eliam started.

"He fought for me," she said, not looking away from Karse's wary eyes. "Against the harpies, again in Malachar's cell, when he could barely stand. The least I can do is try."

The warmth responded to her call more gently this time, perhaps exhausted from healing Eliam, or perhaps simply recognizing that Karse was other in a way that required a different touch. It flowed out in careful tendrils, seeking the cold-damaged core of him.

Karse hissed through his teeth, his body arching slightly. "That's... uncomfortable."

"It's working," Thaine observed, and she could hear genuine surprise in his voice. "His color's improving."

She found Karse's inner fire, barely an ember now, drowning in residual mountain cold. The tendrils wrapped around that ember carefully, feeding it, coaxing it back to life. Not trying to replace it but simply removing what suppressed it, letting his natural heat regenerate.

The scales beneath her palm began to warm, their color shifting from gray back towards an iridescent black-green. Karse's breathing deepened and became less labored.

Briar felt a wave of dizziness wash over her.

"Enough," Eliam said and she felt his hand come to rest on her shoulder.

She pulled back, the warmth retreating readily this time. Karse sat breathing hard, but his eyes were brighter, more alert. When he lifted his hand, small flames danced between his fingers, weak still, but present.

"Well," he said after a moment, his usual drawl returning. "That was intimate."

"That was necessary." She stood, swaying slightly. The healing had taken more than she'd thought, adding to her exhaustion.

Eliam's hand steadied her elbow, but his attention was on Karse. "Can you travel?"

"I can do whatever needs doing." Karse pushed himself to his feet, only wobbling slightly. "Though I'd prefer if it involve burning things. I have some aggression to work out."

"You'll have your chance," Thaine said. "But we need to reach the castle before Malus. The Forest Court needs to be warned, defenses prepared—"

"The Forest Court is divided," Eliam cut him off. "Half think I've gone weak. They won't follow me against Malus without proof of strength."

The words settled over Briar like cold water. Divided. Because he'd left. Because he'd left his post to rescue her from Malachar.

"But that isn't fair, you weren't abandoning anyone," she protested. "You've barely been gone a day or two."

"And you think that matters to them?" He shook his head. "They saw me cast you out, then risk everything to retrieve you. To them, it only confirms my weakness."

Risk everything. The words echoed in her mind. She'd been so focused on her own hurt, her own anger at what he'd done, that she hadn't considered what coming for her had actually cost him.

"Then we make it not about you," Karse said, examining his claws. "Make it about territory. The Forest Court might be divided about you, but they'll unite against an outsider trying to claim what's theirs."

"He's no outsider, and when Malus offers them an alternative to my leadership? They'll turn." Eliam's voice had gone cold. "When he promises them strength without sentiment? I've given them weakness, in their eyes."

He turned from them, facing the dark forest. "The moment I showed care for a human, I lost their respect."

The words stung, but Briar couldn't argue with them.

Silence stretched between them, heavy with implications Briar was only beginning to understand. A fae lord didn't just leave his court undefended. A king didn't abandon his throne to rescue one human, no matter how he felt about her.

Finally, Eliam turned back, his expression set. "We return to the castle. Thaine, you'll coordinate defenses. Karse—"

"I'm not yours to command," the Drak interrupted, though without real heat. "But I have my own score to settle with Malus. He made deals with Malachar about me, about her. That makes this personal."

Eliam was quiet for a moment and then gave a curt nod. "We leave now. The forest paths will be faster than the main roads."

As they prepared to leave, Briar's mind kept circling back to what Thaine had said. The whole court saw him leave to find her. They'd seen their lord abandon everything for a human he'd cast out just days before.

And that abandonment had consequences. Real ones. The kind that could cost him everything.

Because of her.

No, not just her, both of them. She *had* freed Malus, however unwittingly, and even if Eliam had overreacted with the hunt she wasn't innocent of wrongdoing. It was layer upon layer of choices and consequences, tangled too tightly to separate into simple blame.

They moved into the forest, Frederick secure in his bowl in her arms. Eliam took the lead, with Thaine at the rear and Karse moving between.

The forest paths should have welcomed their lord home with eager obedience. Instead, they opened grudgingly, like doors with rusted hinges.

"Something's wrong," she said quietly.

"The forest is... confused," Eliam admitted, though saying it aloud seemed to pain him. His hand pressed against an ancient oak, and for a moment nothing happened. Then, slowly, the path revealed itself, but narrower than it should be.

Briar frowned. *This* was what his rescue had cost. Not just political capital or his court's respect, but his very connection to the forest itself. The land that should have recognized him as its lord was now questioning him.

Behind them, Karse snorted. "Your kingdom doesn't recognize you, Forest Lord?"

"Shut up," Thaine said curtly.

Eliam said nothing.

Instead they moved forward, and Briar watched Eliam struggle with every step. The paths forgot them the moment they passed. Twice, he had to force openings that should have appeared naturally, his jaw tight with frustration.

Each struggle felt like a knife in her chest.

She could stay angry at him. Part of her still was—the hunt had been real, the terror had been real, and his regret didn't erase what she'd endured. But watching him fight for control of his own domain, the anger felt... insufficient. Not wrong, just incomplete.

The path ahead grew more difficult, forcing them to slow. Briar's exhaustion dragged at her with each step, but she pushed forward. Behind her, she heard Karse's breathing grow labored—he was still weak despite the healing.

"We rest," Eliam said without warning. "Five minutes."

"My lord, we should—" Thaine started.

"Five minutes."

They'd reached a small clearing where fallen logs provided natural seating. Briar sank onto one gratefully, setting Frederick's bowl beside her. The sprite made a sleepy sound, clearly as exhausted as she felt.

Eliam moved to the clearing's edge, his back to them, keeping watch, but she saw the tension in his shoulders, the way his hand kept moving to his side where Malachar's wound had been and her magic had healed him.

"I'll scout ahead," Thaine said, disappearing into the shadows.

Karse stretched out on the ground with a groan. "Wake me when it's time to burn things."

Briar closed her eyes, just for a moment. The weight of everything pressed down on her—exhaustion, guilt, lingering hurt, and something else she couldn't quite name. When she opened them again, purple flowers surrounded her feet.

They hadn't been there before. Small clusters of delicate blooms, the exact shade of twilight, growing from bare earth that should have been too cold for anything to thrive.

She looked up.

Eliam still stood with his back to her, apparently watching the forest. But the line of his shoulders had changed—less rigid, as if waiting.

The forest barely obeyed him. The trees argued about whether to let him pass. His own kingdom was fracturing beneath his feet. But he could still make flowers grow for her.

And suddenly, watching him stand there pretending he hadn't just created something beautiful in the middle of their crisis, something clicked into place.

This wasn't about who was right or wrong. This wasn't about deserving forgiveness or earning redemption. This was about two people who'd both made terrible choices, who'd both hurt each other, who were both standing in the wreckage trying to figure out what came next.

She could hold onto her anger. Keep him at arm's length. Make him pay for the hunt, for the cruelty, for every moment of terror she'd endured because of his pride.

Or she could acknowledge that they were in this together. That his mistakes and her mistakes had tangled into something neither of them could have predicted. That moving forward meant accepting the complexity of it all—the hurt and the regret, the guilt and the sacrifice, the anger and the... whatever this was between them.

Briar stood, her legs unsteady. Karse lifted his head slightly, watching, but said nothing.

She crossed to where Eliam stood and took his hand.

He went still, looked down at their joined fingers.

"I freed Malus," she said. "You threw me to the hunt. We both—" She stopped, searching for the right words. "We both made choices that led here."

He shifted his eyes and sighed. "That doesn't make what I did—"

"No. It doesn't." She squeezed his hand. "It doesn't mean that I'm not still angry and hurt. But staying angry won't fix any of this."

He didn't respond, but his hand stayed in hers.

"The rest... well... we can figure it out after," she said. "When this is over."

His eyes lifted again and she could tell he was searching her face, looking for something—sincerity, maybe, or a lie he expected to find. Whatever he saw there made something in his expression crack.

He kissed her.

Not like before, not desperate or demanding. This was careful, almost hesitant, as if asking permission with every movement. His hand came up to cup her jaw, thumb brushing her cheek, and she felt him trembling slightly.

The warmth, for once, was still, as though it too was waiting to see what she would do next. She kissed him back, answering the question he hadn't asked aloud.

When they broke apart, his forehead rested against hers for just a moment. "I'm sorry."

Briar nodded, but before she could say more, Thaine's voice rose from the shadows. "Path ahead is clear. We should move."

Eliam stepped back, his hand sliding from her face. But his eyes held hers for a breath longer, and she saw something in his expression she'd never seen before—something vulnerable and raw.

When he turned, Briar followed, the purple flowers already beginning to fade behind them.

The urgency returned as they drew closer to the castle, but now it felt different—heavier, more ominous. The forest continued its reluctant obedience, paths opening just wide enough for them to pass before closing again like wounds trying to heal. Eliam didn't struggle quite as much now, or perhaps he was simply hiding it better, his expression locked into that cold mask she recognized from court.

They moved faster, harder, the night pressing in around them. No one spoke. The only sounds were their footsteps on packed earth and the whisper of wind through branches that watched them with what felt like suspicion.

The warmth in Briar's chest began to pull in two directions at once—toward Eliam as always, but also recoiling from something ahead. Something wrong. The sensation grew stronger with each step, an uncomfortable stretching that made her press her hand against her sternum.

"Do you feel that?" she asked quietly.

Eliam's jaw tightened. "Yes."

Karse moved closer, flames dancing between his fingers. "I don't like this."

"Neither do I," Thaine said from behind them, his hand on his blade.

When they reached the outer boundaries of the castle grounds, everything felt off. The guards at the gate stood at perfect attention, exactly where they should be, but their eyes slid past Eliam without proper acknowledgment. Not disrespect exactly—more like uncertainty, as if they weren't quite sure who he was anymore.

"Strange night, my lord," one offered, and there was something careful in his tone, something that made the hair on Briar's neck stand up.

The courtyard was eerily normal. Servants crossed with purpose, guards walked their routes, but everything felt rehearsed. Choreographed. Like players maintaining their roles while waiting for a cue that hadn't come yet.

"Something's very wrong," Karse muttered.

The warmth in Briar's chest grew more agitated, the pulling sensation becoming almost painful. She stumbled slightly, and Eliam's hand immediately steadied her elbow.

"What is it?" he asked, low enough that only she could hear.

"I don't know. The warmth—it's pulling toward you but also away from something. Something ahead." She looked toward the castle's main entrance. "Something in there."

"Perhaps we should—" Karse started, but stopped when they heard it.

Laughter from the great hall. Casual conversation. The clink of glasses. The sounds of court as if nothing had happened, as if their lord hadn't been gone for days rescuing a human from the Mountain Court, as if everything was perfectly, horrifyingly normal.

Eliam's expression had gone completely still and Briar's heart began to pound. This was a trap. She could feel it closing around them with every step toward those doors.

"Thaine, take Karse and Briar to the—"

"With respect, my lord," Thaine interrupted, "we should stay together."

Eliam looked like he wanted to argue, but another burst of laughter from the hall made his decision for him. Briar felt his hand curl around hers.

"Stay close to me," he said. "All of you."

They approached the great hall as a group, footsteps echoing in the empty corridor. The warmth in Briar's chest twisted painfully, and she had to force herself to keep walking toward whatever was making it recoil so violently.

The doors stood open, spilling golden light and the sounds of revelry into the hallway.

The hall fell silent the moment they entered. Not suddenly—more like a wave, conversation dying as heads turned one by one to look at them. Dozens of fae lords and ladies, all watching with expressions of polite interest rather than surprise.

As if they'd been expected and this whole thing had been arranged.

There, sitting on the Forest Throne with the casual ease of someone who belonged there, was Malus.

Chapter Fourteen

Malus didn't rise, he didn't need to.

"Brother." Malus barely looked up, his tone casual and disinterested. "And what a menagerie you've brought me."

"Though I suppose I should thank you," Malus continued, his gaze finding Briar with those green eyes that were almost Eliam's but wrong, too bright, too amused by cruelty. "Malachar's halls are miserably cold this time of year. All that ice and grievance. You've saved me from such a tedious journey."

The throne beneath him, ancient wood carved before the forest above existed, dark with age and power, the same throne that had accepted Eliam, that had recognized his claim when he'd taken it, Malus wore it like a second skin, every line of his body relaxed into its embrace as if he'd never left.

Where Eliam had commanded it, Malus simply... inhabited it, with the casual ownership of someone returning to their own bed after a long journey.

"Just what is it you think you're doing, Malus?" Eliam asked, stepping forward to place himself between Briar and the throne.

"The forest recognizes its first king," Malus replied, addressing the assembled court. "As you all do. Don't you?"

The murmur of agreement was soft but undeniable. More than half. Enough to tip the balance through ancient law.

And then Briar felt it—a shifting at her throat, like something alive reshaping itself. The thorned vines of Eliam's mark began to move, writhing against her skin. The white buds that had bloomed along them withered and fell away like ash, and in their place, new growth emerged. Autumn leaves, copper and gold, unfurling along vines that darkened from green to deep bronze. The thorns remained but changed. They grew longer, crueler, turned outward as if to catch rather than protect.

"No." Eliam's voice was barely controlled fury.

"Oh yes," Malus said, watching the transformation with satisfaction. "The bargain recognizes the rightful Forest King. Look how much prettier it is now. Autumn suits her better than your eternal shadow, don't you think?"

The warmth in Briar's chest contracted violently, recoiling from the change, pulling toward Eliam with such desperate force she gasped from it.

"Come here."

Two words. Soft. Casual.

"Eliam," she gasped as her legs carried her forward without permission. She tried to stop, to dig her heels in, but the compulsion forced her closer. Each step was a war inside her body, the warmth raging against the draw, pulling back toward Eliam while her muscles obeyed their new master.

"Don't." Eliam stepped forward, but guards moved to block him, not aggressively, just present, making the situation clear.

"Don't?" Malus echoed with amusement. "She's fulfilling her bargain, brother. The one you made with her. Would you have her break fae law?"

When she reached the throne, he patted his thigh with casual expectation. "You look tired. Sit."

"No." The word escaped before the bargain could strangle it.

His eyebrows rose with genuine delight. "No? How wonderful. Say it again."

"I won't—"

But her body was already moving, the bargain overriding her will with brutal efficiency. She found herself pulled onto his lap, positioned like a trophy, her back against his chest and facing the court. The humiliation burned worse than any physical pain—displayed, claimed, owned in front of everyone who had once seen her as their future queen. Malus's arm settled around her waist, holding her in place with a possessiveness that was entirely for show.

"There we are," Malus said against her ear, loud enough for others to hear. "Much better perspective from here, don't you think?"

The warmth in her chest was going wild, pushing against her skin from the inside. Golden light flickered beneath the surface, creating patterns like veins of sunlight.

Where it touched, Malus's hand on her waist actually pulled back slightly, not burned but... curious.

"Your magic wants him," Malus observed, settling his hands more carefully, avoiding the spots where golden light gathered. "How romantic. And how very unfortunate for you both."

"Let her go." Eliam's voice had dropped to something dangerous. "Your quarrel is with me."

"My quarrel was with you. Past tense. I've won." Malus's fingers found Briar's chin, turning her face toward him while keeping her displayed for Eliam to see. "Now I'm simply enjoying the spoils. You understand spoils, don't you, brother? You enjoyed mine for quite some time."

"If you hurt her—"

"Hurt her? Why would I damage something so intriguing?" His fingers traced the bargain marks at her throat. "Though I suppose you've already done that, haven't you? These marks, this binding—all your handiwork."

Eliam took another step forward, and this time Thaine caught his arm, recognizing the trap being laid.

Golden flowers began blooming along the base of the throne—small, desperate things that withered almost immediately in the autumn-touched air. But where they touched the ancient wood, they left tiny scorch marks, as if their brief existence burned too bright for this new order.

"Oh, now that's interesting," Malus murmured, shifting her on his lap to see better. "They're fighting my influence. Dying, but fighting. What are you, little human?"

"Let them go," Briar managed, though speaking felt like pushing words through broken glass. "You have what you wanted. The throne. The court. Me."

"I have the throne," Malus agreed. "The court is mine by right. But you?" He looked over her head at Eliam, and his smile sharpened. "You're more puzzle than prize at the moment. Though we'll solve that together."

He addressed the guards without looking away from his brother. "Escort the former lord to his chambers. The ones I so recently vacated. They should be... familiar."

The dungeon. Where Eliam had kept him for over a century.

"As for his companions," Malus continued, "the Drak is a guest. Find him quarters. Unpleasant ones—I don't want him getting comfortable. The huntsman can choose his own fate. Serve me or share his master's accommodations."

"I'll take the cell," Thaine said flatly.

"Loyalty. How tedious." Malus waved dismissively. "Take them both then."

As the guards moved toward them, thorns erupted from the floor with all the violence of someone who knew this might be his last chance. Thick vines burst through cracks in the stone, wrapping around guards' ankles, yanking them down. One screamed as a large thorn pierced through his boot and into his calf.

"Oh good," Malus said to Briar, his tone conversational as if they were watching a performance. "He's going to fight. I was worried he'd gone soft."

Eliam moved through the guards, thorns growing from his palms like claws. He caught one guard across the chest, leaving deep gouges. Another found himself wrapped in vines that constricted until his sword arm snapped. Thaine moved with him, their coordination speaking of years fighting together.

"See how the vines are already browning at the edges?" Malus observed, his hand casual on Briar's waist. "The forest doesn't recognize him anymore, so he's forcing growth through will alone. Exhausting."

Three guards converged on Eliam at once. He spun, a wall of thorns erupting between them, but the effort cost him—she could see it in the way he staggered slightly, sweat already beading on his forehead.

"At this rate, maybe five more minutes before he collapses?" Malus continued his commentary. "Forest magic without the forest's cooperation is like trying to grow roses in salted earth."

More guards poured in. Eliam caught one with thorns that erupted from his palm, but another's blade found his thigh. Blood immediately soaked through his trousers.

"First blood to my guards," Malus noted. "Though your lover is doing better than expected."

The vines Eliam summoned were thinner now, the thorns smaller. A guard with a mace caught him across the ribs. She heard something crack. He went down to one knee, hand pressed to the floor, trying to call more growth from stone that wouldn't answer.

"Oh, broken ribs. Those are miserable." Malus sounded delighted. "Makes every breath agony."

Eliam forced himself up, thorns sprouting weakly from his knuckles like a wounded animal's last defense. He dropped another guard, but two more took his place. Thaine was pressed against a pillar, bleeding from multiple cuts, barely keeping three guards at bay.

"Your huntsman won't last much longer either," Malus observed. "Look, he's already favoring that leg. Hamstring, perhaps?"

A blade caught Eliam's shoulder—the same one Malachar had injured. He couldn't suppress the sound of pain, and his left arm dropped, useless. The thorns on that hand withered instantly, falling like dead leaves.

"Stop," Briar whispered.

"What was that?" Malus asked, though she knew he'd heard.

Another guard struck Eliam across the face with a pommel. Blood poured from his nose, and he stumbled. He pressed his palm to the floor, trying to summon vines, but only managed a few weak shoots that a guard crushed underfoot.

"The Drak has the right idea," Malus noted, and Briar saw Karse standing apart, watching but not intervening. "No point fighting a lost battle."

Eliam tried to grow thorns and managed only regular vines, thin as grass. Tried to stand straight and swayed. A guard's boot caught him in the stomach, and he doubled over, coughing blood.

"Please," Briar said louder.

"Please what?" Malus asked mildly.

Thaine went down, a guard's blade at his throat. Eliam saw it, tried to help, and took a mace to the back. He hit the floor hard, his magic failing entirely—no thorns, no vines, just blood on stone.

"Please stop!" The words tore from her throat.

"Why should I?" Malus asked as a guard raised his sword over Eliam's exposed neck. "He attacked my guards. The punishment for that is death."

"Please!" She turned in his lap, grabbing his shirt. "Please, I'll—"

"You'll what?" His attention shifted to her fully, one hand staying her desperation while guards held Eliam down, blood pooling beneath him.

"Anything. I'll do anything, just don't kill him."

The sword stayed poised above Eliam's neck. He was trying to rise, but three guards kept him pinned. His eyes found hers—furious, desperate, already knowing what she was about to sacrifice.

"Anything." Malus tested the word. "Such a foolish answer. You should never offer anything to the fae. We tend to take it literally."

He caught her chin, forcing her to meet his eyes. "Kiss me."

"What?"

"Kiss me. Here, now, in front of him. In front of everyone." His thumb traced her lower lip. "And mean it. Make me believe you want it, and I'll let him live. Fail, and I'll tear his heart out while you watch."

The throne room had gone silent except for Eliam's labored breathing. Everyone watched—the court, the guards, Thaine frozen mid-fight.

"That's sick," Karse said from somewhere to the left.

"That's power," Malus corrected, still watching Briar's face. "Choose quickly. My patience is not infinite."

Briar looked at Eliam, on his knees, blood running from too many wounds, shadows still trying weakly to reach for her. The warmth in her chest was screaming, pulling toward him with desperate intensity. But the bargain, the autumn-touched marks at her throat, they recognized Malus's authority.

She turned back to Malus, and before she could think too much about it, pressed her mouth to his.

He tasted of autumn, of dying leaves and overripe fruit, sweet things beginning to rot. His mouth was colder than Eliam's, crueler in its demands. She tried to make herself respond, to save Eliam's life, but her body recoiled from the wrongness of it.

"You're not trying," Malus murmured against her lips. "I said *mean it.*"

She could feel Eliam watching, feel the rage and anguish radiating from him. The warmth in her chest was thrashing, trying to escape through her skin. But she forced herself to lean into Malus, to part her lips, to kiss him like she wanted it.

He took his time, making sure everyone saw, making sure Eliam saw. His hand tangled in her hair, holding her in place while he claimed her mouth with deliberate thoroughness. She let him, participated even, while tears ran down her cheeks.

When he finally pulled back, he studied her face with satisfaction. "Adequate, if not inspiring. But I suppose you've earned his life."

He waved his hand and the guard withdrew his blade.

"Take him to his new chambers," Malus commanded. "Gently. We wouldn't want him dying after she worked so hard to save him."

As the guards hauled Eliam to his feet, his eyes found hers. The betrayal there, not anger at her choice, but agony at what she'd been forced to do, made the warmth in her chest dim to almost nothing.

"I'll kill you for this," Eliam said to Malus, blood running from his mouth.

"No," Malus said softly, his arm possessive around Briar's waist. "You'll sit in the cell where I sat for centuries, and you'll think about her up here with me. You'll imagine what I'm doing, what she's doing to keep you alive. Because that's so much worse than death, isn't it?"

Eliam's eyes met hers one final time as the guards dragged him and Thaine away. *I'll come for you.*

"He's planning already," Malus said against her ear, amused. "I do hope he tries something dramatic. Don't you?"

The throne room doors closed with finality, and Malus addressed the remaining court while keeping Briar displayed on his lap.

"Tomorrow night, we feast. The return of proper order deserves celebration." His fingers traced her throat, feeling her pulse race. "Wine that tastes of summer's end. Meat so rare it still remembers being alive. And perhaps some entertainment. It's been so long since we've had proper entertainment at court."

The assembled lords murmured agreement, some enthusiastic, others careful. The atmosphere was shifting—becoming older, hungrier, tasting the edges of what had been long forbidden.

The throne room emptied except for them. Malus kept her on his lap for another moment, his fingers tracing the autumn leaves at her throat with possessive satisfaction.

"Come," he said finally, lifting her to her feet but keeping his hand on her lower back. "Let me show you your new accommodations."

The corridors felt different as they walked—the shadows less deep, the air carrying a hint of autumn decay that hadn't been there before. Servants bowed as they passed but wouldn't meet her eyes. The warmth in her chest pulled steadily southward, toward the dungeons, but her body obeyed Malus's guiding touch.

"You're very quiet," he observed as they climbed a spiral staircase she recognized—it led to the tower rooms, the highest quarters in the castle. Where Eliam's chambers were. Had been.

"What would you like me to say?"

"Whatever you're thinking would be a start." His hand shifted to her elbow as they reached a landing. "Though I suspect it's nothing flattering."

He opened a door she'd never seen unlocked before, another room connected to Eliam's chambers through an internal passage. A queen's suite, she realized with a sick feeling. Prepared long ago for a Forest Queen who had never materialized.

The room was beautiful in an ancient way. A massive bed dominated one wall, carved with forest scenes that seemed to move in the firelight—deer fleeing, wolves hunting, seasons cycling in endless wooden loops. Windows overlooked the forest canopy, and she could see storm clouds gathering in the distance. Everything was deep green and gold, but as they entered, she watched those colors shifting subtly—the green fading to brown, the gold brightening to copper.

"The castle responds to its king," Malus said, noticing her attention. "It's already beginning to remember how things were. How they should be."

He guided her to a chair by the fire—no, guided was wrong. The bargain compelled her to sit when he pressed lightly on her shoulder. She sat rigidly while he poured wine from a decanter.

"You said anything," he reminded her, handing her a glass. "Drink."

The wine tasted of autumn fruits, too sweet with an edge of fermentation. She drank because the bargain demanded it, feeling it warm her throat.

"Now," he settled in the chair across from her, completely at ease, "let's discuss your magic."

"I don't understand it myself."

"No, but you can feel it." He leaned forward slightly. "That warmth in your chest—yes, I notice how you keep touching that spot. It pulls toward him, doesn't it? Even now."

There was no point denying what he'd already observed. "Yes."

"But it's not part of the bargain. The bargain binds you to me, yet this magic reaches for him." His eyes sharpened with interest. "Two different magics in one human body. How did he manage it?"

"I don't know."

"Perhaps." But he sounded amused rather than angry. "I believe you know more than you're saying. But we have time. All the time in the world to unravel this puzzle."

He stood, moving to stand behind her chair. His hands settled on her shoulders, and she fought not to flinch.

"The feast tomorrow will be illuminating," he said, his thumbs pressing into the tense muscles of her neck. "The court needs to see that the new order has truly begun. That humans can serve... different purposes than mere entertainment."

"What purposes?" Her voice came out steady despite the revulsion of his touch.

"You'll feed me." His hands stilled. "It's time for the court to remember the old ways, the true ways, when humans were sustenance as well as playthings."

The warmth recoiled so violently she gasped. For a moment, golden light flared beneath her skin, bright enough to cast shadows.

"There it is," Malus breathed, genuinely delighted. "It protects you. How wonderful." His hands moved to her throat, fingers spreading over the autumn marks. "I wonder what would happen if I truly threatened you? Not these small gestures, but real danger?"

"Please don't—"

"Oh, not tonight." He stepped back, moving toward the door. "You've had enough excitement for one evening. But tomorrow, after the feast, we'll explore what triggers this defense. What makes it manifest."

He paused at the door, looking back at her. "Your anything has limits, of course. I won't permanently damage you, you're too valuable. I won't kill your former lover, as promised. But everything else?" He smiled. "Everything else is mine to command."

"What about the others? Thaine? Karse?"

"The huntsman is Eliam's concern. The Drak..." he considered. "The Drak interests me. Fire magic that intense, trapped in such an unstable form. He might be useful. Or dangerous. I haven't decided yet."

He opened the door, then paused again. "The connecting door to my chambers won't lock from your side. Don't bother trying. Sleep well, Lady Briar. Tomorrow will be... educational."

The door closed, leaving her alone in a room that was already forgetting Eliam had ever existed, while the warmth in her chest pulled uselessly toward dungeons she could no longer reach.

She stood on shaking legs and moved to the window, pressing her palm against the cold glass. Somewhere below, Eliam was locked in the cell where he'd once kept his brother. The reversal was so complete it felt scripted, theatrical. But then, fae had always loved their dramatic ironies.

Thunder rumbled in the distance, and she wondered if the approaching storm was natural or if it was the forest itself responding to the change in power. The warmth in her chest pulsed with each thunderclap, as if answering something in the storm.

Rain began to fall, soft at first, then harder, obscuring the forest beyond. She watched it streak the glass, her reflection fragmenting in the water trails. The autumn marks at her throat caught the firelight, looking like real leaves for a moment, ready to crumble at a touch.

The connecting door Malus had mentioned drew her attention. Just a simple wooden door, unremarkable except for the knowledge that it led to his chambers. That it wouldn't lock from her side and he could enter whenever he pleased.

She turned away from it, exhaustion finally winning over fear. The bed was too large, too fine, but her body didn't care. She collapsed onto it fully clothed, curling into herself as the warmth in her chest maintained its steady pull southward.

The rain intensified, drumming against the windows with increasing violence. She closed her eyes and tried not to think about forgotten old ways, about experiments, about the way the court had looked at her like she was something between a curiosity and a meal.

Sleep, when it finally came, brought no peace.

Chapter Fifteen

T he knock came too early, while morning light still struggled through the windows. Briar had barely slept, the warmth in her chest pulling southward all night, making rest impossible.

"Come in," she called, expecting servants.

Instead, Arachne glided in, her spider-silk gown catching the weak sunlight. Behind her came Síocháin, those impossible fingers carrying a basket of silver combs and pins that chimed softly with each step.

"Lady Briar." Arachne's solid black eyes regarded her sympathetically, or perhaps it was merely pity. With the fae, it was almost impossible to tell. "His lordship has chosen your attire for tonight."

Síocháin moved to the bed, laying out the dress with ritualistic care. The autumn colored silk spread across the covers like a sunset bleeding into dusk—brilliant orange at the bodice deepening through burnt orange to burgundy at the hem.

"It's beautiful," Briar said, because what else could she say?

"It's a statement," Arachne corrected, those many fingers already assessing Briar's tangled hair. "The Forest Court's colors remade in autumn's palette. Everyone will understand the message."

"Which is?"

"That summer has ended." Síocháin's voice was still like water over stones, unchanged from when she'd dressed Briar for Eliam. "That harvest time has come."

The two fae exchanged glances, something unspoken passing between them.

"We served the former lord well," Arachne said carefully as she began pulling pins from her basket. "You wore our creations with... dignity."

"Things change," Síochàin added, those pearl-like nails beginning to section Briar's hair. "Courts rise and fall. We adapt. We survive."

"As must you," Arachne said, and there was definitely something meaningful in her tone now. "The old ways Lord Malus speaks of returning to... they were not kind to humans."

"When were the fae ever kind to humans?" Briar asked bitterly.

"There are degrees of cruelty," Síochàin said, her fingers working with mechanical precision. "Lord Eliam's games were possessive but... limited. Lord Malus remembers when humans were currency. Entertainment that could be fully consumed."

"We cannot speak against our king," Arachne added quickly, producing the bodice of the dress. "But perhaps we can speak of... practical matters. This neckline, for instance. It will display your marks prominently."

"The autumn leaves," Briar touched her throat where the transformed bargain marks rustled against her skin.

"Yes. But also..." Síochàin paused in her braiding. "If one were to apply certain oils, certain barriers, the skin becomes less... permeable. Less able to be affected by outside influences."

She produced a small vial from her basket, setting it on the vanity without comment.

"And this particular style of hair," Arachne said as they worked in tandem, "while elaborate, has some practical benefits. These pins, for instance. Very sharp. One might scratch oneself if not careful."

She slipped several into the evolving hairstyle—decorative to look at, but Briar could feel their points, could tell they were meant for more than holding hair.

"You understand," Síochàin said quietly, "we serve whoever rules. We cannot take sides. Cannot offer aid."

"But we remember," Arachne added, cinching the bodice with practiced efficiency. "We remember every human who has worn our creations. Some with more fondness than others."

They worked in loaded silence after that, transforming her into exactly what Malus wanted—an autumn queen, a harvest trophy. The dress fit perfectly, the gradient silk catching light like dying fire. Her hair rose in elaborate coils that left her throat bare, displaying the transformed bargain marks for all to see.

"One more thing," Síochán said, producing something else from her basket. A necklace of delicate copper leaves, each one perfect and sharp-edged. "His lordship's addition."

She fastened it around Briar's throat, the metal cold against her skin. The leaves hung just below the bargain marks, chiming softly when she moved.

"You look beautiful," Arachne said, stepping back. "Like autumn incarnate."

"Like something about to be devoured," Briar corrected.

Neither fae disagreed.

"The feast begins at sunset," Síochán said, gathering their supplies. "We're to escort you when the time comes."

"Until then," Arachne added meaningfully, "perhaps rest. Save your strength. Tonight will be... long."

They left her alone with their warnings, their careful non-help, their sharp pins and protective oils. Briar studied her reflection—the autumn dress, the elaborate hair, the marks at her throat that no longer belonged to the right king.

She looked like exactly what she was: a prize dressed for display, a human prepared for consumption.

The vial Síochán had left sat on the vanity, innocuous and small. Briar uncorked it, sniffing carefully. It smelled of mint and something sharper, something that made the warmth in her chest pulse with recognition. She dabbed it on her wrists, her throat, anywhere skin might be touched. It tingled briefly, then seemed to sink in, leaving nothing visible behind.

Whatever small protection they could offer, she'd take it. Tonight she would need every advantage, no matter how slight.

The copper leaves at her throat chimed with each movement, counting down the hours until sunset.

The great hall blazed with autumn fire. Hundreds of candles floated overhead, their light catching on copper and gold decorations that hadn't existed yesterday. Real leaves drifted from the vaulted ceiling, never quite reaching the floor before dissolving into sparks of amber light.

Briar entered flanked by Síochán and Arachne. The copper leaves at her throat chimed with each step, the sound too bright for how she felt. Her stomach had been in knots since they'd come for her, and the oil on her skin tingled faintly—a constant reminder of the small rebellion she carried.

Conversations quieted as she passed. She kept her eyes forward, not wanting to see who had chosen Malus, who had traded Eliam's steady rule for whatever this would become. The warmth in her chest pulled southward, always southward, toward stone and iron and silence.

Malus sat as if he'd been carved from the wood itself, dressed in burgundy so deep it looked black until the light caught it. His smile when he saw her was pleased, proprietary.

Beside the throne stood something new—a pedestal covered in midnight blue cloth, concealing an object about the length of her forearm. She noticed others glancing at it, curious, but no one asked.

"Exquisite," Malus said when she reached him. "Turn."

Her body obeyed, the gradient silk shifting from flame to wine with the movement. She hated how exposed the plunging neckline made her feel, how the autumn marks at her throat seemed to pulse with foreign life.

"Come." He guided her to the smaller throne beside his, a queen's chair that had gathered dust for generations. The wood felt wrong beneath her hands, too smooth, too eager to accept her. She sat rigid, trying not to think about what the placement meant.

"Are you comfortable?" he asked, loud enough for nearby lords to hear. His hand settled on her wrist, thumb finding her pulse.

"Yes." The word came out because the bargain demanded it, though comfort was the last thing she felt.

The feast began with wine that tasted of overripe fruit. Lord Pendron made the first toast, and she recognized him as one of the oldest at court, his bark-like skin speaking of centuries.

"To the return of proper order," he said, his ancient eyes gleaming. "To the restoration of what was always meant to be."

Others followed. Some toasts were careful, hedging bets. Others, from the older fae, carried an anticipation that made her skin crawl. They spoke in code about traditions and proper ways, but underneath she heard hunger.

"You're trembling," Malus observed, his fingers still on her wrist. "Are you cold?"

"No." This truth the bargain allowed.

"Nervous then?" He leaned closer, his breath autumn-cool against her ear. "You should eat something. Keep your strength up."

He selected food for her—meat so rare it bled onto the plate, fruits that looked beautiful but tasted of fermentation. She ate because he commanded it, each bite sitting heavy in her stomach. The warmth in her chest recoiled from the food, recognizing something wrong in it.

Between courses, lords approached to pay their respects. Some she knew, their faces familiar but their allegiances shifted. Others were strangers, older fae with eyes that held too much history.

"Dance," Malus commanded when the music began. "Lord Tamlin first, I think."

Lord Tamlin's hand was dry as parchment when he led her onto the floor. She remembered him from Eliam's court, always watching from the edges, never quite participating.

"You look lovely," he said as they moved through the steps. "The autumn colors suit you."

She said nothing, concentrating on not stumbling. The music was different than she remembered—slower, with undertones that made her feel off-balance.

"I remember when humans danced differently," Tamlin continued, his grip tightening slightly on her waist. "When they understood their place in the dance. Perhaps we'll see those days again."

The threat was subtle but clear. When the dance ended, another lord claimed her immediately. Then another. Each partner held her a little too close, whispered things that skirted the edge of propriety. One traced the autumn marks at her throat while they turned, murmuring about how much prettier they were than thorns.

She caught glimpses between partners, the fae lord she'd impaled on thorns, watching from the shadows with hatred in his eyes, Lady Corvaine speaking intently with other older fae. Along the edges of the room the Withered stood so still they looked like strange sculptures until their antlered heads turned to track movement.

When she finally returned to her seat, her feet ached and her skin felt crawled over. Malus watched her resettle herself, something pleased in his expression.

"You're quite popular," he said. "Though you're sweating, perspiration doesn't become you."

He traced a finger along her throat, and she saw the moment he noticed it—the faint residue of oil. His expression didn't change, but the temperature around them dropped.

"I—" she started.

"Quiet." The command was soft but absolute. He stood, drawing her up with him. "It's time."

He moved to the pedestal, one hand keeping her close. The hall's attention focused on them, conversations dying. With theatrical deliberation, he pulled away the cloth.

The box beneath was carved from bone, symbols etched into its surface that seemed to hum with a magic that made Briar take half a step back. He opened it, revealing a knife, its blade seeming to shift between silver and something darker.

"Some of you," Malus said, addressing the court, "remember the old ways. When this blade had purpose beyond ceremony."

She felt the shift in the room, anticipation from some, confusion from others. Lord Pendron actually smiled.

"Long ago," Malus continued, lifting the knife and brandishing it for all to see, "before we forgot ourselves, before we pretended to be civilized, we understood what humans were for. Warmth. Fear." He paused, the blade catching candlelight. "Blood."

Murmurs rippled through the crowd. She saw Lord Tamlin take a step back.

"My lord," Tamlin said carefully, "surely you don't mean—"

"I mean exactly what our ancestors meant." Malus turned the blade, admiring it. "The sharing of human essence. The old feast. The true communion. The real reason behind your Wild Hunt."

"This is barbarism," Lord Garrett said from the back, his voice carrying shocked disapproval.

"This is tradition," Lord Pendron corrected, his ancient voice cutting through the murmurs. "This is what we were before we grew soft."

Lord Garrett stepped forward, his young face set with determination. "I didn't support your claim to the throne for this. This isn't restoring proper rule, it's—"

"It's what?" Malus asked softly, still holding the knife. "Do finish your thought."

"It's an abomination." Garrett moved closer, several other younger fae shifting behind him as if building courage. "We're not monsters who feed on humans. That's not what the Forest Court—"

"The Forest Court," Malus interrupted, "existed long before your birth, young lord. Before we pretended to be civilized and forgot our true nature." He set down the knife with deliberate care. "But perhaps you need a reminder of what we truly are. Of what defiance will afford you."

He made a small gesture, barely visible. The Withered moved.

One moment Lord Garrett stood defiant in his court finery. The next, a Withered had stepped from the shadows behind him, one decayed hand settling on his shoulder.

Garrett's scream cut off almost immediately. Where the Withered touched, his shoulder began to age—the fabric of his coat crumbling, then the flesh beneath going gray, then black, spreading like rot. His skin wrinkled, hair whitening and falling out in clumps.

"No," someone whispered. "No, stop—"

But it was too late. The decay spread down Garrett's arm, up his neck. Briar wanted to look away, to close her eyes, but Malus wouldn't allow it.

"Watch," he said, and so she did.

The fae lord aged decades in seconds, centuries in a moment. His eyes clouded, skin pulling tight over bones that brittled and cracked. He tried to pull away but his body was failing too quickly, muscles withering, tendons snapping like old rope.

When he fell, he was already crumbling. Not dead, something worse. He was still aware as his body became dust and memory, consciousness trapped in failing flesh until the last possible second.

The Withered stepped back, returning to stillness. Where Lord Garrett had stood, only the tattered remnants of clothes remained around a pile of gray ash and bone fragments.

The hall was silent.

"Anyone else," Malus asked pleasantly, "have objections to tradition?"

No one spoke. Even Lord Pendron looked unsettled, though whether by the method or the waste of fae blood, Briar couldn't know for sure.

Malus raised the knife to her throat. "Now, where were we?"

The attention in the hall shifted back to Malus, to her. Briar closed her eyes and held her breath, bracing herself for the sting of the cut. The blade touched her skin just below the copper leaves, and slid off.

He tried again, pressing harder this time. The knife skittered across her skin like it was polished glass, leaving nothing behind, not even a scratch.

Briar opened her eyes.

The silence grew heavy. Malus tried once more, this time with enough pressure that even a dull blade should have drawn blood. Nothing.

"My lord?" Lord Pendron's confusion was evident.

Briar saw the moment Malus's control cracked. His jaw tightened, his eyes went flat, and for an instant, rage flickered across his features before he smoothed them.

He set the knife down carefully and turned to her with a smile that didn't reach his eyes. Then he grabbed her throat and slammed her back against the throne.

The violence of it shocked the court. Several fae stepped forward instinctively, but more Withered moved from the shadows, their presence both a threat and a promise to anyone who thought to intervene.

"Someone," Malus said, his voice still casual despite his hand crushing her windpipe, "has been getting creative."

He yanked her forward, then drove her back again. Her head snapped back against the wood leaving her dazed.

Malus leaned in. "Did you think," he said against her ear, fingers tangling in her hair at the nape of her neck, "that parlor tricks would stop me?"

"Don't—!"

He sank his teeth into her throat, tearing through whatever protection the oil provided through sheer savagery. She screamed and her hands came up, striking at his face, his shoulders, anywhere she could reach.

He caught one wrist, pinning it against the throne while using his body weight to trap her. Her free hand clawed at him, drawing blood from his cheek before he grabbed that wrist too, holding both now as he fed.

The warmth in her chest raged, pushing against her skin, trying to manifest. She could feel it building into something violent, something that wanted to shove him away from her, but the oil created a barrier it couldn't breach.

Malus drank deeply, and she felt her strength ebbing. The futility of it, the pain, the violation of being fed upon in front of the entire court. When he finally pulled back with a gasp, she was shaking. Blood ran down her throat, staining the autumn silk.

"What—" He released her wrists to touch his mouth, staring at the blood on his fingers. Then at her. His pupils had dilated strangely. "You taste of forests. Deep forests. Old growth and shadow and—"

His expression shifted from confusion to rage.

"You taste of *him*."

The court erupted in whispers. Malus grabbed her jaw, forcing her to meet his eyes.

"How?" His fingers dug into her skin. "The bargain is mine. The marks are mine. But your blood carries his forest." He inhaled sharply against her hair, her skin. "What did my brother do to you?"

She couldn't answer with his hand crushing her jaw. The warmth in her chest pulsed with something like satisfaction. Even claimed by another, her blood knew its true master.

"My lord," Lord Pendron said carefully, "what does this mean?"

Malus released her face to grab her by the throat again, displaying the savage bite to the court. "It means," he said, "that my brother left more than marks. Her blood carries forest magic. Old magic."

"That's impossible," someone said. "She's human."

"She was human." Malus's grip tightened, and she could feel her pulse pounding against his palm. "Now she's becoming something else. Something that belongs to the forest itself, despite my claim."

He released her suddenly and she collapsed against the throne, gasping, blood still running from the wound. The copper leaves at her throat were splattered with red.

"Clear the hall," he commanded. "Everyone out."

"But my lord—" Lord Pendron began.

"Out!" The word cracked like thunder. Autumn leaves throughout the hall burst into flame, then crumbled to nothing.

The fae fled. Even the ancient ones who'd been eager for blood seemed startled by his fury. Within moments, only the Withered remained, still as death in the shadows.

Malus turned on her, and she saw murder in his eyes.

"You knew," he said. "You knew what you carried."

"I didn't—"

The blow came unexpectedly, the back of his hand connecting with her cheek with such force that it sent her sprawling from the throne. Before she could recover, he grabbed her hair and dragged her to her feet.

"Don't lie to me." He shook her hard enough to make her vision blur. "The oil was one thing. A servant's trick. But this? Blood that rejects me? That sings of another king?" Another violent shake. "What are you?"

"I don't know!" The words came out desperate, but true.

He studied her face, then smiled. It was worse than his rage.

"Then we'll find out together." He started dragging her toward the doors, her feet scrambling to keep up. "In private. Where I can be *thorough*."

The Withered parted as they passed, their antlered heads turning to watch. She caught a glimpse of the great hall, the abandoned feast, overturned chairs, blood on the throne.

Then Malus hauled her into the corridor, toward his chambers, his grip in her hair never loosening.

"You're going to tell me everything," he said as they climbed the stairs, Briar tripping and stumbling in an effort to maintain her footing. "About the warmth in your chest. About when it started, every moment you've felt it react." His fingers tightened. "And if you lie or if you resist, then my brother loses a finger. Then a hand. Then more. Do you understand?"

"Yes."

"Good." He kicked open his chamber door. "Now we begin your lessons in what happens when you try to deceive the Forest King."

Chapter Sixteen

The door slammed behind them with enough force it made the panes of glass in the window rattle. Malus released her hair, shoving her toward the center of the room. She stumbled, catching herself against a chair, her scalp burning where he'd dragged her.

"Sit."

The command hit like a physical force. Her body sank into the chair before she could resist, the bargain asserting itself with brutal efficiency. The warmth in her chest flared in protest, pushing against the compulsion too late.

"Better." He moved to pour himself wine, his movements sharp, agitated. The composed king from the feast was gone. Here, in private, she could see the rage barely contained. "Now. Tell me about the warmth."

Her mouth stayed closed. She hadn't been compelled to speak, just to sit.

He turned, saw her resistance, and something dangerous flickered in his eyes. In two strides he was in front of her, his hand tangling in her hair again, yanking her head back.

"Tell me about the warmth," he repeated, each word precise.

The bargain forced the words out. "It started when I arrived here. In the Oubliette."

"Liar." His free hand struck her across the face, not as hard as before but enough to sting. "Try again."

"That's when I first felt it—"

Another strike that left her gasping. "When did it really begin?"

The compulsion dug deeper, pulling truth from her throat. "I don't know. The Oubliette is when I noticed it, when it saved me, but—"

"But?"

"It felt familiar. Like recognizing something that had always been there."

He studied her face, then released her hair to pace the room. She watched him move, noting how the autumn magic seemed to follow him, leaves appearing in his footsteps only to crumble to dust moments later.

"Stand," he commanded suddenly. "Remove the dress."

Her hands moved to the fastenings before she could think to resist. The warmth surged, and for a moment her fingers stilled, fighting the compulsion. She felt it pushing back against the bargain's hold.

Malus noticed immediately. "Fascinating." He moved closer, watching her internal struggle play out. "It's helping you resist. How much, I wonder?"

He grabbed her wrist, squeezing until Briar could feel the bones grinding against each other, forcing her fingers to continue undoing the dress. The autumn silk pooled at her feet, leaving her in the thin shift beneath. In the firelight, the bite wound on her throat was clearly visible, already beginning to close far too fast for human healing.

"Look." He turned her toward the mirror, standing behind her. "Watch what happens."

He pressed his fingers against the bite wound. She expected pain, but instead felt the warmth recoil violently from his touch. Not just pulling away but actively fighting, pushing against his autumn magic.

"There," he breathed against her ear. "Do you feel it? How it recognizes me as wrong?" His fingers traced the wound's edges. "It knows I'm not the one who should be touching you."

She tried to pull away but he held her still, one arm around her waist, the other hand at her throat.

"When he marked you," Malus continued, his fingers finding the autumn leaves at her throat, "what did you feel?"

"Pain." The word came out without compulsion—her own bitter truth.

"And when these changed? When they became mine?"

She remembered the sensation, the pulling, the way the warmth had raged. "Like being torn in half."

"Because part of you belongs to him." His hand moved to press against her sternum, where the warmth pulsed strongest. "This part. Hidden inside you like a seed."

The warmth flared at his touch, hot enough that he pulled his hand back with a hiss. When she looked in the mirror, she could see a faint golden glow beneath her skin where he'd touched, there and gone in an instant.

"Show me," he commanded. "Make it manifest."

"I can't control it—"

He spun her around, slamming her back against the mirror hard enough to crack it. "Don't lie to me."

"I'm not!" She pushed against his chest, and the warmth responded, golden light flickering across her palms. They both froze, staring at her hands.

"So you can control it," he said softly. "When you're angry enough. When you're threatened enough." He leaned closer, his weight pinning her against the cracked mirror. "What else can it do?"

"I don't know."

His hand wrapped around her throat, not squeezing yet, just present. "Let's find out."

He began applying pressure slowly, watching her face. The warmth responded immediately, golden light spreading from her chest outward, trying to push him away. But it was weak, unfocused, like something not fully awakened.

"More," he murmured, increasing the pressure.

She couldn't breathe. Her hands clawed at his wrist, and the warmth surged stronger. Golden light began seeping from her skin, not just flickering but steady, growing brighter as her need for air became desperate.

Just before she would have passed out, he released her. She collapsed, gasping, the golden light fading as quickly as it had come.

"Interesting." He crouched beside her, tilting her chin up to examine her eyes. "It responds to mortal danger. To protect you." His thumb traced her jaw. "My brother hid something in you. But what? And why?"

She couldn't answer, still trying to breathe properly. Everything hurt—her throat, her scalp, the bite wound that was somehow both healing and burning.

"What bargain did you strike with him?"

"To save my sister," Briar whispered, her hand resting on the bruises forming like a macabre necklace around her throat. "My life for hers, but—"

"But? Speak."

Briar tried to fight it, but the words forced their way out. "He'd already claimed it, my mother made a bargain with him, she thought it was for her life, but it wasn't. It was mine."

"When?"

She clamped her teeth together, fighting the command. Malus lifted his hand and the words tumbled free. "Twenty-five years ago."

"Twenty-five years ago," he mused, standing to pour himself more wine. "I was preparing the ritual to strip Eliam's power. It required innocent blood, a catalyst..."

He trailed off, his expression shifting as he worked through something. She watched him calculate, saw understanding dawn.

"A car accident. Mortal world violence, innocent blood spilled." He turned to look at her. "My ritual was working, pulling at his power."

The warmth pulsed, agitated now.

"But Eliam must have sensed it, must have realized what I was doing."

The room felt suddenly cold despite the fire. Briar pressed back against the wall, the cracked mirror sharp against her spine.

"He intervened," Malus continued. "When your mother was dying, when her blood was spilling, when my ritual was pulling at his power—he made a bargain with her. He saved her life and in exchange..." His eyes gleamed with terrible satisfaction. "He hid part of himself where I'd never think to look. In that unborn child."

"That's impossible—"

"Is it?" He grabbed her chin, forcing her to meet his eyes. "The ritual needed innocent blood and got it. But instead of claiming Eliam's power for me, it created an opening he exploited. He placed a fragment of his essence inside you before you were even born. Let it grow with you, become part of you, until separating it would destroy you both."

The warmth pulsed frantically now, and she could feel the truth of it resonating in her bones. This thing she'd thought was separate, alien—it had been with her since before birth. Growing as she grew. Becoming part of who she was.

"He made you a living sanctuary for his power," Malus continued. "And now, through the bargain, you belong to me." His smile was vicious. "Which means his hidden power belongs to me as well."

"You can't—"

"Can't I?" His hand moved to her chest, pressing flat against her sternum despite the warmth's burning protest. "It's inside you. You're mine. Therefore, it's mine."

The warmth fought violently, golden light flaring so bright that Malus had to squint. But he didn't pull away, his autumn magic pressing against the warmth, trying to contain it, claim it.

"Stop," she gasped, the competing magics making her feel like she was being pulled apart from the inside.

"Submit," he commanded. "Let it recognize me as its master."

The bargain tried to force her compliance, but the warmth—Eliam's essence—wouldn't yield. It had its own will, its own loyalty, and it raged against Malus's touch with increasing violence.

"You can't force it," she managed through gritted teeth. "It's not truly mine to give."

"Then I'll tear it out of you." His fingers dug into her chest, autumn magic trying to hook into the warmth, to drag it from her by force.

The pain was excruciating. She screamed, her back arching, golden light erupting from every pore. The warmth wasn't just fighting now—it was burning, trying to destroy the autumn magic before it could take root.

Malus finally jerked back with a snarl, his hand reddened and blistered where the warmth had burned him.

"Stubborn," he said, examining his injured hand. "Just like him." He looked at her, crumpled on the floor, golden light still flickering weakly beneath her skin. "But I have time. And I have leverage. Tomorrow we'll continue exploring what you really are." He tilted her chin up. "What you can become, with the right motivation."

He left her there, crumpled on his chamber floor, the warmth in her chest flickering like a dying ember. She could feel it—Eliam's essence—trying to comfort her, but it was exhausted from fighting, from protecting her against its false king.

The door to her adjoining chambers stood open. She crawled through it, every movement agony, and collapsed on her bed. The autumn marks at her throat felt like chains, binding her to someone who would tear her apart to get to the power hidden inside her.

But the warmth, weak as it was, still pulled southward, reaching for its true source.

It still remembered who it really belonged to.

The knock came late the next afternoon. Briar had spent the day curled in bed, the bite wound on her throat finally closed but still tender. Every movement reminded her of his hands, his rage, the way he'd tried to tear the warmth from her chest.

"Come in," she called, expecting servants.

Malus entered instead, pausing in the doorway with a tray bearing wine, fruit, and delicate pastries that looked too perfect to eat. He'd changed into softer colors, russet and gold rather than the deep burgundy of last night. His expression was carefully pleasant.

"I thought you might be hungry," he said, entering without invitation. "You missed breakfast. And lunch."

She sat up slowly, pulling the covers higher. The shift she wore felt too thin, too exposed, but she had nothing else. Her dress from the feast lay ruined on his chamber floor.

"I'm not hungry."

"No?" He set the tray on her bedside table, movements unhurried. "My temper got the better of me yesterday. The oil trick, the resistance of your blood—I reacted poorly."

The words sounded like apology but felt like strategy. She watched him pour wine into two glasses, the liquid dark as garnets.

"I've been thinking about what you are," he said, offering her a glass. When she didn't take it, he set it on the table beside her. "What my brother created. A living vessel for his essence. Quite brilliant, actually."

He moved to the window, looking out at the forest that no longer fully answered to him.

"In the old days," he continued, "before the courts split, before we pretended we were better than our nature, human blood served a purpose beyond pleasure." He turned to face her. "Each drop strengthens our magic. Each feeding sharpens our power. The Night Court ruled for millennia on that strength."

"You don't need it to survive," she said, her voice rough.

"No, we don't need it." He moved closer, sitting in the chair beside her bed. "But iron doesn't need to be sharpened to exist—yet a dull blade is useless. We abandoned the old ways and our magic dulled with it. Became... domesticated."

He leaned forward slightly. "Your blood is particularly interesting. Human essence mixed with fae magic. I wonder—does it strengthen twice as much? Or does that forest taint make it poison to anyone but him?"

The warmth in her chest pulsed with alarm, recognizing threat.

"I tasted your fear and pain last night," he continued. "But blood changes with the body's state. Fear makes it sharp. Pain makes it bitter." He paused, studying her face. "And arousal... arousal makes it sweet. More potent. In the old days, the Night Court would keep favored humans, pleasure them thoroughly before feeding. The power gained from willing, aroused blood could last for weeks."

Her stomach turned. "You can't—"

"Can't?" He moved closer, sitting in the chair beside her bed. "Did my brother tolerate such defiance? You belong to me. With a word I could command you to want me." He paused, studying her face which Briar struggled to keep impassive. "But commands are so... inelegant. And they don't produce authentic responses."

"So I'm going to offer you a choice," he continued. "Come to my bed willingly. Give yourself to me. Let me taste your blood in pleasure rather than pain. Show me what sweetness you're capable of."

"No." The word came out firm despite her fear.

"No?" He leaned back, still casual. "Interesting... then I'll have Eliam brought up from the dungeons. You can watch while I remove pieces of him. Fingers first, I think. Then perhaps an eye. He has two, after all."

The warmth contracted violently, and she felt it pulling desperately southward.

"You're lying," she said. "You need him alive."

"Alive, yes. Whole? That's negotiable." He stood, moving toward the door. "I'll have the guards fetch him now. We can conduct this experiment with him watching. Would that be better? Let him see exactly how his essence responds when you're taken by another?"

"Wait." The word escaped before she could stop it.

He paused, hand on the door. "Yes?"

She couldn't look at him. The warmth in her chest was thrashing, knowing what she was about to do, trying to stop her. But she could picture it too clearly. Eliam chained and helpless, Malus with a blade, the blood and screaming.

"If I... if I come willingly," she said, each word a struggle, "you leave him alone?"

"For now." He returned to stand before her. "Though if you resist, if you fight me, if you make this difficult, well, the deal changes."

She stood on shaking legs, the shift falling to mid-thigh. Every instinct screamed to run, to fight, but where would she go? And Eliam would pay the price.

"Your chambers," she said quietly. "Not here."

Not in the bed where she'd been trying to feel safe. Some small boundary she could maintain.

He smiled, pleased by her negotiation. "As you wish."

Briar felt her stomach twist as she she followed him through the connecting door, each step feeling like walking to an execution. His chambers still smelled of autumn, the fire casting shadows that moved wrong.

"Wine?" he offered, gesturing to a decanter.

"No." She wouldn't make this easier for herself. If she was choosing this to protect Eliam, she'd face it clear-headed.

"Proud even now." He moved closer, circling her slowly. "Take off the shift."

Her hands shook as she reached for the hem. The fabric whispered against her skin as she pulled it over her head, each inch of exposure making her stomach clench. The cold air hit her like a slap—her nipples tightening, goosebumps racing across her flesh. She could feel his gaze like touch, cataloguing every mark, every bruise he'd left before.

The warmth in her chest contracted, pulling so deep she could barely sense it, like it was trying to hide from what was coming.

"Lovely," he murmured. "Come here."

Her bare feet were silent on the cold floor. Each step felt like walking through mud, her body fighting the command even as it obeyed. When she reached him, his hands settled on her waist, and revulsion rolled through her so strongly she thought she might vomit. His skin was too cool, too smooth, wrong in every way.

"You're trembling," he observed, his thumbs stroking her hip bones. "Fear? Or anticipation?"

"You know which."

"Do I?" His mouth found her throat, lips resting against her pulse. She could feel him inhale, scenting her. "Your body says you're afraid. But you came willingly. You chose this."

"To protect—"

"Yes, yes, to protect him." His hands moved lower, gripping her hips hard enough to bruise. "But you still chose. That's what matters."

When he kissed her, she held herself rigid, neither responding nor pulling away. His tongue pushed into her mouth, tasting, claiming. He tasted of spiced wine and something metallic. The warmth in her chest recoiled so violently she felt physical pain, like something tearing.

"You're not trying," he said against her lips. "Should I send for Eliam after all? Let him watch what you're willing to do for his life?"

The image of Eliam chained, being forced to watch, broke something in her. She kissed him back, hating herself for the small sound of satisfaction he made. Her hands came up to his chest, feeling the expensive fabric of his shirt, the hard muscle beneath. Nothing like Eliam's body, but she pushed that thought away viciously.

"Better," he murmured. "But not enough."

He walked her backward toward the bed, his mouth moving to her ear. "I need to understand what makes you respond. What makes your blood sing." His teeth caught her earlobe, tugging. "Is it gentle touches?" His hand skimmed up her ribs, barely there. "Or something rougher?"

His other hand tangled in her hair, pulling her head back to expose her throat. The position made her vulnerable, made her heart race with instinctive panic. He licked a line from her collarbone to her jaw, and she shuddered, not with want but with the effort of not pulling away.

"Interesting," he murmured. "Your pulse speeds but your body fights. Let's try something else."

He pushed her onto the bed, but didn't follow immediately. Instead, he stood over her, slowly removing his shirt. "Watch," he commanded when she tried to look away. "I want you to see who's about to take you."

His chest was pale, unmarked by battle or labor. Beautiful in an ethereal way that felt cold and decorative. She watched his hands move to his belt, the leather sliding through loops with a whisper that made her stomach clench.

"Tell me you want this," he said as he removed his boots, then his trousers, taking his time. Making her watch every movement.

"I—" The lie stuck in her throat.

"Tell me, or Eliam loses a finger. Then another. I'll have them brought to you in a box."

"I want this." The words tasted vile, but she made herself hold his gaze as she said them.

"Again. Make me believe it."

She sat up, forcing herself to reach for him even as every cell in her body screamed in protest. "I want you."

He climbed onto the bed then, prowling over her on hands and knees. "Your body tells a different story. Still so tense. So resistant." He nudged her legs apart with his knee, settling between them but not pressing against her yet. Just hovering, making her aware of his presence, his intent.

His mouth found her breast, tongue circling before teeth bit down—not to feed, just enough to hurt. She gasped, her back arching involuntarily. He did the same to the other side, alternating between gentle and sharp until her body didn't know how to respond, caught between flinching and following.

"Better," he said, watching her face. "Your blood is warming. I can smell it changing."

One hand traced down her stomach, lower, until his fingers found her. She wasn't ready—would never be ready for him—but he was patient, clinical, working her body like an instrument he was learning to play. When she remained dry, unresponsive, he made a thoughtful sound.

"Perhaps you need more direct stimulation."

His mouth replaced his fingers, and she nearly screamed, not from pleasure but from the violation of such an intimate act from someone she despised. But her body, treacherous thing, began to respond to the mechanical stimulation. She could feel herself growing wet despite the horror, despite the hatred.

"There we go," he murmured against her. "See how easily the flesh betrays? All that resistance, and yet here you are...."

She pressed her palms against her eyes, trying to disappear into herself, but he stopped immediately.

"Look at me," he commanded. "Be present, or I stop being gentle."

She forced her eyes open, forced herself to watch his face as he returned his mouth to her. The warmth in her chest thrashed weakly, confused by her body's physical response conflicting with her emotional revulsion.

When he finally rose up, positioning himself over her, she could see her wetness on his mouth. He was making sure she could see it, could see the evidence of her body's betrayal.

"Now," he said, pushing just the tip inside, making her feel the intrusion. "Let's see if your blood is finally sweet enough."

He entered her slowly, watching her face the entire time. She couldn't help the sound that escaped—not pleasure but something raw, broken. Her body stretched to accommodate him, and she hated that it knew how, that Eliam had taught it to receive, and now Malus was using that knowledge against her.

He moved with deliberate rhythm, one hand braced beside her head, the other gripping her hip. Not violent, not rough, but almost tender. That made it worse somehow, that he was taking time, taking care to build her body's response.

"You're getting wetter," he observed. "Your body is beginning to want this. I can feel you clenching around me."

She turned her face away, but he caught her chin, forcing her to look at him. "Every. Moment. Present."

He shifted angle, and suddenly he was hitting something inside that made her gasp, made her hips lift involuntarily. He smiled, cold and satisfied, and targeted that spot relentlessly until she was making sounds she couldn't control, her body climbing toward something she desperately didn't want.

"Perfect," he breathed. "Now your blood should sing."

He bit her then, at the curve where neck met shoulder, and drank deeply. She could feel him inside her in two ways—his body taking hers, his mouth taking her blood. The dual invasion made her feel split apart.

The warmth tried to taint her blood, tried to make it bitter, but he'd worked her body too well. She could feel herself climbing toward climax even as she fought it, even as tears ran down her face.

"Yes," he said against the wound. "There it is. Arousal makes it so much sweeter. Like honey and copper and—" He thrust harder, making her cry out. "—submission."

She came with his teeth in her throat, her body convulsing around him in the ultimate betrayal. He groaned against her neck, drinking deeper as her orgasm flooded her blood with exactly what he'd wanted to taste.

He finished moments later, still feeding, and she felt him shudder with more than physical release. When he finally pulled away, from her throat and from her body, his eyes were dilated, almost drunk.

"Exquisite," he said, crimson staining his lips. "Your blood when you come... it's intoxicating. Eliam is a fool for denying himself. Perhaps tomorrow I'll see how fear mixed with arousal tastes. Or pain with pleasure."

He stood, dressing efficiently while she lay shaking on the bed, blood seeping from the bite, her body still pulsing with aftershocks she didn't want.

"Clean yourself up," he said from the doorway. "There will be no court tonight. Ensure you rest well because tomorrow I want to see what else we can discover about your unique blood."

The door closed, and she curled into herself, the sheet sticking to the blood and other fluids on her skin. The warmth in her chest was so quiet she thought it might have died from shame. She could still feel everywhere he'd touched, could still taste him in her mouth, could still feel the echo of him inside her.

But worse than all of that was the knowledge that her body had responded, wanted, and had found pleasure in her own violation.

Minutes ticked by before she finally forced herself to move. She grabbed the sheet, wrapping it around herself, and tried to stand. Her legs shook violently, barely supporting her weight after all her body had been forced to endure. She had to grip the bedpost to keep from falling before she could stumble back to her own chambers.

The moment she crossed the threshold, she collapsed, the weight of what she'd done crushing her. But beneath the violation, beneath the disgust and self-hatred, something else burned.

Rage.

Pure, clean rage that he'd used Eliam against her. That he'd made her complicit through threats rather than force. The warmth in her chest responded to that anger, stirring from its hiding place, feeding on the fury.

She pressed her hand to her chest, feeling it pulse with newfound strength. Not comfort—it was too angry for comfort. But solidarity. It hated him too. Hated what he'd done, what he'd made her do.

"Tomorrow," she whispered to the warmth, to herself. "Tomorrow we find a way to stop this."

The warmth pulsed agreement, and for the first time since entering Malus's chambers, she felt like she might survive this. Not intact, not unharmed, but unbroken.

She was damaged but not destroyed. And that made all the difference.

"My lady?" Síochán's voice was soft, those pearl-like fingers already reaching for the washing basin. "I came to prepare you for evening court, but—" She stopped, seeing the bruises blooming on Briar's throat, the blood on the sheets.

"There is no evening court," Briar said, her voice hollow. "He cancelled it."

Síochán moved closer, her strange fingers gentle as she helped Briar sit up. The sheet slipped, revealing more bruises, bite marks, the evidence of what had been done. Síochán's expression didn't change, but her movements became even more careful.

"Let me help you," she said simply, guiding Briar toward the bathing chamber. "The water will ease the aches."

Briar let herself be led, too exhausted to resist kindness. Síochán drew the bath, adding something that made the water shimmer faintly and smelled of mint and something that cut through the lingering scent of autumn.

"I remember the old days," Síochán said quietly as she helped Briar into the water. "I was young when the Night Court fell. Young enough to survive the transition, old enough to remember what it was like." Her fingers worked through Briar's tangled hair with inhuman gentleness. "The blood-lettings. The hunts that ended in death, not sport. Humans kept like cattle, bled slowly over months until they were husks."

"Why are you telling me this?" Briar asked, sinking deeper into the water.

"Because Lord Malus speaks of returning to tradition as if it were golden." Síochán's voice carried old pain. "But I remember the screaming. I remember humans begging for death as mercy." She paused, her hands stilling. "Lord Eliam was harsh, yes, but he didn't believe in the old ways. His cruelty had limits."

Síochán helped her from the bath, wrapping her in soft towels. The fae woman's impossible fingers worked through Briar's tangled hair, each pull making her scalp ache where Malus had grabbed her the night before.

"Where is Karse being kept?" Briar asked suddenly. The thought of the Drak, unpredictable but fierce, sparked the first hint of hope she'd felt. "The one who came with me from the Star Court."

"The east wing." Síochán's hands didn't pause, but Briar felt her tense slightly. "Why?"

"I need to speak with him." Briar turned, water dripping from her hair onto the stone floor, pooling around her feet. "I need to find a way out of here."

Síochán set down the ivory comb, those pearl-like fingers folding carefully in her lap. "My lady, there's something you should know. Lord Malus has instructed me to prepare you tomorrow evening. For a private dinner. Just the two of you."

Briar's stomach turned, bile rising in her throat. She knew what private dinners meant. What would come after.

"Can you get me to Karse?" Her voice cracked, her desperation was palpable. "Tonight?"

"The wing is watched by Withered." Síocháin reached for the comb again, her movements deliberate, careful. "Even I don't go there unless I must. Their touch, it ages anything living."

"Then a message—"

"My lady, even if I could..." Síocháin said, resuming her work on Briar's hair. "The castle is sealed. Withered at every door. The forest itself obeys Lord Malus now. There's no clear path out. What plan could you make that Malus would not intercept?"

Briar stood abruptly, the towel slipping. She didn't care. She paced to the window, her bare feet leaving wet prints on the cold floor. Outside, autumn had spread further, leaves the color of dried blood stretching as far as the eye could see. The forest looked diseased.

"There has to be something." Her fingers pressed against the glass until her knuckles went white. The cold seeped through, numbing her fingertips. "Poison. Something I could slip into his wine when he isn't looking."

"We wouldn't know which wine until he selects it, should we poison them all?"

Of course. Everything planned, controlled. She turned from the window, pressing her palms against her temples.

"I just need him unconscious. Or distracted. Something. Anything." She looked up at Síocháin, saw something flicker across her face. "What? What are you thinking?"

"Nothing. I shouldn't—" Síocháin stood, moving toward the wardrobe. "Let me find you something to wear."

"No, wait." Briar crossed the room. "Whatever it is, tell me."

Síocháin's hands stilled on the wardrobe's carved handle. For a moment, Briar was afraid she had pushed too hard. When Síocháin spoke, her voice was barely above a whisper.

"There is something. Bloodshade. A sleeping draught. Very potent." She paused, still not turning. "But it doesn't matter, even if you could get him to drink it, it won't work from a cup."

"But there's another way." It wasn't a question. Briar could see it in the rigid line of Síocháin's shoulders.

"It works only when consumed through blood." The words came out reluctantly, like pulling splinters. "If someone were to take it, and then be... fed upon..."

The implication hung between them like a blade. Briar sank onto the bed, her damp skin made her shiver despite the room's warmth, goosebumps rising along her arms.

"I'd have to let him..." Her voice sounded distant to her own ears, hollow. "I'd have to make him want to feed. Quickly."

"More than that." Síochán finally turned, her ageless face troubled. "The bloodshade loses potency quickly once taken. You'd have minutes to get it into his system. You'd have to make him bite you before it becomes too diluted to work."

"I have to seduce him," Briar whispered. "Let him touch me after what he—"

She couldn't finish. Her hand went to her throat, fingers finding the bruises hidden beneath her wet hair.

They stood in silence, the weight of what that meant settling over them. The fire crackled, sending shadows dancing across the walls.

"I don't think I can fake wanting him convincingly enough," Briar said finally. "Not with that kind of pressure. He'll figure it out, he'll know something's wrong."

Síochán moved to sit beside her, careful not to touch. "There are wines. Old vintages from before the courts split. They... affect the body. Make it respond to touch, to proximity. Heighten sensation."

Briar looked at her sharply. "You're suggesting I drug myself?"

"You could take a small amount. Just enough to make your body's responses genuine, even if your mind resists." Síochán's voice was steady but her hands trembled slightly. "The wine would make your seduction believable, give you the time you need to get him to feed before the bloodshade loses its effect. I could make sure it is served at dinner."

The plan was horrifying in its simplicity. Drug herself to endure him. Let him feed. Watch him fall.

"How quickly does bloodshade work?"

"Within minutes. Fast enough that he'd be unconscious before he realized anything was wrong." Síochán stood, pulling a simple brown dress from the wardrobe, soft wool that wouldn't irritate bruised skin. "But you'd have to time it perfectly."

Briar took a deep breath. "Can you get it?"

Síochán was quiet for a moment, then, finally nodded as she helped Briar into the dress. "I'll bring it tomorrow, when I prepare you for dinner."

She began working the laces, careful around the bruises on Briar's back.

"About Karse," Briar said quietly. "I need him to know the plan. To wait in the rose gardens at midnight tomorrow. Tell him... tell him the hunt ends then."

Síochán's fingers paused on the laces. "I told you, I don't go to the east wing."

"Please. There has to be a way."

Síochán was quiet for a moment. "I prepare the meal trays for that wing, even if I don't deliver them. I could hide a message in his food. The servants who carry the trays wouldn't know to look."

"Would he find it?"

"Draks are paranoid creatures when it comes to fae. He'll examine everything before eating." She resumed lacing. "You understand what you're risking? If Lord Malus suspects anything—"

"He'll do worse than kill me." Briar met her eyes in the mirror. "I know."

Síochán finished with the dress and moved to leave, pausing at the door. "My lady... the wine. It will make things easier, but you'll still be aware. Still remember."

Briar thought of Eliam in the dungeons below, of Thaine probably being tortured for sport, of endless nights as Malus's experiment.

"I'll remember anyway. At least this time, it serves a purpose."

The door closed softly, leaving Briar alone with the weight of what she'd have to do. The warmth in her chest pulsed once, weak but present, pulling toward the dungeons. *Tomorrow*, she told it silently. *Tomorrow we get him back.*

Chapter Seventeen

The garden was dying beautifully. That was the worst part—how lovely autumn made everything look even as it killed. Briar sat on a stone bench, watching leaves spiral down like drops of blood and gold, trying to prepare herself for tonight. Her fingers worried at the wool of her dress, picking at a loose thread.

She had to seduce him. Had to make him believe she wanted him. The thought made her stomach clench, made the bruises on her thighs ache with memory.

"Hiding?"

She jerked, her head rising sharply, she hadn't heard him approach. Malus stood behind the bench, close enough that she could smell the autumn on him—dying leaves and smoke and something sweet tainted by rot.

"Just thinking," she managed, starting to stand.

His hand settled on her shoulder, keeping her seated. "No need to get up." He moved around the bench, his fingers trailing along her shoulder, across the nape of her neck. "I've just come from the bone garden. Did you know Eliam cultivated new species there? Flowers that grow from marrow. Quite creative, really. Disturbing, but creative."

He sat beside her, too close. His thigh pressed against hers through the wool dress.

"You look better today," he observed, tilting her chin up with one finger. "Less... fragile."

"I slept," she lied.

"Good." His thumb traced her jaw, found the faded bruise at her throat. "This is healing well. Though I think I prefer you marked."

The warmth stirred in her chest, recognizing the threat. She forced herself to stay still, not pull away. If she showed hesitation now, if she showed fear, it would be harder to convince him later.

"Are you looking forward to tonight?" His hand moved to her throat, fingers spanning the places he'd bitten. Light pressure, just enough to make her pulse jump.

She had to start somewhere. had to begin the performance. "I've been thinking."

"Oh?" His fingers stilled but didn't leave her throat.

"About fighting you and how pointless it is." The words wanted to lodge in her throat but she forced herself to keep speaking. "You won. The throne is yours. Eliam is caged. And I'm..." She made herself meet his eyes. "I'm tired of fighting."

Interest flickered in his expression. His hand shifted, cupping her jaw. "Is that so?"

"He humiliated me. Sent his huntsman to torment me. Then let you take me." Each word carefully chosen, building the lie. "Maybe I've been loyal to the wrong brother."

Malus studied her face, searching for deception. Then he kissed her.

It was different from before—less violent, more testing. She made herself respond, her lips parting under his, her hand coming up to rest against his chest. The warmth recoiled, pulling deep, but she couldn't let him feel her contempt.

His tongue swept into her mouth, tasting, claiming. His hand tangled in her hair, tilting her head for better access. She kissed him back, hating herself, hating the small sound he made of pleased surprise.

When he pulled back, his pupils were dilated. "You taste different. Less afraid."

"I told you. I'm tired of fighting."

"Show me." His hand found her waist, pulled her closer. "Show me how tired you are."

She turned into him, her hand sliding up to his neck before tangling in his hair, and kissed him this time. She made herself the aggressor even as her skin crawled. His surprised exhale against her mouth felt like victory and violation all at once.

His hands roamed, finding the curve of her breast through the wool, her hip, the inside of her thigh. The warmth flared with each touch, golden light threatening to show beneath her skin. She pressed closer, using the movement to hide the light, to distract him.

"Eager," he murmured against her mouth, his hand sliding higher on her thigh.

She caught his wrist, not pulling away but stilling him. "Not here."

"No?" His fingers pressed harder, a warning. "Shy?"

"You deserve better than a garden liaison." She made her voice soft, wanting. "Tonight. When we have time. When I can properly..." She let the sentence trail off, implications hanging.

He studied her, and she saw the moment he decided to believe her. His hand left her thigh to cup her face.

"Tonight then." His thumb traced her lower lip. "Wear something that comes off easily."

"Yes." The word barely made it past her throat.

He stood, pulling her up with him, kissing her once more—possessive and promising. When he released her, she had to catch herself on the bench.

"Don't disappoint me," he said softly. "I'd hate to have to visit Eliam before our dinner. Stress affects the appetite."

The threat was clear. She nodded, unable to speak.

He left her there, autumn wind picking up in his wake. Briar sank onto the bench, wiping her mouth with the back of her hand. She could still taste him, still feel the wrongness of his touch.

But he'd believed her. She'd seen it in his eyes, felt it in the way his hands had grown confident. Tonight. Just a few more hours of this performance, and then they could run.

The warmth pulsed, agitated from his touch, from her allowing it. She pressed her hand to her chest, trying to calm it.

"I know," she whispered. "I know. But it's almost over."

The garden continued its beautiful death around her, leaves falling like a curtain between what was and what would be.

Síochán arrived as the sun began its descent, carrying a covered gown and a basket that clinked softly with hidden glass. She locked the door behind her, something she'd never done before.

"Did you bring it?" Briar asked immediately, her voice tight.

Síochán set down her burdens, pulling the small vial from her basket. The liquid inside was clear as water, innocent looking. "Bloodshade. Tasteless, odorless. Once you drink it, you have perhaps five minutes before it loses potency in your blood."

Briar took it with shaking fingers. Such a small thing to carry such weight.

"I've prepared a wine for you," Síocháin continued, laying out the dress. "It will be in the dining room, the bottle marked with a small nick on the label. It will help you relax, make this easier to bear. Drink as much as you need." She paused. "But not so much you lose your wits. You'll need to time the bloodshade carefully."

The dress unfurled across the bed—deep russet silk that clung rather than structured, held by thin straps that could be slipped off with minimal effort. The neckline plunged low, the back lower still. It was a dress designed to be removed.

"He wanted something that comes off easily," Briar said flatly, touching the fabric.

"And this will. But it also hides things." Síocháin showed her a tiny pocket sewn into the inner seam at the hip, low enough that wandering hands would find skin before they found secrets. "The vial goes here. Don't forget which side."

Briar started undressing, her movements mechanical. "I can do this. It's just one evening. Just him and me. I can make him believe me long enough to—"

"You convinced him in the garden," Síocháin agreed, helping her into the gown. The silk slid over her skin like cool water. "He'll be expecting you willing. Eager, even. Give him that, and he won't think to question."

The dress required no corset—it skimmed her body, relying on the cut rather than structure. Briar felt exposed in a different way than the elaborate gowns. This left nothing to imagination while pretending at simplicity.

"Sit," Síocháin directed, beginning on her hair. "You're shaking."

"I'm terrified." The admission came out raw. "But at least it's private. Just one person to convince. I can focus on him, read his reactions, adjust if something seems wrong."

Síocháin's fingers paused for just a moment before continuing their work. "Yes. Just focus on him."

"What if the bloodshade doesn't work? What if he notices the vial?"

"He won't notice the vial if you keep him distracted." Síocháin pinned another section of hair, weaving it into something elaborate that left her neck bare. "And the bloodshade will work. I've seen it fell fae far older than Malus."

"Before, I wasn't actively participating," Briar said to her reflection. The woman in the mirror looked pale beneath the cosmetics Síocháin applied. "Before, I could blame him entirely. This time I have to make him think I want it."

"This time you're choosing to save Lord Eliam. To save yourself." Síocháin's voice was firm. "That's not participation. That's war."

She stepped back, surveying her work. The kohl made Briar's eyes look larger, darker. The red on her lips matched the undertone of the silk where light caught it. She looked like someone who had made a choice and intended to see it through.

"Remember," Síocháin said quietly, "he needs to believe you've chosen him. That you want to be there. If you tense, if you pull away—"

"I won't." Briar stood, the silk moving with her like a second skin. She checked the vial in its hidden pocket, feeling its small weight against her hip. "I convinced him in the garden. I can convince him tonight. And once we're alone, once he's distracted..." She took a breath. "The wine will help. I'll let him think he's won, drink the bloodshade when he's ready to feed, and then it's over."

"Briar." Síocháin caught her arm. "Whatever happens tonight, whatever he asks of you—the goal is to survive long enough to act. Don't forget that."

Something in her tone made Briar pause. "You sound like you're warning me about more than seduction."

Síocháin's ancient eyes held hers for a long moment. "I'm warning you that Malus never does what you expect. Be ready to adapt."

Before Briar could press further, a knock at the door made them both jump.

"Lord Malus requests your presence," a servant called.

Síocháin squeezed her hand once, then slipped out the servant's entrance. Briar took one last look at her reflection—the exposed skin, the dress that promised everything, the face painted to hide terror—and followed the servant into the hall.

She could do this. A private dinner, the special wine to calm her nerves, and a plan that would end with Malus unconscious and Eliam free. She just had to be convincing for a few hours.

The vial pressed against her hip with each step, a secret weight that would either save them or destroy them all.

The servant led her through corridors she didn't recognize, away from the private wing where she'd expected to dine. Briar's steps faltered as they turned down a wider hallway, one lined with torches and decorated with autumn leaves that rustled despite no breeze.

"Where are we going?" she asked, but the servant didn't answer, just kept walking with that blank-faced efficiency all of Malus's staff seemed to share.

The noise reached her before the doors did. Voices, dozens of them, the clink of glasses and murmur of conversation. Her heart began to pound.

No. This was wrong. This was supposed to be private.

The servant pushed open the great doors, and Briar's carefully constructed composure shattered.

The entire court was assembled. Long tables stretched the length of the hall, filled with fae lords and ladies in their finest attire. Candles floated overhead, casting everything in warm golden light that made the scene look almost beautiful if you didn't notice the hungry eyes turning toward her. At the head of the room, elevated on a dais, sat Malus in a throne-like chair, watching her with an expression of pure, delighted anticipation.

There was no private table. No bottle of wine with a nick on the label. No intimate setting where she could control the situation.

She'd been played.

"Ah, there she is." Malus's voice carried across the sudden silence. He gestured with one hand, a lazy beckoning. "Come, pet. I've been telling everyone how eager you were to join us tonight."

Every eye in the room fixed on her. She felt their gazes pressing against her exposed skin, the plunging neckline, the dress that suddenly felt like nothing at all.

Move, she told herself. You have to move.

Her legs carried her forward somehow, silk whispering against her thighs with each step. The vial pressed against her hip, useless now. There would be no private moment to drink it, no opportunity to let Malus feed while she was drugged. Everything she'd planned was worthless.

The walk to the dais felt endless. Fae whispered as she passed, their words just loud enough to catch.

"...the human pet..."

"...heard she begged him in the garden..."

"...wonder how long before he tires of her..."

Briar kept her chin up, kept her expression smooth. Malus wanted her broken and desperate. She wouldn't give him that. Not yet.

She reached the dais and stopped, unsure what to do. There was no chair for her, no place set at his table. Just Malus, lounging in his throne, watching her with those calculating eyes.

"You look disappointed," he said softly, pitched for her ears alone. "Were you expecting something more... intimate?"

"I was expecting dinner." She was proud of how steady her voice came out.

"And you'll have it." His smile widened. "But first, I thought we might address some concerns my court has raised. They worry, you see, that my new pet isn't quite as tame as I've claimed. That perhaps her earlier displays of affection were... performative."

Ice flooded her veins. "I don't understand."

"Don't you?" He reached out, fingers catching her wrist, and pulled her toward him. "You told me you were tired of fighting. That you'd chosen the winning side. I believed you." His grip tightened. "But belief and proof are different things, aren't they?"

"What do you want me to do?"

The question came out barely above a whisper. Malus's smile turned sharp, cruel, satisfied.

"Prove it." He tugged her forward, off-balance, and she tumbled into his lap. His arm wrapped around her waist, holding her there. "Show my court that you belong to me. Willingly."

The hall had gone utterly silent. She could feel hundreds of eyes on her, could hear her own heartbeat thundering in her ears. Malus's hand splayed across her stomach, possessive and warm through the thin silk.

"I don't—" she started.

"You said you were done fighting." His lips brushed her ear, his voice dropping to something intimate and terrifying. "You said you wanted this. Were you lying to me, Briar?"

The threat hung unspoken. Eliam in the dungeons. What Malus could do to him with a single command.

"No," she whispered. "I wasn't lying."

"Then prove it."

His hand slid lower, fingers trailing across her hip, her thigh. She forced herself not to flinch, not to pull away. The dress's thin fabric hid nothing—she could feel the heat of his palm through the silk.

"Spread your legs."

The command was quiet but absolute. When she hesitated, his other hand gripped her chin, forcing her to look at the assembled court. All those faces, watching, waiting.

"They need to see," he murmured against her neck. "They need to know you're mine. Unless you'd rather I visit the dungeons tonight instead?"

Briar's eyes burned, but she didn't cry. She couldn't cry. Instead, she let her thighs part, just slightly.

"Wider."

She obeyed.

Malus made a sound of approval. His hands found her knees, lifting them, draping her legs over the arms of his chair so she was spread open and displayed. The position pulled her dress up her thighs, exposing far too much. Cool air hit her skin and she had to bite back a sound of humiliation.

"There," he said, satisfaction dripping from every syllable. "Isn't that better?"

His hand returned to her thigh, tracing lazy patterns on her inner skin. Each touch made her want to scream, to fight, to run. Instead, she stayed perfectly still, her body rigid in his lap.

"You're tense." His fingers walked higher, brushing the edge of her smallclothes. "That won't do. You're supposed to be enjoying this."

She couldn't speak. Could barely breathe.

"Look at them," he commanded. "Look at my court while I touch you."

She raised her eyes. The fae watched with expressions ranging from hungry interest to barely concealed disgust. Some leaned forward in their seats. Others whispered behind raised hands. All of them saw her like this, spread and helpless and pretending she wanted it.

Malus's free hand slid up her stomach, over her ribs, until he cupped her breast through the thin silk. He squeezed, testing the weight of her, his thumb finding her nipple and circling until it hardened despite her will.

"The dress was a good choice," he mused, pinching lightly. "So thin. They can see everything."

He was right. She could feel her nipples pressing against the fabric, could see fae eyes dropping to watch his hand knead and shape her. He tugged at the strap on one shoulder, pulling it down until her breast spilled free, bare and exposed to the entire court.

"Lovely," he said, rolling the nipple between his fingers. "Don't you think she's lovely?"

Murmurs of agreement rippled through the hall.

His other hand slipped beneath the fabric of her smallclothes.

The touch was electric, unwanted, and her body jerked in response. He laughed softly, the sound vibrating against her back.

"So responsive," he purred. "And we've barely begun."

He explored her slowly, deliberately, one hand between her legs while the other continued its assault on her breasts, switching from one to the other, pulling the second strap down until she was bare from the waist up. His fingers mapped every fold and curve while the court watched. She felt her face burning, felt shame crawling up her throat, but she didn't fight. Couldn't fight. Every time she started to close her legs, his hand abandoned her breast to grip her thigh in warning, keeping her spread wide.

His hand left her thigh and slid to her hip, fingers toying with the bunched silk of her dress. He traced along the seam, lazy and possessive, and Briar's heart stopped.

The vial. He was inches from the vial.

His fingers dipped beneath the fabric, exploring the curve of her hip, moving closer to that hidden pocket with every passing second. If he found it, if he felt that small glass shape against his fingers—

"Please." The word came out before she could stop it, desperate and breathy.

Malus stilled. His fingers paused their exploration, hovering dangerously close to the vial's hiding spot.

"Please what?" His voice was low, curious, delighted.

She shifted in his lap, arching her back, pressing herself more firmly against his chest. Her hand found his wrist and pulled, guiding his fingers away from her hip and back between her thighs.

"Touch me," she gasped. "I need—please, I need you to touch me."

The court murmured. Malus laughed, the sound rich with surprised pleasure.

"Well, well." His breath was hot against her ear. "Perhaps you aren't pretending after all."

His hand followed where she'd led it, fingers sliding back through her slick folds, and she nearly sobbed with relief even as fresh shame flooded through her. She'd just begged him to touch her. In front of everyone. And he believed it.

"So eager," he purred. "I knew you'd come around eventually."

Malus rewarded her with a stroke that made her hips jerk, his other hand returning to pinch her nipple hard enough to make her cry out. He knew exactly what he was doing, exactly how to make her body respond even as her mind screamed. His fingers circled, pressed, retreated, building sensation she didn't want to feel.

"See how she responds?" he announced to the watching court. He rolled her nipple again, pulling it taut. "And these pretty breasts—look how they flush when she's aroused."

Humiliation burned through her. Her body was betraying her, responding to his touch even as revulsion churned in her stomach. She could feel arousal building despite everything, her hips twitching involuntarily toward his hand.

"That's it," he crooned. "Stop fighting. Let them see how good I make you feel."

His fingers found a rhythm, steady and relentless. She tried to stay quiet, tried to deny him the satisfaction, but small sounds kept escaping—gasps and whimpers she couldn't quite suppress. Each one made his smile grow wider.

"I've imagined this so many times." His breath was hot against her throat. "How you'd sound when you finally stopped fighting. How your face would look when you realized there was nothing left to hold onto." His fingers twisted and she cried out. "Even better than I dreamed. Every fracture, every break—I want to remember all of it."

He shifted beneath her, adjusting the angle of his hand, and the new position made her see stars. His hand left her breast, wrapping loosely around her throat. Not squeezing, just resting there, a reminder of how completely he controlled her.

"Look at them," he commanded. "Look at my court while I take you apart."

She forced her eyes open, forced herself to see the sea of faces watching her degradation. Some looked hungry. Others bored, as if this were just another evening's entertainment. A few wouldn't meet her eyes at all.

The pleasure was building now whether she wanted it or not, coiling tight in her belly, her thighs beginning to tremble.

"You're close," he observed. "I can feel it. All those muscles tightening, your pulse racing." He bit her earlobe, just hard enough to sting. "Come for me, Briar. Come for my court."

She didn't want to. Willed herself not to. But his fingers knew exactly where to press, exactly how to move, and her body didn't care about her dignity or her shame or the eyes watching her fall apart.

The orgasm hit her without warning, sharp and intense, ripping a cry from her throat that echoed through the silent hall. Her back arched against Malus's chest, her legs trembling over the chair arms, completely unable to close or hide. He kept stroking through it, drawing it out, making her writhe and gasp until she was shaking and oversensitive and nearly sobbing.

Only then did he stop.

"Good girl," he murmured, pressing a kiss to her temple that felt like mockery. "See? She's perfectly tame."

Laughter rippled through the court. Scattered applause.

Briar's vision blurred. She couldn't feel her legs. The vial pressed against her hip, completely forgotten and utterly useless.

Malus gripped her jaw and kissed her, deep and possessive, letting the court see his tongue sweep into her mouth. She tasted wine and underneath it, something darker, something wrong.

When he released her mouth, his lips trailed down to her throat.

"Every piece of you that falls away," he said softly. "I'm going to collect. Keep. Rebuild you into something perfect."

Without warning his teeth sank into her neck.

The pain was sharp, immediate as Malus bit deep and drank greedily, his arm locked around her waist as she jerked in his grip.

The court watched that too.

He drank until her vision started to gray at the edges, until her struggles grew weak, until she hung limp in his arms. Only then did he pull back, licking the wound with a tongue that burned like frost.

"Mine," he announced, his voice carrying to every corner of the hall. "Body, blood, and soon enough, soul."

The court erupted in applause.

Briar couldn't move. Could barely think. Her neck throbbed, her thighs ached from their forced position, and somewhere deep in her chest, the warmth that connected her to Eliam flickered weakly, damaged by Malus's feeding.

He kept her there through the entire dinner, legs still spread over the chair arms, her body on display while the court ate and drank and pretended this was normal. Occasionally his hand would return between her thighs, stroking idly, reminding her and everyone else exactly what he'd claimed.

Briar stared at nothing, trying to retreat somewhere inside herself where this wasn't happening. The conversation around them had resumed, stilted at first but growing more natural as wine flowed and the court adjusted to the sight of their king's human pet splayed open before them.

She felt eyes on her. Not just passing glances but a steady, hungry gaze. A fae lord at one of the nearer tables, his golden hair swept back from a sharp-featured face, watched her with an intensity that made her skin crawl even more than it already did.

Malus noticed.

"Lord Liefand, isn't it?" His voice cut through the ambient noise, pleasant and curious. The hall quieted.

The lord startled, then recovered with a bow of his head. "Yes, Your Majesty."

"You seem to be enjoying the view." Malus's hand traced idle patterns on Briar's stomach as he spoke. "I can hardly blame you. She is exquisite, isn't she?"

Liefand's eyes darted between Malus and Briar, uncertainty flickering across his features. "She is, Your Majesty. You are... most fortunate."

"I am." Malus tilted his head, a smile playing at his lips. "Would you like a closer look?"

The hall went utterly silent.

Liefand froze. Briar felt Malus's chest rise and fall against her back, calm and steady. His hand continued its lazy movements on her skin.

"I..." Liefand swallowed. "Your Majesty, I wouldn't presume—"

"It's not presumption if I'm offering." Malus's voice was warm, inviting. "Come. See what all the fuss is about."

A trap. This was a trap. Briar wanted to scream it, to warn the fool, but her voice wouldn't work. She watched in mute horror as Liefand rose from his seat, as he approached the dais with hesitant steps, as greed slowly overtook caution in his expression.

"That's it," Malus encouraged. "Don't be shy."

Liefand climbed the dais steps. Up close, Briar could see the hunger in his eyes, the way they roamed over her exposed breasts, her spread thighs. Revulsion churned in her stomach.

"Go on," Malus said softly. "Touch her."

Liefand's hand extended, trembling with what might have been fear or anticipation or both. His fingers hovered over her knee, then made contact—cold, unwelcome, making her flinch.

Malus moved.

One moment he was relaxed beneath her, the next his hand had shot out and closed around Liefand's throat. The lord made a choked sound of surprise, his hand jerking away from Briar's skin.

"Did you really think," Malus said, his voice still conversational, almost friendly, "that I was offering?"

Liefand's hands scrabbled at Malus's grip, his face reddening. "Your Majesty—I—you said—"

"I said touch her. I wanted to see if you would." Malus's smile didn't waver. "You did."

"Please—"

"Look at her." The friendliness began to bleed away, something colder seeping through. "Look at what you thought you could have."

Liefand's terrified eyes met Briar's. She couldn't look away, couldn't move, couldn't do anything but watch as Malus's expression shifted from pleasant to something terrible.

"She belongs to me," Malus said, and now there was anger beneath the calm, building like a storm. "Every inch of her. Every sound she makes. Every drop of blood in her veins. Mine."

His grip tightened on Liefand's throat. The lord's struggles grew weaker.

"And you thought you could touch her? You thought I would share?"

"Forgive me," Liefand gasped. "Please, Your Majesty, I beg—"

"Watch," Malus commanded Briar, his voice sharp. "Watch what happens to those who touch what's mine."

She couldn't have looked away if she'd wanted to. Malus released Liefand's throat, and for one brief moment hope flickered across the lord's face.

Then Malus placed his palm over Liefand's eyes.

The screaming started immediately. Liefand's hands flew to his face, clawing at Malus's wrist, but Malus held firm. Briar could smell it—decay, rot, the sickly-sweet stench of something dying. She could see the skin around Malus's fingers turning gray, darkening, withering.

"This is what happens," Malus announced to the silent hall, his voice rising over Liefand's shrieks. "To anyone who thinks they can take from me. To anyone who believes my generosity is weakness."

He released Liefand, and the lord crumpled to the dais floor, hands pressed to his face, sounds coming from his throat that didn't sound like language anymore. Dark fluid seeped between his fingers—not blood, something thicker, fouler.

"Let this serve as a reminder." Malus's voice had gone cold, hard, furious. "She is mine. If any of you so much as look at her too long, you will envy Lord Liefand. Because I was merciful tonight. I left him his tongue so he can tell others what happens when you covet what belongs to the Autumn King."

The hall was deathly silent except for Liefand's broken sobbing.

Malus settled back in his throne, his hand returning to Briar's thigh, his touch gentle once more. "Now," he said pleasantly, as if nothing had happened, "where were we?"

Briar couldn't stop shaking. On the floor beside the dais, Liefand continued to weep, his ruined eyes hidden behind trembling hands. Guards eventually dragged him away, leaving only a smear of dark fluid on the stones.

The court resumed eating. Conversation picked up again, forcibly cheerful, studiously avoiding any mention of what had just occurred.

And Briar understood, with horrible clarity, exactly what would happen to Síocháin if Malus ever discovered her betrayal. What would happen to anyone who tried to help her. What would happen to Eliam if she failed.

The vial pressed against her hip, a tiny weight that suddenly felt impossibly heavy.

She had to succeed. There was no other option.

Chapter Eighteen

The days blurred together.

Briar stayed in her room, curtains drawn against the weak autumn light. She couldn't bear to look outside, couldn't stand the thought of seeing those golden leaves drifting past her window when she could still feel Malus's hands on her skin.

The bite on her neck throbbed constantly, a dull ache that spiked whenever she moved wrong. She'd looked at it once, in the mirror, and immediately wished she hadn't. The wound was a vivid reminder of everything that had happened at the feast, of his teeth sinking into her flesh while the court watched and applauded.

She stopped looking in mirrors after that.

Food appeared on trays outside her door. She forced herself to eat a few bites here and there, enough to keep functioning, but everything tasted like ash. Her body felt foreign, like something that belonged to someone else. Every time she closed her eyes, she saw the faces of the court watching her, heard the echo of their applause, felt the phantom pressure of Malus's fingers between her thighs.

And Liefand's screams. Those woke her in the night, gasping and drenched in sweat, certain she could smell the rot of his eyes.

She didn't leave the room. Couldn't. The thought of walking those corridors, of seeing any of the fae who had watched her degradation, made her chest seize with panic. So she stayed in bed, or curled in the chair by the cold fireplace, or paced the same ten feet of floor until her legs ached.

The vial of bloodshade was hidden in her vanity, untouched. A reminder of her failure.

On the second day—or was it the third? She'd lost track—a soft knock came at the door.

Briar froze, her heart immediately racing. She hadn't heard footsteps in the corridor, hadn't had any warning. Was it him? Had he come to—

"It's Síochán."

The breath left her in a rush. She crossed to the door on unsteady legs and opened it just enough to let the older fae slip inside.

Síochán took one look at her and her expression tightened with something that might have been grief. "Oh, child."

"I'm fine," Briar said automatically.

"You're not." Síochán guided her to sit on the edge of the bed, then settled beside her. "I heard what happened at the feast. What he did to you. What he did to Lord Liefand."

Briar's hands began to shake. She pressed them flat against her thighs, willing them to stop. "It doesn't matter. I need to try again."

"Briar—"

"I have to." Her voice cracked. "I can't let it be for nothing. Everything he did, everything I let him do... if I give up now, it was all just... suffering. Pointless suffering."

Síochán was quiet for a long moment. When she spoke, her voice was gentle. "There may be other ways. We could try to get word to the Star Court. Or I could attempt to free Lord Eliam myself, create a distraction while you—"

"No." Briar shook her head. "He'd kill you. You saw what he did to Liefand for touching my knee. What do you think he'd do to you for freeing his brother and helping me?"

"I'm old. I've lived long enough."

"No," Briar repeated, firmer this time. "The plan stays the same. We use the blood-shade. We just have to make sure it's actually private this time."

Síochán studied her face for a long moment. Whatever she saw there made her sigh. "You're certain?"

"Yes." Briar reached out and gripped Síochán's hand. "This is the only way." She swallowed hard. "It will work. It has to work."

"And if he decides to make it public again?"

The question made her stomach lurch, but she forced herself to answer. "Then I'll find a way to get through it and try again. As many times as it takes."

Síocháin squeezed her hand. "You're so much stronger than you know."

"I don't feel strong." The admission came out small, broken. "I feel like I'm barely holding myself together."

"That's what strength is, child. Holding together when everything is trying to tear you apart." Síocháin tucked a strand of hair behind Briar's ear. "I'll make sure the wine is ready. And this time, I'll find out where the dinner is being held before you arrive."

"Thank you." Briar's eyes burned with tears that she refused to let fall. "For everything. For risking yourself for me."

"I told you. Old debts." Síocháin rose, smoothing her skirts. "Rest while you can. Eat something. You'll need your strength."

She left as quietly as she'd come, and Briar was alone again.

But the conversation had kindled something in her chest, a small flame of determination that had been guttering since the feast. She could do this. She would do this. For Eliam. For herself. For everyone Malus would hurt if he remained in power.

She forced herself to eat the bread and cheese that had been left on a tray. It still tasted like nothing, but she chewed and swallowed anyway. Then she bathed, scrubbing her skin until it was pink and raw, trying to wash away the memory of hands that weren't there anymore.

She was sitting by the window, hair still damp, when the door opened.

Not Síocháin slipping in quietly. This was someone who didn't need to knock, who walked in like he owned the space—because he did.

Her blood went cold.

The door swung open, and Malus filled the frame.

He looked immaculate, as always. Dark burgundy jacket over a cream shirt, his copper hair gleaming in the corridor light. His smile was warm, almost tender, and that was somehow worse than if he'd been openly cruel.

"There you are," he said, stepping inside and closing the door behind him. "I was beginning to worry."

Briar rose from her chair, acutely aware of how thin her dressing gown was, how vulnerable she felt. "Your Majesty."

"Malus," he corrected, moving closer. "I think we're past formalities, don't you?"

She made herself smile. It felt like cracking glass. "Malus."

"Better." He stopped in front of her, his eyes dropping to the bite wound on her neck, and something flickered across his expression. "How are you healing?"

"Slowly," she admitted, because lying about something he could clearly see seemed pointless.

"I may have taken too much." He reached out, fingers brushing the edge of the wound. She held herself perfectly still, fighting the urge to flinch. "I got... carried away. You bring that out in me."

He said it as if it were a compliment and draining her nearly to the point of death was something she should be flattered by.

"I haven't seen you these past few days," he continued, his hand moving from her neck to cup her jaw. "I've missed you."

"I haven't been feeling well," she said. "The feeding took a lot out of me."

"Of course it did. You're so delicate." His thumb stroked along her cheekbone. "I've been giving you time to recover. But I confess, my patience has reached its limit."

Her heart began to pound.

"I'd like you to join me for dinner tonight." He continued, his eyes held hers, and beneath the pleasant tone was steel. "Just the two of us."

Private. The word sent a complicated rush through her—relief that it wouldn't be another public spectacle, dread at what private with Malus would actually mean.

"I would like that," she made herself say. The words wanted to stick in her throat, but she pushed them out, softened her expression into something approaching eagerness. "I've been hoping... that is, after the feast, I thought perhaps you were displeased with me."

"Displeased?" He laughed softly. "Dear one, you exceeded every expectation. The way you begged me to touch you..." His eyes darkened with remembered pleasure. "I've thought of little else."

Bile rose in her throat. She swallowed it down.

"Then I'll be there," she said. "Tonight."

"Good." He leaned in and captured her mouth with his. She made herself respond even as her stomach turned. When he finally pulled back, his eyes were bright with anticipation. "I'll send someone to escort you at sunset."

He released her and moved toward the door, then paused, looking back over his shoulder.

"Oh, and Briar? Don't keep me waiting. I'm not nearly as patient as my brother was."

The door closed behind him, and Briar let out a shaky breath.

Briar waited several minutes to ensure he was gone and then crossed to the vanity. She knelt, reaching beneath the heavy wooden frame to the small hollow she'd discovered in the ornate carving. Her fingers found the vial where she'd tucked it away and pulled it free. She turned it over in her fingers. Such a small thing. Such a fragile hope.

But it was all she had.

Síocháin arrived an hour before sunset, her expression carefully neutral.

"I confirmed it myself," she said before Briar could ask. "His private dining room. No court, no audience. Just the two of you."

The relief that washed through Briar was almost dizzying. She sank onto the edge of the bed, her hands pressing flat against the mattress to steady herself. "You're certain?"

"I watched the servants set the table. Two places. The wine I prepared is already there, marked with a nick on the label." Síocháin moved to the wardrobe, opening the heavy doors. "Now, let's get you ready."

She reached for a gown in deep burgundy, the color of dying leaves and autumn wine—Malus's colors. Her fingers brushed the fabric.

"Not that one."

Síocháin paused, glancing back at her. "This would please him."

"I know." Briar stood, crossing to the wardrobe. Her eyes scanned the options until she found what she was looking for. Deep emerald silk with an overlay of black lace at the bodice, the pattern intricate and dark against the green beneath. A high collar of sheer lace, structured corset, and a full skirt embroidered with gold leaves and delicate vines.

Eliam's color.

She pulled it from the wardrobe. "This one."

Síocháin's expression shifted—concern, maybe worry. "He'll notice. He'll be angry."

"I know." Briar reached out and touched the fabric, cool silk sliding beneath her fingertips. "That's the point."

"You want to anger him? After what happened at the feast?"

"I want him to ask why I'm wearing it." She looked up at Síocháin, something hard settling in her chest. "And when he does, I'll tell him it's a reminder. A slap in his brother's face. That I chose to wear Eliam's colors while giving myself to Malus."

Understanding flickered in Síochán's ancient eyes. "You'll turn defiance into flattery."

"I'll turn it into proof." Briar stood, beginning to undress. "He's still testing me. If I can convince him I hate Eliam enough to wear green while seducing his brother..." She let the sentence trail off.

Síochán helped her out of her simple day dress, then lifted the emerald gown. "Arms up."

The fabric slid over her head, settling cool against her skin. Síochán moved behind her to work the laces of the corset, pulling them snug but not painfully tight.

"The vial," Briar said. "It needs to go in the bodice. Somewhere I can reach it easily but he won't find it if he..." She couldn't finish the sentence.

"Here." Síochán's fingers found a spot along the inner edge of the corset, just below her left breast. "There's boning on either side. The vial will sit flat between them, and the lace overlay will hide any shape. You can reach it through the neckline without being obvious."

Briar retrieved the vial from its hiding spot beneath the vanity and handed it to Síochán, who tucked it carefully into place. The glass was cool against her skin, a small hard presence she could feel with every breath.

"Can you feel it?" Síochán asked.

"Yes."

"Can you reach it?"

Briar slipped her fingers along the edge of her neckline, finding the vial easily. She could pull it free in seconds if needed. "Yes."

"Good." Síochán stepped back, surveying her work. "Sit. I need to do your hair."

Briar settled onto the vanity stool, watching in the mirror as Síochán began to work. The older fae's fingers were deft, weaving sections into an elaborate updo that left her neck exposed. Small pins studded with dark gems disappeared into the arrangement, catching the candlelight.

"The wine will be there this time, to help you relax," Síochán said as she worked. "But don't drink too much. You need to stay sharp enough to time the bloodshade properly."

"I remember." Briar's reflection looked pale despite the rich color of the dress. The black lace at her throat did little to hide the fading bite mark, the edges still tinged with yellow and purple. She wondered if Malus would comment on it. Wondered if he'd add another one tonight.

"When he's ready to feed," Síocháin continued, "you'll have only moments. Drink the bloodshade, let him bite, and within minutes he'll be unconscious."

"And then we free Eliam."

"And then you run." Síocháin met her eyes in the mirror. "Don't wait for me. Don't look back. Get Lord Eliam and go."

Briar's throat tightened. "Síocháin—"

"I've made my peace with what may come." Her voice was steady, but her hands paused in Briar's hair for just a moment. "Don't throw away your chance at freedom because of sentiment."

"It's not sentiment. It's—"

"It's unnecessary." Síocháin resumed pinning. "I'll create a distraction if needed, delay any pursuit."

Briar wanted to argue, wanted to insist they would all escape together, but the words felt hollow. She didn't know what would happen tonight. Didn't know if the plan would work or if she'd end up back in that throne room, spread open for the court's entertainment while Malus punished her for her defiance.

She pushed the thought away. She couldn't afford to think like that.

"There." Síocháin stepped back. "You're ready."

Briar looked at her reflection. The woman staring back at her looked regal, dangerous even. The emerald gown made her skin glow and her eyes look darker, deeper. The high lace collar gave her an air of untouchability even as the corset pushed her breasts up in obvious invitation. She looked like someone who had chosen to be here, who wanted this.

She looked like a lie made flesh.

"How do you feel?" Síocháin asked.

Briar stood, the full skirt rustling around her legs. The vial pressed against her ribs, a constant reminder of what she carried, what she planned to do.

"Terrified," she admitted. "But I'm not going to let that stop me."

Síocháin's expression softened with something that might have been pride. She looked like she wanted to say something but they were interrupted by a knock came at the door.

"Lady Briar," a servant's voice called. "Lord Malus is ready for you."

Síocháin squeezed her hand once and then slipped out through the servant's entrance without another word.

Briar took one last look at herself in the mirror. Green silk. Black lace. A hidden vial and a desperate plan.

This time, it would work. It had to.

The walk to the dining room felt endless. Each step echoed in the empty corridor, each heartbeat louder than the last. She kept one hand pressed lightly against her bodice, feeling the small shape of the vial beneath the lace. Still there. Still hidden.

The servant stopped before a set of heavy wooden doors and stepped aside without a word.

Briar drew a breath and entered.

The dining room glowed with amber light from dozens of candles, their flames reflecting off crystal and silver. A small table had been set for two, intimate, too close. The smell hit her first—roasted meat, wine, something sweet that made her stomach turn.

Malus stood by the window, his back to her. The coat he wore was exquisite, deep burgundy velvet with copper roses embroidered along the hem and cuffs, the metallic thread catching the candlelight with every small movement. The layered vest beneath matched perfectly, and the dark trousers and polished boots completed the image of a king dressed for conquest.

"Punctual," he said without turning. "I appreciate that."

She moved into the room, the emerald silk of her skirt rustling with each step. The black lace felt suddenly too thin, too revealing, despite the high collar framing her throat. Her heart hammered so hard she was sure he could hear it.

He turned, and his expression shifted. His eyes traveled from the sheer lace at her throat down to the structured corset, lingering on the way the black pattern contrasted against the deep green silk beneath, then slowly rose back up to her face. Something flickered across his features—annoyance, maybe anger.

"Interesting choice," he said, voice carefully neutral.

"You don't like it?" She made herself step closer, fighting the urge to run.

"My brother's color." His jaw tightened. "You come to my table dressed in forest green."

"Exactly." She touched the bodice, her fingers brushing over the lace just above where the vial lay hidden. She tried not to linger too long, but even now she couldn't help but worry that she might fail again, that she might have to repeat this charade over and over. The very thought made her sick. She dropped her hand back to her side, afraid he might see the way it trembled.

She couldn't risk that kind of mistake.

"I thought it was appropriate. A reminder of what he lost. What you took from him." She met his eyes, forcing steadiness into her voice. "Let him rot in his cell knowing even his colors warm your bed now."

The anger blooming in his expression shifted to something else. Interest, perhaps, and pleasure. He crossed to her, his fingers tracing the edge of the high collar where lace met her skin.

"Clever," he murmured. "Vicious, even. I'm impressed."

"I told you. I'm tired of fighting."

His hand moved to her throat, thumb pressing against her pulse. "Your heart is racing."

"I... it's anticipation," she lied.

"Is it?" He leaned closer, inhaling against her hair. "You smell of fear."

She felt her pulse jump, panic creeping in. He knew she was lying. He was just waiting for a chance to expose her. She lowered her eyes, a gesture she hoped would be seen as show of submission, then let some of the truth slip through. "I wasn't certain this would be... private. After the feast, I thought perhaps—"

"You thought I might parade you before the court again?" His smile sharpened. "Did that embarrass you? Being spread open on my throne while my subjects watched you come apart?"

Heat flooded her cheeks. She couldn't meet his eyes. "It was... unexpected."

"Get used to it." His fingers tightened on her throat, just enough to feel the pressure. "You belong to me now, Briar. I will take you wherever I please, whenever I please. In my chambers. In the throne room. In the middle of the great hall while my court dines around us." He tilted her chin up, forcing her to look at him. "Your comfort is not my concern."

She swallowed against his grip. "I understand."

"Do you?" He studied her face for a long moment, then released her throat and stepped back. "We'll see."

He led her to the table, pulling out her chair. The gesture would have been gallant if not for the way his fingers lingered on her shoulders, cold and possessive.

The food was beautiful and excessive—glazed fowl, roasted vegetables that glistened with butter, bread that steamed when broken. Her stomach was too knotted to eat, but she forced herself to take small bites. Each one threatened to come back up.

"Wine?" He gestured to bottles set in a neat row on the sideboard.

"Please." She stood, smoothing her skirts. "Let me."

She went to the bottles, her back to him. There—the tiny nick on one label, barely visible. She poured from the marked bottle into her own glass, the regular into his. The wine was dark, almost purple, and smelled of blackberries and something earthier.

She brought both glasses to the table, setting his down carefully.

"To new beginnings," he said, raising his glass.

She touched hers to his, the crystal singing. The wine was perfect, not too sweet, not too dry. She took a small sip, then another. Already she could feel it working, warmth spreading through her chest, down her arms. Her skin began to feel sensitive, aware of every brush of fabric.

"You're not eating much," he observed.

"Nervous stomach." The truth, for once.

"You have no reason to be nervous." He reached across the table, fingers encircling her wrist. "Unless you're planning something."

Her pulse jumped under his touch. The wine was making his skin feel too warm against hers, making her aware of every point of contact. "What would I plan?"

"I wonder." His thumb stroked the inside of her wrist. "You were so resistant before. Now suddenly compliant. Wearing his colors. Sharing wine with me."

"I explained about the colors—"

"Yes. Very convincing." He didn't release her wrist. "Tell me, what changed? Really?"

She had to give him something true, something he could taste as honest. "When you kissed me. When you... touched me." She made herself meet his eyes. "I... I didn't hate it as much as I should have."

His pupils dilated slightly. "No?"

"No." The wine made the word easier, made her skin flush with false warmth. "And I hate myself for that. But hating doesn't change it."

He studied her face, then released her wrist to stand. "Come here."

She rose on unsteady legs. The wine was working faster than expected, making everything feel soft-edged and too warm. When she reached him, he pulled her close, one hand at her waist, the other tangling in her carefully arranged hair before pulling her face closer.

"Show me," he said against her mouth. "Show me you don't hate it."

She kissed him, made herself kiss him like she meant it, her arms going around his neck. The wine helped, making her body respond. His mouth was hungry, demanding, and she matched it, letting him taste surrender on her tongue.

When they broke apart, both were breathing hard.

"Better," he said. "Much better." His hands roamed, finding the shape of her through the silk. "But I think you're still holding back."

"The food will get cold," she managed, though her voice came out breathier than intended. The wine was making everything feel like too much—his hands, the silk, the air itself.

"Let it." But he led her back to the table anyway, pulling her onto his lap instead of letting her return to her chair. "I find I'm hungry for something else entirely."

She could feel the vial pressing against her skin. Not yet. Too soon, and the blood-shade would lose potency before he fed. She had to wait, had to endure more of this performance.

His mouth found her throat, kissing where he'd bitten before. She shivered, unable to stop the reaction. The wine made everything feel like fire and ice at once.

"This collar," he murmured against her skin, fingers tracing the delicate lace at her throat. "It hides too much."

Before she could respond, he gripped the sheer fabric and tore. The sound of ripping lace was sharp in the quiet room, and cool air hit her newly exposed throat and collarbone. He discarded the ruined pieces without a second glance.

"Better." His mouth returned to her skin, trailing down to where the lace had been. "Responsive tonight."

She shivered, unable to stop the reaction. "Maybe you're seeing who I really am." The lie came easier with wine warming her blood, making her pliant against him.

"Am I?" His teeth scraped her throat, not biting yet, just threatening. "Or are you performing for me?"

Her heart stopped. But his hand was moving up her thigh, and she realized he was teasing, not accusing.

"If I were performing," she said, turning in his lap to face him properly, "would it feel like this?"

She kissed him again, deeper this time, letting the wine guide her body's responses. His groan of approval vibrated through her chest. The warmth recoiled from the contact, but she pressed closer, using her body to hide its retreat.

"No," he said when they parted. "No, this doesn't feel like a performance."

His hands were everywhere now, possessive and sure. The dress felt like nothing between them, silk too thin to be armor. She could feel his arousal pressing against her, could feel her body responding thanks to the wine, and she hated herself for it.

"Bedroom?" he suggested, voice rough.

"No." She kissed him harder, selling the desperation. "Here. Now. I don't want to wait."

He laughed, dark and pleased. "Eager. I like this change." He lifted her onto the edge of the dining table, the wood cold against her thighs. Dishes clattered as he pushed them aside, a wine glass tipping, spreading burgundy across white linen. His hands ran up her legs, fingers finding the edge of her stockings, the bare skin above. The silk of her dress bunched higher with each touch.

"Beautiful," he murmured, spreading her knees wider, stepping between them.

His mouth followed where his hands had been, lips pressing to the inside of her knee. She jerked at the contact—the wine had made her skin feel too thin, every nerve exposed. His tongue traced higher, teeth grazing the soft flesh of her inner thigh, and she had to grip the table's edge to stay upright.

This was her chance. While his attention focused on her legs, his face buried in silk and skin, she fumbled for the hidden pocket in her bodice. The vial was small, smooth glass warm from her body heat. Her fingers were clumsy—from wine, from what his mouth was doing, from fear.

He bit gently at her thigh, and she gasped, her hand freezing. But he took it for encouragement, his mouth moving higher, tongue finding the edge of her undergarments. The wine made her body respond without her permission, wetness gathering, muscles tensing.

She pulled the cork with her teeth, trying to mask the small pop with a moan. The angle was awkward—she had to tilt her head back, pretend she was arching in pleasure while the clear liquid slipped down her throat. Nothing. It tasted like nothing. Like swallowing air.

Five minutes. Maybe less.

His mouth found her center through the thin fabric, and her body jolted. The empty vial nearly slipped from her fingers. She managed to set it on the table beside her, among the scattered dishes, just as his tongue pressed harder.

"Already so wet," he said against her, satisfaction clear in his voice.

She couldn't speak, could only nod as he pulled her undergarments aside. His tongue was direct, skilled, and the wine made her feel every movement like lightning. Her thighs trembled, her hands white-knuckled on the table's edge. She hated that it felt good. Hated that her hips moved toward his mouth without her permission.

He worked her until she was shaking, until the wine and stimulation had her on the edge of something she didn't want. Then he stood, his mouth wet with her, eyes completely black with desire.

His hands went to his trousers, unbuttoning with practiced ease. She watched him reveal himself—hard, ready—and the warmth in her chest recoiled even as the wine made her body clench with anticipation.

"Come here," he said, pulling her forward to the very edge of the table.

She thought he would take her there, but instead he lifted her, her legs automatically wrapping around his waist to keep from falling. He carried her back to his chair, settling with her straddling his lap. She could feel him pressing against her, separated by nothing now.

"Ride me," he commanded, his hands on her hips, positioning her.

She sank onto him slowly, the wine making her body accept him easily. He was different from Eliam—cooler, smoother, wrong. But the fullness made her gasp, made the warmth in her chest thrash with confusion.

"That's it," he encouraged, guiding her hips into rhythm.

She moved, using the wine's effect to make it convincing. Her body knew the motion, the angle, what felt good even when she didn't want it to. His hands roamed—her waist, her breasts through the dress, her throat. Always possessing, always claiming.

Time was running out. She could feel it like a countdown in her blood. The blood-shade diluting with each heartbeat.

She tilted her head back, exposing her throat as she moved on him, finding a rhythm that made him groan. "Bite me."

"What?" His hands tightened on her hips, forcing her down harder onto him.

"Mark me as yours. So everyone knows. So Eliam knows, if he ever sees me again." The words tasted like betrayal. "Make me forget him."

His eyes went dark, pupils blown wide. One hand tangled in her hair, pulling her head further back. "Say it again."

"Bite me. Feed from me. Make me yours."

He didn't hesitate. His mouth found her throat, and she felt the moment his teeth broke skin. The pain burned red hot, but the wine dulled its edges, made it mix with the heat already in her blood.

He drank deeply, groaning against her throat, his hips thrusting up harder as he fed. She felt him swallow once, twice, three times. The bloodshade was in him now, spreading through his system with each pull of her blood.

His free hand moved to the laces of her dress, trying to expose more skin, and she rolled her hips, keeping his focus on pleasure and blood.

Then he paused.

"You taste..." He pulled back slightly, blinking. "Different."

Fear shot through the wine's haze. "Different how?"

"Sweeter. But also..." He shook his head, as if clearing it. "I feel..."

His grip on her hips loosened. She watched his pupils dilate differently now—not with desire but with confusion. The bloodshade was working.

"What did you..." He tried to lift her off him, to stand, but his legs weren't cooperating properly. His cock was still hard inside her but his movements had become uncoordinated, weak.

She slid from his lap, his hands grasping for her as she backed toward the door, watching him struggle.

"You..." His words were slurring now, eyes struggling to focus. "You poisoned..."

"Not poison. Just sleep." She watched him try to reach for something, anything, but his hands wouldn't obey. "I told you I was tired of fighting. I just didn't specify which fight I was ending."

He tried to speak again, but the words wouldn't form properly. His hands scrabbled at the table's edge, trying to keep himself upright.

"You took everything from me," she said quietly. "Now I'm taking it back."

He collapsed back into the chair, eyes rolling back. The last thing he managed was her name—half-curse, half-question.

Then silence.

She stood there shaking, the wine still making her skin feel too sensitive, her body still warm from his touch. Blood trickled from the bite on her throat, and she pressed her hand to it, trying to stem the flow.

One hour. Maybe two. That's all she had.

She ran.

Chapter Nineteen

The corridors beneath the main castle were colder, older. The stones here wept with moisture that smelled of earth and decay. Briar's torn dress dragged through puddles she couldn't see in the dark, the silk heavy and ruined. Every footstep seemed too loud.

"Left here," she whispered to Karse.

They pressed against the wall as footsteps echoed from ahead. Withered. Two of them, their antlered heads turning slowly as they patrolled. Briar held her breath, feeling Karse's heat behind her, ready to burn if needed. The creatures passed, their decayed robes brushing the floor with sounds like dead leaves.

They moved deeper. The warmth in her chest pulled stronger now, reaching for something below. Her throat still bled sluggishly from Malus's bite, each pulse of her heart sending fresh trickles down her chest.

Another patrol. They ducked into an alcove, Briar's back pressed against Karse's chest. His scales radiated warmth, but she couldn't stop shivering. The Withered passed so close she could smell them—rot and winter and ancient earth.

"How much further?" Karse breathed against her ear.

"Next corridor."

Once the coast was clear, they crept forward and stepped around the corner. The hall stretched on endlessly, ending in darkness and shadow. Briar didn't hesitate, passing the door leading to the oubliette without sparing it a glance. The hall narrowed and Briar slowed, angling her steps until she saw the shimmer. It was still there, just as Briar remembered it from what felt like a lifetime ago.

"Are you planning to walk through solid stone?" Karse asked dryly. "Because while I appreciate optimism, I don't think that's how walls work."

Briar moved to the seemingly blank wall, reaching for where the hidden latch would be. "It's here."

"Of course it is. Invisible doors. Fae can't make anything practical."

"Wait."

The voice came from shadows so thick they seemed solid. Briar's entire body went rigid, ice flooding her veins. She spun toward the sound, the warmth in her chest flaring defensive heat.

She knew that voice.

Ferria stepped into the weak torchlight. Her dark hair hung limp and tangled, nothing like the perfect waves Briar remembered. Her dress was torn at the hem, stained with things Briar had no desire to identify. Hollows carved themselves beneath her eyes, and her hands trembled slightly as she raised them, palms out, empty.

"You." The word ripped from Briar's throat, raw and violent. She took half a step towards her, the warmth surged, responding to her rage, wanting to burn. "All of this is your fault."

"I know." Ferria's voice held none of its usual music. Just exhaustion.

"Do you?" Briar took another step forward, and Karse's hand settled on her arm—not restraining, just present. "Do you know what he's done? What your precious Malus has become?"

"I've been living in the walls for three days." Ferria's eyes stayed steady on Briar's face. "Sleeping in service corridors. Eating scraps. I've heard the screams from the great hall. Seen the blood on servants' clothes. Smelled what the Withered do to anyone who resists." Her voice cracked slightly. "Yes, I know what I helped create."

"Then why are you here?"

"Same reason you are." Ferria's gaze shifted to the hidden door. "Eliam."

Hearing Ferria say it, after everything, made Briar's stomach twist.

"You don't get to—"

"I don't care what I get to do." Ferria's flatness cut through Briar's building tirade. "If I could get him out myself, I would. I'd leave you here to whatever end Malus planned. But the Withered don't respond to illusions, and I can't fight them alone."

The honesty was brutal. No apology, no pretense of redemption.

"She could have raised the alarm," Karse said, doing little to temper Briar's mounting fury. "Could have run to Malus the moment she saw us sneaking around. She didn't."

"The dungeons are guarded," Ferria continued. "Heavily. But I know the castle's secrets. Service passages that run parallel to the main routes."

"Why should we believe you?"

"Because I spent years sneaking through this castle to meet with Malus." Bitterness crept into her voice. "Years of planning, scheming, and for what? He promised me Eliam. Told me once he had power, I could have what I wanted. Instead, he throws Eliam in the dungeons and starts feeding on humans like we're back in the Night Court's glory days."

A door slammed somewhere above them. They all froze.

"We don't have time for this," Karse said. "Either we take her with us or we leave her here, but standing around debating gives Malus time to wake up."

Briar's jaw clenched so tight her teeth ached. Every instinct screamed against trusting Ferria. But Karse was right. And Ferria was here, knowing the risk, offering help they might need.

"One wrong move," Briar said quietly, "one hint of betrayal, and Karse burns you to ash."

"Gladly," Karse added, heat-shimmer rising from his scales.

Ferria nodded.

Briar turned to the hidden door again, finding the latch by memory and pressure. The mechanism clicked, and the door swung inward on silent hinges. Cold air rushed out, carrying the scent of deep earth and old water and something else—despair, maybe. The darkness beyond was absolute.

"I'll go first," Ferria said. "If there are guards at the top of the stairs—"

"I'll torch them," Karse said with a shrug.

They stepped through the door, first Ferria, then Briar, then Karse. The moment Briar's foot hit the first step, her fingers found the wall for balance, brushing against the familiar moss. It flared with pale green light at her touch, just as it always did.

She kept her hand on the wall as they descended, the phosphorescent glow lighting their way before fading back to darkness.

"What is that?" Karse whispered from behind, his voice carrying genuine curiosity.

"Luminous moss," Ferria answered flatly. "It grows throughout the lower levels."

The stairs seemed to go on forever, though Briar knew it was just the exhaustion making each step feel heavier.

Behind her, Karse's breathing was controlled but she could feel his heat, his readiness. Ahead, Ferria moved silently, her illusion magic wrapped around her even though it wouldn't work on the Withered.

The warmth in Briar's chest pulled harder with each step down, reaching desperately for what waited below. It knew how close they were.

The door at the bottom of the stairs hung askew, wood rotted through in places, the ancient hinges barely holding. Briar pushed through, the wood groaning and splintering where she touched it. The sound echoed wrong in the space beyond—too big, too hollow.

The chamber opened before them, vast enough that the moss-light couldn't reach the far walls. More of the luminous growth carpeted the floor here, pulsing in slow waves as they entered, casting everything in that sickly green glow. The air tasted of minerals and damp stone, thick enough to choke on.

Cells lined the walls, carved directly from the rock. Most stood open, their bars long since rusted away or torn free. But at the far end, she could see two that remained sealed. Her heart lurched. Eliam was there. She could feel him through the warmth in her chest, that pull so strong now it physically hurt.

"There," she breathed, already moving forward.

The moss beneath her bare feet was slick and cold, squelching between her toes. Behind her, she heard Karse make a disgusted sound—something about the smell—but she didn't care. Eliam was there, just across this empty chamber, just—

Movement.

Not sudden, but wrong. Shapes that had seemed like shadows or stone pillars began to shift. Straighten. Turn.

Six Withered stepped into the moss-light.

They'd been standing perfectly still against the walls, so motionless she'd mistaken them for architecture. Now they moved with that horrible wrongness—too smooth, too synchronized, like puppets on shared strings. Their antlered heads turned toward the intruders in unison.

Briar's blood turned to ice. They were between her and the cells. Between her and Eliam.

The nearest Withered took a step forward. Where its foot touched, the moss black-ened and died, leaving a perfect print of decay. The temperature dropped, her breath suddenly visible in small puffs.

"Well," Karse said behind her, heat already radiating from his body. "This should be fun."

The Withered didn't speak. They never did. They just started walking forward, closing the distance with inevitable purpose, their robes dragging through the moss and leaving trails of rot in their wake.

"Six of them," Ferria whispered. "Too many."

"Speak for yourself." Karse's voice had gone hard, eager. Fire flickered between his fingers, casting dancing shadows on the walls. "I've been cold for days."

The lead Withered raised one decrepit hand, reaching for Briar. She could see the flesh hanging loose on its fingers, could smell the sweet-sick scent of decay rolling off it in waves. The warmth in her chest flared, defensive, but she knew it wouldn't be enough. Not against six.

"Move!" Karse shoved her aside as he unleashed a torrent of flame.

The fire hit the Withered straight on, and for a moment the creature was entirely engulfed. The heat washed over Briar's face, so intense after the cold that her eyes watered. When the flames cleared, the Withered was gone—nothing left but a pile of ash and ancient bone.

Five left.

They didn't react to their companion's destruction. Didn't pause or reassess. They just kept coming, spreading out now to surround the group.

"Can you do that five more times?" Ferria asked, her hands already weaving illusions that Briar knew wouldn't work.

"We're about to find out," Karse said, grinning wickedly.

The Withered spread out, flanking them with that eerie synchronization. One reached for Ferria, its decayed fingers stretching toward her face. She jerked back, throwing up an illusion of herself that stepped sideways—but the creature's hand passed right through it, still reaching for the real her.

"They don't see illusions," she gasped, stumbling backward.

"Then stay behind me." Karse stepped forward, fire roaring from both hands now. Not the concentrated blast that had destroyed the first one, but a wall of flame that forced two of the Withered back. The moss on the floor charred and smoked, filling the air with an acrid stench that made Briar's eyes water.

But the other three kept coming from different angles. One moved toward Briar with that horrible gliding walk, its antlered head tilting as if considering her. She backed up, her bare feet slipping on the wet moss, and her hand found the rusted remains of a cell bar on the ground—broken off, about the length of her forearm.

Without thinking, she swung it at the creature's reaching hand. The moment the metal connected, the Withered recoiled with the first sound she'd ever heard one make—a hiss like air escaping from a punctured lung. Where the metal had touched, its flesh smoked.

"Iron!" she shouted. "The iron hurts them!"

But there was no time to process this discovery. Another blast of fire erupted from Karse, this one aimed at the cells themselves. He was trying to clear a path, but the angle was wrong. The flame hit the bars of one of the occupied cells, and the metal glowed white-hot before starting to bend.

"Karse, wait—"

Too late. The bars twisted and warped, the ancient metal giving way. Part of the cell wall collapsed inward with a grinding crash.

"Was that supposed to happen?" Ferria asked.

From inside the damaged cell came movement, then Thaine appeared in the twisted opening, having to duck through the half-melted bars. He looked terrible—days without food or water had left him unsteady, his usually immaculate clothing torn and stained, dried blood matting his hair from some unseen wound.

"Were you aiming for me," he rasped, "or was nearly incinerating me just a bonus?"

"You're welcome for the rescue," Karse shot back, sending another gout of flame at an approaching Withered. "Though if you're going to complain—"

"Behind you!"

Thaine's warning came just as a Withered reached for Karse from his blind side. The Drak spun, but not fast enough. The creature's fingers brushed his arm, and where they touched, his scales immediately began to gray and flake.

Karse snarled in pain, fire exploding from him in all directions. Briar threw herself flat, feeling the heat sear over her head. When she looked up, another Withered had been reduced to ash, but Karse was favoring his left arm, several scales now dull and cracked.

"Can you fight?" Ferria asked Thaine, pressing something into his hand—a broken piece of chain from his own cell.

"Do I have a choice?" He swayed on his feet but wrapped the chain around his fist. His movements were weak, uncoordinated, but his eyes burned with fury.

Four Withered left, and they were adapting. They moved more carefully now, using the pillars and shadows, making Karse work for his shots. The air grew thick with smoke and the stench of burned moss. Briar's eyes streamed, her throat burning with each breath.

The warmth in her chest pulled desperately toward the remaining sealed cell. Eliam was there, so close, but the fight had spread across the chamber. There was no clear path.

One of the Withered lunged for Ferria. She threw herself sideways, but it caught her dress, and where its fingers touched, the fabric aged decades in seconds, crumbling to nothing. She screamed, more from shock than pain, and Thaine swung his chain at the creature's head. The impact did little damage, but it turned its attention to him.

"Any time you want to burn the rest of them," Thaine gasped, dodging the Withered's grasping hands.

"Working on it," Karse growled, but Briar could see he was tiring. The cold of the dungeons had weakened him, and each blast of fire took more effort than the last.

They were losing ground. Being pushed back toward the stairs. Away from Eliam.

The fight was spreading, pushing them away from where she needed to be. Another Withered fell to Karse's fire, but three remained, and they were learning—keeping distance, using the shadows.

Briar saw her chance when Karse drove two of them toward the far wall with a sustained blast of flame. The third was focused on Thaine, who was barely managing to keep it at bay with wild swings of his chain.

She ran.

Her bare feet slapped against the wet moss, skidding on the slick surface. The sealed cell was just ahead—twenty feet, fifteen, ten. The warmth in her chest burned so hot it hurt, pulling her forward with desperate need.

She reached the bars, her hands wrapping around them without thinking. The metal was cold and rough with rust, flaking under her grip. Through the gaps, she could see him.

Eliam sat against the far wall, wrists shackled with heavy chains. His head was down, white hair falling forward, but at her approach it lifted slightly. Even in the dim moss-light, she could see how pale he'd become, how the days without eating had already hollowed him out.

"Briar." Her name came out cracked, disbelieving.

"I'm getting you out." She pulled at the bars uselessly. They didn't budge. The lock was massive, ancient, and she had no key. Behind her, she could hear the fight continuing—Thaine cursing, Karse's fire roaring, Ferria shouting warnings.

The warmth in her chest pulsed, almost painful now. It wanted out. It wanted to reach him.

"Go," Eliam said, his voice stronger but still rough. "Get out while they're distracted."

"No." She pulled harder at the bars, her palms tearing on the rust. Blood smeared the metal. "I'm not leaving you."

A crash behind her—someone hit the wall hard. Thaine's voice, pained. They were running out of time.

The warmth surged, and she felt it building like pressure under her skin. Not gentle like before, not subtle. This was desperate, violent almost in its need to reach its other half.

"Please," she whispered, not to Eliam but to the magic itself. "Please."

Heat flooded down her arms. Her hands began to glow, that familiar golden light but brighter, more solid. Then the vines came.

They burst from her palms, from her wrists, even growing up from where her blood had touched the bars. Not delicate things—these were thick, woody, thorned. They wrapped around the bars like living things, growing into the gaps, pushing, pulling.

The metal groaned.

"Briar, stop—" Eliam started, but she couldn't. The magic had taken over, pouring out of her in waves.

The vines thickened, multiplied. Golden flowers bloomed and immediately wilted, their petals falling like tears. The bars began to bend, rust flaking away in sheets. Her vision blurred, dark spots dancing at the edges, but she held on.

With a shriek of tortured metal, two of the bars bent outward, creating a gap just wide enough for a person to squeeze through.

The vines crumbled to dust. The light died.

Briar's knees hit the stone floor hard. Her hands were raw, bleeding where the magic had torn through her skin. Everything spun, her body cold and shaking from the effort. She'd pushed too hard, given too much.

But the way was open.

She crawled through the gap, her dress catching and tearing on the bent metal. The stone floor of the cell was damp, cold against her palms. She could barely lift her head, but she forced herself forward, toward where Eliam sat chained.

"What did you do?" His voice was closer now. She felt his hands on her shoulders, trying to steady her. "Briar, what did you—"

"The keys," she mumbled, her words slurring. "Where are the keys?"

"There are no keys. Malus—" He stopped as another crash echoed through the chamber. "You have to go. Leave me."

"No." She forced her eyes open, made herself focus on the shackles. Old iron, but the locks looked different from the cell door. Smaller. More intricate. "There has to be a way."

Her hands were shaking too badly to be useful. The warmth in her chest was quiet now, exhausted from breaking the bars. She could hear the fight getting closer, they were being pushed back.

"Briar." Eliam's hand touched her face, tilting her chin up. Even weakened, even chained, his touch made the warmth stir slightly. "You magnificent fool. You should have run."

"Shut up and help me think," she managed. "How do I get these off you?"

"Briar..."

She ignored him, her mind spinning. "What if... you could break them."

"I don't have strength left." His words were matter-of-fact, resigned.

"You could." She forced herself to meet his eyes, even though everything was spinning. "If you fed."

The temperature in the cell dropped. Even through her exhaustion, she felt him completely still.

"What did you say?"

"Feed on me." The words came out steadier than she felt. "My blood will give you strength."

His hands tightened on her shoulders, not quite painful but close. "How do you—" He stopped, and she saw the moment he understood. His face transformed, even weakened as he was, fury blazing in his eyes. "Malus. He fed on you."

It wasn't a question.

"It doesn't matter—"

"It matters." The chains rattled as he shifted, leaning closer to examine her throat. Even in the dim light, he could see the bite mark, still not fully healed. "My brother put his mouth on you. Drank from you."

"Eliam, please. They're losing out there." There was another crash, closer now. Thaine's voice rose, sharp with pain. "We need you strong."

"No."

"You have to—"

"I don't feed on humans." Each word was clipped, final. "I have never fed on humans. I won't start with you."

"Then we all die here." She grabbed his face between her bloody hands, forcing him to look at her. The warmth stirred weakly in her chest, responding to the contact. "Karse is exhausted. Thaine can barely stand. Ferria's useless against them. You're our only chance."

"I said no."

A scream—Ferria. The sound of fire sputtering out. They were almost out of time.

"Please." Tears ran down her face, mixing with the blood on her hands. "I know what I'm asking. I know what it costs you. But I can't watch you die. Not when I can save you."

"Briar—"

"My blood is different anyway." She was desperate now, words tumbling out. "You know it is. The warmth, the magic—it's yours. Part of you. You wouldn't be feeding on a human, you'd be taking back what's already yours."

His jaw clenched. She could see the war in his face—principle against necessity, revulsion against need.

"They're dying out there," she whispered. "We're all going to die. Please. Please, Eliam. Just this once."

The sounds of battle were getting worse. She heard Karse roar in pain, heard something heavy hit the ground.

Eliam's hands moved to her throat, fingers ghosting over the mark Malus had left. "This will hurt."

"I know."

"I might not be able to stop."

"You will." She tilted her head, exposing her throat. The warmth pulsed stronger, seeming to understand, to offer itself. "I trust you."

He didn't move and for a moment Briar thought he might continue to fight it. Then his mouth was on her throat, not where Malus had bitten but the other side, and his teeth broke skin.

The pain was sharp but brief. Then came the pull—deep, desperate, nothing like Malus's controlled feeding. Eliam drank like he was drowning, like her blood was air. She felt the warmth respond, flowing toward the wound, offering itself eagerly to its other half.

Her hands tangled in his hair, holding him close even as dizziness washed over her. She could feel him getting stronger with each swallow—his grip steadying, his breathing deepening. The chains around his wrists groaned.

"I can't... please, no more," she whispered, but he didn't seem to hear. The pulling sensation intensified. Her vision started to gray at the edges. "Eliam. Eliam, stop."

With visible effort, he wrenched himself away. Her blood stained his mouth crimson, his eyes had gone completely black, no white visible, and for a moment she didn't recognize him.

Then he blinked, and they were just his eyes again, horrified and grateful and furious all at once.

"Briar—"

The chains around his wrists snapped.

He stood in one fluid motion, power radiating from him in waves. The moss on the walls flared brighter, responding to his presence. The very air seemed to thicken with forest magic.

"Stay here," he commanded, and his voice carried the weight of the Forest King even if he no longer held the title.

Then he was gone and she heard the Withered's hissing screech accompanied by the sound of ancient wood growing where no wood should be, and, finally, silence.

Briar stayed where she was, one hand pressed to her bleeding throat, the other flat against the cold stone floor to keep herself upright. The warmth in her chest thrummed with satisfaction, weaker but content.

They'd done it. He was free.

Chapter Twenty

The silence after violence had a weight to it. Briar could hear her own breathing, harsh and too loud in the sudden quiet. She lay on the cold stone floor of the cell, one hand pressed to her bleeding throat, the other flat against the floor to keep the world from spinning.

Ash drifted down like snow—all that remained of the Withered. The air stank of burned moss and decay, making her already churning stomach worse. She could taste copper in her mouth, feel the sticky warmth of blood trailing down her neck, soaking into the torn silk of her dress.

Footsteps. She forced her eyes open, though the effort felt monumental.

Eliam stood over her, and for a moment she didn't recognize him. His eyes were still completely black, no white visible. Blood—her blood—stained his mouth, his chin. Power radiated from him in waves that made the remaining moss flare brighter, as if bowing to their king.

Then he blinked, and they were just his eyes again. Dark, worried, fixed on her.

"Can you stand?"

She tried to push herself up, got as far as her elbows before the chamber tilted sideways. "Not yet."

He knelt beside her, his hands surprisingly gentle as they checked the bite on her throat. She felt him tense when his fingers came away bloody.

"I took too much."

"You took what you needed." Her voice came out rasping, raw. "We're alive."

"Barely." But his arm slipped under her shoulders, lifting her against his chest. Her head fell against his shoulder, and she breathed in the scent of him—forest and rain and something darker now, something that hadn't been there before.

"The others?" she managed.

"Karse has a burn on his arm. Thaine's upright. Ferria's whole." He stood, lifting her with him as if she weighed nothing. "We need to move."

The world swayed as he carried her toward the chamber entrance. She could see the others through blurring vision—Karse cradling his left arm, several scales blackened and cracking. Thaine leaning heavily against a broken cell door, blood matting his hair. Ferria standing apart, her illusion magic flickering around her like nervous energy.

"Can you all walk?" Eliam's voice carried command even though he looked barely better than the rest of them.

"Better than staying here," Karse said, though his usual snark sounded strained.

They moved toward the stairs, Eliam still carrying her. The moss had gone dark, no longer responding to their presence. Her blood had left a trail across the floor—she could see it in the dying light, dark splatters leading from the cell to where they walked now.

The sound started soft. Slow.

Clap.

Clap.

Clap.

They all froze.

"Bravo," Malus's voice drifted down from the stairway, each word precisely enunciated. "Truly. A magnificent performance."

He descended into view, and Briar's heart sank. He looked perfect. Immaculate. His dark burgundy jacket without a wrinkle, his hair copper-bright in the dim light. No sign that she'd drugged him. No indication that bloodshade had touched him at all.

Behind him came more Withered. Six, eight, a dozen, she lost count as they flowed down the stairs like water, spreading out to block any possible exit.

"I particularly enjoyed the bloodshade," Malus continued, reaching the bottom of the stairs. "Clever. Though you might have used a stronger dose. I was only unconscious for—what? An hour?" He examined his nails, casual as if discussing the weather. "Síocháin suffered beautifully for her part, by the way. Did you know fae as old as her can survive quite extensive damage? We're still discovering exactly how much."

No.

Briar tried to push herself up in Eliam's arms, but he tightened his grip, keeping her still.

"Malus," Eliam said, his voice flat.

"Brother." Malus smiled, and it was all teeth. "How lovely to see you free. And feeding on humans, no less." His gaze fixed on the blood still staining Eliam's mouth. "How the mighty have fallen. All those principles, all those years of refusing to take human blood, and look at you now. Covered in it. Reeking of it."

"Let us pass."

"Let you pass?" Malus laughed, the sound echoing off stone. "After the trouble you've caused? After what she—" his eyes found Briar, "—put me through? No, I don't think so."

The Withered moved closer, their antlered heads turning in unison. The temperature dropped, frost beginning to form on the wet stones.

"Though I must say," Malus continued, his attention still on Briar, "she was delightful. So responsive once properly motivated. Did she tell you how sweetly she submitted? How her body sang when I—"

"Don't." Eliam's voice was barely human, more growl than word.

"Oh, she didn't tell you." Malus's smile widened. "She came to my chambers wearing your colors. Kissed me with such enthusiasm, letting me explore every inch of her while she moaned so prettily. And her blood when aroused—exquisite. Like honey and copper and complete submission."

Briar felt Eliam's arms turn to stone around her. The temperature dropped further, but this cold came from him, from fury so complete it changed the very air.

"Given time," Malus added, almost conversationally, "I plan to train her properly. Teach her to crave my touch instead of just enduring it. She was already on her way to learning, weren't you, dear one?"

She couldn't look at anyone. Couldn't see their faces. The shame burned worse than the wound on her throat.

"Get close to me," Eliam said quietly. Too quietly.

Karse moved first, understanding danger when he heard it. Thaine stumbled over, his hand finding Karse's shoulder for support. Ferria hesitated, then stepped near, her face carefully blank.

"Karse." Eliam's voice stayed level, controlled. "How much fire do you have left?"

The Drak flexed his burned hand, scales scraping. "Enough. If you need it."

"I'm going to need it."

Malus laughed again. "Planning something, brother? While you can barely stand? While holding your bleeding pet?" He gestured, and the Withered began moving forward. "Take them. Don't harm the girl—she's mine. The others are disposable."

The Withered glided across the floor, their robes trailing through puddles of blood and ash. That sweet-sick smell of decay grew stronger, thick enough to choke on.

Eliam set Briar down, carefully, propping her against Thaine who caught her with his good arm. She wanted to protest, but her legs wouldn't hold her. The blood loss made everything feel distant, underwater.

"When I say run," Eliam said under his breath, "you run."

The floor beneath them groaned.

No—not groaned. Grew.

Thorns erupted from the stone, black wood spiraling up between them and the advancing Withered. Not a wall—a maze of brambles, each thorn as long as her hand, weaving and spreading with violent speed. The Withered hit the barrier and immediately began their work, decay spreading wherever they touched.

"Karse," Eliam said. "Now."

Fire roared. Not the controlled bursts from before, but everything Karse had left, a wave of flame that caught the brambles and turned them into a blazing wall. The Withered recoiled—even they couldn't walk through that inferno.

The heat washed over them, so intense Briar's eyes watered. She could hear Malus shouting something, but the roar of flames drowned him out.

Eliam grabbed her again, pulled her tight against him. "Everyone hold on."

Ferria gripped his arm. Karse grabbed Thaine and Eliam's shoulder. The shadows at their feet began to move, to rise, to wrap around them like living things.

"No," Malus's voice cut through the fire's roar. "You don't get to—"

The world tilted.

Shadow-walking felt like drowning in reverse. Like being pulled up through black water, unable to breathe, unable to see. Briar's stomach turned inside out. Her lungs burned. The wound on her throat tore wider from the pressure.

Then air. Cold, clean air that tasted of pine and night.

They collapsed in a heap on frost-covered ground. Trees surrounded them—not the twisted things near the palace but healthy pines, their needles rustling in wind that didn't smell of decay.

Briar rolled onto her hands and knees, dry heaving. Nothing came up—there was nothing in her stomach—but her body tried anyway. Beside her, Thaine was actually vomiting, his body rejecting the violence of shadow travel.

"We're not far enough," Eliam gasped. He was on his knees too, shaking from the effort. Shadow-walking that many people, even just to the forest edge, had cost him. "He'll follow. We need to—"

"Move," Karse finished, dragging himself upright. His burned arm hung useless at his side, but he pulled Thaine up with the other. "Can anyone run?"

"I can." Ferria was already standing, illusions shimmering around her. "I'll hide our trail."

"Won't matter," Eliam said, getting to his feet, pulling Briar up with him. "He'll track my magic."

They stumbled forward through the darkness. Eliam was half-carrying, half-dragging her, and every step sent her vision swimming. The trees pressed close, identical pines that offered no landmark, no sign they were going the right direction.

Behind them, something roared. The sound wasn't human, but it wasn't entirely fae either. It was pure rage given voice.

"He's coming," Ferria said unnecessarily, her illusions flickering weakly around them.

Then Briar heard it. The sound was like dried leaves skittering across stone, but it was wrong somehow. It was too purposeful, and there were too many sources.

"What is that?" Thaine started to ask.

The first creature dropped from the trees onto his shoulder. It was cat-sized, with mottled grey skin and eyes that glowed red in the darkness. Its mouth opened to reveal rows of needle teeth, and Thaine screamed.

Karse grabbed it and burned it to ash instantly, but more were coming. Dozens of them poured from the underbrush and scrambled down tree trunks. Their chittering filled the air like angry insects.

"Run!" Eliam shouted, but there was nowhere to run. The creatures were everywhere, swarming around their feet and leaping for exposed skin.

One latched onto Briar's torn dress and climbed rapidly toward her throat. She tried to bat it away but her movements were too slow and too weak. Its claws dug through fabric to find flesh, and she felt those teeth graze her neck.

Fire burst around them in a protective circle. Karse stood at the center with flames pouring from his good hand, holding the creatures at bay. But she could see the effort was costing him, and he was starting to sway.

"I can't hold this for long," he gasped.

The creatures pressed closer, testing the edge of the flames. Their chittering grew louder and more aggressive. One darted through a gap in the fire and went straight for Ferria. She shrieked and her illusions exploded around her in panic, but the creature passed right through them.

That's when the stars began to fall.

No, not stars, but arrows made of pure light, streaming from the trees ahead. Each one struck true, piercing the corrupted pixies and making them dissolve into shadow and smoke.

"Get down!" a familiar voice commanded.

They dropped to the ground, and more arrows sailed overhead. The creatures scattered with furious chittering, but more light-arrows found them.

Figures emerged from the forest. They were Star Court guards in silver armor that seemed to glow with its own light. At their head stood Arion.

The Star Court prince looked different than he had at court. He wore practical armor that still somehow looked like captured starlight. His expression was cool and focused as he nocked another arrow.

"Can you run?" He didn't wait for an answer. "We need to reach the border because more are coming."

As if summoned by his words, another wave of the creatures poured from the darkness. But now there were Star Court soldiers forming a protective circle around them.

"Move!" Arion commanded.

They ran, or tried to run, while the Star Court forces held the creatures back. Arrows of light flew continuously, and each impact lit up the forest for a moment. The vicious pixies kept coming, wave after wave, but the soldiers were disciplined and their formation held.

Briar struggled to keep up, but it wasn't long before her legs gave out completely. Eliam swept her up without breaking stride, though she could feel him trembling with exhaustion. Around them, the battle continued to move. The Star Court forces were walking backward now, maintaining their defensive line while retreating toward the border.

"How did you know?" Eliam asked Arion between ragged breaths.

"Your water sprite reached us," Arion replied, firing three arrows in rapid succession. "He said you were taken prisoner."

Frederick had made it. Despite everything, the little sprite had gotten through. Briar wanted to cry from relief, but she had no tears left. Her body felt disconnected from her mind, floating somewhere above the pain.

Arion sent another arrow flying into the chaos. "Is it true? Has Malus taken the throne?"

"Yes." Eliam's voice was flat, emotionless, but Briar could feel the tension in his arms, the way his grip on her tightened slightly. "He holds the Forest Court. The lords kneel to him. The forests answer to him."

"Then he's the legitimate Forest King." Arion's tone held something careful, calculating. "If he crosses into Star Court territory now, it's an act of war."

"He won't care," Eliam said. "He wants her back. She belongs to him by law."

The words hit deep. It didn't matter what she did, as long as Malus was king, she belonged to him. By the bargain she'd made, by the marks on her skin, by what he'd taken from her in his chambers.

"The law," Arion said quietly, "is not always the same as what is right."

A pixie broke through the line and launched itself at her face. She couldn't even flinch. Her body had nothing left to give. Arion's hand shot out, and suddenly the creature was simply... elsewhere. Not dead, just gone, relocated to somewhere that wasn't here.

"The border is just ahead," one of the guards called.

Through the trees, Briar could see the standing stones glowing blue in the darkness. So close. After everything, safety was just yards away. The warmth in her chest pulsed weakly, reaching toward those stones like it knew sanctuary waited beyond.

But the chittering behind them was getting louder, and underneath it, she could hear something worse. Footsteps that made the ground shake, and a voice raised in fury that she recognized too well. The same voice that had whispered against her skin, that had commanded her to be present while he—

Malus had arrived.

The trees behind them began to groan and split. Not from physical force but from will alone. Even from here, she could feel his rage like heat from a forge. He was bending his domain, forcing it to reshape around his fury. The Forest King coming to reclaim what he considered his.

Her stomach turned. She pressed her face against Eliam's shoulder, trying to block out the memory of Malus's hands, his mouth, the way he'd made her body respond despite her mind's revulsion. But she could still feel him approaching, like pressure building before a storm.

"Keep moving!" Arion commanded and his soldiers tightened their formation, their arrows of light becoming a constant stream.

They broke through the final line of trees and the standing stones rose before them like ancient sentinels, each one taller than two men and carved with symbols that glowed steady blue in the darkness.

The light they cast was cold and clean, nothing like the sickly green of dungeon moss or the dying gold of corrupted forest magic. Briar could feel the difference in the air even from yards away—it tasted lighter, carried the scent of winter stars rather than decay.

Arion's soldiers tightened their formation around them, a wall of silver armor and drawn bows. Their arrows remained nocked, points of captured starlight aimed back at the tree line where Malus had emerged.

The corrupted pixies circled in the shadows between trees, their chittering a constant background noise that made her skin crawl. But they didn't advance. Something held them back.

Eliam's arms tightened around her as he carried her forward. She could feel his exhaustion in the way his muscles trembled, in how each step seemed to require conscious effort. Shadow-walking that many people should have been impossible. That he'd managed it at all spoke to how much of her blood he'd taken, how desperately her essence had poured strength back into its other half.

The warmth in her chest pulled toward those stones with weak insistence. Safety. The promise of it made her throat tighten, made the tears she'd been holding back threaten to spill over. Just a few more yards. Just across that invisible line and—

"Stop."

Malus's voice carried across the distance between them, cold and precise as a blade. Not shouted. He didn't need to shout. The command in it made even the Star Court soldiers pause, though Arion gestured sharply for them to keep moving.

"I said stop."

This time the words held weight that had nothing to do with volume. Fae magic, the kind that bent reality around a king's will. The ground between them and the stones began to crack, thin fissures spreading across frost-covered earth. Not an attack. A statement. I could stop you if I chose.

They halted. The soldiers' grips tightened on their weapons, but Arion raised one hand and the formation held. Waiting. Briar could feel Eliam's jaw clench where her head rested against his shoulder, could sense him preparing to shadow-walk again if needed, though she didn't know if he had the strength left for it.

Malus stepped fully from the tree line, and the corrupted pixies parted around him. He looked exactly as he had in his chambers—dark burgundy jacket without a wrinkle, copper hair catching what little light remained. His eyes found her immediately, pinning her in place with an intensity that made her stomach turn.

She remembered those eyes above her. Watching her face while he moved inside her. Studying her reactions like she was an experiment to be solved.

Her body tried to curl in on itself, to make itself smaller, but there was nowhere to hide. Eliam's arms were the only barrier between her and that gaze, and they suddenly felt far too thin.

"Arion of the Star Court." Malus's attention shifted, though Briar could still feel the weight of his awareness on her like physical touch. "We find ourselves in an interesting position."

"Lord Malus." Arion's voice carried none of the warmth she'd heard in it before. This was court formality, prince to king, careful and cold. "You stand at the border of Star Court lands. I assume you have a reason for this... visit."

"Visit." Malus's smile was sharp enough to cut. "Is that what we're calling it?" He gestured toward their group, his hand moving with casual elegance. "You shelter my brother, who until recently was considered a criminal in my court. You harbor his huntsman, who abandoned his post. You provide sanctuary to—" his eyes found Briar again, "—property that belongs to me by law and binding contract."

Property. The word made bile rise in her throat. Because it was true. By every law that governed the fae courts, she was his. The bargain she'd struck, the marks on her throat that even now rustled like real autumn leaves when the wind picked up—all of it bound her to him as surely as chains.

"The girl came to us seeking sanctuary," Arion said, his tone still carefully neutral. "As did your brother. We do not turn away those who request our protection."

"Protection." Malus took a step closer to the border, and Briar felt Eliam tense, ready to move. "From what, exactly? From facing the consequences of theft? Of assault? Of poisoning a king?" Each word was measured, precise. "She drugged me. Attacked me in my own chambers. Freed my prisoners and fled with them into the night. These are not the actions of someone seeking protection. These are crimes."

The autumn marks at her throat tightened slightly, responding to his words, to his proximity. Not painful yet, but present. A reminder that he could reach her even from across the border, even through distance and stone and wishful thinking.

"Crimes," Arion repeated, and something shifted in his voice. Still formal, but with steel beneath it now that Briar hadn't heard before. "Or self-preservation? I've heard interesting reports from the Forest Court. About changes in tradition. About a return to old ways that many thought best left forgotten."

Malus's smile widened. "Ah yes. The Star Court's famous moral superiority. How comfortable it must be, to judge from your pristine halls, never having faced real hardship, real hunger, real need." He took another step, close enough now that Briar could see the decay beginning to form on the ground at his feet. "Tell me, Prince Arion, have you ever gone without? Ever felt your power dimming, your essence depleting, your very self fading because you refused to take what you needed to survive?"

"We survive without feeding on humans," Arion said flatly. "As your brother has for centuries."

"My brother." Malus's attention shifted to Eliam, and the temperature dropped further. "My dear, principled brother. Who stands before me now with human blood staining his mouth. Who reeks of it. Who broke his most sacred rule because—what? Desperation? Or did you finally accept that your high-minded principles were nothing but performative nonsense?"

Briar felt Eliam's arms turn rigid around her. The shadows at their feet stirred, responding to his rage, but he said nothing. His jaw worked like he was physically holding words back.

"Nothing to say?" Malus pressed, his voice carrying across the distance with cruel amusement. "No defense of your choices? No explanation for why you, who spent centuries lecturing me about the sanctity of human life, and then locked me away for it, would drain this particular human nearly to death?"

"She gave it willingly," Eliam said, his voice rough and low. "To save her own life and ours. That's the difference."

"Is it?" Malus tilted his head, considering. "Because from where I stood—or rather, from where I lay unconscious because she poisoned me—it looked quite similar. You took what you needed. You fed. You let her blood make you strong again." His smile turned vicious. "Welcome to reality, brother. We're not so different after all."

"Though I must say," Malus continued, his eyes still fixed on Eliam, "you're missing out on the full experience, brother. Her blood is exquisite, yes, but you really should try it when she's properly... receptive." His smile turned predatory. "When her body is warm and wanting, when she's arching beneath you—that's when it truly sings. The fear you tasted? That's bitter. But arousal?" He made a small sound of appreciation. "Like honey and sunlight and complete submission all at once."

The warmth in Briar's chest recoiled violently, pulling so deep inside her that she felt it like a physical withdrawal. She wanted to press her hands over her ears, to unhear his words, but her arms wouldn't cooperate. The blood loss had left her weak and shaking, barely able to hold herself upright even in Eliam's arms.

"I'll be dreaming of it," Malus added, his gaze sliding back to her. "Of the next time. Of all the ways I'll make that sweet blood flow for me again. And you'll be there in my dreams too, won't you, dear one? Feeling me call to you through those pretty marks on your throat."

Eliam's whole body trembled with the effort of not moving, not attacking. The shadows around their feet had grown thick and restless, reaching toward Malus like grasping hands before Eliam forced them still.

"You've made your position clear," Arion said, his voice cutting through the tension before Eliam could respond. "What exactly are you proposing?"

Malus's attention shifted back to Arion, and Briar saw the calculation in his eyes. The careful weighing of options, of risks and rewards. His jaw tightened almost imperceptibly before smoothing back to that pleasant mask.

"What I'm proposing," he said slowly, each word chosen with precision, "is that you return what is mine. Immediately. Before this becomes... complicated."

"Complicated," Arion repeated. "You mean before it becomes war."

"If you prefer that term." Malus spread his hands in a gesture that might have looked reasonable if not for the decay still spreading from his feet, creeping toward the border stones. "Though I find it strange that the Star Court would risk open conflict over one human woman. Surely she's not worth the lives that would be lost. The destruction. The years of bloodshed that would follow."

The corrupted pixies chittered in the trees behind him, a rustling chorus that sounded almost like laughter. Several of them crept closer to the border, testing, their red eyes reflecting the blue glow of the standing stones. The Star Court soldiers shifted, arrows tracking the movement, but the creatures didn't cross. Not yet.

"You speak of war," Arion said, his tone still carefully measured, "as if invading Star Court territory would not be an act of aggression itself."

"Invading?" Malus's eyebrows rose in mock surprise. "I stand at the border, as is my right. I make no aggressive moves. I simply request the return of stolen property." His eyes found Briar again, and she felt the autumn marks pulse in response. "Though if you choose to keep what belongs to me, if you choose to harbor criminals and thieves, then yes. That would constitute an act of war. One that you would be starting, not I."

The words were carefully chosen, she realized through the fog of exhaustion and blood loss. He was framing it so that any conflict would be the Star Court's fault, to make Arion the aggressor, not him.

"The Forest Court just regained its rightful king," Malus continued, his voice carrying that reasonable tone that made her skin crawl. "After years of... mismanagement. My lords and ladies are still adjusting to proper rule. Still remembering what it means to have a king who doesn't let sentiment cloud judgment." His gaze flicked to Eliam.

There it was, the real reason behind his hesitation. He couldn't afford to look weak and risk his newly reclaimed throne by starting a war over her. Not when he'd criticized Eliam for caring too much about a human.

But she could see the rage in him, barely contained beneath that pleasant mask. The way his fingers flexed at his sides, the slight tension in his jaw. He wanted to cross that border. Wanted to tear through the Star Court soldiers and take her back. The only thing stopping him was politics.

"So you're giving us a choice," Arion said. "Return her willingly, or face war."

"I'm giving you an opportunity," Malus corrected. "To avoid unnecessary conflict. To be reasonable." His smile was sharp as broken glass. "After all, what is one life weighed against thousands? What is her comfort—her preference—compared to the safety of your people?"

Briar felt Eliam's arms tighten around her, felt Karse shift closer, his good hand radiating heat. But she also felt the weight of truth in Malus's words. How many would die if the courts went to war? How many families destroyed, how many lives ended, all because she didn't want to go back?

"Think carefully, Prince Arion," Malus said, his voice dropping lower, more intimate. "You built the Star Court on principles of protection and sanctuary. Noble ideals. But are those ideals worth watching your people burn? Worth seeing your beautiful halls reduced to rubble?"

He paused and when no one spoke he continued.

"I'll make this very simple," he said. "I am the legitimate Forest King. She belongs to me by binding contract and fae law. If you keep her, you commit an act of theft against a ruling monarch. That is grounds for war." He paused, letting that sink in. "The question is whether you're willing to face those consequences."

The chittering of the pixies grew louder, more agitated. The cracks in the ground between them and the stones widened slightly, frost crawling along their edges. The temperature continued to drop, her breath misting in the air, and she realized with cold clarity that he was showing them what war would look like. The corruption spreading. The decay. The slow death of everything the Star Court had built.

"Think about it," Malus said, his voice almost kind now, which made it worse somehow. His eyes found hers again, and she felt the autumn marks pulse against her throat. "Is she really worth it?"

The question wasn't just for Arion. It was for all of them. For Eliam, who held her against his chest with arms that still trembled from exhaustion. For Karse, whose burned arm hung useless at his side. For Thaine, barely able to stand. All of them broken and bleeding because of her choices, her mistakes, her desperate attempt to escape what she'd bargained herself into.

"You have no answer?" Malus's smile turned cruel. "How telling. Perhaps you're already realizing the inevitable." He stepped back from the border, just one step, but it felt like a concession pulled from him against his will. "When you come to your senses, you know where to find me. My patience is not finite, don't make me wait long."

His gaze locked on Briar one final time, and when he spoke, his voice carried across the distance as clearly as if he whispered directly in her ear. "And you, dear one. You can run to whatever sanctuary you like, hide behind whatever court offers protection. But you're mine and every night when you close your eyes, I'll be there. Waiting. Calling. Until you remember that your place is with me."

The marks tightened suddenly, not quite painful but impossible to ignore. A promise and a threat wrapped together. She could feel his magic through them, testing the distance, the barriers, looking for any weakness to exploit.

Then he turned, his coat swirling around him, and walked back into the forest. The corrupted pixies followed, their chittering fading as they disappeared into the darkness between trees. The cracks in the earth remained, frost-filled and wrong, a reminder of what stood just beyond the border.

For a long moment, no one moved. The Star Court soldiers kept their arrows trained on the tree line, waiting for another attack that didn't come. Briar could hear her own breathing, harsh and uneven, could feel Eliam's heart hammering where her cheek pressed against his chest.

"Move," Arion said finally, his voice tight. "Get them across. Now."

They crossed the border in a rush, soldiers forming a protective barrier as they passed between the standing stones. Briar felt the change immediately, the oppressive weight of Malus's presence lifting. The blue glow of the stones washed over her, and the warmth in her chest pulsed with something like relief.

But the autumn marks at her throat remained. Still pulling, still reminding her that no matter how many borders she crossed, she carried her chains with her.

The moment they were fully on Star Court land, her body decided it had endured enough. The darkness that had been creeping at the edges of her vision rushed in all at once, and she felt herself going limp in Eliam's arms.

She heard voices, Arion shouting orders, Karse cursing, someone running, but they sounded distant, underwater. The last thing she was aware of before consciousness left completely was the warmth in her chest settling, content now that it was near its other half, even as the autumn marks at her throat whispered promises she didn't want to hear.

Then nothing.

Chapter Twenty-One

Consciousness returned in fragments, like pieces of a shattered mirror slowly reassembling. First came awareness of warmth—not the oppressive heat of Malus's chambers or the cold bite of healing magic, but something alive. A heartbeat that wasn't hers, steady and strong beneath her ear. Arms wrapped around her middle, holding her against a chest that rose and fell with each breath. The scent of forest and rain and something darker, something that made the warmth in her chest pulse with recognition.

Eliam.

She kept her eyes closed, not ready to face whatever came next. Not ready to see his expression, to deal with questions or the aftermath of everything that had happened. Her throat ached where Malus had bitten her, where Eliam had fed. Her body felt heavy, disconnected, like it belonged to someone else entirely.

The room around them was quiet except for their breathing. She could hear wind beyond windows, the soft crackle of a dying fire. The bed beneath them was impossibly soft, furs and silk that smelled of winter flowers. Star Court chambers, then. Safety, or at least the illusion of it.

She felt the moment Eliam's breathing changed, the subtle shift from sleep to waking. His arms tightened around her reflexively, pulling her closer, and she heard him draw in a sharp breath through his nose. His whole body went rigid against her back.

"You're awake," he said, his voice rough from sleep but carrying something else underneath. Not quite relief. Not quite anger. Something raw that she couldn't name.

She didn't answer, couldn't find words. The silence stretched between them, filled only by the crackle of dying embers and the wind beyond the windows.

His hand moved from her waist, sliding up to her throat with careful deliberation. His fingers found the bite marks—both of them. Malus's on one side, his own on the other. She felt him go completely still as he traced the wounds with his fingertips, mapping the damage with a gentleness that felt wrong coming from him.

"How long?" Her voice came out cracked, barely recognizable.

"A day and a half." His hand didn't leave her throat, fingers resting against her pulse. "Your body needed time to recover from the blood loss."

From feeding him. From giving him enough of herself to break those chains, to shadow-walk them all to safety. The memory made her throat tighten, made the marks pulse with a dull ache.

"The others?" she managed.

"Alive. Recovering." His thumb stroked along the side of her neck, almost absently, like he was reassuring himself she was real. "Karse's arm is healing. Thaine is being insufferable about his heroics. Ferria is... present."

The way he said Ferria's name carried weight. They would deal with her betrayal later. There were too many other things to process first.

She tried to sit up, needing to see him, but his arms locked around her like iron bands.

"Don't," he commanded, his voice dropping to something darker. "Don't move."

"Eliam—"

"I said don't." His grip tightened almost painfully before he forced himself to loosen it. She could feel the tremor running through his muscles, the barely controlled violence of whatever he was holding back. "Just... stay still. Let me—"

He didn't finish. His hand remained on her throat, fingers pressing against her pulse like he needed to count each beat, to confirm she was alive and whole and here.

The silence stretched again. His breathing was too controlled, too measured. The kind of control that came from holding something massive back, from keeping emotions at bay through sheer force of will.

"I fed on you," he said finally, the words coming out flat, emotionless in the way that meant he was feeling too much.

Her heart lurched. Here it was. The thing she'd been dreading. The acknowledgment of what had happened in that cell, when she'd tilted her head and offered her throat and let him drink from her.

"I know," she whispered.

His hand on her throat tightened slightly, then loosened again. "I've never—" He stopped. Started again. "Human blood. I don't take human blood."

"I'm sorry," she said, the words escaping before she could stop them.

His whole body went rigid. "What?"

"I—I didn't know what else to do. How to save you." Her voice cracked. "Malus said it made him feel stronger so I thought that it would help—but after everything he did to me, my blood was—was ruined. Tainted. I'm—"

He moved so fast she didn't have time to finish. One moment he was behind her, the next he'd turned her roughly to face him, his hands on her shoulders, his face inches from hers. His eyes were completely black, pupils blown wide with rage or anguish or both.

"Stop," he said, the word coming out harsh. "Stop talking."

She stared at him, her heart hammering. His grip on her shoulders was almost painful, his whole body tense like a coiled spring ready to snap.

"You think—" He stopped, his jaw clenching. "You think that I'm disgusted by what I tasted?"

"Aren't you?" The question came out small, broken.

His hands moved from her shoulders to her face, cupping her jaw with a gentleness that contrasted sharply with the violence she could see barely contained in his expression.

"I'm furious," he said, each word deliberate and controlled. "I'm so angry I can barely think straight. But not at you."

She blinked, confused. "Then—"

"At myself." His thumbs traced her cheekbones, his touch achingly gentle. "At my brother. At every single lord who supported his claim to the throne, the entire situation that put you in his chambers in the first place."

The rawness in his voice made her chest tighten. This wasn't the cold, controlled Forest King. This was something else entirely. Something wounded and furious and barely holding together.

"When you were there," he continued, his voice dropping lower, rougher, "I felt it. Here." He brought her hand to his chest. "I could feel your fear. Your pain. Something was hurting you, terrifying you, and I couldn't reach you. Couldn't stop it. I was going mad trying to understand what was causing it, trying to break free, and I couldn't." His hand tightened on her face. "And now I know. Now I know exactly what he did, what you had to endure, and I want to tear him apart. I want to make him suffer for every second of fear I felt from you, for every moment of pain."

Not at you. He wasn't angry at her, wasn't disgusted or blaming her for what her body had done, for the choices she'd made to survive.

The tears came without warning, hot and fast, spilling down her cheeks before she could stop them. Great, shaking sobs that tore from her chest and made her whole body tremble. She tried to pull away, to hide her face, but his hands held her steady.

"Briar—" His voice held uncertainty now, the kind that came from someone who didn't know how to handle this. "Don't—you don't need to—"

But she couldn't stop. The tears kept coming, days of fear and violation and shame finally breaking through the walls she'd built around herself.

For a moment he just stared at her, his hands still cupping her face, clearly at a loss. Then he pulled her against his chest. His arms wrapped around her, crushing her close, one hand coming up to cradle the back of her head.

"Stop crying," he commanded, but there was no force behind it. Just helplessness. "I don't—I can't—" He made another frustrated sound. "Just stop."

But he held her tighter even as he said it, his hand stroking her hair with unexpected gentleness.

Eventually, the tears began to slow and his hand continued stroking through her hair, like he was petting something wild that might bolt if he stopped.

"Humans," he said finally, "are absurdly fragile. Emotionally and otherwise. I should probably just keep you wrapped in cotton and locked in a room somewhere."

Despite everything, Briar huffed a laugh. "Deal with it," she managed, her voice muffled against his chest.

"I'm trying." His hand moved from her hair to her jaw, tilting her face up to his. Her eyes were swollen, her cheeks blotchy and wet, and she probably looked terrible, but he just studied her with that intense focus he brought to everything. "You're a disaster."

"Your disaster," she said without thinking.

Something shifted in his expression. His thumb traced along her jaw, then lower, finding the pulse beneath the bite marks. For a moment they just looked at each other, and she could see him weighing something, deciding something.

Then he kissed her.

It wasn't gentle, it was desperate and claiming and full of everything he couldn't put into words. His mouth moved against hers with an intensity that spoke of fear and relief and possessive need.

Her body went rigid.

She couldn't help it. The memories crashed over her without warning—Malus's mouth on hers, his hands holding her in place, the wine making her body respond while her mind screamed. The taste of autumn and rot and wrongness. The way he'd smiled against her lips, knowing exactly what he was doing to her.

Eliam felt it immediately. He pulled back like she'd burned him, his hands releasing her face, his whole body going still.

"Briar—"

She stared at him, her heart hammering, her breath coming too fast. The fear was still there. The memory of Malus's violation, the way he'd taken her choice, her control, her body's responses and twisted them into weapons against her. She could still feel the phantom weight of him, still taste that wrong autumn sweetness.

But she could also feel Eliam pulling away, could see him withdrawing, closing himself off, and she realized with sudden, fierce clarity that this was exactly what Malus would want. For her to flinch from Eliam's touch and the trauma to poison what they had, for it to continue violating her even now, even here, even safe in Star Court chambers.

He'd taken enough from her. Her dignity. Her sense of safety. Her body's autonomy. But he wouldn't take this. Wouldn't take Eliam, not again.

She grabbed Eliam's face between her hands and pulled him back down, crushing her mouth to his before fear could win.

Her hands rose to tangle in his hair, her body pressing against his. When his lips parted in surprise, she deepened the kiss. She poured everything into it—defiance and determination and a desperate need to replace Malus's touch with something that was hers.

Eliam made a sound against her mouth, half moan and half something darker. His hands came to her waist, and after a moment of letting her lead, something shifted. His grip tightened, turning possessive, and he took over the kiss with an intensity that stole her breath. His tongue swept into her mouth and she felt herself responding despite the lingering fear.

His hands moved from her waist to her hips, pulling her flush against him, and she gasped at the contact. The kiss turned rougher, his teeth catching her lower lip hard enough to sting. One hand slid up her back to tangle in her hair, tilting her head to give him deeper access.

She wanted this. Her body was responding, the warmth in her chest singing with recognition and need. But underneath it, anxiety threaded through like a dark current. The memory of hands that took without asking, of her body responding when she didn't want it to, of pleasure twisted into a weapon.

The kiss slowed.

He pulled back just enough to look at her, his eyes still dark with desire but searching her face. She opened her mouth to apologize, to explain, but he just shook his head. His hands released her hair, her hip, moving instead to pull her against his chest.

"You need more rest," he said, his voice rough. "Before I can properly bed you."

The words struck her as odd. She'd been half-drowned and hypothermic after the river, and that hadn't stopped him. This? This was different.

His mouth found her throat. His teeth scraped against the bite marks Malus had left there, then bit down. The pressure was hard, deliberate, and she gasped, her hands clutching at his shoulders.

"You're mine," he said against her throat. He bit again, lower this time, marking her collarbone. "Always mine."

Each bite was firm enough to leave a mark, firm enough to hurt. Even as he pulled back she could feel the bruises forming, a constellation of possession across her throat and shoulder.

He settled her back against the pillows, pulling her into his arms with a firmness that suggested argument would be useless. One arm wrapped around her waist, holding her against his chest, while his other hand splayed possessively across her stomach.

"Sleep now," he demanded. "You're still recovering."

A thought crept in unbidden. What if he was lying? What if he didn't want her anymore, not really, and this was just—

"If you don't stop thinking whatever you're thinking," he said against her hair, "I'll take you right now and make sure the entire Star Court hears it."

The threat was so unexpected that she let out a startled laugh. His arms tightened around her.

"I mean it," he continued. "I'll have you screaming my name loud enough that Arion comes running. Let everyone in this pristine, proper court know exactly who you belong to."

She huffed out a small laugh against his chest. "I'm sure that would go over well."

"I don't particularly care what goes over well in the Star Court." His hand on her stomach pressed possessively. "Now sleep or keep thinking foolish thoughts and suffer the consequences. Don't say I never gave you choices."

She closed her eyes, letting herself relax against him. His heartbeat was steady beneath her ear, his arms solid around her, and for the first time since Malus had taken her, she felt like maybe, eventually, she might be okay.

She slept, finally, without dreams.

Briar woke to the weight of being watched. Even before she opened her eyes, she knew Eliam was there, that particular intensity of his attention a physical thing she could feel even through sleep. She snuggled further into downy blankets piled over her body while the warmth in her chest pulled steadily—no longer desperate but constant.

"How long will you pretend to be asleep?"

Pushing the blanket down, Briar turned to see Eliam sitting in a chair beside the bed, fully dressed in clothes that were undoubtedly borrowed from the Star Court's wardrobe. They fit him well enough, but something about seeing him in cream and blue instead of his usual jeweled tones felt wrong, like he was wearing someone else's skin.

He was watching her with that particular intensity that meant he'd been doing it for a while. His expression was unreadable, caught somewhere between possession and something darker, more complicated.

"How long have you been sitting there?" Her voice came out rough from sleep.

"Long enough." His eyes tracked her movement as she pushed herself upright, the blankets falling away from her shoulders. "Arion sent word three hours ago. Everyone's gathering in the council room."

Three hours. The words hit her with sudden panic. She threw the covers back, her body protesting the quick movement.

"Three hours?" She swung her legs over the edge of the bed, her feet finding the cold floor. "Why didn't you wake me? They're all waiting, I've kept everyone—"

"Stop." The command in his voice made her freeze mid-movement. He stood from the chair, crossing to her in two strides. His hands found her shoulders, firm enough to keep her in place. "Your recovery is the top priority. If that means they wait three hours or three days, they'll wait."

"Eliam, if Arion gathered everyone—"

"I don't jump because the Star Court prince says so." His thumbs pressed against her collarbones, grounding and possessive. "You needed rest. Everything else can wait."

She stared up at him, seeing the steel in his expression, the absolute refusal to compromise on this particular point.

"You can't just make people wait because—"

"I can, and I did." His hands slid from her shoulders to cup her face, tilting it up to his. "They'll wait as long as I decide they need to wait. Your body needed time to recover from what I took from you, from what he did to you. A few hours of their inconvenience means nothing measured against that."

The arrogance of it should have irritated her, but instead she felt something warm settle in her chest that had nothing to do with the fragment of his essence living there. He was being completely unreasonable and absolutely unmovable, and somehow that steadiness felt like safety.

"Are you ready now?" he asked, his tone shifting slightly, becoming less command and more question. "Or do you need more time?"

She considered his words. Her body felt heavy, disconnected, but functional. The worst of the exhaustion had faded with sleep, leaving behind only the bone-deep weariness that she suspected wouldn't leave for days yet.

"I'm ready," she said. "We need to figure out what to do about... everything."

His expression darkened and his hands dropped from her face. He offered a curt nod and moved to the wardrobe across the room.

"The Star Court provided clothes," he said, opening the ornate doors to reveal an array of gowns in various shades of blue and silver and white. Colors that would mark her as belonging to this court, to Arion's protection. He stood there for a moment, his hand resting on one of the silver dresses, then moved past it with clear dismissal.

His fingers found a gown near the back, pulling it free from the others. The fabric was a deep sage green, darker than the vibrant emerald of his Forest Court but unmistakably green nonetheless. Not his color exactly, but close enough to make a statement.

"This one," he said, laying it across the bed. Then, quieter, "You look best in green."

She looked at the dress, understanding what he was doing. Marking her as his even here, even wearing borrowed clothes in another court's territory. It was possessive in a way that would have made most people balk, but for Briar it was proof that nothing fundamental had changed between them, that Malus hadn't succeeded in poisoning what they had.

"Alright," she said quietly, a small smile tugging at the corners of her mouth.

She stood, reaching for the hem of the oversized sleep shirt someone had dressed her in, but her arms felt leaden and uncooperative. The simple act of lifting the fabric over her head became a struggle, her muscles protesting.

Eliam was there immediately, his hands covering hers. "Let me."

There was a moment where her body went rigid, instinct screaming at the memory of hands on her, removing clothes, controlling her movements. But this was Eliam. Not Malus. The difference mattered.

She lowered her arms and let him draw the shirt up and over her head, the fabric whispering against her skin. The cool air of the room hit her bare skin and she fought the urge to cover herself, to hide the bruises that still shadowed her ribs, the healing bite marks that decorated her throat and shoulder.

His eyes tracked over her body, cataloging every injury with an expression that went completely cold. She saw his jaw clench, saw murder flash through his eyes before he forced it away.

"I'm going to kill him," he said quietly, almost conversationally. "Slowly."

"Get in line," she managed, trying for levity and falling short.

His hands found her waist, steadier than hers would have been, and he guided her arms into the dress sleeves one at a time. The fabric was soft against her skin, cool silk that warmed quickly. He moved behind her to work the laces, his fingers deft and practiced.

"I've dressed you before," he said, his voice dark with amusement. "Though usually I was more interested in the reverse."

Despite everything, she felt her lips quirk slightly. "I remember."

His hands worked the laces and when he finished, his fingers lingered at the small of her back, pressing gently through the fabric.

"Turn around," he said.

She did, and found him watching her with that intense focus he brought to everything. His hands rose to her hair, finger-combing through the tangles with unexpected gentleness. She'd expected him to leave it, to declare it fine as it was, but instead he gathered it carefully, his touch light against her scalp.

"What are you doing?" she asked.

"You can't go to a council meeting looking like you just woke from a three-day fever dream." His fingers twisted her hair into something simple, securing it with pins that had been left on the bedside table. "Even if that's exactly what happened."

The intimacy of it caught her off-guard. This wasn't desire or possession or claim. This was care, quiet and practical and utterly focused on her comfort rather than his wants.

When he finished, his hands framed her face, thumbs brushing her cheekbones. "Better."

She realized she wasn't afraid of his touch right now, wasn't fighting the urge to pull away or brace for something unwanted. The panic that had gripped her when he'd kissed her earlier had faded, leaving behind only exhaustion and the steady warmth of his presence.

He noticed. She saw it in the way his expression shifted, something easing in his shoulders.

"Progress," he said softly, almost to himself.

"Small steps," she agreed.

His hands dropped from her face and he stepped back, offering his arm with surprising formality. "Ready to face the disaster waiting for us?"

She took his arm, feeling the solid strength of him beneath her fingers. "As ready as I'll ever be."

The walk to the council room took longer than it should have. Briar's legs felt disconnected from her body, each step requiring conscious effort. The day and a half of unconsciousness had let her wounds heal, but her body still remembered the blood loss, the trauma, the violation. Everything moved too slowly, like she was underwater.

The Star Court hallways gleamed around them, all crystalline surfaces and captured starlight that felt too bright, too clean after the decay of Malus's court. Her bare feet made no sound on the smooth floors, but Eliam's boots clicked with each step, marking their progress.

They reached the council room doors and Eliam paused, his hand sliding from her back to her waist. His grip tightened slightly, possessive and protective both.

"If you need to leave," he said quietly, "just say it."

She nodded, though leaving felt impossible. They needed to decide what to do, needed to plan, and she was at the center of every problem they faced. Running from this conversation wouldn't make any of it less real.

The doors opened.

The room beyond was smaller than she'd expected, more intimate than the grand halls she'd seen in the Star Court. A long table dominated the space, carved from what looked like a single piece of pale wood that seemed to glow from within. Windows lined one wall, offering a view of gardens blooming in colors that shouldn't exist together.

Everyone was already there.

Sian stood near the windows, her water-sprite nature making her seem like she might dissolve into mist at any moment. When she saw Briar, her face transformed with relief and she crossed the room in three quick steps, arms already reaching.

Briar felt Eliam tense beside her, but he didn't stop Sian from wrapping her in a careful hug. The embrace was gentle, mindful of injuries, and smelled of fresh water and something floral that Briar couldn't name. It lasted only a moment before Sian pulled back, her hands lingering on Briar's arms.

"I'm so glad you're alright," Sian said, her voice thick with genuine emotion. "We were so worried."

"Thank you," Briar managed, her throat tight. The simple comfort of the hug had made something crack in her chest, threatening tears she couldn't afford right now.

Arion stood near the head of the table, and she saw him notice the exchange. Something flickered in his expression before he smoothed it away. He moved toward them, slower than Sian had, more conscious of the territorial fae lord between them.

"Briar." His voice held warmth but also careful respect for Eliam's presence. "It's good to see you awake."

She saw him wanting to reach for her, to offer comfort the way he had before, but Eliam's hand on her waist turned to iron. The warmth in her chest pulsed, reaching toward Arion with weak recognition, and she felt Eliam go completely rigid beside her.

"Prince Arion," Eliam said, his tone perfectly neutral in a way that meant nothing was neutral at all. "Thank you for your hospitality and for sending aid when Frederick reached you."

The formal words hung in the air, a reminder of debts and politics and the careful dance they all had to perform.

Karse stood against the far wall, his burned arm wrapped in what looked like spider-silk bandages. His golden eyes found hers immediately, assessing, calculating. He gave a single nod that acknowledged her presence without offering comfort or sympathy. Drak didn't traffic in either.

Thaine occupied the opposite corner, looking better than he had any right to after everything. The blood had been washed from his hair, and someone had given him fresh clothes, though she noticed he still favored his right side where the worst injuries had been. When their eyes met, he offered a slight smile that held approval. She'd survived. That was enough.

Halian sat at the table, his usual gentle demeanor strained. His eyes kept flicking to the corner where Ferria stood, guarded by two Star Court soldiers. Her brother's distress was palpable, a war between loyalty and knowing what his sister had done.

Ferria herself wouldn't meet Briar's eyes. She stood perfectly still between her guards, her face carefully blank. The illusion magic that usually shimmered around her was absent, suppressed or simply abandoned. Without it, she looked smaller somehow, more vulnerable, but Briar knew better than to trust that appearance.

"Please, sit," Arion said, gesturing to the chairs. "We have much to discuss."

Eliam guided Briar to a seat, his hand never leaving her until she was settled. Then he took the chair beside her, close enough that their arms brushed, close enough to make his claim obvious to everyone in the room.

The tension was thick enough to choke on.

Arion remained standing at the head of the table, his expression settling into something more formal, more princely than the warm friend she'd known in their brief time together.

"We're here to address several urgent matters," he began, his gaze sweeping the room before they landed on Ferria, and his voice hardened. "We'll start with you."

The room went silent, waiting. Ferria stood perfectly still between her guards, her face carefully blank.

"You are accused of conspiring with Malus to overthrow the Forest Court," Arion said, his tone carrying the weight of formal judgment. "Of betraying the Star Court's trust by acting as his agent while under our protection. Of manipulating Briar Washington through deception and coercion, providing her the means and motive to release

Malus from his imprisonment. Of participating in the capture and torture of Lord Eliam of the Forest Court." He paused, letting each accusation settle. "Do you deny any of these charges?"

"I never—!" She stopped, gaze sweeping the room again. The silence stretched as everyone waited for her to speak, to defend herself, to offer some explanation for the betrayal. "It wasn't supposed to be like this. Eliam was never... I helped them escape," she said finally, her voice steady. "That should count for something."

The words landed wrong, too calculated, too focused on shifting blame away from everything she'd done before.

"You helped him escape after participating in his capture," Arion said, his tone sharp. "After working with Malus to overthrow the Forest Court. After lying to us all."

"Malus used me too," Ferria said, her voice growing desperate. Briar felt rage spike hot in her chest. "He promised me things, told me what I wanted to hear. I was as much a victim of his manipulation as the human girl was."

The comparison was too much.

"No." The word came out harsh, louder than Briar intended. Every eye in the room turned to her. "You were not a victim the way I was a victim. Don't you dare try to compare the two."

Ferria's jaw tightened, but she didn't respond.

"You chose to work with him," Briar continued, her hands fisting in her lap. "You chose to lie to me to give me the means and the motive to find Malus and release him. You knew I was desperate... ignorant. You told me yourself that if you could have freed Eliam without me, you would have left me there. You made choice after choice, and now you want to act like you had no control over any of it?"

"I was trying to survive," Ferria said, her voice rising slightly. "Trying to protect myself in an impossible situation."

"Survive?" Briar's voice cracked. "You have no idea what surviving is."

"I freed Eliam," Ferria repeated, desperate now to prove herself against the weight of the crimes she'd committed. "I got him out. That means—"

"It means you have a sense of self-preservation," Eliam said, his voice cold enough to freeze. "It means you realized Malus wouldn't need you anymore once he had what he wanted. It doesn't absolve you of anything."

Halian shifted in his seat, his distress obvious. "She's still my sister," he said quietly, though the words sounded like they cost him. "Whatever she's done, she's family."

"Family who committed treason against this court," Arion said, his tone gentler when addressing Halian but no less firm. "She aided in the torture and imprisonment of a sovereign lord. She manipulated and endangered others to serve her own interests."

"Kill her," Eliam said flatly. "She's earned that much."

"No!" Halian stood abruptly. "Exile her. Lock her away. But not death. Please."

Arion's expression suggested he was calculating political equations Briar couldn't fully grasp. The Star Court's relationship with the Forest Court, the delicate balance of power between courts, the message any judgment would send.

"She's a member of the Star Court," Arion said finally. "Technically, she falls under my jurisdiction, and killing her without proper trial would create complications we don't need right now."

"Then hold the trial," Eliam said, voice calm though Briar could feel the tension radiating off of him in waves.. "Find her guilty. Execute her."

"We don't have time for a full court trial," Arion countered. "Not with everything else we're facing."

"So she walks free?" The edge in Eliam's voice could have cut stone.

"No." Arion's gaze returned to Ferria. "She'll be imprisoned. Held in secure chambers under guard until this situation with Malus is resolved. After that, we'll decide her ultimate fate."

"You're imprisoning me?" Ferria's carefully neutral expression cracked slightly. "For how long?"

"As long as necessary," Arion said. "Be grateful Halian loves you enough to plead for your life, because I'm inclined to agree with Eliam's assessment."

He gestured to the guards. "Take her to the lower chambers. No visitors, no communication with anyone outside. If she tries to use magic, you have permission to bind her completely."

The guards moved to escort Ferria out. She went without resistance, but as she passed Briar, she finally met her eyes. What Briar saw there wasn't remorse or apology. It was calculation, a promise that this wasn't over.

Then she was gone, the door closing behind her with a soft click that felt too quiet for the magnitude of what had just happened.

The room breathed out collectively.

"One problem addressed," Arion said, returning to the head of the table. "Now for the harder ones."

Chapter Twenty-Two

The silence after Ferria's departure felt heavier somehow, weighted with all the problems they still had to solve. Briar watched Arion return to his position at the head of the table, his expression settling into something grimmer than before.

"The second matter," he said, his gaze moving to Briar, "is the bargain that binds you to Malus."

The autumn marks at her throat seemed to rustle in response to being mentioned, copper leaves chiming softly against her skin. She resisted the urge to touch them, to feel how deeply they'd rooted themselves into her flesh.

"I don't understand how he can claim her," Arion said, frustration threading through his voice. "The bargain was with you, Eliam. How does overthrowing you give him rights to it?"

"The wording," Eliam said, his voice flat. "When Briar made the bargain, it wasn't with me specifically. It was with 'the Forest King.'" He paused, letting that sink in. "Words matter in fae law. The bargain doesn't care who I am. It cares about the title. Malus holds the title now, so the bargain is his."

"That can't be right," Sian said, her voice carrying more hope than certainty. "Surely there's some clause, some way to—"

"There isn't." Thaine's tone was gentle but firm. "Fae bargains are absolute. Once made, they stand."

Arion's expression darkened. "So transferring the throne transferred the claim."

"Yes." The word came from Eliam, sharp and bitter. "And as we saw at the border, he has no intention of releasing it."

Briar felt Eliam's hand find hers under the table, his fingers lacing through hers with almost bruising pressure. The warmth in her chest pulled toward him, seeking comfort, seeking home.

"There has to be a way to break it," Sian said, though her voice carried more hope than certainty.

"The only ways out are death of the bargain holder, willing release, or completion of terms," Eliam said. "But her bargain has no completion terms. She gave her life. That means it holds until she dies."

The words settled over the room like a shroud. Until she dies. Decades, if she was lucky. A lifetime of belonging to Malus.

"So we kill him," Karse said from his position against the wall. "Problem solved. Next?"

"He's the legitimate Forest King now," Eliam said. "Protected by laws and loyalties I no longer command. Getting close enough to kill him would require an army."

"Which would mean war," Arion said. "Something we're trying to avoid."

Briar found her voice, though it came out smaller than she wanted. "What if I just... went back? Maybe if I cooperated, if I didn't fight him—"

"No." Eliam's response was immediate, absolute. His hand tightened on hers. "That's not an option."

"But if it would prevent war—"

"I said no." His eyes had gone dark, that possessive fury she'd seen before rising to the surface. "I don't care if it would prevent the apocalypse. You're not going back to him."

"What about another bargain?" Halian suggested carefully. "If Briar made a new bargain that superseded the old one—"

"With who?" Karse asked. "And what would she trade that she hasn't already given? She bargained her life. There's nothing larger than that."

"She could bargain with me," Arion said quietly.

The room went completely still. Briar felt Eliam go rigid beside her, his hand turning to stone around hers.

"No," Eliam said, his voice deadly calm.

"It's an option we should consider," Arion continued, his eyes on Briar rather than Eliam. "I have the authority as a ruling prince. A bargain made with me could poten-tially—"

"She's not making a bargain with you." Eliam's words carried the weight of absolute refusal.

"There might not be another solution," Arion said, finally meeting Eliam's gaze. "If she's bound to Malus and we can't break that binding, then perhaps binding her to another court—"

"Would just add another chain," Eliam cut him off. "She'd still belong to my brother and to you. That's not freedom, that's making things worse."

Arion was quiet for a moment, and when he did speak again, his voice low.

"And when exactly did you start caring about her freedom? You kept her in your court, in your bed, under your control for months. You marked her, claimed her, paraded her in front of your entire court as your possession. So forgive me if I find your sudden concern for her autonomy a bit convenient."

The temperature in the room dropped. Eliam went completely still.

"Careful," Eliam said, his voice deadly quiet.

"No, I don't think I will be careful." Arion leaned forward, his expression harder than Briar had ever seen it. "Because this isn't about her freedom at all, is it? This is about the fact that she doesn't belong to you anymore. That Malus has what you consider yours."

"Arion—" Halian started, but the prince held up a hand.

"Tell me I'm wrong," Arion pressed. "Tell me that if I offered her a bargain that gave her actual choice, actual freedom to leave any time she wanted, you'd support it. Tell me you wouldn't fight just as hard against that as you're fighting against this."

Eliam stood slowly, his chair scraping against the floor. "Say one more word and hospitality won't save you."

Briar felt the warmth in her chest pulling frantically between them, confused and distressed by the conflict. She opened her mouth to speak, to stop this before it escalated further, but Sian beat her to it.

"This isn't helping," Sian said firmly, her voice cutting through the tension. "Fighting about who's wronged her more doesn't solve the problem of Malus."

"She's right," Thaine said quietly. "We need to focus on the actual issue."

Arion and Eliam continued to stare at each other across the table, neither willing to back down. Briar could see the argument wasn't really about her, or not just about her. It was about something else, something in how the warmth responded to both of them.

"Eliam," Briar said quietly, squeezing his hand. "Sit, please."

For a moment she thought he might refuse, might let his rage carry him into something he'd regret. Then his jaw clenched and he sank back into his chair, though his posture remained rigid, ready to lash out if the occasion called for it.

Arion followed suit, but his expression stayed hard.

"The bargain transferred once already," Thaine observed quietly. "When the title changed hands. Could it transfer again?"

"To who?" Karse asked. "His majesty there doesn't have the title anymore."

"Not officially," Thaine agreed. "But I've seen the forest respond to him for centuries. Titles are political constructs. The forest itself might see things differently."

Eliam shook his head. "The forest answers to Malus now. It's letting him rule, letting him command its full power. That's answer enough."

"Is it?" Thaine pressed. "The forest took years to fully accept you after you took the throne. What if it simply hasn't decided yet?"

"That's speculation," Eliam said flatly.

"Most solutions to impossible problems start as speculation," Karse said from the wall.

Eliam's jaw worked, his hand still gripping Briar's. She could feel him thinking, working through possibilities with that sharp mind that had ruled a court for centuries.

"A new bargain could work," he said finally, reluctantly. "Worded to acknowledge the existing one but allowing the forest to choose who holds it. If the forest recognizes me despite the political situation, the bargain would transfer back. If it doesn't..." He stopped, his expression darkening.

"If it doesn't?" Briar prompted.

"Then the existing bargain would fight the attempt," Eliam said, his voice carefully controlled. "It would interpret a new bargain as an attack, a violation. The marks would defend themselves."

"How badly would it hurt her?" Arion asked, voicing what everyone was thinking.

Eliam's hand tightened on hers. "I felt it when the bargain first transferred to Malus. The marks changing, reshaping themselves. The pain was..." He paused, clearly choosing his words carefully. "Considerable. And that was the bargain accepting a legitimate transfer. Forcing it against its nature would be worse."

"How much worse?" Briar needed to know.

His eyes found hers, and she saw the war happening behind them. The desire to protect her from pain fighting against the knowledge that she deserved the truth.

"The marks would constrict," he said finally. "They'd try to enforce the existing bargain, to punish what they see as rebellion. It would feel like drowning, like being crushed."

The room had gone silent, everyone processing what that meant.

"But if it works?" Briar pressed. "If the forest chooses you?"

"Then the marks would change again," Eliam said. "They'd recognize me as the rightful holder of the bargain."

Briar thought about Malus's voice at the border, the way he'd promised to call to her through the marks, to make her feel him no matter where she ran. She thought about belonging to him for the rest of her life, about what he would do with that power, with that kind of access.

"I want to try," she said.

"Briar, you're still recovering," Sian protested.

"I want to try," she repeated, meeting Eliam's eyes. "Because doing nothing means I'm his until I die. At least this way there's a chance."

She saw him wanting to argue, saw him ready to refuse, but something in her expression made him stop. His jaw clenched, and she watched him wrestle with the desire to protect her from pain and the knowledge that protection wasn't what she needed right now.

"The wording would need to be precise," he said finally, the words coming out rough. "Acknowledging the existing bargain while asking the forest to choose. Something like..." He paused, working through it. "'My life was given to the Forest King in bargain. I ask the forest to show me its true king, and to that king alone shall I belong.'"

"Would that work?" Halian asked.

"Maybe." Eliam's expression suggested he had doubts. "If the forest is willing to choose. If it recognizes the distinction between title and truth. If a dozen other things go right that I can't predict."

"And if they don't?" Karse asked.

"Then she suffers for nothing," Eliam said bluntly. "And we're back where we started, except she's been put through agony for my arrogance in thinking I could outsmart a binding I created in the first place."

Briar squeezed his hand, drawing his attention back to her. "It's not arrogance to try. It's arrogance to assume we can't even attempt to fix this."

Something shifted in his expression, the harsh lines softening slightly.

"Alright," he said finally. "But the moment it starts to go wrong, I'm stopping it. I don't care if we're halfway through, if there's still a chance. The moment you're in too much pain, we stop."

"Agreed," Arion said before Briar could argue.

Eliam stood, Briar's hand still wrapped in his, and pulled her up with him. "Everyone else step back. If this goes badly, I don't want anyone close enough to interfere."

The others moved away from the table, giving them space. Briar felt her heart hammering, felt the autumn marks at her throat already seeming to sense something was coming. They rustled against her skin, copper leaves chiming soft warning.

Eliam turned to face her fully, both his hands finding hers now. His expression was focused, intense, but underneath she could see his fear. Not for himself. For her.

"Ready?" he asked quietly.

She nodded, not trusting her voice.

"Then repeat after me," he said. "My life was given to the Forest King in bargain."

"My life was given to the Forest King in bargain," she echoed, her voice steadier than she felt.

The autumn marks pulsed once, acknowledging the truth of the statement.

"I ask the forest to show me its true king."

Briar took a steadying breath. "I ask the forest to show me its true king." The marks pulsed again, but this time there was resistance in it. A warning.

"And to that king alone shall I belong."

"And to that—" Briar felt the marks beginning to stir. "To that king alone shall I—"

The marks seized her throat, cutting off air before she could finish the words. The copper leaves turned sharp as blades, pressing into her skin with brutal force. She couldn't breathe. Couldn't speak. Her hands flew to her throat as though she could somehow stop what was happening through force alone.

Eliam's own marks flared in response, burning across her shoulder and arm where he'd claimed her. Fire meeting constriction, two competing magics warring for dominance while her body became the battlefield.

She tried to scream but no sound came out. The marks were squeezing tighter, tighter, cutting off air, cutting off everything. Her vision started to gray at the edges, black spots dancing across her sight.

Through the agony, she felt Eliam's hands on her face, heard him shouting something, but the words were distant, underwater. The warmth in her chest was thrashing, trying to help, trying to fight, but it was too weak, too depleted from everything they'd already endured.

The autumn marks squeezed harder.

Then Eliam's magic surged.

It poured through their connection with violent force, shadows and thorns and forest power crashing against the autumn marks like a wave against stone. Not trying to destroy them but to force them back, to make them loosen their grip just enough for her to breathe.

The competing magics screamed against each other, the autumn marks fighting viciously, recognizing the challenge, refusing to yield. Eliam's power pushed harder, and somewhere in the chaos she heard him speaking, commanding, pouring authority and will into words she couldn't quite hear.

The marks loosened. Just slightly. Just enough.

Air rushed into her lungs and she gasped, the sound harsh and desperate. Her knees buckled and Eliam caught her, pulling her against his chest, one hand cradling the back of her head while the other pressed flat against her back.

"No more," he commanded, and she realized he was talking to the magic, to the bargain, to everything that was trying to tear her apart. "Enough!"

Finally the autumn marks settled back against her skin, no longer actively trying to kill her but still there, still claiming her for Malus. Briar stayed pressed against Eliam's chest, shaking uncontrollably.. Her throat felt raw, bruised, like invisible hands had tried to strangle her.

"I've got you," Eliam said against her hair, his voice rough. "You're alright. I've got you."

Sian appeared at her elbow with a glass of water, her expression stricken. "Here. Small sips."

Briar took the glass with trembling hands, barely able to hold it steady. The water burned going down her abused throat, but it helped. She managed a few swallows before her stomach threatened to rebel.

"It didn't work," she said finally, her voice coming out as barely more than a rasp.

"No," Eliam agreed, his arms still tight around her. "The forest either can't choose or won't. The bargain stays with Malus."

"So we're back to killing him," Karse said, his tone carrying no sympathy, just cold practicality. "I did mention that was the simplest solution."

"Getting close enough to kill him isn't simple," Arion said, though he sounded tired now, the earlier anger drained out of him. "Not with the entire Forest Court protecting him."

"Then we find a way to get close," Karse said. "Or we accept that she belongs to him and start a war. Personally, I'm okay with either."

"We're not accepting anything," Eliam said, his voice carrying that cold authority that meant the discussion was over. "But we're also not solving this tonight. Briar needs rest."

"I'm fine," Briar protested, pulling back to look at him. "We need to figure out what to do, we need—"

"You need rest," Eliam cut her off. "You just survived having a bargain try to strangle you. You're done for today."

"Eliam—"

"Not a discussion." He stood, pulling her up with him, one arm staying firmly around her waist when her legs wobbled. "We'll reconvene tomorrow. The problems will still be there, and you'll be in better shape to face them."

"But—"

He simply turned toward the door, his arm around her the only thing keeping her upright. She wanted to argue, to insist she could keep going, but her body betrayed her. Her legs felt like water, her throat ached with every breath, and exhaustion was crashing over her in waves now that the adrenaline was fading.

"Tomorrow," Arion said, and she couldn't tell if he was agreeing with Eliam or just acknowledging the inevitable. "Get some rest, Briar."

Sian touched her arm gently as they passed. "I'll check on you later."

Eliam guided her out of the council room, his hand never leaving her waist. The hallway felt impossibly long, each step requiring more effort than the last. By the time they reached the chambers Arion had given them, she was leaning heavily against Eliam's side, her pride the only thing keeping her from asking him to carry her.

He shut the door behind them with a soft click that felt like a barrier against the world. The room was warm despite the open terrace doors, a fire crackling in the hearth and candles floating overhead in that distinctly Star Court way that made everything feel ethereal and slightly unreal.

A table had been set near the terrace, laden with food that steamed gently in the cool air flowing through the open doors. Someone had anticipated their needs, or perhaps

Arion had sent word ahead. Either way, the sight of actual food made Briar's stomach clench with sudden, desperate hunger.

"Come," Eliam said, his hand at the small of her back guiding her toward the table. "You need to eat."

She wanted to argue, to say she was fine, but her body betrayed her with a stomach growl loud enough to make him raise an eyebrow. Heat crept into her cheeks as she let him pull out a chair for her.

Through the open doors she could feel winter in the wind that drifted through carrying a bite that hadn't been there days ago.

"It'll snow soon," she said, the observation coming from nowhere, from the need to fill silence with something safe and mundane.

"Inevitably." Eliam said as he sat across from her, already filling a plate with bread, cheese, and fruit. He set it in front of her before preparing his own. "The Star Court keeps winter at bay within its borders, but you can feel it waiting beyond."

She picked up a piece of bread, tearing it into smaller pieces more from habit than intention.

The meeting kept replaying in her mind—Ferria's deflection, the failed bargain attempt, the way the autumn marks had tried to strangle her. Arion's accusation that Eliam didn't actually care about her freedom.

"Eat," Eliam said, his tone carrying command but also something gentler underneath. "Or do you require my assistance?"

She forced herself to take a bite, then another. The food was good, simple and real in a way that made her realize how long it had been since she'd eaten anything. After all she'd been through, her body needed fuel even if her mind was too chaotic to care.

They ate in silence for a while and soon Briar felt the exhaustion creeping back in now that she'd stopped moving. Her throat still ached from where the marks had constricted, and every swallow reminded her that she belonged to Malus, that nothing they'd tried had changed that fundamental truth.

She reached for her water glass and paused, her hand hovering over it.

Something Malus had said seemed to drift like a phantom to the forefront of her mind. It had been in his chambers, when he'd been trying to understand what the warmth was, what it meant. The words had gotten buried under everything else, but now, in the quiet, they surfaced with crystalline clarity.

He placed a fragment of his essence inside you before you were even born.

Her hand trembled slightly as she picked up the glass, took a sip. The water felt cold going down her bruised throat.

"Briar?" Eliam's voice cut through her thoughts. "What's wrong?"

She set the glass down carefully, not wanting to spill it.

"I think,,," she said quietly, lifting her eyes to meet his gaze. "I think I know why Malus wants me back so badly."

Eliam went completely still, his fork halfway to his mouth. He set it down slowly, his eyes locked on her face. "What do you mean?"

"He bit me and he... he was so angry," she explained, memories of that night rising unbidden. The fear and the hopelessness. She pressed her hand to her chest, feeling the warmth pulse beneath her palm. It grounded her. "My blood, he said it tasted of the old forest, of you. He was trying to understand why." Her fingers spread over her sternum. "Why it protects me, why it reacts the way it does."

"And?"

"He thinks he knows," she said, lowering her eyes.. "He thinks you hid something in me. That when you saved my mother's life, you put part of your essence inside me." She swallowed hard. "Before I was even born."

The silence that followed was absolute.

Eliam's expression went blank, that careful neutrality he used when his mind was racing too fast to show anything on his face. His hand on the table had curled into a fist.

"That's impossible, I—" He stopped, his jaw clenching, muscles working beneath skin. She could see him trying to reach for the memory, to grasp at something that wasn't there. The frustration that crossed his face was raw, unguarded.

"If I had done something like that," he said finally, "put part of myself in an unborn child, I should remember."

He stood abruptly, moving to the terrace doors, bracing himself against the frame. His back was rigid, tension radiating from every line of his body.

"Malus said you were trying to protect it," Briar continued, needing to get all of it out. "He was doing something that night... some ritual or something... and you hid part of your power where he wouldn't think to look. In me."

"A ritual." Eliam's voice was distant. "Twenty-five years ago."

"He was trying to strip you of your power."

She watched his shoulders tense further, watched him process implications she couldn't fully see.

"If that's true," he said slowly, not turning to face her, "if you're carrying part of my essence, part of my power—"

"Then that's why he wants me." The words came out steadier than she felt. "Not just because of the bargain."

Eliam turned then, and his expression was terrible. Not angry. Worse. The kind of cold calculation that came before violence.

"He won't stop," Briar said, voicing what they both knew. "He can't afford to. This isn't about pride or the bargain or punishing you. If I have access to your power, if he can get it through me—"

"Then he gets what he's always wanted." Eliam crossed back to her, his hands finding her shoulders. "And knowing my brother, he'll do anything to make that happen."

The weight of it settled between them. The border confrontation made more sense now. Malus's barely contained rage, his threats, his refusal to let her go despite the political complications. She wasn't just a human he owned. She was the key to something bigger.

"What does he need your power for?" she asked. "What's he planning?"

Eliam's hands tightened on her shoulders, then released. He stepped back, running a hand through his hair in a gesture of frustration she rarely saw from him.

"I don't know," he said.

The autumn marks at her throat rustled, responding to something. A shift in the air, a change in temperature. Briar's hand went to them automatically.

"We tell the others tomorrow," Eliam said, his voice settling back into that controlled authority. "We will figure out what he's planning and how to stop him. But right now..." He moved to her, pulling her to her feet. "Right now you should rest."

"I don't think I can," she admitted. He said nothing, his hands were already working the laces of her dress. She didn't stop him from undressing her, enjoying the warmth of his touch as she let him guide her into the sleep shirt and then let him pull her into bed with possessive care. His arms wrapped around her, solid and warm, and the warmth in her chest settled, recognizing its other half.

"Sleep," he commanded, pressing a light kiss against her hair.

Tomorrow they would figure out what it meant. What Malus wanted with it. How to keep him from taking it.

Chapter Twenty-Three

Something pulled her from sleep. Not sound or touch, but *cold*.

It as the biting kind—winter air against bare skin, stone beneath her feet where smooth wood should be, wind that carried the sharp scent of snow.

Briar's eyes opened to darkness punctuated by soft blue light.

Standing stones rose around her, tall as trees, carved with symbols that glowed with steady azure luminescence. The border. She was at the border of the Star Court, the same stones they'd crossed fleeing from Malus, and she had no memory of how she'd gotten here.

Her heart stuttered in her chest. She was barefoot, wearing only the thin sleep shirt Eliam had dressed her in. Overhead she could see white drifting down from the sky.

Snow.

The first snow of winter. It would have been enchanting if Briar wasn't so confused. What was she doing outside and why was she standing so close to the edge of safety?

She tried to move back, to turn around, to run, to do anything, but her body wouldn't respond. Her feet stayed planted, her weight already shifting forward, preparing for that final step.

No.

Panic flared hot in her chest. The warmth pulsed frantically, trying to push back against whatever held her, but it was weak, exhausted from the day's trials. Her foot lifted, bare toes pointing toward the invisible line between safety and—

Movement in the snow beyond.

A figure stepped into view between the standing stones, and her blood turned to ice that had nothing to do with the temperature.

Malus stood just beyond the border, snowflakes catching in his copper hair, his dark coat pristine despite the weather. He looked exactly as he had at their last confrontation—immaculate, composed, terrible in his beauty. But his eyes held something different now. Hunger. Triumph.

He smiled and extended his hand toward her, palm up, beckoning.

"Come here, dear one," he said, his voice carrying across the distance with unnatural clarity. "You've kept me waiting long enough."

Her foot moved forward another inch. The autumn marks at her throat were burning now, pulling her toward him with inexorable force. She could feel the compulsion wrapping around her like invisible chains, dragging her step by step toward the border.

"No, please," she tried to say, but her mouth wouldn't form the words. Her body belonged to the bargain, and the bargain belonged to him, and he was calling her home.

Another step. Then another. The blue glow of the standing stones washed over her skin, and she was so close now she could see the individual snowflakes falling beyond, could see the way Malus's breath misted in the frozen air.

"That's it," he murmured, his voice like honey and poison. "Just a few more steps. Come to me."

The warmth in her chest was screaming now, raging against the compulsion with everything it had left. Golden light flickered beneath her skin, trying to manifest, trying to stop her, but the autumn marks squeezed tighter in response. She couldn't breathe. Couldn't think. Couldn't do anything but walk.

One more step and she'd cross the border.

One more step and the Star Court's protection would mean nothing.

One more step and she'd be his.

Her foot lifted—

A hand clamped around her wrist spinning her away from the border with force that nearly took her off her feet.

She crashed into a solid chest, arms wrapping around her, and she fought. Her hands came up to shove, to claw, anything to get free because Malus was right there, she had to go to him, the marks were burning and pulling and demanding—

Lips crashed against hers.

The kiss was hard, demanding, nothing gentle about it. Strong hands cupped her face, holding her still, and the warmth in her chest exploded outward with violent recognition.

It surged outward, enveloping the person kissing her like it had been drowning and just found air. Golden light erupted from her skin, flooding through her in waves that made her gasp against his mouth. The autumn marks recoiled, their hold shattering under the onslaught of warmth that knew—that recognized—that sang with joy at finding—

Finding what?

The compulsion broke.

Briar's knees gave out and she would have fallen if the arms around her hadn't tightened, holding her up. The kiss gentled, became something less desperate, and when it finally ended she was left gasping, her forehead pressed against a chest that wasn't Eliam's.

Arion.

She jerked back, or tried to, but his arms stayed firm around her waist.

"Easy," he said, his voice rough. "You're safe. You're still on Star Court land."

Her mind was spinning, trying to process too many things at once. She'd been walking to Malus. Arion had stopped her. *Arion* had kissed her.

She looked back toward the border stones, toward where Malus had been standing.

Empty. Just snow falling beyond the barrier, peaceful and quiet.

Had he even been there? Or had she dreamed it all, sleepwalked to the border in some nightmare she couldn't remember?

"We need to get you inside," Arion said quietly, his arm still around her waist. "You're freezing."

He was right. Now that the adrenaline was fading, she could feel how numb her bare feet were, how the thin sleep shirt did nothing against the wind. She nodded, not trusting her voice, and let him guide her away from the stones.

They'd barely made it ten feet when a figure appeared in the garden path ahead of them.

Eliam.

He was fully dressed, his hair slightly disheveled like he'd thrown clothes on in a hurry. His eyes went immediately to Arion's arm around Briar's waist, then to her bare feet, her thin nightgown, the way she was leaning against the Star Prince for support.

His expression went absolutely cold.

"Take your hands off her." The words were quiet, controlled, which made them more dangerous than if he'd shouted.

"Eliam, she was—" Arion started.

"Now."

Arion's arm loosened but didn't fully release her. "She was sleepwalking. Heading toward the border. I found her at the stones."

Eliam crossed the distance between them in three strides. His hand found Briar's arm, pulling her away from Arion and against his chest with possessive force. She felt him trembling with barely controlled rage, of perhaps fear, as his arms wrapped around her.

"Are you hurt?" he asked her, his voice still too controlled.

"No, I—" Her teeth were chattering now, the cold and shock catching up to her. "I don't know what happened. I woke up and I was at the border, and Malus was there, or I thought he was, but then—"

She felt Eliam go completely rigid.

"Malus was here?" His eyes cut to Arion. "On Star Court land?"

"Beyond the border," Arion said. "He must have been calling to her through the marks."

Eliam's hand moved to her throat, fingers finding the autumn marks with careful precision. They were warm to the touch, warmer than they should be, like they'd been actively working.

"He tried to pull you across," Eliam said, and it wasn't a question.

Briar nodded against his chest. "I couldn't stop. I tried to turn around, to go back, but my body wouldn't listen. The marks were—" She stopped, swallowing hard, unable to finish.

"And how exactly did you stop her?" Eliam's attention shifted back to Arion, his voice dropping to something lethal. "From crossing."

Arion met his gaze steadily. "Does it matter? She's safe."

"It matters." Eliam's arms tightened around Briar. "Because the warmth just flared. Violently. Enough to wake me from three floors away. So I'll ask again. What. Did. You. Do?"

The silence stretched between them, heavy with things unsaid.

"I broke the compulsion," Arion said finally. "However I could."

Briar felt the moment Eliam understood. Felt his whole body turn to stone around her, felt the temperature drop as shadows began pooling at their feet.

"You kissed her."

It wasn't a question this time either.

Arion didn't deny it.

The gardens erupted.

Thorns burst from the ground between them, black and vicious, driving straight for Arion's chest. The Star Prince moved, light forming a barrier that shattered the thorns into dust, but more were already growing, spreading across the path in a wave of violent wood.

"Eliam, stop—" Briar tried, but he'd already released her, shadows pouring from him like living things.

Arion raised his hands and light exploded outward, not attacking but creating distance, pushing the shadows back. "I'm not fighting you."

"Then you're going to die standing still." Eliam's voice was barely human. Thorns erupted from his palms, launching toward Arion with lethal speed.

More light, forming shields, deflecting. Arion moved backwards, his expression was hard. "She was going to cross the border. I did what I had to do."

"By putting your mouth on her?" Vines shot forward, wrapping around Arion's ankles, yanking him off balance. He hit the ground hard, light flaring as he severed the vines, rolling to his feet.

"By breaking Malus's hold however I could!" Arion's hands spread, light forming restraints that shot toward Eliam. They wrapped around his wrists, his chest, trying to bind him in place.

Eliam shattered them with a snarl, thorns growing through the bindings, breaking them apart. "There are a hundred ways to break a compulsion that don't involve touching what's mine."

"She's not a possession!" Arion's voice finally rose, anger bleeding through his careful control. Starlight gathered in his palms, forming chains that lashed out, trying to restrain Eliam's arms, his legs, anything to stop the assault without causing real damage.

"Isn't she?" Eliam dissolved into shadow, reforming behind Arion, thorns wrapping around the prince's throat. Not tight enough to choke but present, threatening. "You want her. You've wanted her since the moment you pulled her from that river. Don't pretend this was just about saving her."

Arion's hand came up, light burning against the thorns, forcing them back. He spun, and his expression was cold now, truly cold. "And you cast her out. Sent her into the Wild Hunt to die. So forgive me if I question your right to play the possessive lover."

Eliam's control cracked further, shadows spreading across the ground, swallowing the light from the floating lanterns. The garden plunged into darkness broken only by Arion's defensive magic.

"I made a mistake—"

"You always make mistakes with her!" Arion's restraints shot forward again, light wrapping around Eliam's wrists, yanking them apart, trying to stop him from forming more weapons. "You claim her, you hurt her, you throw her away, and then you rage when someone else tries to pick up the pieces!"

Eliam broke the restraints with brute force, thorns erupting from the ground in a circle around Arion, growing inward, trying to cage him. "Help? Is that what you call it? Kissing her?"

"She was going to him!" Arion's light burned brighter, shattering the thorns before they could close completely. "Another second and she would have crossed, and you would have lost her forever. So yes, I kissed her. I broke the compulsion. I saved her life."

"You had no right—"

"I had every right!" Arion's composure finally shattered. Light exploded from him, not restraining now but pushing, forcing Eliam back several feet. "Someone had to! You were asleep, comfortable and safe while she walked barefoot through the gardens toward her death. So don't you dare tell me I had no right to save her."

The warmth in Briar's chest was going wild, pulling toward both of them with equal desperate intensity. She could feel it trying to stop this, trying to make them understand something she couldn't grasp.

Footsteps on the garden path. Thaine appeared, taking in the destruction with wide eyes. "What in the seven hells—"

"Stay out of this," Eliam snarled, not taking his eyes off Arion.

More footsteps. Karse emerged from the shadows, assessing the situation with lazy interest. His gaze found Briar, shivering in her thin nightgown, and he crossed to her without a word.

"Come here," he said, his good arm wrapping around her from behind, pulling her against his chest. Heat radiated from him, blessing of the Drak, and she couldn't help but lean into it. "Let the fae have their tantrum."

"They're going to kill each other," she said, her teeth still chattering.

"Probably not." Karse's chin rested on top of her head, his arm tightening around her middle. "The pretty one's not even trying to hurt him. Just playing defense. Interesting, that."

He was right. Every attack Arion made was restraint-based, trying to bind or push back rather than harm. While Eliam was throwing lethal force with every strike.

"Eliam, stop!" Thaine tried again, moving closer. "This isn't—"

A thorn shot past his head, close enough that he felt the wind of its passage. Thaine froze.

"I said stay out of it."

Arion used the distraction to send bands of light around Eliam's chest, yanking him forward and off-balance. "You want to be angry at someone? Be angry at Malus. He's the one who tried to steal her tonight. He's the one controlling her through those marks. Not me."

"I know exactly who to be angry at." Eliam shattered the bands, shadows coiling around his arms like serpents. "And right now, it's the fae who thought he had the right to kiss my—"

He stopped, the word dying on his lips. Not quite willing to say it.

"Your what?" Arion pressed, light forming a barrier between them as Eliam advanced. "Your prisoner? Your property? What exactly is she to you, Eliam? Because from where I stand, you've never actually decided."

"She's mine." The shadows surged forward, crashing against Arion's barrier. "That's all you need to know."

"She's a person!" Arion's light pushed back, driving the shadows away. "With her own will, her own choices. You don't get to decide what's best for her and then rage when someone else offers her kindness."

"Kindness." Eliam's laugh was bitter. "Is that what we're calling it?"

"What would you call it?" Arion's barrier strengthened, turning solid, forcing Eliam to stop his advance. "I saved her. I brought her back. I kept her safe when you—" He stopped, seeming to realize he'd gone too far.

"When I what?" Eliam's voice dropped to something deadly quiet. "Say it. When I cast her out. When I sent her to die. When I failed her." Shadows began building behind him, massive and dark. "You think I don't know? You think I haven't thought about it every moment since?"

"Then why are you fighting me instead of him?" Arion's hands spread, light gathering. "I'm not your enemy. Malus is."

"You kissed her." The words came out flat, final. "That makes you my enemy."

The shadows launched forward with devastating force, and Arion's barrier shattered under the impact. He went down hard, light forming shields above him as thorns rained down, but one got through, slicing across his shoulder.

Blood, bright and red against his pale clothing.

Eliam froze, staring at it.

"Enough!" Thaine stepped between them, his hand on Eliam's chest. "Enough. You made your point. He made his. This solves nothing."

Briar felt the warmth in her chest split, pulled equally toward both of them, and the sensation was so painful she gasped. Karse's arm tightened around her.

"Steady," he murmured. "Breathe through it."

Eliam's eyes found hers across the destroyed garden, and she saw the moment reality crashed back in. His shadows receded, pulling back into him, and his expression shifted from rage to something rawer.

Arion stood slowly, one hand pressed to his bleeding shoulder. His light had dimmed, but his eyes stayed locked on Eliam.

"I would do it again," he said quietly. "If it meant keeping her safe." He paused, his eyes meeting Eliam's directly. "And you're right. About the river. About me wanting her. I offered her sanctuary after you cast her out. Hoped she'd stay, that she'd choose the Star Court. Choose me."

His jaw tightened slightly. "She didn't. Even without saying the words, I knew. She'd already decided to go back to you."

"But that doesn't mean I've stopped wanting her," Arion continued, his hand still pressed to his bleeding shoulder. "So I'll take any opportunity I can to change her mind. The next time you hurt her, the next time you make her question whether she belongs with you, I'll be right there offering her something better. Consider that fair warning."

Eliam's shadows surged again, but Thaine's hand on his chest held firm.

"Enough," the huntsman said quietly. "He's made his position clear. You've made yours. This is done for now."

Karse released Briar with a small sound of amusement. "Fae," he said, like it explained everything. Then to Briar, "Can you walk?"

She nodded.

Eliam was there immediately, his arm around her waist, supporting her weight. He didn't say anything, didn't look at Arion, just turned and began leadding her back toward the residence halls.

She looked back once, seeing Arion still standing in the destroyed garden, Thaine moving to check his shoulder. The Star Prince's eyes met hers, and something passed between them. Understanding, perhaps, definitely confusion. The same question she had no answer for.

Why had the warmth responded to his kiss that way?

Why did it still pull toward him even now?

What did it mean?

Eliam guided her back to their room in silence, his grip on her waist possessive and tight. When they reached the door, he swept her up without a word, carrying her inside despite her protest that she could walk.

He set her on the bed and immediately began layering blankets over her, his movements sharp and controlled in a way that meant he was barely holding his temper.

She watched him move around the room, stoking the fire higher, checking that the terrace doors were locked, his shoulders rigid with tension. When he finally climbed into bed beside her, he pulled her against him, his arms wrapping around her like he was afraid she might vanish.

The silence stretched between them, filled only by the crackle of the fire and their breathing.

"Was it true?" he asked finally, his voice rough. "What he said. Before Malachar took you, had you already decided to come back?"

She felt him holding himself completely still, waiting for her answer.

"Yes," she said quietly.

His arms tightened fractionally around her. "Why?"

Briar studied him a moment. She could give him a dozen reasons that were all true—the bargain, the marks, the way the warmth pulled her toward him. But none of those were the real answer.

"Because I love you," she said, the words coming out steadier than she felt.

He went completely still behind her. She felt him stop breathing for a moment, could sense the war happening inside him between what he wanted to say and what he was capable of saying.

His hand moved from her waist to turn her to face him, and when she met his eyes, they were black and intense and full of things he couldn't put into words.

"Say it again," he demanded, his voice dropping to something rough and possessive.

"I love you."

His mouth crashed against hers, and the kiss was desperate and claiming and full of everything he couldn't say. His hands moved to her face, holding her like something precious and breakable, while his tongue swept into her mouth with an intensity that stole her breath.

When he pulled back, his forehead pressed against hers, his breathing ragged. "You're mine," he said, and it wasn't a question or a command. It was a statement of fact, of truth, of something fundamental that existed between them. "Always mine."

"Yes," she agreed, and felt the warmth in her chest surge with recognition and relief.

His hands moved to the hem of her sleep shirt, drawing it up and over her head with careful deliberation. The firelight painted her skin in shades of gold and shadow, and she watched his eyes track over every bruise, every mark, cataloging each one.

"He touched you," Eliam said, his fingers tracing the autumn marks at her throat. "Called to you. Tried to take you from me."

"It didn't work."

"Because of Arion." The name came out like gravel, and she saw murder flash through his eyes before he forced it away. "Because another man put his hands on you, his mouth on you."

"To save me," she said, her hands finding his face. "That's all. Nothing more."

His jaw clenched under her palms. "I should have felt it. Should have known you were in danger. The warmth should have woken me the moment you left the bed."

"You're here now."

"Not good enough." His hands moved to her waist, fingers pressing into her skin with possessive need. "I want to replace every touch that isn't mine. Every kiss. Every moment you spent afraid or cold or thinking I wasn't coming for you."

He pulled her closer, his mouth finding her throat, teeth scraping against the autumn marks with deliberate pressure. She gasped, her hands tangling in his hair, and he bit down harder, marking over Malus's claim with his own.

"This is mine," he said against her skin, moving lower to her shoulder. Another bite, hard enough to bruise. "Every inch of you."

His hands were already working the fastenings of his clothes, stripping them away impatiently. When he settled back over her, skin against skin, she felt the full weight of his need, his fear, his desperate possessive claim.

"Tell me again," he demanded, his hand sliding between her thighs.

"I love you," she gasped as his fingers found her, already slick and ready.

He made a sound low in his throat, something between satisfaction and need, and his mouth claimed hers again. The warmth in her chest was singing now, reaching for him, recognizing its other half, and she felt it flowing between them in waves that made her arch against his hand.

"Eliam—"

"Not yet." His thumb found her clit, circling with maddening pressure while his fingers moved inside her. "I want you desperate for me. Want you begging."

She was already close, her body responding to his touch with an intensity that made her shake. But he knew her too well, knew exactly when to ease back, to keep her on the edge without letting her fall.

"Please," she managed, her nails digging into his shoulders.

"Please what?" His teeth found her earlobe, biting gently. "Tell me what you want."

"You. I want you."

He positioned himself at her entrance, but didn't enter, just pressed against her with agonizing slowness. "Say it again. Tell me who you belong to."

"You," she gasped, trying to shift her hips to take him in, but his hand on her waist held her still. "I belong to you."

He thrust into her in one smooth motion, and they both cried out at the sensation. He didn't give her time to adjust, didn't ease into it, just took her with desperate possessive need that spoke louder than any words.

His hand fisted in her hair, pulling her head back to expose her throat, and his mouth found the marks there again, biting and sucking hard enough to leave new bruises over the old ones. Claiming. Marking. Making absolutely certain that anyone who looked at her would know who she belonged to.

She wrapped her legs around his waist, pulling him deeper, and he groaned against her throat, his rhythm becoming harder, more demanding. One hand moved between them, finding her center again, and the dual sensation made her vision white out.

"Come for me," he commanded, his voice rough. "Let me feel it."

The warmth in her chest exploded outward as she shattered, golden light flooding through her, through him, binding them together in waves of pleasure that seemed to go on forever. She felt him follow her over the edge, felt him pulse inside her as he buried his face against her neck, his whole body shaking with the force of his release.

They stayed like that for a long moment, tangled together, breathing hard, the warmth settling between them like a living thing.

When he finally moved, it was only to roll them so she was draped across his chest, his arms wrapped around her with possessive care. His hand stroked through her hair, gentle now, all the desperate violence drained away.

"You're not allowed to almost die again," he said against her hair. "Or walk toward borders in your sleep. Or let other princes kiss you."

Despite everything, she felt her lips quirk. "I'll try to avoid all of that."

"See that you do." His arms tightened around her. "Because I'm not letting you go. Not to Malus, not to Arion, not to anyone. You're mine, and I keep what's mine."

Chapter Twenty-Four

S he woke to warmth and the soft light of early morning filtering through the windows. For a moment, she just lay there, taking inventory. Her body ached in ways that had nothing to do with Malus or failed bargains. The pleasant soreness of being thoroughly claimed.

Eliam's hand was tracing idle patterns across her stomach, his chest warm against her back. She could tell by his breathing that he'd been awake for a while.

"Good morning," she said, closing her eyes again, content to lay wrapped in his arms.

"I was... too eager last night," he murmured, lips brushing against her ear, his voice still rough from sleep.

She opened her eyes and turned her head to look at him, confused. "What?"

"Rushed. Desperate." His hand slid lower, fingers spreading across her hip possessively. Briar felt her heart skip in her chest. "I only made you come once and then took what I needed like some untried boy with no control."

Briar didn't know what to make of the admission and felt warmth creeping into her cheeks. "Oh... it's... fine."

"Don't. You deserve better." He shifted, rolling her onto her back, settling over her with deliberate slowness. The morning light painted his features in soft gold, and she could see the intensity in his eyes. "You deserved to be worshipped. Taken apart slowly."

His hand moved between her thighs, fingers ghosting over her with maddening lightness, not quite touching where she was already starting to ache for him.

"At least three or four times," he continued, his voice dropping lower. "Maybe more. Until you're shaking and oversensitive and begging me to stop." His fingers finally made contact, the barest brush against her center. "That's what you deserved."

"Eliam—"

"So that's what you're getting now." He shifted down her body, his mouth finding her breast, teeth closing around her nipple with enough pressure to make her gasp. His hand between her legs remained still, just resting there, a promise of what was coming.

He took his time with her breasts, alternating between gentle suction and sharp bites, never quite giving her what she needed. When he finally moved lower, pressing kisses along her ribs, her stomach, she was already breathing hard.

But he didn't go where she wanted, instead, his mouth found the inside of her thigh, high up where the skin was sensitive, and he bit down. Not gently. Hard enough that she cried out, hard enough to leave a mark that would last days.

"Mine," he said against the reddening skin, then bit the other thigh just as hard.

Her hands twisted in the sheets as he worked his way higher, marking her inner thighs with bruises and teeth marks, each one a declaration of ownership. By the time his breath finally ghosted over her center, she was trembling, desperate for his mouth on her.

He made her wait.

His tongue traced along the crease where her thigh met her body, then the other side, deliberately avoiding where she needed him. When she tried to shift her hips, to guide him where she wanted, his hands clamped down on her thighs, holding her in place.

"Stay still," he commanded, his voice muffled against her skin. "Or I'll stop entirely and leave you like this."

Briar forced herself to do as he said, though every muscle in her body was taut with need. Finally, his tongue dragged up her center in one long, slow stroke that had her back arching off the bed.

Then he stopped and she whimpered in frustration.

"This isn't worship," she gasped. "This is torture."

"Look at me," he demanded.

She forced her eyes open, looking down to find him watching her, his eyes black with desire. The sight of him between her thighs, mouth wet with her, staring at her with that possessive intensity, sent heat flooding through her.

"I want to watch you," he said, his breath hot against her oversensitive flesh. "I want to see your face when you come undone. So keep your eyes on me."

His tongue returned, and she had to struggle to keep her eyes open as he worked her with deliberate precision. He knew exactly what she liked, exactly where to focus his attention, and he used that knowledge mercilessly. But every time she got close, every time her breathing hitched and her thighs started to tremble, he would pull back.

"Eliam, please—"

He hummed against her, the vibration making her gasp, but didn't increase his pace. Just kept that same slow, deliberate rhythm that kept her hovering without letting her fall.

His fingers joined his mouth, sliding inside her with agonizing slowness. One, then two, curling to find that spot inside that made her moan. But still he kept that steady, controlled pace, never quite giving her enough to push her over.

She was shaking now, her hands twisted so tight in the sheets her knuckles had gone white. The pleasure was building and building with nowhere to go, and she could feel herself getting desperate, needy in a way that would have embarrassed her if she could think past the sensation.

He knew it, could feel it through the warmth.

"Beg me," he said against her, his voice dark and commanding.

"Please," she gasped. "Please, I need—"

"You need what?" His fingers stilled inside her. "Be specific, little thief,"

"I need you to let me come," she managed, her voice breaking. "Please, Eliam, I need—"

He sealed his lips around her clit and sucked, hard, at the same time his fingers found that perfect angle inside her, and she shattered with a cry that bordered on a scream. The orgasm hit like a wave, crashing through her with an intensity that made her whole body convulse.

He didn't let up. His mouth stayed on her, his fingers kept moving, drawing out her pleasure until she was gasping and trying to pull away from the oversensitivity.

But his hands on her thighs held her in place, and he started building her up again before the first orgasm had even fully faded.

"Too much," she managed, her hands finding his hair, trying to pull him away. "I can't—"

"You can." His fingers curled inside her again, finding that spot with unerring accuracy. "And you will."

The second orgasm built faster, her body already primed, every nerve oversensitive. But this time he didn't ease her into it. His free hand pressed down on her lower stomach, adding pressure that made everything more intense, while his mouth worked her with focused purpose.

When she came the second time, it was harder, more desperate, her whole body going rigid as pleasure crashed through her. She heard herself making sounds she'd never made before, desperate and broken and utterly his.

He pulled back slightly, giving her a moment to breathe, but his fingers remained inside her, moving in slow, lazy circles that kept her on edge despite the oversensitivity.

"One more," he said, and there was dark satisfaction in his voice.

"I can't—" But even as she said it, she could feel her body responding to him, the need building again despite her protests.

He shifted his position, kneeling between her legs, and used his free hand to hook one of her legs over his shoulder. The new angle let his fingers go deeper, and when he added a third, stretching her, she gasped at the sensation.

His thumb found her clit again, circling with firm pressure while his fingers worked inside her, and his mouth dropped to her inner thigh, biting down hard enough to make her cry out.

The combination of pain and pleasure, of being stretched and filled while he marked her skin with his teeth, pushed her toward the edge faster than she thought possible. But this time, instead of the sharp peak of before, the orgasm built slowly, a rolling wave that seemed to go on and on, leaving her shaking and gasping and completely undone.

When it finally faded, she was boneless, her whole body trembling with aftershocks. Eliam withdrew his fingers carefully and moved up to gather her against his chest, his hand stroking through her hair.

"Three," he murmured against her temple. "Better. But I'm not finished with you yet."

Not finished? What more could he possibly—

Before she could speak he was already shifting, rolling onto his back and pulling her on top of him in one smooth motion. His hands settled on her hips, positioning her so she straddled him.

She could feel how hard he was beneath her, and despite her body's protests that it was too much, too sensitive, she felt heat pooling low in her belly again.

His hands guided her up slightly, positioning her over him. "Take me in," he commanded. "Slowly."

She lowered herself onto him with trembling thighs, gasping at the stretch. She was so sensitive that every inch felt magnified, pleasure bordering on too much but not quite crossing that line. When she was fully seated, she had to pause, breathing hard, adjusting to the fullness.

"Look," Eliam said, one hand leaving her hip to turn her face to the side.

She'd forgotten about the mirror. It stood near the wardrobe, tall and ornate, and from this angle she could see everything. See herself straddling him, her thighs spread wide, her body marked with his teeth and fingers. See the way her breasts moved with each ragged breath, nipples still red from his attention. See the flush that spread across her chest and throat, the autumn marks standing out stark against her skin.

See the way he looked at her, eyes dark with possession and hunger.

"Watch yourself take me," he said, his voice rough. "I want you to see what you look like when you're mine."

His hands on her hips urged her up, then pulled her back down, and she watched in the mirror as her body moved, as she took him deep. The sight was obscene and intimate all at once, and she couldn't look away.

She found her pace, rolling her hips in a way that had them both gasping. The oversensitivity from before made every movement almost unbearably intense, pleasure building faster than she thought possible after already coming three times.

One of his hands left her hip to slide between her legs, finding her center. She cried out at the contact, her rhythm faltering.

"Don't stop," he commanded, his fingers circling with firm pressure. "Watch while you fall apart on me."

She forced her eyes to stay on their reflection, watching as her body moved over his, as his hand worked between her legs, as her expression shifted from concentration to desperation. She could see the exact moment the pleasure became too much, see her mouth fall open, see her back arch—

The fourth orgasm hit differently than the others. Deeper. More consuming. She felt it in every part of her body, felt herself clenching around him, felt the warmth in her chest explode outward in waves of golden light that made her skin glow.

Eliam groaned beneath her, his hands gripping her hips hard enough to bruise as he thrust up into her, chasing his own release. She watched in the mirror as he came, his head thrown back, his whole body going rigid. The sight of him losing control beneath her sent another wave of pleasure through her already oversensitized body.

She collapsed forward onto his chest, gasping, completely spent. Her whole body was shaking with aftershocks, and she could feel him still pulsing inside her.

His arms came around her, holding her close while their breathing slowly returned to normal. One hand stroked through her hair with unexpected tenderness.

"Four," he said with deep satisfaction. "That's more like it."

She couldn't even form words to respond, just lay against his chest feeling thoroughly, completely claimed in every possible way. Her body was marked inside and out, painted with bruises and bite marks and the lingering sensation of his touch.

"Say it again," he said softly, pressing a kiss to the top of her head.

Briar almost asked what he meant but the previous evening came flooding back to her. "I..." she began, suddenly feeling shy despite the intimacy. "I love you."

He pulled her closer, burying his face against the curve of her throat. "Rest now. It's still early, barely dawn."

Briar closed her eyes again, feeling the warmth in her chest settle between them, content and sated.

Briar woke to the scent of food and the sound of water running in the adjoining bathing room. For a moment she just lay there, sore in places she'd forgotten could be sore, marked inside and out, but feeling more rested than she had in days.

The bed beside her was empty, though she could hear Eliam moving around in the other room.

She sat up slowly, wincing at the pull of muscles that had been thoroughly used. The bruises on her inner thighs were dark and obvious, the bite marks on her shoulders and throat even more so. She looked like she'd been in a fight, though the kind of fight was decidedly different from the ones involving Malus or border confrontations.

"You're awake," Eliam said from the doorway. "Good."

He crossed to her, his eyes tracking over her body with possessive satisfaction. The marks he'd left were clearly visible, and she saw his expression settle into something smug.

"How do you feel?" he asked.

"Sore," she admitted.

"As you should be." He pulled back the blankets without asking permission, ignoring her protest as he scooped her up. "Bath first."

The bathing room was filled with steam, a large tub already filled with water that smelled of herbs and something floral. He set her on her feet beside it, his hands steadying her when her legs wobbled slightly.

"I can manage," she said, though the thought of climbing into the tub on her own made her muscles ache in protest.

"Can you?" His tone suggested he doubted it, but he stepped back, leaning against the doorframe with his arms crossed. Clearly not leaving, but giving her space to handle it herself.

She let the sleep shirt fall to the floor, too tired to be modest about his watching. His eyes tracked over every mark, every bruise, cataloging his work with clear satisfaction.

The water was almost too hot, but in the best way. She sank into it with a groan of relief, feeling her muscles begin to unknot immediately. The heat soaked into her sore thighs, her aching back, all the places that bore evidence of the previous night and morning.

For a few moments, she just let herself float in the warmth, eyes closed, breathing in the herbal steam. It smelled like lavender and something sharper, something that helped clear the fog from her mind.

A small splash near her elbow made her eyes open.

Frederick surfaced from beneath the water, his translucent form shifting from blue to pleased green. His gill-fronds waved excitedly, creating tiny currents around her arm.

Despite everything, she felt herself smile. "Frederick. You found me."

The water sprite did a little loop, his whole body flashing brighter green before settling back to his usual translucent clarity. He swam in circles around her, clearly delighted to see her.

"I heard you made it to the Star Court," she said quietly, running her fingers through the water near him. "That you're the reason they came for us."

Frederick's color shifted to an even brighter green, his movements becoming more animated. He pressed against her hand like he was seeking affection, and she felt that strange sensation of cool silk against her skin.

"You did so well," she told him, and he practically glowed with pride, doing another little spin that sent ripples across the bath.

"The sprite has been living in the main fountain," Eliam said from the doorway. "Arion lets it swim wherever it wants."

Frederick released a stream of bubbles that looked almost indignant, his color flickering toward defensive blue before settling back to green. He swam protectively around Briar's arm, his gill-fronds waving in what Briar translated to mean he did not approve of Eliam's dismissiveness.

"He has a name," Briar said. "And he helped save your life. Be nice."

Eliam made a noncommittal sound, but Frederick seemed satisfied, returning to his pleased green and doing lazy circles while she washed.

She reached for the soap, and Frederick immediately investigated it with apparent suspicion, his color shifting to cautious yellow as he swam around the bar. When she lathered it in her hands, he darted away, then cautiously approached the bubbles with what looked like fascination.

"I don't think he's seen soap before," she observed.

"Water sprites are easily entertained," Eliam said, but there was less dismissal in his tone than before. Maybe because Frederick had, in fact, saved them all.

She worked the soap through her hair, her arms protesting the movement. Everything ached in a way that was going to make today interesting. Frederick watched with rapt attention, occasionally poking at the soap bubbles with his gill-fronds, which only made more bubbles, which delighted him further.

When she dunked her head under to rinse, she opened her eyes beneath the water to find Frederick right there, eye-spots wide, his whole body doing an excited shimmy. She surfaced with a laugh, water streaming down her face.

"He's very enthusiastic," she said.

"He's a nuisance," Eliam corrected, but without any real heat.

Frederick did a loop, flashed blue, then dove deep into the tub, disappearing from view. A moment later, he popped up near the edge, perched on the rim like he was surveying his domain.

Briar finished washing, taking her time, letting the heat work into her sore muscles. When she finally stood to get out, Frederick did one more cheerful loop and dove back under, presumably off to find another fountain to explore.

Eliam was there immediately with a towel, wrapping it around her before she could reach for it herself. His hands were careful as he dried her off, mindful of the marks he'd left, though his expression suggested he had no regrets about putting them there.

"Can you walk?" he asked.

"Yes," she said, though her legs still felt unsteady.

He kept one hand on her elbow anyway as she moved back into the bedchamber. A fresh sleep shirt lay on the bed, soft and oversized, and he helped her into it with the same careful attention he'd used with the towel.

"Now food," he said, guiding her to the table by the windows.

The tray held more than she could possibly eat—bread, cheese, sliced fruit, cold meat, honey, butter. Simple but substantial. Her stomach reminded her that she'd burned a lot of energy in the past twelve hours.

She sat and began eating while he poured water from a pitcher, setting the glass in front of her with a firmness that suggested he'd be monitoring how much she drank.

"Eat all of it," he said, settling into the chair across from her.

"I can't possibly—"

"You can and you will." His tone left no room for argument. "Your body needs fuel to recover."

She picked up a piece of bread, tearing it into smaller pieces. The food was good, and once she started eating, she realized how hungry she actually was. She made her way through the bread and cheese, then the fruit, while Eliam watched with that intensity he brought to everything.

"More," he said when she slowed, pushing the plate of meat toward her.

"I'm full—"

"You're not." He leaned back in his chair, arms crossed. "You've barely eaten in days. You need more than fruit and bread."

She sighed but took a piece of the meat. He was right, annoyingly. Her body needed the protein, needed to rebuild after everything it had been through.

The silence was comfortable as she ate, broken only by the clink of her fork against the plate and the distant sound of wind beyond the windows. When she finally pushed the plate away, genuinely full, he seemed satisfied.

"Better," he said.

She looked out the windows for the first time, really looked, and saw what she'd barely registered in the panic of last night. The Star Court gardens were blanketed in white, snow covering the impossible blooms and turning everything into a winter scene that looked like something from a dream.

"It's beautiful," she said, unable to keep the wonder from her voice.

"It's cold and wet..." His tone suggested he didn't enjoy it.

She pressed her hand against the glass, feeling the cold seep through. The snow was still falling, soft and steady, covering everything in pristine white.

"I want to go out," she said, the words escaping before she could think them through.

Eliam's expression shifted to something between disbelief and refusal. "You're recovering. You should be in bed."

"I've been in too many beds lately," she said, still watching the snow fall. "Too many rooms with locked doors. I want to be outside. Just for a little while."

Eliam moved to stand behind her, his hands settling on her shoulders. "You're exhausted. Your body needs rest."

"My body needs to move," she countered. "To feel something other than fear and pain for five minutes."

His hands tightened slightly on her shoulders. "The cold won't help with that."

"Maybe not. But being trapped inside will make it worse." She turned to face him, tilting her head back to meet his eyes. "Please."

Something flickered across his expression—surprise, maybe, or something softer. "You've gotten remarkably comfortable making demands of me."

"Is that a problem?"

"Prince Arion seems to think you're not my possession," he said, his voice carrying that dangerous edge. "That you have autonomy and choices."

Her heart sank slightly, the moment of lightness evaporating. Of course. She was still just—

"He's wrong, of course," Eliam continued, his hand moving to cup her face. "You are mine. Which means I'm responsible for keeping you alive and well." His thumb brushed her cheekbone. "So if we're going outside, you'll wear something warm. And you won't overexert yourself. And the moment you start looking tired, we're coming back inside. Do you understand?"

The relief that flooded through her was almost dizzying. Not a refusal. Not dismissal of what she needed. Just... conditions. Reasonable ones, even.

"I understand," she said.

"Good." He released her and moved to the wardrobe, pulling it open to reveal the array of clothes. His hands moved past the lighter dresses, settling on a heavier one in a warm chestnut brown trimmed with white. "This one. And you'll need stockings, proper boots, and a cloak."

She watched him gather the items, laying them out on the bed like he was preparing for battle rather than a walk in the garden. When he turned back to her, she was smiling despite herself.

"What?" he asked, his eyes narrowing slightly.

"Nothing. Just... thank you."

His expression suggested he didn't quite know what to do with her gratitude, so he did what he always did—turned it into action. "Come here. Let me help you dress before you decide to argue about that too."

She crossed to him, letting him pull the sleep shirt over her head. The cool air raised goosebumps on her skin, but his hands were warm as he helped her step into the stockings, drawing them up her legs with careful attention to the bruises on her thighs.

The dress came next, the fabric soft and warm against her skin. He worked the laces carefully, his knuckles occasionally brushing her spine as he secured them.

"Sit," he said, gesturing to the bed.

She sat, and he knelt to help her with sturdy boots lined with fur. They were perhaps a size too large, but thick socks would solve that problem. He laced them with the same methodical care he brought to everything, then stood and retrieved the cloak.

It was heavy, lined with what felt like rabbit fur, and when he settled it around her shoulders, the warmth was immediate and encompassing. He fastened it at her throat, his fingers brushing the autumn marks there. She saw something dark flicker through his expression at the contact—possession and frustration both, that these marks bound her to someone else.

"Ready?" he asked.

"Yes."

He guided her to the door, his hand at the small of her back, and they stepped out into the quiet hallway. The Star Court was beautiful even in the corridors—crystalline surfaces catching light, tapestries that seemed to shift and change as they passed. But Briar's attention was on the windows they passed, each one showing more snow falling, more white covering the gardens.

When they finally stepped outside, the cold hit her immediately despite the cloak. Sharp and biting, making her breath mist in the air. But it was the good kind of cold, the kind that made her feel alive and present rather than trapped in her own fear.

The snow was falling steadily now, accumulating on the garden paths, weighing down the impossible blooms. Everything looked softer under the white blanket, quieter, like the world was holding its breath.

She walked ahead of Eliam, her boots crunching through the fresh snow, and for a moment she could almost forget about Malus and bargains and the marks at her throat. Could almost pretend she was just a girl walking through a winter garden.

Behind her, she heard Eliam's measured footsteps. When she glanced back, he was watching her with that intensity he brought to everything, but something about his expression was softer than usual. Not quite bored, despite his earlier protests about the cold and her need for rest.

She turned back to the garden, breathing in the cold air, feeling some of the weight lift from her shoulders. The snow kept falling, peaceful and clean, covering everything in white.

Then the weight came crashing back.

She remembered Malus standing in snow just like this, calling to her through the marks. Remembered walking toward him, unable to stop, unable to fight the compulsion. Remembered his hand outstretched, beckoning, promising that she would come back to him eventually.

The marks at her throat pulsed once, as if responding to the memory, and suddenly the peaceful snow felt threatening. A reminder of how close she'd come to crossing that border, to being taken.

Her hands clenched into fists at her sides. She could feel panic building in her chest, the warmth starting to pulse frantically in response to her fear.

No.

She wasn't going to let him take this too. Wasn't going to let the memory of him poison every moment of peace she tried to find.

Briar bent down without thinking, scooping up a handful of snow, and threw it at Eliam before she could talk herself out of it.

It hit him square in the chest.

He stopped walking, looking down at the snow on his jacket, then up at her with an expression of complete disbelief.

"Did you just—" He stopped, his eyes narrowing dangerously. "My property just struck me?"

His tone was serious, but there was something underneath it. Something that wasn't quite anger.

"Your property is cold and trying not to think about last night," she said, surprising herself with her honesty. "And she needed something to do with her hands."

His expression shifted, something flickering across his features that she couldn't quite name. Understanding, maybe. Or recognition of what she was really doing, fighting back against fear the only way she knew how.

"I see," he said slowly, taking a step toward her. "And you thought assaulting your king would help with that?"

"Jury's still out," she replied before she bent down and scooped up another handful of snow. "I need to gather more evidence." She threw it at him before he could close the distance. This one hit his shoulder.

He stopped again, staring at the snow like she'd done something incomprehensible. Then his lips curved into something that was almost—not quite, but almost—a genuine smile. Not the predatory smirk or the possessive curve she was used to. Something lighter.

"You dare strike me twice?" He bent down, gathering his own handful of snow with deliberate precision. "That requires punishment."

The snowball hit her middle with surprising accuracy, and she let out a surprised laugh, already gathering more ammunition. The sound of her own laughter startled her—when was the last time she'd laughed? Really laughed, not the bitter or desperate kind, but something genuine?

She threw her next attack before he could ready himself, and satisfaction flooded through her when snow exploded against his chest. He looked down at the white splatter, then back at her, and that almost-smile curved his lips again.

He bent smoothly, gathering snow with quick efficiency, and she was already moving, trying to put distance between them while she fumbled for more ammunition. Her throw went wide, sailing past his shoulder into a hedge.

His didn't.

The impact made her stumble, and she was laughing again before she could stop herself, the breathless kind that came from somewhere lighter than the places she'd been living in.

She scooped up more snow, her hands clumsy in the cold, and launched it in his general direction. It fell short by several feet. His next throw caught her as she was bending for more, and she felt the cold impact through the heavy cloak.

"You're showing off," she said, trying to pack the snow tighter.

"I'm merely competent." Another throw, and she barely dodged it, the snowball hitting the ground where she'd been standing a moment before.

She threw two in rapid succession, wild and uncoordinated. Both missed. His answering shot didn't, and she felt it hit somewhere near her shoulder, snow cascading down from the impact.

Her lungs burned from the cold air and laughter. Snow clung to her hair, melted against her face, and her fingers were going numb, but she felt present in a way she hadn't since she had first come to this world. Like she was fully in her body instead of trapped in her head with fear and memories.

Eliam was holding back—she could tell by the way his throws were precise but never too forceful, by the way he aimed for the cloak rather than anywhere more vulnerable. When one of her shots actually connected with his side, she saw genuine surprise cross his face before something else replaced it. Something warm.

She bent to gather more snow, still catching her breath, when she noticed the figure standing motionless on one of the garden paths.

Thaine was staring at them with an expression of pure confusion, like he'd walked into a scene that couldn't possibly be real.

Eliam followed her gaze and immediately straightened, his expression shuttering back to something more controlled. But there was color in his cheeks from the cold and exertion, the gleam of snow in his white hair, and he looked more alive than she'd seen him in days.

"Thaine," Eliam said, his voice returning to its usual controlled tone. "Was there something you needed?"

Thaine's mouth opened, then closed. He looked between them, clearly trying to process what he'd just witnessed. The Forest King. Throwing snowballs. *Smiling.*

"Prince Arion has called for everyone to gather," Thaine finally managed. "He said it's urgent."

"We'll be there shortly," Eliam said, his hand finding her waist, pulling her against his side.

Thaine nodded and retreated, but not before giving them one more confused look over his shoulder.

They walked back toward the residence in silence, the playfulness from moments before evaporating like the snow melting on her cheeks. Eliam's expression had returned to its usual intensity, though his hand stayed warm on her waist.

"What do you think Arion wants?" she asked quietly.

"To discuss what happened last night. What Malus attempted." His jaw tightened. "And probably to push his case for why you should bind yourself to the Star Court instead."

She remembered Arion's declaration from last night, his promise that he'd take any opportunity to change her mind. The tension between him and Eliam hadn't been resolved, just postponed.

"We need to tell them," she said, her hand rising to her chest. "About the warmth. About what Malus said it is."

"I know." His arm tightened around her.

They reached the hallway leading to the council room, and Briar could hear voices from within. Her stomach tightened with apprehension.

"What aren't you telling me?" she asked, stopping him before they reached the door. "About what Malus might want with your power? You know something."

His expression went carefully neutral. "I have suspicions. But I'd rather confirm them before spreading fear."

"Eliam—"

"We'll discuss it," he cut her off, his hand finding hers, squeezing once. "After we hear what Arion has to say. After we understand what happened last night and why the marks were able to call to you through Star Court wards."

He was right. They needed information first. But she could see the worry in his eyes, the calculation happening behind them.

They walked the rest of the way in silence. When they reached the council room doors, Eliam paused, his hand still holding hers.

"Whatever happens in there," he said quietly, "whatever Arion says or offers, remember that you're mine. Not his. Not anyone else's. Mine."

"I know," she said, and felt the warmth in her chest pulse in agreement.

Chapter Twenty-Five

T he council room doors opened to reveal everyone already assembled. Snow
had accumulated on the window ledges outside, casting strange blue shadows
across the floor. Arion stood near the windows, and Briar noticed the way he held
himself—careful, controlled. A faint line of dried blood marked his collar where Eliam's
thorn had caught him. Sian and Halian flanked him, their usual ease replaced with
something tighter, watchful. Thaine leaned against the far wall, still looking at them
both with that bewildered expression he'd worn in the garden.

Karse was sprawled in a chair in the corner, one leg thrown over the armrest. His
amber eyes tracked them as they approached, lingering on the possessive spread of
Eliam's fingers against her waist. His lips curved into something that wasn't quite a
smile. "You smell like sex."

Heat flooded Briar's face. Beside her, she felt Eliam go rigid, but not with embarrassment. With warning.

"Is there a point to that observation?" Eliam's voice was dangerously calm.

"Just noting that someone had a better morning than the rest of us." Karse's tone
carried amusement but no actual judgment. "Though I suppose that's one way to deal
with attempted kidnapping and ah... *territorial* disputes."

"Karse," Thaine said, his tone suggesting this wasn't helpful.

The Drak shrugged, clearly unbothered. "What? We're all thinking it."

"We're not *all* thinking it," Sian said firmly, though her cheeks had gone pink. "And
it's not relevant to why we're here."

Arion's jaw tightened, but he said nothing. His eyes found Briar's for a moment, and she saw something complicated there—hurt and resignation and that same determined intensity from last night. The warmth in Briar's chest suddenly pulled in two directions—toward Eliam at her side and, disturbingly, toward Arion by the window. She pressed her hand against it, trying to quiet the sensation.

He finally looked away, focusing on the room at large.

"Thank you for coming," Arion began, his tone formal. His gaze met Eliam's briefly before settling on Briar. "We need to discuss what happened last night."

"Malus tried to steal her through the marks," Eliam said flatly. "The discussion should be about how to prevent it happening again."

"The discussion," Arion said, his jaw tightening, "should be about why it was possible at all. The Star Court's wards should have prevented any external compulsion. Yet he still reached her. If I hadn't been in the gardens, she would have crossed the border."

Briar felt the weight of everyone's attention shift to her. She touched her throat self-consciously, feeling the autumn marks rustle beneath her fingers.

"What do you remember?" Sian asked gently.

"Waking up at the stones," Briar said. "I was already there, already moving toward the border. I couldn't stop. My body wouldn't respond to what I wanted, only to what the marks were telling me to do." She swallowed hard. "Malus was there. Beyond the border. Waiting."

"He knew it would work," Thaine said quietly. "He knew he could call you through the marks and you'd have no choice but to obey."

"This happened because your wards failed," Eliam's voice carried an edge of accusation. "So much for the vaunted protection of the Star Court."

"They didn't fail." Halian stepped forward, his usual cheerfulness replaced by concern. "That's what's troubling. The wards are intact, stronger than ever. Whatever Malus did, he didn't break through them."

"Then how—" Briar started, then stopped as understanding dawned. "The marks. They're not external magic."

"No," Sian said quietly. "They're part of you now. Woven into your being through the bargain. The wards can't protect you from something that's already inside."

The warmth in Briar's chest pulsed with agitation, responding to her spike of fear. She felt Eliam's hand tighten on her waist.

"Which means," Karse said lazily from his corner, "that as long as those pretty marks decorate her throat, the copper-haired one can call to her whenever he pleases."

"Not if she's properly warded," Arion said, moving closer. "Individual protections, layered and reinforced daily."

"Temporary measures," Eliam countered. "Bandages on a severed artery."

"Better than letting her bleed out." Arion's light flickered faintly around his fingers. "Or would you prefer to wait until Malus succeeds in stealing her?"

The temperature in the room dropped as Eliam's shadows began to gather. Briar pressed her hand against his chest before another fight could erupt.

"Stop," she said quietly. "Both of you. This isn't helping."

"She's right," Thaine said, pushing off from the wall. "You're too busy marking territory to focus on the real problem."

"Which is?" Eliam's tone suggested Thaine was walking on dangerous ground.

"That Malus knows something we don't." Thaine's dark eyes were serious.

Silence fell over the room. Briar felt the warmth pulse again, stronger this time, as if responding to being discussed.

"There's more," Halian said reluctantly. "When I was reinforcing the wards this morning, I noticed something. A foreign energy signature from the eastern boundaries match the residue Malus left behind when he attacked the first time."

"He's been testing our defenses," Sian added. "For days, maybe longer."

"Looking for weaknesses," Arion said, his expression grim. "Planning."

"The question is what he's planning," Karse said, examining his fingers with apparent boredom.

"Does it matter?" Eliam's voice was cold.

"It matters if we want to stop him," Thaine said. "Know your enemy's desires and you know his moves."

Briar's hand rose involuntarily to her chest, feeling the warmth pulse beneath her palm. Everyone's attention shifted to the gesture.

"We should tell them," she said quietly.

"Tell us what? What exactly are you keeping to yourselves?" Arion asked, his gaze fixed on Eliam. "Or rather what secrets are you forcing her to keep?"

"Nothing that concerns you, brightling," Eliam sneered.

"Ever since I arrived I've felt a warmth, a pull, that I didn't understand," Briar said, interrupting Arion before the argument could escalate again. "Ever since... ever since the Wild Hunt, it's been getting stronger. Reacting to things. To danger, to emotions, to..." she glanced at Arion, then away, "to certain people."

"It has always recognized me," Eliam said, his tone carrying a note of possession. "Responded to me, but I couldn't figure out what it was."

"Malus when he fed from me... he said I tasted of old magic, of the forest..." she glanced towards Eliam. "He said it was because of a piece of Eliam's essence that had been hidden inside me. The night he made the bargain with my mother."

"But it responded to me too," Arion said quietly. "Last night. When I..." He didn't finish, but everyone understood.

Eliam's shadows surged before he controlled them. "A fluke. Desperation."

"Was it?" Arion's gaze stayed on Briar. "Or is there something more to this magic than simple recognition?"

"What do you mean?" Sian asked.

"I mean," Arion said slowly, "that if Eliam hid something in her, then we need to understand what it is and why it's been getting stronger. What exactly did you do that night?"

Eliam hesitated. "I don't remember clearly. Making the bargain with her mother, yes. But what happened before, why I was there..." Frustration bled through his controlled tone. "There are gaps."

"Malus said he was conducting a ritual," Briar explained. "Something meant to strip Eliam's power. That Eliam must have intervened when my mother was dying."

"A ritual?" Arion questioned, gaze flickering towards Eliam.

Eliam had gone very still. Briar looked up at him, seeing the calculation in his eyes, the pieces he was putting together that he wasn't sharing.

"What aren't you telling us?" she asked.

He met her gaze, and she saw the conflict there. The desire to protect her from knowledge that might hurt her, warring with the necessity of information.

"There are... stories," he said finally. "Old ones. About fae who split their power to protect it."

"Protect it from what?" Halian asked.

"From being stolen. Destroyed. Corrupted." Eliam's jaw tightened. "From family members who might try to take what isn't theirs."

Understanding rippled through the room.

"You think you knew," Arion said. "You think you knew Malus would come for your power."

"I think," Eliam said carefully, "that my brother has always been ambitious. And that hiding something valuable where he wouldn't think to look would be exactly the kind of thing I would do."

"Inside a human," Sian said softly. "Brilliant. Insane, but brilliant."

"Except now Malus knows," Thaine pointed out. "So the hiding place isn't hidden anymore."

"Which is why he's testing the borders," Halian said, understanding dawning.

"He talked about taking me apart," she said, her voice smaller than she intended. "About seeing how I work."

Eliam pulled her against him, his arms wrapping around her protectively. "That won't happen."

"Won't it?" Karse asked, his tone deceptively mild. "He got her to walk to the border in her sleep. What happens next time? Or the time after that?"

"I think the better question is, what did Malus want with your power, Eliam?" Thaine's voice cut through the tension.

Eliam's jaw tightened. "Power is power. Does he need another reason?"

Karse straightened in his chair for the first time since they'd entered. "Power for power's sake? No. The copper-haired one has plenty of his own."

"Unless he needs yours specifically," Thaine said, pushing off from the wall. "Forest Court magic for something only Forest Court magic can accomplish."

"There are things sealed in the Wildwood," Eliam said, choosing each word with extreme care. "Old things. Dangerous things."

"The Night Court," Sian breathed.

The air in the room seemed to shift and grow heavy.

Briar looked between them. The way they'd all gone still, the way even Karse's casual sprawl had tensed—whatever the Night Court was, it terrified them.

"What's the Night Court?" she asked. "The books you made me study... they only spoke of five courts."

"There used to be six," Arion said quietly. His light had dimmed, drawing inward. "The Night Court was destroyed centuries ago."

"Not destroyed," Eliam corrected. "Sealed."

"What's the difference?" Briar asked, though the warmth in her chest was already pulsing with dread, as if it knew the answer would be terrible.

"Destroyed things stay dead," Karse said. His claws had extended slightly, catching the firelight. "Sealed things can be released."

The fire in the hearth popped, sending sparks up the chimney. Everyone flinched.

"They were fae once," Sian explained, her voice barely above a whisper. "The Night Court. But they changed, became something else. Something... wrong. They fed on humans first and then—" She stopped, swallowing hard.

"Fae," Eliam finished. "They began to hunt and consume their own, they discovered that blood could enhance their magic exponentially, but it was temporary and each time required more to satiate their growing hunger. They stopped being fae as we understand it and became what we called the Unseelie."

Briar's hand rose to her throat, to the marks that still carried the memory of Malus's feeding. The warmth in her chest contracted violently.

"The other courts united against them," Arion said. "The only time in our history all the courts worked together. It took everything we had to seal them away."

"And the Forest Court holds that seal," Eliam said. The shadows at his feet had spread to touch the walls now. "Has held it for centuries. It requires Forest King magic to break it—but not just any Forest King's magic. The seal was designed to need more power than any single ruler could possess."

The pieces clicked into place with sickening clarity.

"That's why he needs your magic too," Briar said, understanding. "Malus has his own Forest King power, but it's not enough. He needs both."

"That's insane," Halian said immediately, but his voice cracked on the word. "Even he couldn't be that—"

"My brother has always been fascinated by dark and dangerous things," Eliam interrupted. "By power. When he approached me about releasing them, when he tried to convince me that the Unseelie deserved freedom, that we could control them—" His jaw clenched. "I refused. When it became clear he wouldn't stop trying, that he'd been collecting old texts, seeking ways to break the seal, I had no choice. I imprisoned him."

"But imprisonment wasn't enough," Thaine said slowly. "He was looking for other ways."

"The ritual he mentioned," Briar said, her mind whirling with possibilities. "Could have have been trying to steal your powers to open this seal?"

"And I stopped him," Eliam said. "Barely. The ritual was already in progress when I arrived. I couldn't prevent it entirely, only—" He stopped, jaw clenching.

"Only save a fragment," Briar finished. "By hiding it somewhere he'd never think to look. Inside the human woman you were making a bargain with."

"But that shouldn't be possible," Sian said, her brow furrowing. "Humans can't hold fae magic. It burns them from the inside out."

"Yet, she's held it for twenty-five years," Arion pointed out, his gaze intense on Briar.

"The warmth," Briar said quietly. "It's been getting stronger. Ever since the Wild Hunt, it's been... changing. Manifesting in ways it never did before."

"What kind of ways?" Halian asked.

"Giant thorns... golden blooms..." She pressed her hand against her chest, feeling the warmth pulse. "It responds to danger, protecting me... or maybe protecting itself."

"That's not just stored magic," Thaine said slowly. "That's magic that's learned. Adapted."

"Or merged," Karse said, straightening in his chair. His amber eyes were sharp, calculating. "Twenty-five years of fae essence sitting inside human flesh. Like leaving metal in water until it rusts, except..."

"Except instead of destroying either element, they've combined," Eliam said. His voice was carefully controlled, but Briar felt his tension through the warmth. "The fragment didn't just hide inside her. It's been slowly transforming her."

"Into what?" Briar asked, though she wasn't sure she wanted the answer.

Silence stretched through the room. The fire had burned lower, casting long shadows that seemed to reach toward her.

"Something new," Sian said quietly.

"That's why Malus was so fascinated when he fed from you," Arion said, understanding dawning. "He could taste it. Not just the fragment, but what you're becoming."

"She's not just carrying Forest Court magic anymore," Thaine said, his dark eyes wide. "After twenty-five years of it seeping into every part of her..."

"She IS Forest Court magic," Karse finished. "In a form Malus can use. Not quite human, not quite fae, but something between. Something that could help him break the seal."

Briar's stomach twisted. The warmth in her chest pulsed frantically, as if confirming their words. "I'm not human anymore?"

"You're something unprecedented," Eliam said, his arm tightening around her. "Something that shouldn't exist but does."

"Which is why he's so desperate to get her back," Sian said. "It's not just about reclaiming the fragment—"

"It's about what the fragment has become," Arion concluded. "What she's become."

"There is something I don't understand," Thaine said. "How did Malus manage to conduct any sort of ritual when he was locked in your dungeons?"

Eliam frowned. "He must have had help."

"Who would know about such a ritual?" Arion demanded. "This isn't common knowledge."

"Someone with access to old texts," Eliam said. "Forbidden knowledge. Someone who'd been studying—"

"Ferria," Halian said suddenly, his face paling. "She's been requesting access to the restricted archives for years. Said it was for historical research."

"We need to question her," Arion said immediately. "Find out what she knows, what she told Malus—"

"Bring her here," Eliam commanded, his voice carrying the authority of a king despite being in Star Court territory.

Halian hesitated, torn between defending his sister and acknowledging the threat she represented. Finally, he nodded and left the room.

They waited in tense silence. The fire had burned low, casting long shadows that seemed to move on their own. Outside, the snow had thickened, reducing the world to white nothing. Briar found herself counting heartbeats, feeling the warmth pulse with each one.

Footsteps in the corridor. Too fast. Too many.

Halian burst through the door, and Briar knew immediately something was wrong. Snow clung to his hair—he'd been outside. His face was white, his breathing ragged.

Halian returned, his expression troubled. "She's gone."

"What?" Eliam's voice went flat.

"Ferria. Her cell's empty. The guards are unconscious but alive." Halian's jaw tightened. "She must have had help from the inside, or..." He trailed off, unwilling to voice the alternative—that his sister had capabilities they hadn't known about.

"She'll go to Malus," Briar said quietly. The warmth in her chest pulsed with unease.

"Likely," Eliam agreed. "But she's been locked up. She doesn't know our plans."

"She knows about the ritual," Arion pointed out. "She helped design it."

"And she hates me," Briar added, remembering the venom in Ferria's eyes. "If she reaches Malus, she'll make sure he knows exactly how to hurt me."

"Let her," Eliam said coldly. "She's a tool, nothing more. Malus already knows where we are, what we have. Ferria changes nothing."

"Except now he has someone who understands the ritual's mechanics," Sian said quietly. "Someone who might be able to tell him why it didn't work completely."

Silence settled over the room. Outside, the snow continued to fall steadily, muffling the world.

"We need to secure the seal," Arion said finally. "Before Malus makes his move."

"Easier said than done," Thaine said. "The heart of the wildwood isn't exactly mapped. Most who go looking for it don't come back."

"The fae don't come back," Karse corrected from his corner. His tone carried an edge that made everyone turn toward him. "Because you don't know the old paths. Don't know how to read the forest's warnings."

"And the Drak do?" Eliam asked, skepticism clear.

Karse's laugh was bitter. "Who do you think lived there before you turned it into a wasteland? Before you sealed your mistakes in our hunting grounds and let the corruption spread through the trees?"

The temperature in the room shifted. Not colder—tenser.

"The Unseelie seal," Arion said slowly, "is in Drak territory?"

"Was." Karse's claws extended slightly. "Until the corruption from your sealed monsters poisoned the land. Drove out the game. Made the water run black. We had to abandon territories we'd held for millennia because the fae courts couldn't be bothered to actually destroy their enemies."

"We couldn't destroy them," Sian said defensively. "They were too powerful—"

"So you made them our problem instead." Karse stood, his movements fluid and predatory. "Sealed them away and left us to deal with the consequences."

"You know where it is," Eliam said. Not a question.

"Every Drak knows where it is." Karse's amber eyes burned. "We mark it on our maps as forbidden ground. Pass the warnings down through generations. Stay away from the heart where the fae buried their shame."

"Could you take us there?" Arion asked.

Karse was quiet for a long moment, his gaze moving over each of them before settling on Briar. "The question isn't whether I could. It's whether I should. Why would I help the courts that destroyed Drak lands?"

"Because if Malus breaks that seal," Thaine said quietly, "the corruption you've lived with will seem like nothing compared to what gets released."

"And because," Eliam added, his shadows stirring, "we could add other protections. Layer magic from multiple courts. Make it so no single power could ever break it."

"Pretty promises," Karse said. "The fae are good at those."

"What do you want?" Briar asked suddenly. Everyone looked at her, but she kept her eyes on Karse. "For your help. What would make it worth it?"

Karse tilted his head, studying her. "When this is over, if we survive, the courts acknowledge what they did. Publicly. And work to heal the corruption they caused."

"That could take decades," Halian said.

"Then you'd better get started." Karse's smile showed teeth. "Those are my terms. Take them or find the seal yourselves. Good luck getting there in time."

Eliam and Arion exchanged a look, Arion offered a short nod.

"We agree to your terms, Drak," Eliam said, his shadows stirring ominously. "But if you betray us, I'll flay you alive. Very slowly."

Karse smirked, showing far too many teeth. "Promises, promises. Though if I wanted to watch you all die horribly, I'd just let you wander into the corruption without a guide. Much less effort on my part, and probably more entertaining."

"Comforting," Thaine muttered.

"I'm pragmatic," Karse said with a shrug. "Betraying you gains me nothing. Helping you might actually fix the wasteland your courts created. Simple mathematics."

"Just remember the flaying," Eliam said flatly.

"How could I forget? You've made it sound so appealing." Karse's amber eyes glinted with amusement. "Though I should mention, Drak skin is remarkably difficult to flay. Something about the scales. You'd need special tools."

"I'll manage."

"I'm sure you would." Karse stretched lazily.

"If we're done with the threats, we should discuss preparations. We'll need at least three days to gather what we need," Arion said, already shifting into planning mode. "Supplies for the journey, cold weather gear—"

"Two days," Eliam countered, his eyes moving to the marks peeking out from beneath Briar's dress collar. "We don't have the luxury of time."

"Two days then." Arion's light flickered with frustration but he didn't argue further. "We should keep the group small. The old paths won't accommodate a large party."

"Agreed," Eliam said. "The four of us and Thaine for tracking."

"I'm going too," Sian stepped forward, her usually gentle demeanor replaced with steel.

"It's too dangerous—" Arion started.

"The corruption poisons water first," Sian interrupted. "Rivers, streams, even morning dew becomes tainted near the seal. You'll need someone who can purify water sources, or you'll die of thirst before you even reach the heart of the wildwood."

"She has a point," Karse said lazily. "The corruption spreads through water like blood through veins. Every stream near the seal runs black. Without an Undine to cleanse it..."

"We'd have to carry all our water for two weeks," Thaine concluded. "That's not feasible."

"Exactly." Sian's chin lifted. "My magic can separate the corruption from clean water. It's exhausting, but possible. Unless you'd prefer to test what corrupted water does to someone who's part Forest Court magic?" She looked pointedly at Briar.

"I'm going too," Halian said quietly.

Everyone turned to look at him.

"Halian—" Arion began.

"You'll need a healer," he began.

"We'll manage," Eliam countered, his tone dismissive.

Halian wasn't going to be deterred.

"My sister helped create this mess," he said. His jaw was tight, hands clenched at his sides. "I should have seen it, should have paid more attention. She never wanted to leave the Forest Court, I made her come with me... I had no idea she was meeting with Malus."

"No one blames you," Sian said gently.

"I blame me." The words came out sharp. "She's my family. My responsibility. I failed to stop her, the least I can do is help fix what she's done."

"Your guilt won't help us," Eliam replied.

"No, but my magic might." Halian's usual cheerfulness was completely absent. "I know defensive spells, ward construction. If we're going to reinforce the seal, you'll need someone who understands magical architecture."

"He's not wrong," Arion admitted reluctantly. "Adding new layers to an existing seal requires precision. Halian's studied magical theory more extensively than any of us."

"Seven then," Thaine said from his position against the wall. "Should be manageable."

"This is either going to be very effective or a complete disaster," Karse observed. "Seven people who barely trust each other, traveling through corrupted territory to stop an insane fae lord from releasing ancient monsters. What could possibly go wrong?"

"When you put it like that, it sounds almost impossible," Halian said, some of his usual dry humor returning.

"Almost?" Sian asked.

"Well, we have the power of three courts, a Drak who knows the territory, the best tracker in the Forest Court, and whatever Briar is becoming." Halian glanced at her. "I'd say we have slightly better than impossible odds."

"Slightly better than impossible," Thaine muttered with a shake of his head. "How reassuring."

"Two days to prepare," Arion said, bringing them back to practical matters. "We'll need cold weather gear, provisions for at least two weeks—"

"Two weeks?" Sian asked.

"The paths aren't straight," Karse explained. "And if we encounter corruption, we'll need to go around it."

"What about weapons?" Thaine asked.

"Star metal, if you have any," Eliam said, looking at Arion. "The Unseelie corruption recoils from it."

Arion's expression tightened. "We have a few pieces. Old blades from before... from when we needed them last. They're kept in the deep vaults."

"Star metal?" Briar asked.

"Forged with metal that fell from the sky," Sian explained. "It holds properties that are antithetical to Unseelie magic. But it's rare. Most of it was used during the war."

"I can retrieve what we have," Halian offered. "Three, maybe four blades."

"Better than nothing," Karse said. "The corruption has a way of turning regular weapons useless. They rust, decay, sometimes turn on their wielders."

"Comforting," Briar muttered.

"We'll need to coordinate our magic," Sian said. "Different courts' magic doesn't always blend well. We should practice working together before we're in actual danger."

"Tomorrow," Arion agreed. "After we've gathered supplies." He looked around the room. "Everyone should get rest tonight. We have two days of intense preparation ahead."

His gaze settled on Briar. "What about the compulsion? If Malus tries again—"

"I have a temporary solution," Eliam said curtly, his hand tightening on Briar's waist. "It's handled."

"What kind of solution?" Arion pressed, concern evident in his voice.

"The kind that works." Eliam was already guiding Briar toward the door. "We have preparations to make."

"Eliam—" Arion started.

"Two days, princeling. Focus on your supplies."

Without waiting for a response, Eliam steered Briar out of the room, leaving the others to their planning. She could feel the tension in his hand against her back, the purposeful stride that meant he had something specific in mind.

"What temporary solution?" she asked once they were in the corridor.

"You'll see," was all he said, and something about his tone made her stomach flutter with equal parts anticipation and concern.

Chapter Twenty-Six

T he door closed behind them with a soft click. Briar watched as Eliam moved through their room with methodical precision, his shadows spreading from his fingertips to trace patterns across the floor, up the walls, around the windows. The marks he left glowed faintly before fading into invisibility, but she could feel them—a subtle pressure in the air, a tingle against her skin.

"What are you doing?" she asked, though she already suspected.

"Wards." His voice was flat, controlled in that way that meant he was furious about something he couldn't immediately fix. "They'll alert me if anything crosses them."

She watched him work, noting how the patterns seemed to concentrate around the bed, the door, the terrace. All the places she might try to leave from. The warmth in her chest pulsed with unease.

"Anything," she repeated. "Or just me?"

He paused, his hand hovering over the windowsill. "Both."

At least he was honest about it. She crossed her arms, trying for levity despite the fear crawling up her spine. "Why not just put a bell around my neck? Save yourself the magical effort."

The joke fell flat. He turned to look at her, and his expression was so serious it made her stomach drop.

"Don't." The word came out sharp. "Don't make light of this. You walked to him in your sleep. You almost—" He stopped, jaw clenching.

"I know." The fear she'd been trying to suppress with humor came flooding back. "I know, I just… I can't stop thinking about it. What if he tries again tonight? What if the wards aren't enough? What if—"

Eliam crossed to her in three quick strides, his hands finding her face, tilting it up to meet his eyes. "He won't take you. I won't let him."

"You can't stay awake forever," she pointed out, her voice smaller than she intended. "And if he calls when you're sleeping—"

"Then the wards will wake me." His thumbs brushed across her cheekbones. "Every ward I'm placing is tied to me. The moment you cross one, I'll know."

"A magical leash," she said, trying for bitter but landing on resigned.

"A necessity." He didn't deny it, didn't try to soften it. "Until we deal with Malus, until we break his hold on you, this is what we have."

She pulled away from his hands, moving to sit on the edge of the bed. The fear was still there, coiled in her stomach, making her hands shake slightly. She pressed them against her thighs, trying to still the trembling.

"I can't stop thinking about it," she admitted. "Standing at those stones, seeing him there, wanting to go to him even though I knew what he'd do to me. My body just… wouldn't listen."

The bed dipped as Eliam sat beside her. His hand found hers, fingers interlacing. "You're afraid."

"Terrified," she corrected. "What if next time you're not there? What if next time the wards fail? What if—"

"Stop." His voice was gentle but firm. "You're spiraling."

"I'm being realistic."

"You're torturing yourself with possibilities." His hand tightened on hers. "None of which are happening right now."

"But they could—"

"Many things could happen," he interrupted. "Most of them won't. Right now, you're here. You're safe. You're with me."

She looked at him, saw the intensity in his dark eyes, the controlled way he was holding himself. "How are you so calm about this?"

"I'm not." The admission was quiet. "When I woke up and you were gone, when I realized what was happening…" His free hand clenched into a fist. "I've never felt fear like that."

The warmth in her chest pulsed, responding to his emotion, and she felt it then—the terror he was keeping locked down, the rage at his brother, the desperate need to keep her safe.

"But being afraid won't help," he continued. "So I'm doing what I can. Wards. Plans. Keeping you close."

"And if that's not enough?"

He turned to face her fully, his hand releasing hers only to slide up her arm, across her shoulder, to rest at the back of her neck. "Then I'll find another way. And another. As many as it takes."

"Eliam—"

"You're mine," he said, the words carrying that possessive weight she was learning to recognize. "And I protect what's mine. Always."

The warmth in her chest surged toward him, seeking comfort, and she found herself leaning into his touch despite everything.

"I need to stop thinking about it," she said. "Just for a little while. I need my mind to stop running through all the ways this could go wrong."

His thumb traced along her hairline, a gentle touch at odds with the intensity of his gaze. "I could help with that."

"How?"

His hand tightened slightly in her hair, not enough to hurt but enough to make her breath catch. "By giving you something else to focus on."

Heat that had nothing to do with the warmth in her chest spread through her. "That's your solution? Distraction through—"

"Through reminding you who you belong to," he said, already pulling her closer. "Through making you think about nothing but my hands on you, my mouth on you, until you can't remember why you were afraid."

Her breath hitched. "That's not exactly addressing the problem."

"No," he agreed, his mouth hovering just above hers. "But it's effective."

She wanted to argue, to point out that avoiding the fear wasn't the same as conquering it. But his lips brushed against hers, barely a touch, and her thoughts scattered.

"Let me," he murmured against her mouth. "Let me take you apart until the only thing you can think about is how I'm putting you back together."

The fear was still there, coiled in her stomach. But now there was heat too, spreading lower, making her shift closer to him.

"Yes," she breathed, and felt his satisfaction through the warmth as he claimed her mouth properly.

His kiss was possessive, demanding, leaving no room for thoughts of Malus or marks or midnight compulsions. There was only Eliam, his hands in her hair, his tongue sweeping into her mouth, the solid presence of him grounding her in the present moment.

When he pulled back, she was breathing hard, her hands fisted in his shirt.

"Better?" he asked, though the satisfied curve of his lips said he already knew the answer.

"Getting there," she managed.

"Then I'll have to work harder." His hands moved to the laces of her dress. "Until you can't remember anything but this. But me."

And for the first time since waking at the border stones, the fear loosened its grip, replaced by something much more immediate and infinitely more pleasant.

His fingers worked the laces with deliberate slowness, each pull making the dress loosen incrementally. The anticipation built with every movement, making her breath come shorter, her skin hypersensitive to every brush of his knuckles through the fabric.

"You're going too slow," she complained, though her voice came out breathier than intended.

"Am I?" His mouth found her throat, teeth scraping over her pulse point. "I told you I was going to take you apart. That requires patience."

The dress finally fell loose enough that he could push it from her shoulders. The cool air raised goosebumps across her exposed skin, but his hands followed immediately, warm and possessive as they traced the curve of her shoulders, down her arms.

His mouth moved lower, tracing the edge of where her dress still clung to her chest. Each kiss was deliberately placed, mapping territory he'd already claimed but seemed determined to mark again. When his teeth closed over the soft skin above her breast, biting down hard enough to leave a mark, she gasped and arched beneath him.

"Every time you feel afraid," he said against her skin, "I want you to touch these marks and remember who you belong to. Remember whose bed you're in. Whose hands are the only ones allowed to touch you."

His fingers hooked into the dress, pulling it down and off with more impatience now. She was left in only her undergarments, and those didn't last long under his focused attention.

"Still thinking about him?" he asked against her ear, and she could hear the dark satisfaction when her breath hitched.

"Trying not to," she admitted, because the image of Malus waiting beyond the border kept flickering behind her eyelids.

"Then I'm not doing my job properly."

He turned her suddenly, pressing her face-down onto the bed. The unexpected movement made her gasp, her hands twisting in the sheets. "Beautiful," he murmured and she felt him move behind her, solid and warm, his hands running down her spine with possessive intent.

"Up," he commanded, his hands finding her hips, guiding her to her knees while keeping her chest pressed to the mattress.

The position made her feel exposed and vulnerable. She could feel his gaze on her, taking in every inch of exposed skin, and her face flushed hot against the sheets.

His hands traced the backs of her thighs, up over the curve of her ass, deliberate and claiming. When he pulled her undergarments down and off, the cool air against her heated flesh made her shift restlessly.

"Stay still," he said, one hand pressing between her shoulder blades to keep her in place.

She tried, but the anticipation was too much. She could feel him behind her, still clothed, just watching. The power dynamic—her naked and exposed while he remained in control—made the warmth in her chest pulse frantically. It should have frightened her, but instead, it grounded her. This was Eliam. This was safe. This was choosing to give up control instead of having it stolen.

When his fingers finally touched her, sliding through her the wetness between her thighs, she moaned into the mattress. The angle let him go deeper, find spots that made her whole body jerk with sensation.

"Such sweet sounds you make," he said with dark satisfaction. "I'll never get enough."

She wanted to respond, to say something clever, but then his thumb found her clit and her thoughts scattered. He worked her with focused intent, building her up with steady pressure that had her pushing back against his hand, seeking more.

"Please what?" His thumb circled her clit with barely-there pressure. "Tell me what you need."

"You," she gasped. "I need you."

"You have me." Another circle, still too light. "Be specific."

"I need you inside me," she managed, her face flushing at the words. "I need you to stop teasing and just—"

She heard fabric rustling, felt him shift behind her. When he pressed against her entrance, she tried to push back, take him in, but his hands on her hips held her still.

"My pace," he said, and pushed in slowly, letting her feel every inch.

The stretch was intense from this angle, deeper, more overwhelming. She pressed her face into the sheets, muffling the sounds escaping her throat. Her fingers twisted in the fabric, knuckles white, as he set a rhythm that drove every coherent thought from her mind.

The warmth in her chest pulsed with each thrust, golden light flickering beneath her skin. She could feel it reaching for him, recognizing its other half, and the sensation layered with the physical pleasure until she couldn't separate them. The fear she'd carried all day dissolved under the onslaught of sensation—his hands gripping hard enough to bruise, the sound of his breathing getting rougher, the way he filled her completely.

"That's it," he said, voice rough. "Stop thinking. Just feel."

One hand slid around to find her clit, finger teasing until he shattered her completely. She came with a cry that might have been his name, her whole body convulsing, the warmth exploding outward in waves of golden light that painted the walls.

He didn't slow down, using his grip on her hips to hold her steady as he chased his own release. The continued stimulation when she was oversensitive had her gasping, caught between too much and not enough. When he finally came, pulling her hips back against him and holding her there, she felt it through the warmth—his pleasure mixing with hers until she couldn't tell where one ended and the other began.

They collapsed together, him turning her and pulling her against his chest before she could even catch her breath. She could feel his heart racing beneath her ear, could feel the possessive way his arms wrapped around her.

The fear that had been choking her earlier felt distant now, buried under layers of endorphins and exhaustion. She knew it would return, but for now there was only this: skin against skin, his marks fresh on her hips, and the absolute certainty that nothing could take her from this room while he held her like this.

"Better?" he asked against her hair.

She nodded against his chest, not trusting her voice yet.

"Sleep," he commanded softly. "The wards will hold. I'll hold. Nothing touches you tonight except me."

The courtyard was empty when Briar arrived, her breath misting in the cold morning air. Fresh snow blanketed the ground, pristine and undisturbed, though the sky had cleared to a pale winter blue. She pulled the fur-lined cloak tighter around herself, grateful for the practical clothing—woolen pants tucked into tall boots, a fitted leather vest over a warm tunic. The outfit was distinctly Star Court in its pale grays and silver embroidery, but functional in a way her previous dresses hadn't been.

She turned in a slow circle, wondering why Eliam had told her to meet him here before rushing off without explanation. The courtyard was large, surrounded by high walls that blocked the wind, with archways leading to various parts of the Star Court residence. But there was no sign of—

Movement caught her eye. Eliam emerged from one of the archways, and he wasn't alone. He was leading a horse—massive, white with gray dappling across its flanks, its breath steaming in the cold. The animal's hooves crunched through the snow with measured steps, clearly well-trained despite its size.

Briar's stomach dropped. "No."

"You don't even know what I'm going to say," Eliam said, though the slight curve of his lips suggested he knew exactly what her objection would be. He was smiling more often now and Briar wasn't sure what to make of it.

"You're going to tell me I need to learn to ride that thing."

"That thing has a name. This is Phaeon." He stopped a few feet from her, the horse towering over them both. "And yes, you need to learn."

"I really don't." She took a step backward, eyeing the horse warily. It turned its massive head to look at her, dark eyes far too intelligent for her comfort. "I can just ride with you. It worked fine before."

"It worked when we had no other option." His free hand caught her wrist before she could retreat further, pulling her closer to both him and the horse. "If we're traveling into the Wildwood, you need to be able to ride independently."

"Why? We managed—"

"We weren't being hunted by my brother." His voice had gone serious. "What happens if we're separated? If something happens to me? If we need to split up to evade pursuit?" His thumb brushed across her pulse. "Or would you prefer to be pressed against me for days on end, feeling every movement, every shift of muscle?"

Heat crept into her cheeks at the suggestion in his tone. "That's not—"

"Because I recall you finding it rather... distracting last time." His voice had dropped to that particular register that made her stomach flutter. "All that friction, the rhythm of movement, my thighs wrapped around—"

"Fine!" She cut him off, face burning. "Fine, I'll learn. But when this giant thing throws me and I break my neck, that's on you."

"Phaeon won't throw you." He released her wrist only to place his hand on the small of her back, guiding her closer to the horse. "I was assured he's well-trained and patient. Unlike some horses I could mention."

The horse snorted, as if offended by the comparison to others. Up close, it was even more intimidating—all muscle and power barely contained.

"First," Eliam said, his hand still warm on her back, "you need to let him know you're not a threat."

"I'm pretty sure I'm the one who should be worried about threats," Briar muttered, but she let Eliam guide her hand to the horse's neck.

The coat was softer than she expected, warm under her palm. Phaeon turned his head slightly to look at her, but didn't move otherwise.

"See? He's accepting you." Eliam's hand covered hers, showing her how to stroke along the horse's neck. "Horses can sense fear. Confidence is essential."

"Fake confidence still counts?"

"It's a start." He moved behind her, his chest almost touching her back. "Now, the first thing you need to learn is how to mount properly."

She turned her head to look at him and found his face much closer than expected. "Are you going to make suggestive comments about everything?"

"I haven't decided yet." His expression was perfectly controlled, but she could see amusement in his dark eyes. "Does it bother you?"

"It's distracting."

"Good. You need to learn to focus despite distractions." He stepped back, taking the reins. "Watch."

He demonstrated the proper way to mount—foot in stirrup, hand on the saddle, smooth motion up and over. He made it look effortless, of course. Sitting atop the horse, he looked every inch the fae lord—commanding, powerful, entirely in his element.

"Your turn," he said, dismounting with the same fluid grace.

Briar approached the stirrup with considerably less confidence. It was higher than she'd expected, the angle awkward. She got her foot in, grabbed the saddle, and tried to pull herself up.

She made it halfway before her arms gave out and she slid back down, nearly losing her balance entirely. Eliam's hand shot out to steady her waist.

"Less pulling, more pushing off with your grounded leg," he instructed. "Use your momentum."

She tried again. This time she made it farther but ended up sort of hanging off the side of the horse, one leg over, the other dangling uselessly.

"This is dignified," she gasped, struggling to right herself.

"Tremendously." His hand found her dangling leg, guiding it over until she was properly seated. "But you're up."

She was. She was also very high off the ground, and the horse hadn't even moved yet. Her hands gripped the saddle horn with white knuckles.

"Relax," Eliam said, one hand on Phaeon's neck to keep him still, the other on her thigh. "You're too tense. The horse can feel it."

"Easy for you to say. You're not the one sitting on top of a creature that could kill you with one kick."

"Phaeon has excellent manners. Unlike his rider, apparently." His hand squeezed her thigh once before moving to adjust her posture. "Sit up straighter. Shoulders back. Look ahead, not down."

She tried to follow his instructions, but everything felt wrong. The saddle was hard and unfamiliar, the height dizzying, and she could feel the horse's power coiled beneath her, waiting.

"Now," Eliam said, handing her the reins, "we're going to walk."

"Walk?" Her voice pitched higher. "Already?"

"Would you prefer to start with a gallop?" Eliam's tone was dry, but his hand remained on Phaeon's neck, keeping the horse still.

"I'd prefer to start with both feet on the ground."

"Too late for that." He positioned himself at Phaeon's head, one hand on the bridle. "Hold the reins loosely. Don't pull unless you want him to stop."

"Pulling means stop. Got it." She gripped the reins like a lifeline.

"Loosely," he reminded her. "You're not trying to strangle them."

She forced her fingers to relax slightly, though every instinct screamed at her to hold on tighter. Eliam made a soft clicking sound, and Phaeon took a step forward.

The motion rocked through her entire body. She immediately tensed, grabbing the saddle horn.

"Don't." Eliam's voice was calm but firm. "Move with him, not against him."

"I don't know what that means!"

"Feel the rhythm." He kept walking, leading Phaeon in a slow circle around the courtyard. "Let your hips follow the movement."

She tried, but everything felt wrong. She was bouncing slightly with each step, her thighs already starting to ache from gripping the saddle too tightly.

"You're fighting it," Eliam observed. He stopped Phaeon and moved to her side, his hand finding her thigh again. "Relax here." His touch was warm through the wool. "You're going to exhaust yourself."

"This is relaxed," she lied.

His eyebrow arched. "Is it?" His hand moved to her calf, which was indeed rigid with tension. "And this?"

"Fine, I'm terrified. Happy?"

He squeezed her calf gently before returning his hand to her thigh. "Think of it like when I'm inside you."

She nearly choked. "What?"

"You heard me." His voice dropped to that particular tone that made her breath catch. "You know how to move your hips in rhythm. How to anticipate motion and match it. How to let someone else guide the pace while you follow."

Her face burned. "That's not—"

"The same principle applies." His hand pressed against her thigh, demonstrating the rhythm. "You don't think about it when you're in bed with me. This is no different."

"It's completely different. One involves a massive animal that could kill me."

"And the other involves me," he said with dark amusement. "I fail to see the distinction."

Despite her terror, she found herself laughing. "You're terrible."

"But effective." He adjusted her foot in the stirrup. "Weight in your heels, not your toes. Like when you're bracing against the bed when I—"

"I get it!" she cut him off, face flaming.

"Do you?" His lips curved slightly. "Then show me. Move with him the way you move with me."

He started walking, Phaeon following placidly. This time, Briar tried to focus on the motion instead of her fear. The horse's gait was steady, predictable. She found herself starting to anticipate the movement, her hips beginning to follow the motion naturally.

"Better," Eliam said, and there was approval in his voice that made her stomach flutter. "Now, you're going to steer."

"What? No, you're steering. I'm just sitting here."

"I'm leading. You're going to steer." He stepped away from Phaeon's head, though he stayed close to her leg. "Use the reins. Gentle pressure in the direction you want to go."

She pulled lightly on the left rein. Phaeon's head turned, but he kept walking straight.

"With your legs too," Eliam instructed. "Press with your right leg to go left."

She tried again, adding leg pressure this time. Phaeon turned left in a wide arc. The success sent a little thrill through her.

"I did it!"

"You turned left. Congratulations." But she could hear the amusement in his voice. "Now right."

She tried the opposite, pulling the right rein while pressing with her left leg, and Phaeon obligingly turned right.

"Can you make him stop?" Eliam asked, stepping back further.

She pulled back on both reins. "Whoa?"

Phaeon stopped so abruptly she nearly pitched forward over his neck. Eliam's hand shot out to steady her.

"Gently," he said. "He's well-trained. You don't need to haul on his mouth."

"You could have mentioned that before."

"How else would you learn?" He moved back to Phaeon's head. "We're going to try a trot."

"We're absolutely not."

"We are." He was already adjusting her posture again, hands on her hips to position them correctly. "It's actually easier once you find the rhythm."

"Easier than walking?"

"Different. Post with the motion—rise and fall with his gait."

Before she could protest further, he made that clicking sound again followed by a command she didn't catch. Phaeon moved into a trot.

She immediately started bouncing hard in the saddle, her teeth clicking together with each jolt.

"Post!" Eliam called. "Up, down, up, down!"

She tried to rise with the motion, but her timing was completely off. She was coming down when she should be going up, the impacts jarring her spine. Her thighs burned with the effort of trying to grip and lift at the same time.

"I can't—" she gasped.

Eliam's hand found her knee, pressing in rhythm. "Up... down... up... down..."

She tried to follow his guidance, and suddenly—for just a moment—she found it. The rhythm clicked, and she was moving with Phaeon instead of against him.

Then she lost it again and bounced hard enough to bite her tongue.

"Ow!"

Eliam brought Phaeon back to a walk with a word. "You found it for a moment."

"Before I lost it again." She could taste blood in her mouth.

"That's how learning works." He stopped Phaeon completely and moved to help her dismount. "Swing your right leg over."

She did, but when she tried to lower herself down, her legs had turned to jelly. She would have collapsed if Eliam hadn't caught her, pulling her against his chest.

"My legs don't work," she said against his shoulder.

"They will." His arms stayed around her, supporting her weight. "You used muscles you've never used before."

"I may never walk again."

"Dramatic." But his hand rubbed her lower back where the muscles had seized. "You did well for a first lesson."

"I barely managed a trot."

"You stayed on." He pulled back enough to look at her face. "That's more than most manage their first time."

"You're just saying that."

"I don't say things I don't mean." His thumb brushed across her cheekbone. "You were determined. Even terrified, you kept trying."

The warmth in her chest pulsed, responding to his approval, and she felt heat rise in her cheeks that had nothing to do with exertion.

"Tomorrow we'll work on your seat," he said, and there was something in his tone that made the innocent statement sound like anything but.

"My seat is fine," she said, then realized what she'd said. "I mean—"

"I know what you meant." His lips curved in that way that meant he was highly amused. "But your riding seat needs work. You're too stiff."

"Because I was terrified."

"Among other reasons." His hands shifted to her hips, thumbs pressing into the sore muscles there. "You'll be sore tomorrow."

"I'm sore now."

"It will be worse tomorrow," he promised. "But we'll continue anyway. By the time we leave for the Wildwood, you'll be competent enough to not fall off at a walk."

"Such high praise."

"Would you prefer I lie and say you're a natural?"

"Maybe?"

"You're terrible," he said bluntly. "But you're stubborn enough to get better."

Despite everything, she found herself laughing. "That might be the worst compliment I've ever received."

"It wasn't a compliment. It was an observation." His hands stayed on her hips, supporting her until her legs steadied. "Tomorrow, same time. Don't be late."

"What if I can't walk by then?"

"Then I'll carry you to the horse." His tone suggested this wasn't a joke. "You're learning whether your legs cooperate or not."

She groaned. "You're a tyrant."

"Yes." He guided her toward the archway leading back inside, his hand firm on her lower back. "And tomorrow, you'll be a slightly less terrible rider because of it."

Phaeon nickered behind them, and Briar could have sworn it sounded like laughter.

"Even the horse thinks I'm hopeless," she muttered.

"The horse has good instincts." Eliam steered her through the doorway, out of the cold. "But he'll tolerate you anyway."

"How generous of him."

"It is, actually. I was told that Phaeon doesn't suffer fools." He glanced down at her, and there was something almost like amusement in his expression. "You should be flattered he didn't throw you."

"There is always tomorrow," she pointed out.

"True," he agreed. "And tomorrow's lesson will be worse."

And somehow, despite the threat in those words, despite her aching legs and the terror of being on horseback, she found herself looking forward to it. Even if it meant she'd probably end up face-first in the snow.

Chapter Twenty-Seven

B riar's legs trembled with each step back toward the residence, muscles she'd forgotten existed screaming in protest. The second day of lessons had gone better—she'd managed to stay on during a canter for almost a full circuit of the courtyard before losing her balance. Progress, but hardly mastery. In two days, she'd gone from complete terror to merely moderate fear, which would have to be enough.

Eliam had stayed behind to return Phaeon to the stables and speak with Thaine about route preparations. He'd sent her to their rooms to rest and she'd been grateful for the solitude, needing time to process the strange mix of accomplishment and inadequacy. She could ride now, barely, but the thought of navigating the corrupted paths of the Wildwood still made her uneasy.

Lost in thought, she rounded a corner too quickly and collided with someone coming the other way. Strong hands caught her arms, steadying her before she could fall backward, and she found herself staring up into Arion's startled face.

For a moment, neither moved. His hands were warm through her sleeves, his chest close enough that she could feel the heat radiating from him. The last time they'd been this close, his lips had been on hers, breaking Malus's compulsion with desperate intensity.

"I'm sorry, I wasn't—" she started.

"Are you hurt?" he asked at the same time.

They both stopped. His hands were still on her arms, and she could see something shift in his expression—a flicker of uncertainty that looked strange on someone usually so composed.

He released her and stepped back, the careful distance feeling more significant than it should.

"How are the preparations going?" she asked, defaulting to safe ground.

"Well enough." His tone was neutral, controlled. "Everyone's gathered what they need. Sian's been practicing corruption cleansing. Halian's reviewing ward construction theory."

"And you?"

"I was just heading to the vaults. To retrieve the star metal weapons." He paused, something crossing his face that she couldn't read. "Would you like to come? You should see what we'll be working with."

She nodded, curious despite the awkwardness. He turned and led the way through corridors she hadn't explored before, their footsteps echoing off crystalline walls that gradually gave way to stone as they descended.

"I didn't think the Star Court had underground spaces," she said, trying to fill the weighted silence.

"Even the brightest lights cast shadows," Arion replied. "We keep our dangerous things below."

There was something in his tone that made her want to ask more, but they'd arrived at a heavy door marked with symbols that seemed to absorb light rather than reflect it.

Arion pressed his hand against the wood, and his light flared briefly. The symbols responded, glowing white before the door swung open silently.

The vault beyond was small, circular, with walls of polished white stone. In the center stood a display holding four weapons that seemed to pull at her attention. They gleamed with an inner light that had nothing to do with Arion's magic—something cold and distant, like starlight on winter snow.

Two swords, long and elegant, their blades inscribed with patterns etched into their surfaces, a glaive with a wicked curved blade that seemed to slice the air around it, and a pair of twin daggers, smaller but no less mesmerizing, their handles wrapped in what looked like silver wire.

"Star metal," Arion said quietly. "Forged with fragments of metal that fell from beyond the sky. The Unseelie can't tolerate even the smallest amount, it burns them, disrupts their very essence."

Briar stepped closer, drawn despite herself. The weapons were beautiful in an alien way, but there was something else that caught her eye. Set into the wall above the display was a pendant—a starburst design with fragments of the same strange metal woven throughout.

"What's that?" she asked.

Arion followed her gaze. "A protection amulet. One of the last made before we ran out of sufficient star metal for forging." He moved to retrieve the weapons, carefully lifting each one. "It was meant for royalty, but never worn. Star metal is... uncomfortable for most fae. We can wield it briefly, but prolonged contact burns."

"Then how—"

"We'll manage," he said, but she noticed he was already wrapping the sword hilts in thick leather. "The corruption is far worse than a little discomfort."

He reached for the pendant last, hesitating before taking it from its setting. Tiny crystals embedded in the metal caught the light, throwing prismatic patterns across the walls.

"Here," he said, turning to her with it in his outstretched hand. "You should wear this."

"I couldn't—you just said it was meant for royalty."

"You're the only one of us who can wear it without pain." His expression was serious. "You're not fae, even if fae magic lives inside you. The star metal won't burn you the way it would us. And you'll need every protection we can offer."

She took it carefully, surprised by how light it was. The metal felt cool against her palm, almost pleasant, with none of the burning he'd described.

"Let me," Arion said, moving behind her to fasten the chain around her neck.

His fingers brushed her nape as he worked the clasp, and she felt him pause, his breath warm against her hair. The touch lingered longer than necessary, and when he spoke, his voice had dropped to something lower than she was used to from him.

"About what happened that night at the border—"

"You saved me," she said quickly. "I'm grateful."

"Grateful." He finished with the clasp but didn't step away. Instead, his hands settled on her shoulders, holding her in place. "Is that what you felt when I kissed you? Gratitude?"

The directness of the question startled her. This wasn't like Arion, he was usually careful, respectful of boundaries.

"I—" She tried to turn, but his hands tightened slightly, keeping her facing away.

"The warmth responded to me," he continued, and there was something almost possessive in his tone that reminded her unsettlingly of Eliam. "It reached for me like it was desperate. Like it recognized something in me that it needed."

Now she did turn, his hands falling away, and found his expression intense in a way she'd never seen before. The usual controlled calm was cracking, something hungrier showing through.

"Arion—"

"He's manipulating you." The words came out flat, certain. "The marks, the blood bargain, the way he's isolated you—you think you're choosing him, but are you? Really?"

"That's not true."

"Isn't it?" He stepped closer, backing her against the display case. "When was the last time you made a decision he didn't influence? When was the last time you were away from him long enough to think clearly? His essence *lives* inside of you. Did you ever think that if it wasn't there, you wouldn't be so easily swayed?"

Her back hit the cold stone, and he braced his hands on either side of her, caging her in. The light around him flickered erratically, not the steady glow she was used to but something sharper, almost aggressive.

"You're scaring me," she said quietly.

Something flickered across his face, surprise, maybe, or recognition, but it was quickly replaced by that unsettling intensity.

"Good," he said. "You should be scared. Of him. Of what he's turning you into. His possession, his thing." His hand rose to touch the pendant where it rested against her chest. "You deserve better than being someone's property."

"And what would I be with you?" The question came out sharper than intended.

"Mine." The word escaped before he seemed to catch himself, and she saw him blink, confusion crossing his features as if he wasn't sure why he'd said it. He stepped back abruptly, running a hand through his hair. "That's not—I didn't mean—"

"You sounded like him just then," Briar said, studying his face. "Exactly like him."

Arion's expression grew darker. "I'm nothing like him."

But even as he said it, she could see the uncertainty in his eyes. Something was changing in him, something he didn't understand any more than she did. The usual warmth of his light had taken on an edge, and the way he looked at her now—possessive, hungry, determined—was far from the gentle patience she'd come to expect.

"When he hurts you again," Arion said, his voice dropping back to that darker register, "and he will, because it's what he does—I won't pretend to be noble about it. I won't wait patiently or respect your space." He moved close again, though not quite as aggressively as before. "I'll take you away from him. Make you see what you could have with me instead."

"That doesn't sound like a choice."

"Neither does staying with someone who throws you to the wolves on a whim." His hand rose to her throat, fingers ghosting over the autumn marks. "Who marked you like property. Who would rather see you dead than free."

The warmth in her chest pulsed, pulling toward him with an intensity that made her gasp. His eyes widened, and she felt him lean into it, drawn by the same force.

"It wants me," he said softly, wonder and satisfaction mixing in his voice. "Whatever you want to call it, whatever it is—it recognizes me as much as it recognizes him."

"Why?" The question escaped before she could stop it. "Why both of you?"

"I don't know." His thumb traced along her jaw. "But I intend to find out. And when I do—"

Footsteps echoed in the corridor outside. Arion stepped back so quickly she almost stumbled, his court mask sliding back into place with visible effort. But she could still see it—the darkness lurking at the edges, the hunger he was trying to control.

"We should go," he said, his tone forcibly neutral as he gathered the wrapped weapons. "The others will be waiting."

As they left the vault, Briar couldn't shake the feeling that something fundamental had shifted.

The staging area was bustling with activity. Sian sorted through medical supplies while Halian checked and rechecked ward stones. Karse lounged against a wall, seemingly bored but his eyes tracking everything. Thaine was examining maps spread across a table.

Briar entered with Arion, the wrapped star metal weapons in his arms. The pendant lay cool against her chest, hidden beneath her cloak.

She'd barely taken three steps when Eliam strode in, Thaine close at his heels. He moved with that controlled stillness that meant he was furious.

"I returned to our rooms and you weren't there." His voice was perfectly even, which made it worse. His eyes tracked over her, checking for damage, before fixing on her face with an intensity that made her stomach tighten. "I thought I told you to return there."

The phrasing wasn't a question.

"She was helping me retrieve the star metal weapons," Arion said before Briar could respond, setting them down with deliberate casualness. "For tomorrow's journey. You know, the one where we all try not to die?"

Eliam's gaze never left Briar's face. "I wasn't aware my instructions required your interpretation, princeling."

"Instructions?" Arion stepped slightly closer to Briar. Not touching, just... present. "Interesting choice of words for someone who claims to care for her wellbeing."

"My words are my own concern."

"As are Briar's choices." Arion's light flickered with that newer, sharper edge. "Or did you forget that she's a person, not a possession to be ordered about?"

The temperature dropped a degree. Eliam's shadows didn't surge or writhe—they went perfectly, unnaturally still.

"Careful," Eliam said softly.

"Of what?" Arion's tone was mild, almost curious. "You're in my court, you have no titles, your power is diminished, and Briar..." He paused, letting his words sink in. "Well. She's here by choice, isn't she? Her own choice?"

Eliam took a step closer and Briar moved to intercept, placing a hand on his chest to still him further. He looked down and for a moment she thought he might back down.

Briar's cloak fell open and the star metal pendant caught the light. Eliam's eyes locked onto it, and for just a moment, something raw flashed across his face before the mask slammed back down.

"What is that?"

"Protection," Briar said quickly. "For the journey. Star metal repels corruption—"

"I am well aware of what star metal does." His voice had gone even flatter and his gaze shifted to Arion. "Star Court royalty doesn't share such treasures lightly."

"No," Arion agreed, unbothered by the implication of Eliam's words. "We don't."

Around the room, everyone had gone silent, watching.

"How generous of you," Eliam said, and there was something underneath the words that Briar couldn't quite identify. Not just anger. Something more uncertain. "To mark her with your court's protection."

"Someone should protect her," Arion said quietly. "Properly. Without conditions or consequences."

"The way you protected her at the border?" Eliam's hand clenched at his side. "With your mouth?"

"It worked, didn't it?" Arion's light brightened slightly.

Briar felt the warmth in her chest pulling between them, not violently but insistently, and she pressed her hand against it.

"Stop," she said. Both men looked at her, and she saw something almost identical in their expressions—want, fear, and something else neither of them seemed able to fully grasp.

"We leave tomorrow," she continued. "We need to work together."

"She's right," Sian said, relief evident in her voice. "Save the territorial displays for after we prevent the apocalypse."

Eliam shifted, his hand finding the small of her back. Not grabbing, not dragging, but the pressure was unmistakable.

"We should go," he said. "You need rest."

It wasn't a command, not quite. As he guided her toward the door, Arion's voice followed them, quiet but clear.

"Think about what I said earlier, Briar. About choices."

Eliam's hand tightened slightly against her back, and they walked in silence back to their rooms. She could feel tension radiating from him, controlled but present. He was angry about the pendant, about finding her with Arion. His silence was one Briar had grown to recognize, it was the kind that came before storms.

The fire had burned down to embers, casting the room in shadows and faint orange light. Beside her, Eliam slept with the stillness of someone who never questioned his right to anything—not power, not possession, not her. His arm lay heavy across her waist, and normally the weight would be comforting. Tonight it felt like a chain.

Arion's words wouldn't leave her alone.

His essence lives inside of you. Did you ever think that if it wasn't there, you wouldn't be so easily swayed?

Briar stared at the ceiling, trying to trace back through her memories. The first time she'd seen Eliam in the forest, the immediate pull she'd felt—was that her or the essence recognizing him? When he'd saved her from the river, the way she'd trusted him despite having every reason not to, was that instinct or magical influence?

The warmth pulsed gently in her chest, a constant presence she'd grown so accustomed to she barely noticed it anymore. But now she was acutely aware of it, of how it responded to Eliam even in sleep, reaching toward him like a plant toward sunlight.

Twenty-five years. It had been inside her for twenty-five years, since before she could form memories. How could she possibly separate what was her from what was it?

She thought about every moment with Eliam. The way her body responded to his touch, the pull she felt toward him even when he frightened her, the forgiveness that came too easily after he'd cast her out. Had any of that been real? Or was she just a puppet dancing to the essence's pull?

But no—she'd resisted him. Multiple times. She'd been furious when he'd sent her to the Wild Hunt, had tried to escape, had fought against the bargain. If the essence controlled her, wouldn't she have simply accepted everything?

Unless that was part of it too. The illusion of resistance to make the surrender feel like choice.

Her chest tightened with something approaching panic. Every emotion she'd thought was hers could be questioned now. The love she'd confessed, was it love or magical compulsion? The desire she felt, was it attraction or the essence seeking its other half?

She turned her head to look at Eliam in the dim light. Even in sleep, there was something predatory about him, something dangerous. Why had she been drawn to that? She'd never been attracted to danger in her old life, had dated safe, boring men who would never dream of throwing her to wolves or marking her as property.

But then she thought about Arion, and the warmth pulled toward him too. She felt that same physical draw, that recognition. Yet she didn't love him. She could acknowledge he was beautiful, that there was attraction, but it didn't go deeper.

Or was that just what she was telling herself to make this bearable?

Eliam shifted in his sleep, his arm tightening around her, and the warmth surged with contentment. She felt it like a separate entity almost, pleased by the contact. Was any of what she felt actually hers?

The spiral of doubt pulled her deeper. Every kiss, every touch, every moment of tenderness—all of it could be false. She was corrupted by magic she'd never asked for, bound to a man who might only want her because of what she carried. What had started as a curiosity, a thing to be discovered, had become an obsession.

Would Eliam even look at her twice if the warmth hadn't been there? Or would she just be another human, insignificant and forgettable?

She pressed her hand against her chest, feeling the warmth pulse under her palm. It was part of her now, woven so deeply she'd probably die if it was removed. She'd never know what she would have chosen without it. Never know if this love was real or manufactured.

The thought made her feel hollow, like something had scooped out her insides and left only questions behind.

"Whatever you're thinking about, don't," Eliam murmured against her shoulder, startling her. She hadn't realized he'd woken.

"Sorry," she whispered. "I didn't mean to wake you."

His hand moved to cover hers where it pressed against her chest. "What troubles you?"

She couldn't tell him. Couldn't voice the doubts that would sound like betrayal. So she said, "Tomorrow. The journey. Everything."

He was quiet for a moment, and she wondered if he sensed the lie. Then his lips found her neck, pressing against the marks there.

"Sleep," he commanded softly. "Whatever tomorrow brings, you'll face it better rested."

The warmth pulsed at his touch, reaching for him eagerly, and she wanted to cry. Because she couldn't tell anymore if the comfort she felt was hers or its. Couldn't tell if she turned into his embrace because she wanted to or because the magic somehow demanded it.

But she turned anyway, burying her face against his chest, trying to lose herself in his solid presence. Even if it wasn't real, even if it was all magical manipulation, it was all she had.

The doubt had taken root though, spreading through her like corruption of a different kind, and she didn't know how to stop it.

Chapter Twenty-Eight

T he courtyard was organized chaos.

Briar stood near Phaeon, checking his saddle for the third time even though she knew it was secure. Her hands needed something to do, some task to focus on that wasn't the weight of doubt pressing against her ribs, or the star metal pendant cold against her skin beneath her cloak.

Around her, the group prepared to leave with varying degrees of efficiency. Sian moved between packs with quiet purpose, redistributing weight, while Halian fussed over ward stones that were already perfectly organized. Thaine checked weapons with methodical precision, his dark eyes tracking everything even as his hands worked. Karse lounged against the courtyard wall, watching the fae scramble with barely concealed amusement.

"If you tighten that girth any more, you'll suffocate the poor beast," Eliam said from behind her.

She jumped slightly, then forced herself to still. "Just making sure it's secure."

"It's secure." His hand covered hers on the leather strap, warm despite the cold morning. "You've checked it twice already."

Had she? The morning felt fragmented, her attention scattered across too many things. The doubt that had kept her awake most of the night, turning over Arion's words like poisoned candy. The way Eliam had held her tighter than usual when she'd finally fallen asleep, as if he could sense something pulling away.

She pulled her hand from under his, busying herself with adjusting her cloak. "I want to be prepared."

"You are prepared." His voice carried that edge of controlled frustration she was learning to recognize. "What's wrong?"

"Nothing. Just nervous about the journey."

The lie sat bitter on her tongue. She felt him studying her profile, weighing her words against her tone, and forced herself to meet his eyes.

"Briar—"

"Is everyone almost ready?" she asked, looking past him to where Arion was emerging from the residence, head low as he spoke to an attendant.

She felt Eliam tense beside her, his hand falling away from where it had been reaching for her face. When she glanced at him, his expression had shuttered into something carefully neutral.

"Almost," he said, and moved away to check his own horse.

The loss of his warmth felt more significant than it should have. Briar pressed her hand against her chest, feeling the warmth there pulse in response. Seeking him even when she was pulling away. Was that her or the magic? Did it matter anymore?

"Good morning."

Arion's voice made her turn. He stood close, too close really, holding a small wrapped bundle that steamed slightly in the cold air. His light flickered around his fingers in that new, sharper way she'd started noticing.

"I thought you might be hungry," he said, offering the bundle. "It's not much, just some bread and cheese wrapped to stay warm. You didn't eat much last night."

She hadn't realized he'd been paying that close attention. She took the bundle, feeling the warmth seep through the cloth into her cold fingers.

"Thank you," she said, surprised by the gesture.

His fingers brushed hers as she took it, the contact lingering a moment too long. His hand was warm, his eyes holding hers with an intensity that made her breath catch.

"Anytime." His smile was gentle, concerned. "Did you sleep well?"

"Well enough."

Another lie. They were stacking up like kindling, waiting for a spark. She could see him noticing, reading the tension in her shoulders, the way she wouldn't quite meet his eyes.

"If you need to talk—"

"She doesn't." Eliam's voice cut between them, sharp and cold. He'd moved back without her noticing, now standing close enough that she could feel the barely contained violence in his stillness. "And you should focus on your own preparations, princeling."

Arion didn't step back and didn't acknowledge the threat in Eliam's tone. Instead, his light brightened slightly, a challenge.

"I was merely offering—"

"I know what you were offering." Eliam's hand found Briar's lower back, firm and possessive. "And she doesn't need it."

"Perhaps she should decide that herself."

"Perhaps you should remember whose—"

"If you're all quite finished," Karse's drawl cut through the mounting tension, "we should leave before noon. Unless you'd prefer to measure who has the bigger—"

"Karse," Sian said sharply.

The Drak grinned. "I was going to say territory. What did you think I meant?"

Despite everything, Briar felt her lips twitch. The absurdity of it—two fae lords posturing over her while they prepared to journey into corrupted wilderness to prevent an apocalypse. The situation would be funny if it didn't make her want to scream.

"He's right," Thaine said, already mounted. "We're losing daylight."

The group began final preparations with renewed urgency. Briar moved to Phaeon, grateful for the excuse to put distance between herself and both Eliam and Arion. The horse nickered softly as she approached, his breath steaming in the cold.

"At least you're simple," she murmured, stroking his neck. "No complicated feelings. Just carrots and apples and not being kicked."

"Talking to the horse now?"

She turned to find Halian leading his own mount over, his usual cheerfulness dimmed but present. Of everyone, he seemed the most affected by Ferria's escape—guilt written in the tight line of his mouth, the shadows under his eyes.

"Horses are better conversationalists than fae sometimes," she said.

"Fair point." He paused, then: "I'm sorry. About my sister. About everything she's done."

"It's not your fault."

"Everyone keeps saying that," his hand clenched on his reins. "But I should have seen it. Should have paid more attention. She hated that I made her leave the Forest Court, that I turned her into an outcast. I thought she would get over it. I guess I was wrong."

Briar didn't know what to say to that. What comfort could she offer when Ferria had helped orchestrate so much pain?

"We'll stop her," she said finally. "And Malus. We'll fix this."

Halian managed a weak smile. "Your optimism is refreshing. Possibly misguided, but refreshing."

"Mount up," Eliam called, already on his horse. "We're leaving."

The group assembled with the practiced efficiency of people who'd traveled together before—except Briar, who still needed two attempts to get into Phaeon's saddle and nearly slid off the other side before Eliam's hand shot out to steady her.

"Careful," he said, and she hated how her body responded to even that simple touch, warmth flooding through her that might be hers or might be the magic or might be so tangled together she'd never separate them.

"I'm fine," she said, adjusting her seat the way he'd taught her.

His hand lingered on her thigh for a moment before he pulled back, and she saw uncertainty flicker across his face. As if he could feel her pulling away and didn't understand why.

I don't know what's real, she thought. *I don't know if I chose you or if something inside me did it for me.*

But she couldn't say that. Not here, not now, maybe not ever.

The group formed a loose column with Thaine at the lead, followed by Eliam and Briar, then Arion, Sian and Halian, and Karse ranging somewhere behind. The formation felt deliberate with Eliam positioning himself between her and Arion, a physical barrier to match the emotional one building between them all.

They moved through the Star Court gates as the sun crested the horizon, pale winter light painting everything in shades of blue and silver. Briar looked back once, seeing the crystalline spires catching the light, the gardens still impossibly blooming despite the snow. Safety. Warmth. Everything they were leaving behind.

When she turned forward again, Eliam was watching her.

"Second thoughts?" he asked.

"No." That, at least, was true. Whatever doubts plagued her about her feelings, she knew this journey was necessary. "Just... saying goodbye."

"We'll come back."

It sounded like a promise, but Briar heard the uncertainty underneath. They were riding into corrupted wilderness to reinforce a seal holding back ancient horrors, with a mad king hunting them and Ferria escaped to gods-knew-where. Coming back felt more like hope than certainty.

"You're quiet this morning," Eliam said after they'd been riding for a while, the Star Court now just a glimmer behind them.

"Just tired."

"You barely slept."

"How would you know?"

"Because *I* barely slept." His hand found her waist, steadying her as Phaeon navigated a rough patch. "And because I know you."

Do you? she wanted to ask. *Or do you know the warmth and assume you know me?*

But she said nothing, just let him guide her horse with practiced ease, his body close enough that she could feel his heat even through layers of winter clothing.

They rode in silence after that, each lost in their own thoughts. Soon the Star Court had disappeared behind them, the crystalline spires swallowed by distance and trees. The landscape had shifted gradually from the manicured gardens and careful pathways to something wilder, denser. True forest now, the kind that had grown without fae hands shaping it.

The trees here were massive, their trunks wider than three men standing shoulder to shoulder, their canopy so thick that the sunlight filtered through in scattered beams. Moss covered everything—rocks, fallen logs, the lower branches of trees. The air smelled of earth and decay, the natural rot of leaves and wood returning to soil.

It was beautiful in a raw way, untamed and ancient. But there was something else too, something Briar couldn't quite name. A heaviness to the atmosphere, a sense of watching eyes. The forest felt aware, though whether it was hostile or simply indifferent she couldn't tell.

"How much further today?" Sian asked from behind them.

"Another few hours," Thaine called back. "We'll make camp before dark. I know a clearing ahead with good water."

Briar shifted in her saddle, her thighs already aching from the constant motion. Phaeon plodded along steadily beneath her, unbothered by the rough terrain or the close press of trees on either side of the narrow path.

"Doing alright?" Eliam asked quietly.

"Sore, but fine."

His hand found her leg, thumb rubbing small circles through the wool of her pants. The touch was meant to be comforting, she knew, but it just made the warmth pulse in response, made her question whether her body's reaction was hers or the magic's.

She shifted slightly away, pretending to adjust her seat, and felt him tense beside her.

The afternoon wore on. They stopped once to rest the horses and eat a cold meal of bread and dried meat. Briar wandered a short distance from the group, stretching her legs, trying to work out the soreness from hours in the saddle.

"First day is always the hardest," Sian said, appearing beside her with a water skin. "Tomorrow will be worse, but by the third day your body starts to adapt."

"Comforting," she muttered, but took the water gratefully.

"I try." She glanced back toward where Eliam and Arion stood on opposite sides of the small clearing, both watching her with identical intensity. "They're not subtle, are they?"

"Not even a little."

"For what it's worth," Sian said carefully, "I've known Arion for a very long time. I've never seen him act like this about anyone."

Briar didn't know what to say to that, so she said nothing. Just drank her water and tried not to think about the way Arion's light had flickered when she'd pulled away from his touch this morning, or the hurt in Eliam's eyes when she'd shifted away from his hand on her leg.

"Mount up," Thaine called. "We've still got a ways to go before dark."

The rest of the afternoon passed in a blur of trees and shadows and growing fatigue. By the time Thaine finally called a halt in a small clearing beside a stream, Briar was ready to fall off her horse. She managed to dismount with only minor awkwardness, her legs protesting every movement.

"You did well," Eliam said, already moving to unsaddle Phaeon before she could do it herself.

"I sat on a horse for eight hours. Not exactly an achievement."

"You didn't complain once." He pulled the saddle free, setting it aside. "That's more than most would manage their first full day."

The warmth in her chest pulsed at the praise, and she hated that she couldn't tell if the pleased flush was her own or its response to his approval.

"I'll help set up camp," she said, moving away before he could say anything else.

The group broke off into their respective roles—Thaine and Karse scouting the perimeter, Halian placing ward stones, Sian checking the water source and beginning to prepare a meal. Briar helped where she could, gathering firewood, laying out bedrolls, trying to be useful despite her exhaustion.

By the time the fire was lit and food was cooking, full dark had fallen. The forest around them was alive with sounds—wind through branches, the distant call of an owl, the rustle of small creatures in the underbrush.

They ate in relative quiet, everyone too tired from the day's travel for much conversation. But as the meal finished and people began settling in for the night, Halian cleared his throat.

"Since we have some time," he said, "and since not all of us know the full history... perhaps we should discuss what we're actually riding toward."

Briar looked up from where she'd been staring into the fire. "The Night Court?"

"Yes." Halian glanced around the circle. "I've studied the historical texts, but academic knowledge is different from lived memory." His gaze settled on Thaine. "You're the only one here old enough to have been alive when they were sealed."

Thaine's expression didn't change, but something flickered in his dark eyes. "I was young. Barely a century old."

"But you remember," Sian said quietly.

"Some things you don't forget." Thaine's hands stilled on the weapon he'd been cleaning. "Even when you wish you could."

The fire crackled in the silence that followed. Briar watched the flames dance, feeling the weight of history pressing down on the clearing.

"What were they like?" Briar asked. "Before getting sealed away?"

Thaine was quiet for a long moment, his hands going still on the weapon he'd been cleaning. The firelight caught the planes of his face, made the shadows under his eyes look deeper.

"They were monsters, but they were beautiful in their monstrosity," he said finally. "That's what made it so terrifying and so effective."

He set the weapon aside, his movements careful and deliberate.

"The Unseelie could glamour themselves to look like other fae. Not perfect, not up close, but from a distance..." He paused, taking a breath. "Convincing enough."

No one spoke, everyone was waiting with baited breath.

"It was my bonding celebration." The words came out flat. "Isania and I had just completed the ceremony. There were guests, music, the usual..." He trailed off, one hand rising to his throat before he seemed to realize and dropped it back to his lap. "After the ceremony, I saw her slip away into the gardens. I thought she wanted..."

He stopped, as though the memory of it consumed him for a moment, and then started again.

"So I followed her. Kept catching glimpses through the hedges, her dress, her hair. She was laughing, playing. So I chased her deeper."

Thaine's hands had curled into fists.

"When I finally caught up to her, caught her..." His voice dropped. "The glamour held until I touched her. Then it just... fell away."

The fire crackled. Thaine stared at it, not seeming to see the flames.

"Pale. That's what I remember first. Pale as death, with a touch of green, like—" He shook his head. "Like something that belonged underwater, not walking around wearing my wife's face."

He had to stop again, throat working.

"Her eyes were terrible, bottomless, hungry things. Black until the torchlight caught the crimson underneath." He swallowed hard. "I couldn't look away, couldn't move. It was like being held, pinned in place by her gaze alone. My body just... stopped listening to me."

Thaine closed his eyes and took a deep breath.

"She had raven feathers woven into her hair. Black feathers, dozens of them, and it's absurd but I remember thinking that was wrong, Isania didn't wear feathers, she hated how they felt, and then..."

His hand went to his throat again, pressed against the scars there.

"Then she bit me."

"Thaine," Sian said softly, but he kept going.

The words came out rough. "I felt her teeth break skin, felt her drinking, and I could hear screaming starting from the pavilion. There was so much screaming... and all I could think was that I'd left them, I'd left Isania. I'd followed this thing into the gardens like a fool while—"

He stopped and took a deep breath.

"I had a dagger. Ceremonial thing, mostly decorative, but sharp enough. I stabbed her." His voice had gone cold. "Over and over until she dropped me. Until she fled."

No one moved.

"I staggered back to the pavilion and found..." He struggled to finish the sentence. "Isania, the real Isania, was already gone. Everyone was. There were more of those things, dozens of them, feeding on the guests. Beautiful until they weren't. Until the glamours failed and you could see what they really were."

His jaw clenched so hard Briar could see the muscle jump.

"That's what Malus wants to free," he said finally. "That's what we're trying to keep sealed."

Briar watched him, saw the way his shoulders had gone rigid, the way he wasn't quite looking at any of them anymore.

Silence stretched across the clearing. Halian looked stricken. Sian had her hand over her mouth. Even Karse had lost his usual lazy amusement, his expression dark.

"Their glamours," Arion said at last, his voice quiet. "They fail during feeding?"

"Eventually." Thaine picked up his weapon again, hands moving automatically through the cleaning motions, anything to do that wasn't looking at their faces. "Takes concentration to hold. When they're caught up in it, in the blood, that's when you see the truth. But by then..."

He didn't finish, he didn't need to.

"We should set watch rotation," he said, and his tone had shifted back to his usual practical, distant tone that said without saying that he was done with this conversation. "Two people per shift. No one goes anywhere alone. Karse and I will take the first watch."

The group dispersed slowly after that, moving to bedrolls with considerably less ease than before. Eliam guided her to their shared bedroll, his hand warm on her lower back. She settled onto the blankets, pulling her cloak tighter around herself as he moved to check the perimeter one more time.

The fire had burned low, casting the camp in deep shadows broken only by ember-glow. Around them, she could hear the quiet sounds of people trying to settle—shifting bodies, whispered conversations, the rustle of blankets being adjusted.

But no one seemed to be actually sleeping.

Briar lay on her side, staring at the dying embers. She couldn't stop imagining it. The thing wearing Isania's face, the glamour falling away to reveal the monster underneath. The way Thaine's hand had gone to his throat over and over, five hundred years later and he still carried those scars. Still saw it when he closed his eyes.

That's what they were riding toward. Hundreds of those things, sealed away, waiting.

Her chest felt tight, breath coming shallow. The darkness beyond the firelight suddenly seemed full of possibilities—movement that might be wind or might be something else, shapes that could be trees or could be wearing faces she trusted.

"You're not sleeping," Eliam said quietly, the bedroll shifting as he returned and settled behind her, close but not quite touching yet.

"Can't," she admitted.

Briar felt him move closer, his chest warm against her back, his arm coming around her waist. She should probably pull away, maintain the distance she'd been trying to keep all day. But she was cold and scared and tired of fighting herself.

Instead, she turned in his arms and pressed her face against his chest.

His arms tightened around her immediately, one hand moving to her hair. He didn't say anything. Didn't ask what was wrong or tell her everything would be fine. Just held her.

"I keep seeing it," she said against his shirt. "What Thaine described. The way it looked like someone he loved until it didn't."

"I know."

"We're riding toward that. Toward hundreds of those things." Her fingers curled into his shirt. "What if Malus is already there? What if we're too late and they're already—"

"We're not too late." His voice was certain, solid. "We would know. The corruption would be spreading faster, consuming everything. The seal still holds."

"For now."

"For now," he agreed, and she appreciated that he didn't lie to her. Didn't promise safety he couldn't guarantee.

She pressed closer, feeling his heartbeat steady beneath her ear. The warmth in her chest pulsed, reaching for him, and for once she didn't fight it. Didn't question whether this need for comfort was hers or the magic's. She was scared and he was here and that was enough.

"I'm terrified," she whispered.

His hand stilled in her hair for a moment, then resumed its gentle movement. "Good. Fear keeps you careful. Keeps you alive."

"Is that supposed to be comforting?"

"No." His lips pressed against the top of her head. "But it's true."

She felt him shift, pulling her even closer until there was no space between them. One of his legs hooked over hers, anchoring her against him.

"Sleep," he said quietly. "I'll keep watch."

"You need rest too."

"I'll rest when you do." His hand moved from her hair to her back, tracing slow circles that gradually began to ease the tension from her muscles. "Right now you need this more."

She wanted to argue, to point out that he couldn't stay awake all night just because she was scared. But the steady rhythm of his breathing, the warmth of his body, the solid presence of him was already pulling her toward sleep despite her fear.

"Eliam?" she said, her voice already drowsy.

"Mm?"

She almost said it. Almost let the words slip out that had been sitting in her chest since the night she'd confessed in his bed. But doubt crept back in, that persistent question of what was real and what was magic, and the words stuck in her throat.

"Thank you," she said instead.

His arms tightened fractionally around her. "Sleep, Briar."

She closed her eyes, letting his presence chase away the images of pale skin and crimson eyes and raven feathers. Let herself trust, just for tonight, that this feeling of safety was real even if she didn't know what else was.

The warmth settled between them, content, and she felt him relax slightly as she finally began to drift off.

Just before sleep took her, she felt his lips against her hair again, felt him whisper something too quiet for her to hear. But the tone carried through—possessive and protective and something softer underneath that she was too tired to analyze.

Tomorrow she could go back to questioning everything. Tonight, she just let herself be held.

Chapter Twenty-Nine

The second day bled into the third with little to mark the difference. More trees, more narrow paths, more endless riding that left everyone sore and irritable. The forest had grown denser, darker, the canopy so thick that even midday felt like twilight.

Briar noticed the shift in the group's dynamics around midday on the third day. Small things at first—Sian snapping at Halian when he asked about the water supply, Thaine's responses to questions growing shorter and more clipped.

Then Arion questioned Karse about the route.

"Are you certain this is the right direction?" The Star Prince's tone was carefully neutral, but the implication was clear. "We've been traveling for days."

Karse, who'd been ranging ahead as usual, stopped and turned. His golden eyes had gone flat. "Are you questioning whether I know my own lands?"

"I'm questioning whether you remember them," Eliam interjected, his voice cold. "It's been centuries since your people abandoned these territories. Landmarks change."

"Landmarks don't forget." Karse's claws had extended slightly. "The trees remember. The stones remember. I remember."

"Then perhaps you could share where exactly we're going," Arion pressed. "Because from where I stand, we're just wandering deeper into the wilderness with no clear destination."

"Would you prefer I provide you with a map?" Karse's tone had gone dangerous. "Perhaps mark it with a nice dotted line so you can follow along like children?"

"That's not what he meant—" Sian started.

"Isn't it?" Karse turned to face them all. "You want me to guide you to the seal, but you don't trust that I actually know where it is. You think what? That I'm leading you in circles for entertainment?"

"No one said that," Thaine said carefully.

"You didn't have to." Karse's lip curled. "I can see it in how you all keep checking the sun's position, how you mark the trees as we pass. You're tracking our route because you don't trust mine."

"Can you blame us?" Eliam's shadows had begun to pool at his feet. "Your people have every reason to want the fae courts dead. Leading us into the wilderness and abandoning us would be efficient."

The temperature dropped several degrees. Karse went perfectly still, and Briar saw his hand move to the weapon at his side.

"If I wanted you dead," he said softly, "I wouldn't need to abandon you in the forest. I'd just slit your throats in your sleep and be done with it."

"Try it," Eliam said flatly.

"Enough." Arion's light flared between them. "We're all tired. We're all on edge. This isn't helping."

"No, let's hear it," Karse said, his attention still fixed on Eliam. "If you don't trust me to guide you, why did you agree to my terms? Why bring me at all?"

"Because we had no choice," Eliam said. "Not because we trust you."

Something flickered across Karse's face—hurt, maybe, or rage so deep it had gone cold. "Then perhaps you should find your own way to the seal. See how far you get before the corruption takes you."

He turned and stalked into the trees, leaving the group in tense silence.

"That went well," Halian muttered.

"Someone should go after him," Sian said, but no one moved.

Briar watched from Phaeon's back, saying nothing. The fractures in the group that had been hairline cracks were widening into chasms. Fear and exhaustion were turning them against each other, and they hadn't even reached the corrupted zones yet.

The rest of the day passed in uncomfortable quiet. Karse didn't return until they were making camp, appearing from the shadows without a word. He took the food Sian offered him but sat apart from the group, pointedly not looking at any of them.

No one suggested gathering around the fire for conversation. People ate quickly, separately, barely speaking. The usual routines of watch rotation and ward-setting happened with minimal interaction, everyone just wanting the day to be over.

Briar settled into the bedroll beside Eliam, feeling the exhaustion in every muscle. Three days of riding, three nights of tension, and they hadn't even reached the danger yet.

"Sleep," Eliam said quietly, pulling her against him. "Tomorrow will be better."

She wanted to believe him, but the tight set of his jaw suggested he didn't believe it either.

She closed her eyes and let exhaustion pull her under.

The throne room materialized around her with the logic of dreams—she wasn't walking toward it, she was simply there, standing before the autumn throne as if she'd always been there.

Malus sat in the seat that should have been Eliam's, one leg crossed over the other, looking perfectly at ease. The copper leaves in his hair caught the light from hundreds of candles that hadn't been burning a moment ago.

"There you are," he said, his smile sharp. "I was beginning to think you'd learned to hide from me."

Briar's hand went to her throat, to the marks that suddenly burned like brands. "No. This isn't real."

"Isn't it?" He stood, descending the dais with predatory grace. "You're here. I'm here. Seems real enough to me."

She tried to step back and found she couldn't move her feet. The marks flared hotter, holding her in place.

"You left the Star Court," he continued, circling her slowly. "I felt it the moment you crossed their borders. The pretty wards the Star Prince built around you, all that careful protection—it doesn't extend beyond his territory." His fingers trailed across her shoulders as he moved behind her. "Now you're in the wilderness. Exposed."

"You can't find me." The words came out more confident than she felt.

"Can't I?" His breath was warm against her ear. "I'm inside your head right now, dear one. You don't think that gives me some indication of where you are?"

The throne room flickered, and for a moment she saw trees, darkness, and heard the sound of wind through branches. Then it solidified again, Malus's hand on her shoulder turning her to face him.

"Tell me where you're going," he said, and she felt the compulsion push through the marks, trying to force the words from her throat.

Her jaw clenched. The compulsion pulled, insisted, but nothing came out. The dream space wavered slightly.

Malus's eyes narrowed, a mixture of amusement and fury floating in their depths. "Interesting. The bargain doesn't hold as well in dreams." His hand moved to her throat, fingers tracing the marks. "But these still burn, don't they? Still pull you toward me even when you're asleep?"

"Let me go."

"Why would I do that?" His other hand found her waist, pulling her closer. "You're finally somewhere I can reach you. No wards, no court protections, just you and me and the connection you can't sever."

Briar tried to pull away but his grip tightened, and the marks flared with heat that made her gasp.

"You're heading toward something," he mused, studying her face. "Something important. My brother wouldn't risk taking you into the wilderness otherwise."

She pressed her lips together, refusing to answer.

"It doesn't matter." His smile widened. "Wherever you're going, you won't reach it in time. I'm already so close, dear one. So close to having everything I need." His hand on her throat squeezed slightly. "Including you."

"I'll never help you."

"You won't have a choice." His thumb brushed across the marks. "These make sure of that. And once I have you back, once I extract what's hidden inside you..." He leaned in, his lips nearly touching hers. "We'll have all the time in the world to explore what you've become. How sweet hope must make your blood."

The throne room began to darken, shadows creeping in from the corners.

"Sweet dreams, my lady," he whispered. "I'll be seeing you soon."

The marks on her throat suddenly burned white-hot, searing, and she screamed—

Briar jolted awake, gasping, her hand flying to her throat. The marks were on fire, actually burning, and she couldn't breathe, couldn't think past the pain.

"Briar." Eliam's voice, urgent. His hands on her face, turning her toward him. "Briar, look at me."

She focused on his eyes, dark and intense in the dim firelight.

"Breathe," he commanded. "Just breathe."

She sucked in air, her chest heaving, the marks still burning but starting to fade from white-hot to merely painful. Tears streamed down her face from the intensity of it.

"He was in my head, I could feel his hands, the mark," she managed. "Malus. He—"

"I know." His thumb brushed away her tears. "The marks were glowing. Burning through your skin. I tried to wake you but you wouldn't respond."

She pressed her hand over his where it cupped her face, anchoring herself in his solid presence. The dream was already fragmenting the way dreams do, but Malus's words echoed: *I'm already so close.*

"He knows we left the Star Court," she said. "He felt it. He's looking for us. For me."

Eliam's jaw tightened. "Can he see where we are? Through the dream?"

"I don't think so. He tried to make me tell him but the compulsion didn't work right." She touched her throat again, feeling the marks still hot beneath her fingers. "But he knows we're in the wilderness. He knows we're heading somewhere."

Around them, the camp was stirring. The others had noticed something was wrong—her scream had been audible, and the way Eliam had moved had been urgent enough to wake the lighter sleepers.

"What happened?" Sian appeared at their bedroll, concern clear on her face.

"Malus reached her through the marks," Eliam said, anger edging his words. "In her dreams."

"That's not possible," Halian protested, but his voice lacked conviction. "The wards should prevent—"

"We're not in the Star Court anymore," Arion said quietly. He'd risen from his own bedroll, his light dim but present. "The protections don't extend this far."

Karse appeared from the shadows where he'd been on watch. "Can he find her with those things?"

All eyes turned to Eliam whose grim expression spoke louder than any words could have. He gave a short nod and Karse swore under his breath.

"We can't waste any more time," Eliam continued, already beginning to pack their bedroll. "No more leisurely pace. We push hard, reach the seal before he can intercept us."

"We can't outrun him if he's already close," Thaine pointed out.

"We can try." Eliam's voice left no room for argument.

Briar sat in the center of the activity, her hand still pressed to her burning throat, Malus's words echoing in her head: *I'll be seeing you soon.*

She believed him.

Her throat still ached where the marks had burned. She'd checked it in the pre-dawn light, half expecting to see blistered skin, but there was nothing visible. Just the copper leaves, innocuous and terrible, and the phantom heat that lingered beneath them.

She couldn't shake the feeling of Malus's hands on her. The way his fingers had traced her throat, the pressure of his grip on her waist. Her mind knew it had been a dream, but her body remembered the touch as if it had been real.

They rode north. Or what Karse assured them was north, though the thick canopy made it impossible to track the sun's position with any certainty. Briar found herself checking over her shoulder constantly, scanning the trees for movement that wasn't wind, for shapes that didn't belong.

Everything looked wrong now. Every shadow could hide something. Every rustle of leaves could be approach rather than breeze.

"Stop," Eliam said quietly beside her.

She realized she'd been twisting in the saddle again, neck craned to look behind them. "I can't help it."

"You're exhausting yourself. And Phaeon can feel your tension." His hand found her leg, steadying. "If something comes, we'll know. Thaine is watching our back trail."

She tried to relax, to focus forward, but her shoulders stayed rigid. The exhaustion sat heavy in her bones, made heavier by the sleepless night and the adrenaline that still hadn't fully faded.

The morning wore on. They stopped once to rest the horses and eat a cold meal that no one seemed to have any appetite for. Briar chewed bread that tasted like dirt, swallowed water that didn't ease the dryness in her throat.

When they mounted again, her legs trembled as she climbed back into the saddle. The world swayed slightly, the edges going soft.

"Briar?" Eliam's voice came from very far away.

She blinked, found herself tilted at a wrong angle, Phaeon's neck rushing up to meet her face. Then strong hands grabbed her waist, hauling her back upright, and she was moving through air before settling against a solid chest.

Eliam had pulled her onto his horse. She sat sideways across his lap, her head against his shoulder, his arm iron-strong around her waist.

"I'm fine," she tried to say.

"You were falling off your horse." He made a gesture and Thaine moved forward to take Phaeon's reins, leading the horse alongside them. "You're riding with me."

She wanted to protest, to insist she could manage, but the exhaustion was crushing. Her eyes kept trying to close despite her efforts to keep them open.

"Sleep if you need to," Eliam said against her hair. "I have you."

"Can't. What if he comes back—"

"Then I'll wake you." His arm tightened. "But you're useless like this. Your body needs rest."

She meant to argue more, but his heartbeat was steady beneath her ear, and the rocking motion of the horse was lulling despite her fear. Her eyes drifted closed.

She didn't dream. Or if she did, she didn't remember it. When she woke, the quality of light had changed, grown dimmer, and she realized hours had passed.

"Better?" Eliam asked, feeling her stir.

"A little." Her neck ached from the angle she'd been sleeping at, and her mouth was dry. But the crushing exhaustion had eased to merely bone-deep tired.

He shifted her slightly, adjusting her position to something more sustainable, and she finally looked around properly.

The forest had changed.

It was subtle at first, easy to miss if you weren't looking for it. The leaves on that oak weren't quite the right shade of green, the color muted as if someone had drained the vibrancy away. The bark on the ash tree held an undertone of gray that didn't belong.

And the stream they were following, she could see it through breaks in the trees, had patches where the water caught light wrong, reflecting with an oily sheen that made her stomach turn.

"When did it start?" she asked quietly.

"About an hour after you fell asleep." Eliam's voice was grim. "It's been getting worse."

She watched a bird flit between branches, noticed how its movements were slightly jerky, not quite right. Another landed nearby, and she saw its feathers held that same wrongness, colors that should have been vibrant rendered dull.

"Karse?" Arion called from ahead.

The Drak had stopped, standing in his stirrups to scan the forest around them. His expression was troubled.

"It's spread," he said finally. "Last time I came this far, the corruption didn't start for another day's travel north. Now..." He gestured at the discolored trees, the oily water. "It's creeping outward. Claiming more territory."

"How much further to the seal?" Thaine asked.

"Three days at our current pace." Karse settled back into his saddle. "Maybe two if we push hard. But the corruption will only get thicker from here."

They rode on. The changes became more pronounced as afternoon faded toward evening. Whole trees with bark that wept dark sap. Mushrooms growing in spiraling patterns that made no sense. The undergrowth had taken on shades that existed somewhere between brown and green and gray, colors that didn't quite resolve into anything natural.

When they stopped to refill water skins, Sian had to spend long minutes cleansing each container, her magic pushing back against whatever taint tried to seep through.

"Don't drink anything I haven't cleared first," she said, and no one argued.

By the time Karse called for them to make camp, everyone was on edge. They'd found a small clearing that seemed relatively untouched, the grass still mostly normal colored, no visible signs of corruption in the immediate area.

Eliam helped her down from his horse, and her legs nearly gave out again when her feet hit the ground. She caught herself against his chest, feeling his hands steady her automatically.

"Easy," he said.

"I'm fine. Just stiff." She forced herself to stand on her own, to move away and help with setting up camp even though every muscle protested.

The group worked in tense silence. Ward stones placed with more care than usual, Halian murmuring over each one as he strengthened the protections. Sian cleansed the ground where they'd lay bedrolls, pushing back the subtle wrongness that tried to seep up from the soil itself.

Briar gathered firewood from the edge of the clearing, staying within sight of the others. Even dead branches felt wrong in her hands, the bark too smooth in some places, too rough in others, textures that shifted when she wasn't looking directly at them.

The fire took longer to catch than it should have. The wood burned with smoke that was too dark, too thick, and the flames themselves were tinged with colors that didn't belong. Green at the edges, purple in the depths, orange that was too bright and too dim at the same time.

No one commented on it. Everyone had seen enough by now to know that nothing here would behave the way it should.

They ate in silence, food that had been perfectly good that morning now tasting faintly of metal, of something spoiled. Briar forced herself to swallow each bite, knowing her body needed fuel even if her stomach protested.

The forest around them was too quiet. No bird calls, no rustle of small creatures, no normal night sounds. Just wind through branches that creaked wrong, and the distant sound of water moving over stones with a viscosity that water shouldn't have.

Briar sat with her back against a log, Eliam beside her, and tried not to think about how exposed they were. How easy it would be for something to approach through the corrupted wilderness, for Malus to find them here in the dark.

The marks on her throat pulsed once, as if responding to her thoughts. She pressed her hand over them, trying to calm the sensation.

"First watch," Thaine said, already moving to the perimeter. "Karse, you're with me."

The others began settling in, but no one looked comfortable. Sian kept glancing at the tree line, her hands fidgeting with her water skin. Halian rechecked the ward stones twice. Even Arion, usually composed, had his light flickering erratically around his fingers.

Briar leaned against Eliam, feeling the solid presence of him grounding her against the wrongness pressing in from all sides. The warmth in her chest pulsed, agitated and uncomfortable in this place.

She was just beginning to think she might be able to sleep despite everything when the first sound came from the trees.

A crack. Sharp and loud, like something large stepping on dead wood.

Everyone froze.

Another crack, from a different direction. Then a third, and a fourth, surrounding them.

Thaine was on his feet, weapon drawn. "Something's out there."

There were more sounds, whatever it was not trying to be quiet now, crashing through undergrowth, multiple sources, coming from all directions at once.

Karse moved to stand back-to-back with Thaine. "I count at least six. Maybe more."

The fire flickered wildly, throwing shadows that moved wrong, that seemed to reach too far. Briar scrambled to her feet, her hand going to the small knife at her belt even though she had no idea how to use it properly.

Eliam was already in front of her, thorns erupting from the ground at his feet, spreading outward in a defensive barrier.

A shape burst from the trees to their left. Dark and twisted, moving on too many legs, its form shifting in the firelight until Briar couldn't tell if it was animal or something else entirely. It lunged toward Halian with a sound caught between a scream and the sound of the wind rushing through a hollow space.

Halian threw up a ward. The creature hit it and recoiled, but more were coming, erupting from the trees on all sides. Things with wrong proportions, with limbs that bent at impossible angles, with faces that were almost familiar but distorted beyond recognition.

The camp dissolved into chaos.

Thaine moved with lethal efficiency, his blade catching firelight as he engaged the nearest creature. Karse fought beside him, his claws extended, tearing into something that bled dark liquid that steamed when it hit the ground.

Arion's light flared bright enough to hurt, forming weapons of pure starlight that he drove into anything that got close. Sian and Halian worked together, wards and cleansing magic trying to hold back the tide.

And Eliam's thorns spread like a living thing, erupting from the ground in waves to impale, vines snaring limbs to drag creatures down, roots bursting through soil to trip and tangle anything that approached their position.

But something was wrong.

Briar watched Thaine's blade pass through a creature without resistance, watched the thing dissolve into smoke and reform a moment later. Watched Karse's claws tear into flesh that felt like fog, insubstantial.

The sounds were real. The movement was real. But the creatures themselves—

A hand clamped over her mouth from behind.

She tried to scream, but the hand pressed harder, and she felt herself being pulled backward, away from Eliam, away from the fire. She kicked, tried to twist free, but whoever had her was strong.

The chaos of the battle surrounded them, everyone too focused on the attacking creatures to notice her being dragged into the shadows. She caught a glimpse of long, dark hair, felt magic wrap around her like invisible chains.

Ferria.

The creatures fighting the group flickered, their forms becoming less solid. Illusions. All of them illusions.

Briar managed to get her teeth into Ferria's palm and bit down hard. The fae woman hissed but didn't let go, just tightened her grip and pulled Briar further from the fire's light.

She tried to reach for the warmth, to make it manifest, to do something, but panic was making it hard to focus. Her hands clawed at Ferria's arm, trying to break free.

Something hard struck the side of her head. Pain exploded white-hot behind her eyes, and the world tilted sideways. Her knees buckled, but Ferria's grip kept her upright, kept dragging her backward.

Through the ringing in her ears, Briar felt the knife at her belt again. Her fingers fumbled for it, clumsy and desperate, vision swimming.

She got it free and drove it backward into Ferria's arm with all the strength she could manage.

Ferria's scream was sharp and genuine. Her grip released, and Briar stumbled forward, trying to run, trying to shout for help. But her legs wouldn't cooperate, wouldn't hold her weight properly. The blow to her head had left everything spinning and disjointed.

She made it three steps before Ferria caught her again, yanking her back by her hair. Briar tried to swing the knife again but Ferria caught her wrist, twisted until her fingers opened and the blade fell into the corrupted undergrowth.

"Stupid girl," Ferria hissed, blood running down her arm where the knife had caught her.

Briar opened her mouth to scream, managed to draw breath—

The second blow caught her temple, harder than the first. The world went dark at the edges, closing in like a tunnel. She felt herself falling, felt Ferria catch her, felt the ground moving beneath her as she was dragged away from the light, away from the camp, away from safety.

The sounds of fighting grew distant. She tried to hold onto consciousness, tried to move her limbs, but everything was slipping away like water through her fingers.

Then the world went black, and she knew nothing at all.

Chapter Thirty

B riar woke to pain.

Her head throbbed with each heartbeat, a steady pulse of agony that made her stomach turn. She tried to move and found her body unresponsive, limbs heavy and disconnected. The world spun even with her eyes closed.

She forced her eyes open anyway, squinting against light that felt too bright despite being dim. Stone walls curved around her, smooth and seamless. The air held that particular quality of stillness she recognized, the weight of magic pressing in from all sides.

A safe haven.

Memory returned in fragments. The camp. The creatures attacking. Ferria's hand over her mouth. The blow to her head. Fighting back, the knife driving into flesh. Then darkness.

"Finally awake." Ferria's voice came from somewhere to her left. "I was beginning to think I'd hit you too hard."

Briar turned her head, the movement sending fresh waves of pain through her skull. Ferria sat on what looked like a root formed into a bench, wrapping a bandage around her forearm. Blood had soaked through the fabric in several places, dark and wet.

The knife wound. Briar had done that.

"Where—" Her voice came out rough, throat dry. She swallowed and tried again. "Where are we?"

"Somewhere safe." Ferria tied off the bandage with sharp, efficient movements. "Somewhere your protectors can't reach you. Not immediately, anyway." She looked up, and her smile was cold. "Do you remember this?" Ferria said, watching her face.

"We hid in one like this once." Her smile turned cold. "Though I may have been... less careful with the wards that time. This one is better protected. Much better. Malus will be here soon, and we can't have interruptions before then."

The words penetrated slowly through the pain fogging Briar's thoughts. Malus. Coming here. For her.

She tried to sit up and found she could move now, though her head spun with the effort. Her hands were unbound, but her body felt wrong, sluggish, like she was moving through water.

"I wouldn't try anything sudden," Ferria advised. "You took two solid hits to the head. You're concussed at minimum. Sudden movements will only make you vomit and I'd rather not be trapped in here with that smell."

Briar pressed her hand against the ground, using it to steady herself as she pushed into a sitting position. Her stomach rolled in protest, but she swallowed hard against the nausea.

"Why?" The word came out hoarse. Briar's throat was dry, her mouth tasting of copper. "Why are you doing this? I've never done anything to you. I—"

Ferria turned back, and her smile was cold, vicious. "Haven't you?"

"I don't understand."

"Of course you don't." Ferria was quiet for a moment, studying her with amusement. "Do you know what I find fascinating about humans? How much value you place on life. Your mortality makes you weak. Not just because you die so easily, but because you're so desperate to protect what little time you have. It makes you easy to manipulate."

She stood, moving closer, and Briar instinctively tried to scoot backward. The movement made her head spin, and she had to stop, pressing her palm flat against the floor again to keep from falling over.

"It was so very easy. All it took was making your sister sick," Ferria continued, her tone casual. "One small spell and suddenly you were desperate enough to come back here. To make a bargain. To put yourself exactly where we needed you."

Briar's eyes widened at the revelation. "It was you? You made Allegra sick?"

"Yes." There was no remorse in Ferria's voice as she crouched down, bringing herself to eye level with Briar.

"But why? Why torment a child?" Briar's chest felt tight, breath coming short.

"Because your mother stayed away. It was her we wanted. She made the first bargain after all and we needed to know what it was and why it caused so many... problems. Instead we got you. Desperate and willing. Unfortunately, Eliam got to you first, struck his bargain."

The nausea had nothing to do with the head injury now. Briar thought of Allegra's pale face, her labored breathing, the way she'd grown weaker and weaker until Briar had been willing to trade anything to save her. All of it manufactured. All of it deliberate.

"You're a monster," she whispered.

"I'm practical." Ferria stood again, moving back to her bench. "Malus needed answers and freedom, and I needed something from him in return. It was a simple exchange."

"What could he possibly give you that would make this worth it?"

Ferria's expression shifted, something softer bleeding through the cold calculation. "Eliam."

The single word hung in the air between them.

"Malus promised me that when this is over, when he has what he needs and can reunite what was fractured, I'll have Eliam. Whole and complete. Finally able to see me the way I've always seen him."

Briar stared at her, trying to make sense of the words. "Reunite what was fractured?"

There was silence and then Ferria laughed, the sound sharp and devoid of any real joy. "You really don't know, do you? About what happened that night? About what Malus's ritual actually did." She tilted her head, studying Briar with renewed interest. "How much has Eliam told you about that night?"

"He doesn't remember it clearly." The words came out automatically, and Briar immediately wished she could take them back. She didn't want to give Ferria anything, didn't want to engage in this conversation.

But Ferria's smile suggested she already knew that. "Of course he doesn't. How could he? His mind was split along with everything else."

Briar's hand pressed against her chest, feeling the warmth there pulse with agitation. Split? "What are you talking about?"

"The ritual." Ferria settled back on her bench, clearly prepared to enjoy this. "Malus was conducting a ritual to strip Eliam's power, but Eliam sensed it, felt what was happening, and he intervened."

She paused, as if considering how much to reveal.

"It was already in progress when Eliam arrived, that's what we needed your mother for, innocent blood spilled in tragedy. We assumed he would figure out what was happening, but also knew that even if he did, it would be too late. He wouldn't be able to stop it. Unfortunately, we underestimated his... ingenuity."

"He made a deal and as a result the ritual didn't just fail," Ferria continued. "It backfired. Instead of stripping Eliam's power, it fractured him. Split his very being into two separate entities. The darkness, the control, the possession—all of that stayed in Eliam. But the rest?" Her smile widened. "The capacity for joy, for genuine warmth, for actual connection without constant control—all of that was torn away and given form."

The safe haven suddenly felt smaller, the air harder to breathe. Briar could feel where this was going, could see the shape of it forming before Ferria even said the words.

"Arion," she whispered.

"Yes." Ferria's eyes gleamed with satisfaction. "Prince Arion of the Star Court. Beautiful, kind, controlled Arion who appeared with no memory of his past, no family, nothing but an innate understanding of magic and a personality that felt hollow until he was near his other half." She leaned forward. "Arion isn't a separate person. He's the missing piece of Eliam, walking around in his own body, completely unaware that he's incomplete."

The warmth in Briar's chest was pulsing frantically now, responding to something in Ferria's words. The way it had always reached for both Eliam and Arion, the way it recognized them equally. Because they weren't two people. They were one.

"That's impossible," Briar said, but her voice lacked conviction.

"Is it?" Ferria gestured at Briar's chest, where the warmth pulsed visibly through her clothing. "You've felt it. The way your magic responds to both of them." She stood again, pacing now. "That's what Malus needs. Both pieces in one place, the essence you carry as the catalyst. When he has you, he can force reunification. Restore Eliam to what he was before the fracture. And with the complete Forest King's power, he can break the seal."

Briar's mind was racing, trying to process the implications. Every interaction with Arion suddenly made horrible sense. The way he'd looked at her with want he didn't understand. The way his light had grown sharper, more aggressive. The way he'd kissed her at the border and the warmth had surged with recognition.

Because he was Eliam. Had always been Eliam.

"And when Malus reunites them," Ferria smiled, "when Eliam is whole again, complete and powerful, Malus will give him to me. The bargain is already made. I've waited centuries for Eliam to see me, and he never has. But when he's whole, when he's restored to what he should be..." She trailed off, her expression distant.

The delusion in her voice was clear even through Briar's pain and shock. Ferria actually believed that forcing Eliam back together, that delivering him to her through Malus's bargain, would somehow make him love her.

"You're doing all of this for Eliam?" Briar's voice was sharp with disbelief. "You think reuniting him will make him want you? If it weren't for the piece of him inside me, he wouldn't even—"

She stopped, realizing what she'd just said. But it was too late.

Ferria's expression shifted, something predatory sliding across her features. "Wouldn't even what?" She moved closer, scenting weakness. "Look at you? Want you?" Her smile was cruel now, delighted. "Is that what you tell yourself? That it's only the essence he wants?"

Briar said nothing, but her face must have given something away.

"Oh, this is perfect." Ferria's laugh was sharp and bitter. "You actually believe it. You think the magic is the only reason." She circled Briar slowly, savoring this. "I've watched him for centuries. Seen him with countless others—fae, humans, it doesn't matter. He uses them, controls them, throws them away."

She stopped directly in front of Briar.

"He's never taken the eye of a Great Lord for one of them. He's never abandoned his court to save one. The magic didn't create that."

She leaned in close, her voice soft and edged with amusement. "Malus doesn't intend to let you go." Ferria's smile was one of satisfaction as she returned to the bench. "You'll have plenty of time to reflect on your mistakes. To watch Eliam whole and finally mine, and know exactly what you wasted."

The words cut deep, because Ferria was right. Briar had been so caught up in questioning, in doubting, that she lost sight of what truly mattered. She had let Arion's words worm their way under her skin and fester.

The realization should have brought relief. Instead, it just made everything worse. Because now she knew it was real, and she was going to lose it anyway.

"He'll never love you," Briar said, the words escaping before she could stop them.

Ferria's expression went cold. "What?"

"You could have him for eternity. You could force him whole, could have Malus deliver him bound and helpless, and he would still never choose you." The anger was building now, cutting through the nausea and pain. "You've watched him for centuries and you still don't understand. He doesn't love you because he can't. Because there's nothing in you worth loving."

"Careful." Ferria's voice had dropped to something dangerous.

But Briar couldn't stop, wouldn't stop. The revelation about Allegra, about everything being orchestrated, about this woman's obsession destroying lives, it was too much to contain.

"You made my sister sick. You manipulated everything. You helped fracture Eliam and now you're helping Malus destroy the world, all because you're so desperate for someone who doesn't want you."

"He doesn't know what he wants," Ferria snapped. "He's incomplete. Fractured. When he's whole again, when he's restored—"

"He'll still hate you." Briar forced herself to stand, using the wall for support, ignoring the way the room spun. "Because the problem isn't that he's incomplete. The problem is that you're pathetic."

Ferria moved faster than Briar could track, crossing the space between them in two strides. Her hand caught Briar's throat, slamming her back against the wall hard enough to make stars burst behind her eyes.

"Pathetic?" Ferria's voice was soft, dangerous. "You call me pathetic when you've spent days doubting the one thing I would give anything to have? When you've thrown away his devotion because you couldn't see past your own fear?" Her grip tightened. "At least I know what I want. At least I'm not too stupid to recognize when I have it."

She released Briar's throat, shoving her away dismissively.

"He'll come for me," Briar said, voice rough. "Eliam will find me."

"I'm counting on it." Ferria moved to the entrance of the safe haven, checking something Briar couldn't see. "Malus needs both pieces in one place, remember? Eliam will follow, and Arion will follow Eliam. They always do, drawn to each other even when they don't understand why. And when they're all here, when we have everything we need..." She trailed off, satisfied.

Briar pressed her hand against her chest, feeling the warmth there pulsing with fear and rage and grief all tangled together. Ferria had confirmed what she had doubted. Eliam's love was real. And she was going to lose him anyway.

Unless she could find a way out of this. Unless she could fight.

The warmth pulsed once in response to her unspoken thoughts. It had saved her before. If she could figure out how to use it. How to make it manifest the way it had during the hunt, or when Malachar had attacked. The way it wanted to now, she could feel it pushing against her skin, trying to respond to her fear and rage.

She closed her eyes, focusing on that sensation. Reaching for it consciously instead of letting it react on its own. The rage that had been building finally found its focus. Briar took a step toward Ferria, then another, ignoring the way her vision swam with each movement.

"What are you doing?" Ferria asked, uncertainty mixing with annoyance.

"You're wrong," she said quietly.

"About what?"

"Eliam," Briar took another step, and Ferria actually backed up slightly, hand moving toward a weapon at her belt. "You think reuniting him will make him what you want. But you're forgetting something."

"And what's that?"

"The piece of him that's inside me." Briar pressed her hand against her chest. "You said I'm the catalyst. That means I'm part of the reunification too. Whatever happens when Eliam becomes whole, I'll be there. Part of it. Connected to it." She saw understanding dawn on Ferria's face. "You won't get him the way you think you will. Because I'm woven into what he is now. Into what he becomes."

It was a guess, a desperate theory formed from fragments of information. But she saw it land. Saw Ferria's expression shift from cruel amusement to something darker.

"Malus will extract you," Ferria said, but her voice had lost its certainty. "He'll separate the essence from your body, use it without your interference—"

"Will he?" Briar took another step. "Twenty-five years, Ferria. I've carried this essence for twenty-five years. It's not separate from me anymore. It's woven into every part of who I am. You can't extract it without extracting me. And if I'm part of the reunifica tion..." She let the implication hang.

Ferria's hand closed around her weapon. "You're lying. Trying to manipulate—"

"Am I?" Briar felt the warmth pulse in agreement, felt it confirming what she'd guessed. "Or are you just realizing that your precious bargain with Malus isn't going to give you what you want?"

The silence stretched between them, heavy with implications neither wanted to voice.

"There's one more thing," Briar continued.

Ferria moved before Briar could finish, drawing her weapon in one smooth motion and lunging forward with intent that was unmistakably lethal.

Briar's body reacted before her mind caught up. The warmth surged in response to the threat, and she reached for it consciously this time, imagining the thorns she'd seen Eliam create, wanting them to manifest, to protect, to stop Ferria before—

Golden light erupted from her skin. Not formless and diffuse the way it had been before, but focused. Sharp. Deadly.

Thorns burst from the ground between them, three feet long and wickedly pointed. Ferria tried to dodge but she was already mid-lunge, momentum carrying her forward onto the spikes.

One went through her shoulder. Another through her thigh. A third caught her side, just below her ribs.

She screamed, the sound sharp and terrible in the enclosed space. Her weapon clattered to the ground, and she tried to pull herself off the thorns, but the movement only drove them deeper.

Briar stood frozen, watching golden light fade from her hands, watching Ferria struggle and fail to free herself. The thorns held her suspended, growing from stone that shouldn't have been able to support plant life, anchored with magic Briar had called consciously for the first time.

"I'm not weak," Briar said, her voice coming out steadier than she felt.

Ferria gasped, trying to respond, perhaps beg for mercy, but blood was filling her mouth, making speech impossible.

Briar watched her struggle, watched the light fade from her eyes as blood spread across her clothing, and felt nothing but cold certainty. This was necessary, this was survival.

When Ferria finally went still, Briar couldn't let herself turn away, wouldn't. She had made a choice, a terrible choice, and would not shy away from the truth of it. The thorns were already beginning to fade, returning to whatever place they came from when Briar's will no longer sustained them. Ferria's body slumped to the ground, blood pooling beneath her.

She looked down at her hands, still shaking slightly, and tried to process what had just happened and what it meant. What she'd become in a single act.

Time stretched strangely in the safe haven's artificial quiet. Briar stood frozen, staring at Ferria's body, at the blood pooling beneath it, at her own hands still shaking and stained red. The golden light had faded from her skin, but she could still feel the warmth pulsing in her chest, satisfied in a way that made her stomach turn.

Voices penetrated the silence, distant at first, then growing closer, calling her name with increasing urgency. The entrance to the safe haven shimmered into existence, that strange fold in reality that marked the boundary between here and the real world.

Eliam burst through first, shadows writhing around him in violent agitation. His eyes swept the space, taking in the blood, the body, finding her standing in the center of it all. The wildness in his expression shifted to something else entirely when he confirmed she was upright, breathing.

He crossed to her in three strides, his hands finding her face, fingers checking for injuries even as his eyes stayed locked on hers.

"Are you hurt?" His voice was controlled but she could feel the tremor underneath, the barely leashed violence looking for a target.

She shook her head, not trusting her voice. His gaze tracked over her anyway—noting the rope still binding her wrists, the bruising on her throat where Ferria had choked her, the blood that wasn't hers.

The others were crowding through the entrance now. Arion's light blazed bright enough to hurt, illuminating every corner of the space. Thaine had his weapon drawn, scanning for additional threats with professional efficiency. Sian emerged next, her water already gathering defensively around her. Karse hung back by the entrance, his amber eyes taking in everything with that unsettling stillness.

Then Halian entered, and the world seemed to stop.

His gaze found Ferria immediately, and all color drained from his face. The cheerful demeanor he wore like armor cracked and fell away entirely.

"No." The word came out broken, barely audible. He moved forward in a daze, his legs giving out as he dropped to his knees beside his sister's body. "Ferria. Please, no—"

His hands hovered over her, trembling, as if touching her would make it real. When he finally pressed his fingers to her throat, searching for a pulse that wasn't there, his whole body seemed to crumple.

"She dragged me here," Briar said, her voice rough and strange. "She attacked me. I didn't mean—" The lie stuck in her throat. She had meant it. In that moment, she'd wanted Ferria dead. "She was going to kill me."

"You don't have to explain," Eliam said, his thumbs still tracing her cheekbones, keeping her focused on him rather than Halian's grief. "She's been betraying us from the beginning. This should have been done when we learned of her deception."

"She's my sister." Halian's voice cracked on the word. His hands were on her shoulders now, shaking her gently as if she might wake up, as if this might be some terrible mistake. "She was my sister."

Blood was seeping into the knees of his pants where he knelt in it. His sister's blood. Briar watched him try to smooth Ferria's hair back from her face, his hands so gentle, and felt something break inside her chest.

"She made choices, Halian," Sian said quietly, moving to kneel beside him. Her hand found his shoulder, water gathering and falling away repeatedly as her own composure wavered. "Terrible choices that led to this."

"I know." His voice was hollow. "I know what she did. Who she was. But she was still—" He stopped, pressing his palms against his eyes. "She was all the family I had left."

The safe haven felt too small suddenly, the warm light that had seemed comforting now oppressive. Briar could smell the blood, metallic and wrong, could see how it had splattered across the root-bench where Ferria had been sitting. Could see the holes the thorns had left, ragged and fatal.

"You did what you had to," Thaine said quietly from behind her. She turned to find him studying the scene with a hunter's eye, reading the evidence of struggle in the disturbed dust, the blood patterns. "She would have killed you or delivered you to Malus. Either way, you'd be dead."

"Doesn't make it easier," Briar said.

"No," he agreed. "It doesn't."

"She said Malus was coming here," Briar said suddenly.

Karse moved from the entrance, circling the space once before stopping near Halian. "We need to move. There's no telling how long it will be before he shows up."

"Give him a moment," Arion said sharply, his light flickering with emotion.

"A moment to grieve won't bring her back." Karse's tone wasn't cruel, just practical. "And staying here might get the rest of us killed."

Eliam's hands dropped from Briar's face to her wrists, working at the rope binding them. The rough fibers had rubbed her skin raw, and she hissed as they pulled away. He caught her hands immediately, examining the damage with dark focus.

"Can you ride?" he asked quietly.

She nodded, though she wasn't sure it was true. Everything felt distant and unreal, her body moving without her conscious direction.

Halian stood slowly, his movements mechanical. He wouldn't look at Ferria's body again, keeping his eyes fixed on the middle distance. "We should burn her," he said, voice empty. "She deserves that much."

"We don't have time—" Karse started.

"We'll make time." Sian's voice carried unusual steel. "She was one of us once. Whatever she became, she deserves proper rites."

They filed out of the safe haven in silence, Halian carrying Ferria's body with a care that made Briar's chest ache. She'd done this. She'd taken someone's sister, someone's family, and ended them with thorns and golden light.

The worst part was knowing that given the choice again, she'd still do it. Ferria would have handed her over to Malus, would have watched her die to get what she wanted. Self-defense, survival, necessity—all true.

But Halian's grief was true too, and Briar would carry the weight of causing it for the rest of her life.

The smell of smoke still clung to Briar's hair, even though the pyre had burned down to embers an hour ago. She stood at the edge of their makeshift camp, watching Halian methodically pack his sister's few remaining possessions—a silver hair comb, a ring with a stone the color of deep water, a small leather journal he didn't open. His movements were mechanical, precise, the kind of careful control that came when the alternative was complete collapse.

The corrupted forest pressed in around them, wrong-colored leaves rustling in wind that felt too thick, too warm for the season. Every shadow seemed to shift when she wasn't looking directly at it, every sound carried an undertone that made her skin crawl. The safe haven had been a bubble of normalcy in this twisted landscape, but now they were exposed again, vulnerable.

"We need to move." Karse's voice cut through the uncomfortable silence. He'd been ranging their perimeter for the last twenty minutes, his agitation growing with each pass. "The smoke will draw attention. Things hunt here that shouldn't exist."

"Five more minutes," Sian said quietly, her hand still on Halian's shoulder.

"We don't have five minutes." Karse's golden eyes reflected the dying firelight as he turned to face them fully. "Can't you feel it? The corruption is moving. Spreading. Something's stirring it up, making it aggressive."

Briar pressed her hand against her chest, feeling the warmth pulse in response to his words. It had been agitated since she'd used it to kill Ferria, alternating between satisfaction and what felt like hunger. The sensation made her stomach turn, made her wonder what she was becoming, what price she'd pay for consciously wielding power that had always moved through her without her direction.

Eliam's hand found her lower back, steadying her. He'd been hovering since they'd left the safe haven, never more than arm's reach away, his shadows coiling restlessly around his feet. The protective gesture should have been comforting, but all she could think about was Ferria's revelation. Arion wasn't a separate person. He was part of Eliam, torn away and given form.

She looked across the clearing to where Arion stood talking quietly with Thaine, his light flickering in patterns that seemed to mirror Eliam's shadows. How had she not seen it before? The way they moved with the same predatory grace, the way their magic resonated on the same frequency, the way the warmth in her chest reached for them both with equal desperation.

"Briar." Eliam's voice was quiet, meant only for her. "What did she tell you? In the safe haven, before..."

Before she killed her. The words hung unspoken between them.

"Later," she said, not trusting herself to lie convincingly, not trusting herself to tell the truth either. How could she explain that he was incomplete? That the cousin he'd been circling warily was actually the piece of himself he'd lost? That Malus needed all three of them together to break the seal?

His jaw tightened, but he didn't push. They'd been together long enough now that he recognized when she was deflecting, but also when pushing would only make her retreat further.

A branch cracked in the forest, too loud, too deliberate. Everyone went still, hands moving to weapons, magic gathering in the air like static before a storm. The horses shifted nervously, ears flat against their heads, nostrils flaring at some scent humans couldn't detect.

"How many?" Thaine asked quietly, his blade already free of its sheath.

Karse had gone perfectly still, that unnatural Drak stillness that meant he was tracking something. "Twelve. Maybe more. They're good at masking their numbers."

"Corrupted?" Sian's water was already condensing from the humid air, forming protective barriers.

"No." Karse's expression had gone strange, a mixture of recognition and dread. "Drak."

Chapter Thirty-One

The word had barely left his mouth when they emerged from the trees. Drak warriors in traditional battle garb—leather and bone armor, weapons that looked primitive but hummed with old magic, their scales painted with symbols that seemed to shift and writhe in the firelight. They moved with coordinated precision, surrounding the group before anyone could properly react.

"Nobody move," Karse said sharply, his hands carefully visible and away from his weapons. "These are Ka'tar Drak. Elite warriors. If they wanted us dead, we'd already be bleeding out."

One of the warriors stepped forward, and Briar's breath caught. This Drak was massive, scales so dark they seemed to absorb light, eyes that burning gold of molten metal. Scars crossed his chest in deliberate patterns, ritual markings that spoke of battles won and blood spilled. When he spoke, his voice carried the rumble of distant thunder.

"Karse Isragan," the warrior said, and the name sounded like both greeting and condemnation. "The Exile returns."

"Veroc," Karse replied, inclining his head slightly. Not quite a bow, but acknowledgment. "It's been a long time."

"One hundred and eighty two years." Veroc's gaze swept over the group, lingering on each face with calculating intensity. "You return now, at the corruption's peak, bringing fae to our sacred lands." He bared teeth that were too sharp, too many. "The Council will want to know why."

"I come to fulfill my purpose," Karse said carefully. "To see the seal reinforced, the corruption contained."

Veroc laughed, the sound like grinding stone. "Your purpose? You abandoned your purpose when you chose comfort over duty. When you left us to rot while you played pet to fae lords."

The temperature dropped as Eliam's temper flared, shadows spreading across the ground like spilled ink. "Watch your tongue, lizard."

Three spears were immediately pointed at his throat, the warriors moving so fast Briar barely saw them. The metal points glowed with heat that made the air shimmer.

"No!" Karse stepped between them, hands raised. "Nobody fight. Please." He turned to Veroc. "They're with me. They're necessary. The seal can't be reinforced without them."

"That remains to be seen." Veroc made a gesture, and more warriors emerged from the trees. Twenty. Thirty. Too many to fight even if they weren't exhausted and grief-worn. "You'll come with us. The Council will determine your fate."

"We don't have time for politics," Arion said, his light brightening in warning. "The corruption is spreading. Every hour we waste—"

"Is another hour you're alive at our sufferance," Veroc cut him off. "You entered Drak lands without permission, without tribute, without respect. The fact that you're breathing is already more mercy than you deserve."

Briar felt the warmth in her chest pulse, responding to the threat, wanting to manifest. She pressed her hand against it, trying to keep it contained. The last thing they needed was her accidentally revealing what she could do, accidentally starting a fight they couldn't win.

But Veroc's eyes tracked the movement, noticed the way she was holding herself. His nostrils flared, and his expression shifted to something speculative.

"That one," he said, pointing at her. "She carries something. Power that doesn't belong to her."

Eliam moved to step in front of her, but three warriors blocked him, spears pressing against his chest hard enough to draw drops of blood through his shirt.

"Don't," Thaine warned quietly, his own weapon half-drawn but frozen as two warriors held blades to his throat.

"Bind them," Veroc ordered. "All of them."

The warriors moved with practiced efficiency, producing restraints that looked like twisted metal but felt alive against Briar's skin when they closed around her wrists. The moment they locked, her connection to the warmth dimmed, like trying to reach something through thick glass. Magic-suppressing restraints, designed to hold even powerful fae.

Eliam fought when they tried to bind him, shadows lashing out, thorns erupting from the ground. It took six warriors to subdue him, and even then only when one pressed a blade to Briar's throat, using her as leverage.

"Stop," she said, meeting his eyes across the chaos. "Please."

The please did what violence couldn't. He went still, allowing them to lock the restraints around his wrists, though his expression promised retribution. The shadows retreated reluctantly, coiling around his feet like angry cats.

Arion submitted more peacefully, though his light flickered in dangerous patterns. Sian and Halian were bound without resistance, Halian still too deep in grief to care what happened. Thaine required four warriors and took two down before they managed to restrain him, leaving one warrior with a broken nose and another clutching a dislocated shoulder.

Only Karse remained unbound, Veroc studying him with disappointment.

"You won't fight for them?" Veroc asked.

"Fighting you would only get them killed," Karse replied. "I know better than to challenge Ka'tar warriors on their own ground."

"You've grown soft." Veroc's contempt was palpable. "The Karse I knew would have fought anyway, just for the glory of it."

"The Karse you knew was young and stupid."

"And now you're old and weak." Veroc gestured to the warriors. "Bind him too. The Council will decide if he's even still Drak enough to stand trial."

They bound Karse without resistance, though Briar saw the way his claws extended slightly, the way his muscles coiled with suppressed violence. He was choosing not to fight, choosing to submit, and she wondered what that cost him.

"The weapons," Veroc ordered.

The warriors stripped them of everything—swords, daggers, even the small knife Briar had hidden in her boot. They were particularly interested in Thaine's blade, passing it between them with reverent touches, speaking in their own language with tones of recognition.

"Star-metal," one said in accented common. "Old. Blooded."

They handled the weapons with respect at least, wrapping them carefully rather than tossing them aside. Small comfort, but Briar would take what she could get.

"Move," Veroc commanded, and the warriors formed up around them in a pattern that was both escort and cage.

They were force-marched through the corrupted forest at a pace that had Briar stumbling within minutes. Her body still hadn't recovered from the confrontation with Ferria, from the expenditure of power that had killed her. Every step sent pain shooting through her skull, the concussion Ferria had given her making the world swim in and out of focus.

She tripped over a root that seemed to move deliberately into her path, would have fallen if not for the warrior assigned to her. He caught her arm, steadying her with surprising gentleness, though his expression remained stone.

"Keep up," he said, not unkindly. "It's three hours to the settlement. Four if you slow us down."

Three hours. Briar's legs already felt like water, her breath coming too fast, too shallow. The magic-suppressing restraints seemed to be draining more than just her connection to the warmth—they were sapping her physical strength too, making every movement feel like swimming through mud.

The forest grew worse as they traveled. Trees wept black sap that smelled of rot. Flowers bloomed in colors that hurt to look at directly. The air felt wrong, too thick, too warm, carrying whispers on wind that felt both cold and hot at the same time.

And through it all, Veroc's warriors moved without hesitation, following paths invisible to outsider eyes. They knew this corrupted land, had been living alongside it for centuries. The thought of what that must have been like, watching your territory slowly consumed by wrongness you couldn't stop, made Briar's chest tight with unexpected sympathy.

An hour in, Halian collapsed.

He went down hard, knees hitting the corrupted earth with a sound that made Briar wince. The grief and exhaustion had finally overwhelmed him, leaving him unable to continue.

"Get up," the warrior assigned to him said, prodding him with a spear butt.

Halian didn't move, didn't even try. He knelt there in the wrong-colored grass, head bowed, shoulders shaking with silent sobs.

"He just burned his sister," Sian said sharply. "Give him a moment."

"We don't have moments," Veroc said, but he gestured to two of his warriors. "Carry him if necessary."

They hauled Halian to his feet, supporting him between them when his legs wouldn't hold his weight. The sight of proud, cheerful Halian being practically dragged through corrupted wilderness made Briar's eyes burn with tears she refused to shed.

This was her fault. All of it. If she hadn't killed Ferria—but no, that thinking led nowhere good. Ferria had made her choices. They all had.

Another hour passed in misery. Briar's world narrowed to the next step, the next breath, the constant effort of not falling. The warmth in her chest pulsed weakly, trying to reach through the restraints, trying to help, but the magic suppression was too strong.

She was so focused on walking that she almost missed when the forest began to change.

The corruption faded gradually, wrong colors shifting back toward normal, twisted growth straightening into proper trees. The air grew cleaner, easier to breathe. And then, between one step and the next, they crossed some invisible boundary and the corruption was simply gone.

Before them rose a settlement unlike anything Briar had expected.

Massive trees had been shaped into living structures, their trunks hollowed and carved into homes that rose dozens of feet into the air. Bridges of woven vines connected them, creating a network of pathways through the canopy. Light came from crystals embedded in the bark, glowing with warm amber that reminded her of Karse's eyes.

But what struck her most was the evidence of struggle. Entire sections of the settlement stood empty, trees blackened and dead where corruption had spread too far. Defensive walls had been built and rebuilt, each iteration pushed back as they lost more territory. And the Drak themselves—she could see them now, watching from windows and walkways—many bore scars that looked like corruption burns, patches where scales had been replaced with scar tissue.

They'd been fighting this battle for six hundred years, and they were losing.

The warriors marched them through the settlement's main thoroughfare, and Briar became aware of the attention they were drawing. Drak of all ages emerged to watch them pass—elders with scales gone gray with age, adults with the same warrior bearing as their escorts, children who peered from behind their parents with curious eyes.

The children made her chest ache. Several bore corruption scars, marks that showed even the youngest hadn't been spared. One little girl, no more than six or seven, had an entire arm covered in the telltale scarring, her scales twisted and wrong where the corruption had touched her.

"Outsiders," someone spat.

"Fae," another hissed, the word carrying centuries of accumulated hatred.

But when they saw Karse, the anger became something more complex. Some looked at him with hope—the exile returned to save them. Others with deeper hatred—the traitor who'd abandoned them coming back too late.

"Is that really him?" a young Drak asked, scales bright green with youth.

"The Exile," an elder confirmed, leaning heavily on a carved staff. "Come home to face judgment at last."

They were brought to the center of the settlement, where the largest tree Briar had ever seen rose into the sky. Its trunk was easily a hundred feet across, its branches spreading to shelter half the settlement. Carved into its base was an entrance large enough for dragons to pass through.

Inside was a vast chamber, the tree's hollow interior shaped into what could only be a judgment hall. Seven ancient Drak sat on a raised platform, their scales so dark with age they looked like living obsidian. These must have been the Council Veroc had spoken of, the eldest of the Drak, survivors of the seal's creation who remembered what the world had been before.

Veroc forced them all to their knees before the Council, though Eliam resisted until a warrior pressed a blade to Briar's throat again. The message was clear—submit or watch her bleed.

The centermost elder studied them with eyes that had gone milky with age but still seemed to see everything. When she spoke, her voice carried the weight of centuries.

"Karse Isragan," she said, the name sounding like judgment already passed. "You return to us after almost two hundred years of exile. Why?"

Karse raised his head, meeting her ancient gaze without flinching. "To fulfill my duty, Elder Mor'va. To reinforce the seal before it breaks completely."

"Your duty." Another elder, male with a scarred throat that made his voice rasp. "You abandoned your duty when you chose comfort over your people."

"I left to find solutions," Karse said steadily. "To learn about the courts, their magic, their weaknesses. The seal was made with fae magic—I thought understanding them would help us fix it."

"And did it?" Mor'va asked.

"Yes." Karse gestured to the bound group. "These fae have the power to reinforce the seal properly. To fix the corruption and return our lands to their former glory."

"Fae." The word dripped with contempt from a third elder. "Fae who broke the world. Who created this corruption that has eaten our lands for six centuries. And you bring them here, to our last sanctuary?"

"To fix what was broken," Karse insisted.

"Too late!" A younger Drak in the crowd shouted. "Where were you when the corruption took the eastern groves? When it consumed the spawning pools? When our children were born twisted and wrong?"

Others took up the cry, anger building like a physical force in the chamber. Briar could feel the rage, centuries of it, pressing against her from all sides.

"Silence," Mor'va commanded, and the crowd obeyed, though the anger remained palpable. She turned her attention to the group. "You bring strange company, Exile. The Forest King who rules through cruelty. The Star Prince who offers false hope. Warriors and water-workers and—" Her gaze settled on Briar. "Something else. Something that shouldn't exist."

The warmth in her chest pulsed in response to the scrutiny, pressing against the restraints, wanting to react.

"She's the key," Karse said quickly. "Without her, the seal can't be reinforced. She carries—"

"I can sense what she carries," Mor'va cut him off. "Old magic. Dangerous magic. The kind that breaks worlds." She studied Briar with those ancient eyes. "You've killed recently, child. I can smell it on you. Fae blood, freshly spilled."

Briar said nothing. What could she say? That she'd killed in self-defense? That Ferria had deserved it? The truth wouldn't matter to people who'd suffered for six centuries because of fae actions.

"They're all killers," the scarred elder said. "Look at them. Soaked in blood and violence, bringing their wars to our door."

"We're trying to help," Arion said, speaking for the first time.

The Council's attention shifted to him, and something strange passed across Mor'va's face. She studied him for a long moment, then looked at Eliam, then back again.

"Interesting," she murmured. "Very interesting." She stood, moving with surprising grace for her age. "The charges against Karse Isragan are thus: abandonment of duty, collaboration with the enemy, and bringing threats into sacred land." She looked at each of them in turn. "The charges against the fae are: trespass, bearing weapons in our territory, and carrying magic that could destroy what little safety we have left."

"Elder Mor'va," Karse started.

"The traditional punishment for these crimes is death," she continued as if he hadn't spoken. "However, given the unusual circumstances, I propose an alternative."

The other elders shifted, some nodding, others frowning. Whatever she was about to suggest, not all of them agreed with it.

"A trial," Mor'va said. "Ancient law states that those accused may prove their innocence through ordeal. Success means safe passage to the seal. Failure means death."

"What kind of trial?" Eliam asked, his voice carefully controlled.

Mor'va smiled, showing teeth worn down by centuries but still sharp. "There is a cave to the north. For the past fifty years, we've sent warriors there seeking something that might help us fight the corruption. None have returned." She paused, letting that sink in. "The Exile will enter. If he survives and retrieves what lies within, you may all continue to the seal. If he fails, his body joins the others who thought themselves strong enough."

"I accept," Karse said immediately, his voice steady despite what she was asking of him.

"Of course you do," the scarred elder said with satisfaction. "Finally, the Exile faces consequences."

Briar's mind raced. Karse was their guide, the only one who knew where the seal was, how to navigate the corrupted lands. Without him, they'd never make it. Without him, Malus would win. The memory of freeing him during the Hunt surfaced—her hands working the locks on his chains while hunters closed in, giving him the chance to escape. And afterward, how he'd twisted it, claimed she belonged to him until the debt was paid...

"Wait," she said, the words tumbling out before she'd thought them through. "Karse owes me a life debt."

The chamber went silent. Every Drak turned to stare at her, and she felt the weight of their attention like a physical thing.

Karse's head snapped toward her, his golden eyes wide with horror. "No. Don't—"

"I saved his life during the Wild Hunt," Briar continued, desperate now, thinking she'd found a solution. "I freed him from iron chains when he was captured, dying.

He would have been killed by the hunters if I hadn't freed him." She looked at Mor'va, hoping the elder would understand. "He said it himself afterward—my life belongs to him until the debt is paid. But that's backwards, isn't it? He owes me. Can't I... refuse to let him risk himself? Demand he stay safe until the debt is paid?"

Mor'va's ancient eyes narrowed, and surprise flickered across her features. "You invoke the law of life debt?"

"Stop talking," Karse hissed desperately. "You don't know what you're—"

"I invoke it," Briar said firmly. "His life belongs to me until the debt is paid, doesn't it? So I say he can't face this trial."

The other elders exchanged glances, some looking surprised, others calculating. The scarred elder actually smiled.

"The human invokes our oldest law," Mor'va said slowly, as if savoring each word. "How unexpected. Tell me, child, do you understand what you've just claimed?"

"I've claimed his life debt," Briar said, though uncertainty was creeping in at the expressions around her. "He can't throw his life away if it belongs to me."

"The debt was already settled," Karse said desperately. "I decided the terms—she belongs to me until—"

"You decided?" Mor'va's voice cut through his protest like a blade. "The debtor decides the terms of his own debt?" She turned to the other elders. "Have our laws changed so much in your absence, Exile?"

"A life debt belongs to the one who saved the life," the scarred elder said with obvious satisfaction. "The debtor cannot dictate terms. You knew this, Karse Draven. You perverted our law for your own purposes."

Briar's stomach dropped. Something was wrong. Karse looked like he might be sick, his scales actually paling.

"You stupid, ignorant girl," he whispered.

"Indeed," Mor'va said, standing with surprising grace. "By invoking the life debt, you've claimed ownership of his life. Which means, under our most ancient law, you've claimed responsibility for his actions. His crimes become yours to answer for."

The blood drained from Briar's face. "What? No, that's not what I—"

"You invoked the law," Mor'va said simply. "If his life belongs to you, then you must answer for how he's lived it. The abandonment. The collaboration. All of it." Her ancient eyes gleamed. "The trial is now yours to face, human."

"No!" Eliam's roar shook the chamber, shadows exploding outward despite the restraints. It took eight warriors to hold him down. "She didn't know! She didn't understand what she was saying!"

"Ignorance of the law is not absolution," the scarred elder said with clear satisfaction. "She saved the Exile's life. She claimed the debt. She faces his trial."

"This is insane," Thaine said flatly. "She's human. She's injured. She had no way of knowing—"

"Then she dies," Mor'va said simply. "And you all die with her, as conspirators in the Exile's crimes."

Briar stood frozen, her mind struggling to process how badly she'd miscalculated. She'd been trying to save Karse, to keep their guide alive, and instead she'd condemned herself. The looks on everyone's faces—Eliam's rage, Arion's horror, Karse's guilt and fury—all confirmed what she'd done.

"I take it back," she said desperately. "I didn't understand—"

"The law is spoken," Mor'va cut her off. "It cannot be unspoken."

Karse turned on her, his golden eyes blazing with a combination of fury and anguish. "Why couldn't you just stay quiet? Why did you have to invoke something you don't understand?"

"I was trying to help—"

"You've killed yourself!" His control shattered completely. "Do you understand that? You've volunteered to die for my crimes, you ignorant—" He cut himself off, pressing his palms against his eyes. When he spoke again, his voice was hollow. "You've killed us all. Without you, the seal can't be reinforced. Without you, everything ends."

"Perhaps the Exile should have thought of that before he perverted our laws," Mor'va said mildly. "Before he claimed to own someone who saved his life, twisting the debt to his advantage." She looked at Karse with ancient eyes that had seen too much. "Your dishonor has found its price, Karse Draven. That it falls on an innocent makes it all the more fitting."

The weight of what she'd done crashed down on Briar. Not just her own death, but the failure of their mission, the breaking of the seal, Malus's victory. All because she'd tried to be clever with laws she didn't understand.

"When?" she asked quietly, her voice barely audible.

"Tomorrow at midday," Mor'va said. "You'll be given a night to prepare, though I doubt it will help. The cave has killed warriors far stronger than you."

She gestured to Veroc. "Take them to the holding cells. Make sure they're fed and watered. If the human is to die for us tomorrow, she should at least do it with a full stomach."

The warriors hauled them to their feet, marching them out of the judgment hall. Briar caught Karse's eyes as they walked, saw the guilt and horror and rage warring in them.

"I'm sorry," she whispered. "I didn't know—"

"Ignorance and good intentions," he said bitterly. "The two things that have killed more people than any war."

The warriors separated them then, but she could still feel the weight of everyone's stares. She'd doomed them all with her ignorance.

And for that, she would pay for it with her life.

Chapter Thirty-Two

The holding cells were carved directly into living trees, the wood shaped by magic into small chambers with barred windows. They'd separated the group—Briar could hear Eliam's voice from somewhere above, the low rumble of threats that the guards were ignoring. Arion was in the cell beside hers, his light casting strange shadows through the wooden walls. The others were scattered throughout the structure, close enough to hear but too far to see or touch.

The cell itself was simple. A sleeping platform grown from the wood itself, covered with woven grass mats. A basin carved into one corner where water trickled constantly from somewhere above. A waste hole in the opposite corner that led to depths she didn't want to contemplate. The bars were living wood, still growing, impossible to break or burn.

Briar sat on the sleeping platform, her back against the wall, trying to stop her hands from shaking. The reality of what she'd done kept hitting her in waves. Tomorrow at midday, she would walk into a cave that had killed trained Drak warriors. Tomorrow, she would die.

"Briar." Arion's voice came through the wall, quiet and strained. "Can you hear me?"

"Yes."

"Are you..." He stopped, probably realizing how stupid it was to ask if she was alright. "We'll find a way out of this. Eliam's already trying to negotiate, offering trades, threats—"

"They won't listen." Her voice came out steadier than she felt. "I invoked their law. There's no taking it back."

Silence stretched between them. She could feel his light pulsing through the wall, agitated and desperate.

"What did Ferria tell you?" he asked suddenly. "In the safe haven, before you... before she died. You've been different since then. Distant."

Briar pressed her hand against her chest, feeling the warmth pulse in response. Should she tell him now? That he wasn't real, wasn't separate, was just a piece of Eliam walking around in his own body? What good would it do when she was going to die tomorrow anyway?

"It doesn't matter now," she said.

"Everything matters now." His voice was fierce. "If you're going to—if tomorrow—then tell me. Whatever it is, tell me."

Before she could respond, she heard footsteps approaching. Veroc appeared at her cell, carrying a tray of food and a bundle of cloth.

"Eat," he said, passing the tray through a gap in the bars. "Real food, not prisoner slop. The condemned deserve that much."

The tray held meat that smelled of herbs and smoke, roasted vegetables, flatbread still warm from baking. Her stomach turned at the sight of it.

"I'm not hungry."

"Eat anyway." His golden eyes studied her. "You'll need strength tomorrow. The cave doesn't kill quickly."

"How comforting."

He set the bundle on the floor. "Traditional clothes for the trial. They'll protect you better than what you're wearing now." He paused. "Not much better, but some."

"Why?" Briar looked up at him. "Why are you helping?"

"I'm not." His expression was unreadable. "I'm following protocol. But..." He glanced around, then leaned closer to the bars. "You saved Karse's life. Actually saved it, expecting nothing in return. That matters."

"It's why I'm going to die tomorrow."

"Yes." He didn't soften the truth. "But it still matters. Karse was my clutch-brother before he left. We were raised together, trained together. I hated him for leaving, but you gave him the chance to come home." He straightened. "The cave tests more than strength. Remember that."

He left before she could ask what he meant.

Briar forced herself to eat despite her lack of appetite. The food was good, better than anything they'd had on the road. She wondered if this was what condemned prisoners felt like eating their last meals.

After she finished, she examined the bundle Veroc had left. The clothes were Drak-made—leather pants that would actually protect her legs, a tunic of some scaled material she didn't recognize, boots that fit better than anything she'd worn since leaving home. There were even gloves, thin but tough, and a belt with loops for weapons she wouldn't be given.

She changed slowly, her body still aching from the confrontation with Ferria. The clothes fit surprisingly well, as if they'd been made for someone her size. She wondered whose they'd been, if their original owner had died in the cave she'd face tomorrow.

"Briar?" A different voice this time. Sian, from somewhere below.

"I'm here."

"I can feel water in the cave from here. It's... wrong. Corrupted. But it's there. If you can stay near it, I might be able to—"

"You won't be there." Briar's voice was emotionless. "I go alone."

"We'll be at the entrance. If you can get close enough—"

"Sian." Briar cut her off gently. "Thank you. But we both know I'm not coming out of that cave."

"You don't know that."

But she did. She could feel it in the way everyone had gone quiet when Mor'va described it. Fifty years of warriors entering and none returning. She was human, untrained, already injured. The math was simple.

Night fell properly, the amber lights in the tree structure dimming to almost nothing. Briar lay on the sleeping platform, staring at the ceiling, trying not to think about tomorrow. The warmth in her chest pulsed steadily, almost like it was trying to comfort her.

She must have dozed, because suddenly Eliam's voice was in her cell, though she knew that was impossible.

"Briar."

She sat up, heart racing. But no, he was above her, his voice carrying through the wood itself somehow.

"I'm here," she said.

"Move to the western wall."

She did, pressing her hand against the smooth wood. She felt it warm under her touch, and then suddenly the wood was thin as paper, her hand pressing through to meet his. Not breaking the cell, not creating an escape, just thinning the barrier enough for contact.

His fingers interlaced with hers immediately, desperately.

"I'm going to kill them all," he said, his voice deadly calm. "Every last one of them. For this."

"No, you're not." She squeezed his hand. "You're going to get to the seal. You're going to stop Malus. That's what matters."

"You matter." The words came out raw. "You matter more than any of it."

"Eliam—"

"I should have stopped you. Should have known you'd do something stupidly noble. Should have—" He cut himself off, his grip tightening. "There has to be another way."

"There isn't."

"Then I'll go into the cave with you."

"They won't let you."

"I don't care what they let—"

"Eliam." She pressed her other hand to the wood, wishing she could see him. "If you interfere, they'll kill everyone."

"If you fail they'll kill us anyway."

Briar was quiet. "I know you'll figure something out."

His silence was answer enough.

"Promise me," she said. "Promise me you'll get to the seal. That you'll stop Malus. That this won't be for nothing."

"Briar—"

"*Promise me.*"

She felt him lean his forehead against the wood, felt his breath through the thin barrier.

"I promise," he said finally. "But I'm not saying goodbye."

"You don't have to."

"Eliam..."

She thought about telling him the truth, about what Arion was, but she couldn't. Instead she let her forehead fall to rest against the cool wood.

"I'm sorry." And she *was* sorry. Sorry for letting her compassion get the better of her again. Sorry for letting her doubts make their last days spent together strained and distant. Sorry that she hadn't trusted herself enough to know her own heart before it was too late. "I love you."

They stayed like that, hands pressed together through the wood, until she heard guards approaching his cell. The wood thickened immediately, her hand meeting solid barrier again, and Eliam's cursing told her they were moving him somewhere else. Probably to prevent exactly what he'd just done.

The rest of the night passed in restless dozing and sharp waking. Every time she closed her eyes, she saw the cave, imagined what could kill warrior after warrior without remorse. When dawn finally came, filtering gray through her barred window, she was almost relieved.

Veroc came for her as the sun reached its peak.

"It's time," he said simply.

She stood, legs steadier than she expected. The traditional clothes did make her feel more protected, more capable. Not enough to survive, but enough to walk to her death with some dignity.

They led her through the settlement, and it seemed the entire population had turned out to watch. Drak of all ages lined the paths, their expressions ranging from sympathy to satisfaction to curiosity. The children were the worst, watching with wide eyes as she passed, some clutching their parents' hands.

The others were already at the cave entrance, held back by guards but there. Eliam's expression was murderous, shadows writhing around him despite the bright sunlight. Arion's light was sharp enough to hurt the eyes. Thaine stood perfectly still, the kind of stillness that preceded violence. Even Halian had shed his grief enough to look ready to fight.

Only Karse looked defeated, his shoulders slumped, his golden eyes dull.

The cave mouth yawned before them, a jagged opening in the hillside that looked entirely natural except for the wrongness emanating from it. The air around it was colder, and Briar could smell something sweet and rotten, decay and flowers mixed into something stomach-turning.

Mor'va stood beside the entrance, the other elders arranged behind her.

"Briar of the Forest Court," she said formally. "You stand accused of crimes through the law of life debt. You face the trial of the cave. Enter, survive, retrieve what lies within, and all crimes are forgiven. Fail, and you join those who came before."

"What am I supposed to retrieve?" Briar asked.

"You'll know if you find it," Mor'va replied. "No one has gotten far enough to see it clearly."

"Helpful."

"The trial begins when you enter," Mor'va continued. "You go alone, with no weapons, no aid from your companions. If you do not emerge by sunset, you are declared dead and your companions will meet your same fate."

"Without completing our mission." Briar looked at the elder steadily. "Without reinforcing the seal that protects you too."

"That is no longer your concern."

Briar turned to look at her friends one last time. Eliam's face was a mask of controlled fury, but his eyes... she saw everything there he couldn't say. Arion was gripping Sian's arm to keep himself from moving forward. Thaine gave her a single nod—warrior to warrior, acknowledging what she was about to do.

"Briar." Karse's voice was rough. "I'm sorry. For all of it."

She met his golden eyes, saw the genuine anguish there. "I know."

She turned back to the cave, squared her shoulders, and stepped forward.

The darkness swallowed her whole.

Not the gradual dimming of walking from sunlight into shadow, but immediate, absolute blackness that pressed against her eyes with physical weight. The cave mouth could have three steps behind her or three miles, the darkness erased all sense of distance, direction, space.

Briar kept one hand on the cave wall, using it to guide herself forward. Her footsteps echoed strangely, sometimes sounding far away, sometimes so close she flinched from her own movement.

Then light began to seep in. Not from any source she could identify, but a sickly phosphorescent glow that seemed to come from the stone itself. Pale green-white, just enough to see by, just enough to wish she couldn't.

Bodies.

The first one made her stumble. A Drak warrior, scales still gleaming despite death, slumped against the cave wall. No wounds, no blood, no signs of violence. He looked like he'd simply sat down and decided not to get up again. His eyes were open, staring at nothing, and his expression was... peaceful. Resigned.

The second body lay a few feet further. Another warrior, this one younger, curled on his side with his hands tucked under his head. Sleeping, except for the stillness that meant he'd never wake.

More bodies as she went deeper. All Drak, all warriors, all dead without a mark on them. Some sat against walls, some lay flat, some were curled in protective balls. But every single one looked like they'd simply... given up.

The cave tunnel widened into a larger chamber, and Briar stopped at its entrance, her breath catching. Dozens of bodies here, scattered across the floor in various positions of surrender. Warriors who'd made it this far and no further, all wearing the same expression of defeat.

The phosphorescent light grew brighter, and she saw something else. Writing on the walls. Messages carved into stone by desperate claws.

It knows what you are

You cannot fight yourself

The truth is worse than dying

I am nothing I am nothing I am nothing—this one repeated until it became scratches, then nothing.

The warmth in her chest pulsed, agitated, warning. But warning against what? There was nothing here but death and surrender.

She picked her way between bodies, trying not to look at their faces, trying not to see the tear tracks dried on scaled cheeks. Whatever had killed them, they'd been crying when it happened.

The chamber narrowed into another tunnel. She followed it because there was nowhere else to go, the luminous light growing brighter with each step. Her shadow appeared on the wall beside her, and she tried not to notice how it didn't quite match her movements, how it seemed to have too many angles.

Then she heard it.

"Worthless."

Her mother's voice, clear as if she stood beside her. Briar spun, but the tunnel was empty.

"Always were worthless. It's your fault we fought, your fault he's dead."

"That's not—" Briar's voice cracked. "You're not here."

"Might as well have killed him yourself." Her mother's voice came from ahead now, from the darkness beyond the phosphorescent glow.

"Stop."

"Twenty-five years of burden." The voice was behind her again. "Twenty-five years of watching you fail. Too weak to work hard enough. Too stupid to see what was right in front of you. Too selfish to just disappear and stop dragging everyone down."

Briar pressed her hands over her ears, but the voice came from inside her head now.

"You think I *loved* you?" Laughter, cold and bitter. "I could barely stand to look at you. You had his face, but none of his strength. His eyes, but none of his courage. A pale imitation I had to feed and clothe and pretend to care about."

"You did care," Briar whispered, but doubt began to creep in. Had she? Or had her mother just been trapped by obligation, forced to raise children she'd never wanted after the man she'd loved died?

Briar stumbled but pressed her hand against the wall to keep from falling. Ahead of her the tunnel opened into another chamber, this one perfectly circular. The unnatural light was brilliant here, showing every detail in stark relief. In the center of the room stood a figure.

Herself.

But wrong. This Briar's eyes were flat, dead. Her skin had a grayish cast, and dark veins traced patterns under the surface. The marks at her throat weren't copper but black, spreading like infection up her jaw, down into her bare chest. The warmth that pulsed in the real Briar's chest was visible in this version—a sickly, muted glow that looked like rot, like disease.

"Look at yourself," the other Briar said, and her voice was perfectly normal, which made it worse. "Look at what you're becoming."

"No," she shook her head as though that might be able to dislodge the image. "Y-you're not real."

"I'm the only real thing in your pathetic life." The shadow-Briar moved closer, and Briar saw that her fingernails had grown into long claws, that her teeth were slightly too sharp. "I'm what's under the skin. What the magic is making you. What you were always going to become."

"No."

"Denial doesn't make it any less true." Shadow-Briar smiled, and blood dripped from her teeth. "You killed Ferria and you enjoyed it. *We* enjoyed it. That moment when the thorns went through her, when her blood spilled? I can still *smell* it, still feel the satisfaction. For the first time since you came here you felt complete."

Briar's stomach turned because it was true. In that moment, she had felt satisfaction, she had wanted Ferria dead and felt nothing but rightness when it happened.

"You're not even human anymore." Shadow-Briar reached out, and her touch was ice-cold on Briar's cheek. When she tried to pull away, the fingers tightened, the clawed nails digging painfully into her face. "The magic has been changing you, cell by cell, breath by breath. Soon there won't be anything left of the girl who saved her sister. You're going to be just another monster wearing a human face."

"I'm not—"

"You are." Her mother's voice joined Shadow-Briar's. "Monster. Burden. Worthless thing that should have died instead of him."

More voices joined in. Allegra: "You ruined my life. I never asked you to save me."

Seraphin: "I was punished because of your selfishness, your need to have something from your old life."

Finally Eliam: "You thought I could care for a human? You think I'd want you after Malus used you? You're just a vessel for power. Once I have what's inside you, you're nothing."

"No, please…" Briar gasped. "Stop." She fell to her knees, the voices pressing down on her. Each word driving deeper than the last, each one something she'd always known but tried not to acknowledge.

Shadow-Briar knelt in front of her, gripping her face, forcing her to look into those dead eyes.

"Stop resisting. This is what you are," she said softly. "This is all you've ever been and all you'll ever be. A burden who got lucky. A worthless girl who stumbled into power she doesn't deserve. A killer who pretends at kindness. It would be better for everyone if you died in this cave."

The shadow's hands moved to Briar's throat, over the marks which suddenly burned with an intensity that left Briar gasping on her hands and knees.

"You can't even love properly. You were right. Everything you feel is the magic, pulling you toward them. Without it, they'd never look at you twice. Without it, you're nothing but a broken girl whose mother couldn't stand her, whose sister resented her, who kills anyone who shows her kindness."

Briar felt tears running down her face.

"Just give up," Shadow-Briar said gently, almost kindly. "Like the warriors did. It's easier than fighting what you know is true. Easier than pretending you're worth saving."

Briar caught sight of more bodies, all in that same position of surrender. They too had faced their shadow selves and couldn't bear what they saw.

"You want to." Shadow-Briar's voice was hypnotic now. "I can see how tired you are of fighting for every scrap, for every breath. It's okay to give up, to be tired of trying, of failing. Just let go. Just stop. Do something right for once in your pitiful, pointless life and die."

She *was* beyond tired, the exhaustion had worked its way deep into her bones. Her body hurt from the fight with Ferria, from the march through corrupted lands, from the constant fear and tension. It would be so easy to give in, to lie down like the warriors had. To let the truth of her worthlessness finally win.

"That's it," Shadow-Briar crooned and Briar felt herself sinking lower, her trembling arms simply giving up, pitching her forward. Shadow-Briar caught her, laying her gently on the cool stone floor. "The sooner that you accept that you've always been nothing the better it will be for everyone."

More tears slid down Briar's cheeks as eyes started to close. Maybe if she just rested for a moment...

"No one will mourn you," her mother's voice said. "They'll be relieved."

"The world will be better without you," Allegra's voice agreed.

"You're just another mistake that needs correcting," Eliam's voice added, cold and dismissive.

Briar's eyes closed, the tension eased from her muscles.

"That's it..." she felt the clawed fingers biting into her flesh. "It will all be over soon."

Then the warmth in her chest pulsed.

Not the sick golden glow that Shadow-Briar showed, but real warmth. And with it came a different memory.

Eliam's hand in her hair while she slept. Gentle, careful, like she was something precious.

Another pulse, another memory.

Arion's voice through the wall: "Everything matters now."

Sian teaching her how to help the water sprites migrate.

Thaine's expression when he caught her and Eliam throwing snowballs.

Karse, carrying her through the forest on his back when she couldn't walk.

Briar's eyes fluttered open. "No... you're wrong..."

"You're lying to yourself," Shadow-Briar hissed. "The magic making them care. Without it—"

"Without it, Thaine still helped me," Briar said, her voice rough. "Without it, Sian still befriended me. Without it, Halian was still kind."

"Stop—"

"My mother was ill." The words came stronger now and Briar began to push herself upright. "Sadness made her distant. That wasn't about me. That was about *her* pain."

"You're worthless!"

"I saved my sister's life." Briar raised her head, meeting Shadow-Briar's dead eyes. "I worked three jobs to keep my family fed. I survived everything the fae courts threw at me."

"You're a killer!"

Shadow-Briar sounded desperate now and for some reason that gave Briar strength. She got to her hands and knees, muscles trembling from exertion.

"Yes." The admission came easily. "I killed Ferria. I'd probably kill again. But I killed to survive, to protect, not for pleasure."

"You enjoyed—"

"I was surviving." Briar pushed herself up from the floor. "I enjoyed not being helpless. That's human, not monstrous."

Shadow-Briar's face contorted with rage. "You're nothing without the magic—"

"Maybe." Briar stood fully now, facing her shadow self straight on. "But with it? With it, I'm connected to something larger than myself."

"That's not you, that's the power—"

"The power is part of me now." Briar pressed her hand to her chest, feeling the warmth pulse in response. "Twenty-five years, it's been part of me. Changing me, yes. But I'm changing it too. Making it mine."

"You're becoming a monster—"

"No. I'm becoming something new." She took a step toward Shadow-Briar, who actually backed away. "Something that hasn't existed before. Human and fae and something else entirely. And that terrifies you."

"I am you—"

"Yes." Briar saw it clearly now. "You're my fear. My doubt. Everything I'm afraid of becoming. But fear isn't truth. It's just fear."

Shadow-Briar's form flickered, wavered.

"You're losing yourself," she tried one more time. "Everything human about you is dying."

"Everything human about me is transforming." Briar reached out, grabbed Shadow-Briar's wrist. It was solid, cold, real. "And I choose what I become. Not the magic. Not Eliam. Not Malus. *Me*."

"You can't—"

"I can." She pulled Shadow-Briar closer, until they were face to face. "You're right about one thing. I am becoming something else. But you're wrong about what that means."

"You'll lose everything!"

"I've already lost everything. Multiple times. And I survived." She looked into those dead eyes, saw her own fear reflected back. "I survived my father's death. My mother's illness. Giving up my freedom for my sister. Being hunted. Being marked. Being claimed."

"And it broke you—"

"And I'm still here." Briar's voice was steady now. "Broken or not, I'm still standing. Still fighting. Still choosing."

Shadow-Briar's form was definitely wavering now, edges becoming indistinct.

"You don't love them," she said desperately. "It's just the magic—"

"Maybe it started as magic." Briar didn't let go of the shadow's wrist. "But I choose to let it become real. I choose to love them, all of them. I choose to believe they could love me back, magic or not."

"That's delusion—"

"That's hope." Briar pulled the shadow even closer, until there was no space between them. "And hope is the one thing you can't understand. Because shadows don't hope. They just fear."

"I am you—"

"You're part of me," Briar corrected. "The scared part. The doubtful part. The part that believes every cruel thing ever said to me. But you're not all of me."

She wrapped her arms around Shadow-Briar, embracing her shadow self fully.

"And I'm not going to be afraid of you anymore."

Shadow-Briar screamed, thrashed, tried to pull away. But Briar held on, held tight, accepting this dark part of herself instead of fighting it. The shadow's form began to dissolve, melting into black smoke that smelled of copper and dying flowers.

"You can't..." Shadow-Briar said weakly.

"I can and I do. I accept you," Briar said simply. "I accept that I have these fears. These doubts. This darkness. It's part of me. But it doesn't control me and it won't define me."

The shadow dissolved completely, black smoke swirling around her, through her. For a moment, Briar felt it all—every fear, every doubt, every cruel thought she'd ever had about herself. The weight of it was crushing.

Then it settled into her chest, alongside the warmth. Not gone, but integrated. Part of her, but not controlling her.

The chamber changed. The phosphorescent light shifted from sickly green to softer white, less oppressive. She could move now without the weight of surrender pressing down on her.

She looked at the Drak warriors scattered throughout the chamber. They'd died here facing their own shadows, unable to accept what they saw. Their families would never know what happened to them, would never have closure.

Unless.

Briar moved to the nearest body, an older warrior whose scales had gone grey at the edges. Around his neck hung a pendant, carved bone with symbols she couldn't read. His family would want this. She took the pendant carefully, tucking it into her belt.

The next warrior wore a ring of twisted metal. She took that too. Another had a braided cord around his wrist with beads woven through it. A younger warrior had a small knife with an ornate handle, more ceremonial than practical.

She moved through the chamber methodically, taking something from each body. A pendant here, a weapon there, pouches with personal items—a child's drawing on scraped hide, a lock of hair, a small carved figure.

The items grew heavy quickly. Her pockets bulged, her belt sagged with the weight, she had to carry some in her arms. Each stop cost her energy she didn't have, her body already exhausted from the confrontation with her shadow self.

She made her way back through the tunnel, the phosphorescent light dimming as she moved away from the chamber. The bodies she'd passed on the way in were still there, and she stopped at each one, taking tokens. More pendants, more weapons, more personal effects.

By the time she reached the first warrior she'd seen, the one slumped peacefully against the wall near the entrance, her arms were full. The weight made walking difficult, each step requiring conscious effort. Her muscles shook with exhaustion.

But she couldn't leave them. These warriors had died for their people, and their families deserved something back.

The cave mouth appeared ahead, actual sunlight filtering through. Late afternoon light, gold and red. Had it been hours? It felt like days, but the sun suggested otherwise.

She stumbled out of the cave, arms full of tokens, legs barely holding her.

The crowd that had gathered fell silent.

She stood there, swaying, clutching the belongings of the dead, blinking in sunlight that seemed too bright after the cave's phosphorescent glow. The tokens clinked softly as her arms trembled from the weight.

Then recognition rippled through the crowd as they saw what she carried. Someone made a wounded sound—a parent recognizing a pendant, a spouse seeing a familiar weapon.

Mor'va stepped forward, her ancient eyes taking in the burden Briar carried.

"You honored them," she said quietly.

"They deserved to be remembered," Briar managed, her voice rough.

One by one, Drak began coming forward. An elderly female took a pendant with shaking hands, pressing it to her chest. A young warrior retrieved his brother's knife, tears running silently down his scaled face. Each token found its way to family, to friends, to those who'd been waiting.

Through it all, Briar stood there, gradually emptying her arms, watching grief and gratitude play across faces. When the last token had been claimed, her legs finally gave out.

Eliam caught her before she hit the ground, pulling her against him, holding her upright. She sank into his warmth, savoring the feeling of his arms around her. She wanted nothing more than to live in that moment forever.

"The trial is complete," Mor'va announced. "She survived the cave. She honored our dead. The crimes are forgiven."

The crowd erupted in sound—roars, clicks, and calls in the Drak language that Briar couldn't understand.

Karse appeared in front of her, his expression a mixture of shame and relief.

"The debt—" he started.

"Is paid," Briar cut him off, too exhausted for a longer discussion. "We're even."

He stared at her for a long moment, then nodded slowly. The tension he'd been carrying since she'd invoked the life debt seemed to drain from his shoulders.

Arion pushed through the crowd to reach them, his hand finding her shoulder, gentle but needing the contact, needing to confirm she was real and standing.

"What happened in there?" he asked quietly.

"Later," she managed. "Too tired now."

"The human needs rest," Veroc said, appearing at Mor'va's side. "And food."

"She'll have all of it," Mor'va said. She raised her voice to address the crowd. "Tonight, we celebrate."

"We need to leave now," Thaine protested. "The seal—"

"Will still be a threat tomorrow," Mor'va cut him off. "The Shadow Walker can barely stand. She faced something in that cave that Drak twice her size failed. She needs rest, or she won't survive the journey to the seal."

Shadow Walker. The title rippled through the crowd, and Briar wondered what it meant to them.

"Prepare the celebration," Mor'va commanded, and Drak began scattering to follow her orders. She turned back to the group. "Take them to their quarters, bring food, drink, whatever they need." Her ancient eyes settled on Briar. "You did something I didn't think possible, human. You survived what shouldn't be survivable. And you honored our dead while doing it."

Briar wanted to respond, but exhaustion was pulling at her, making everything feel distant and unreal. She felt Eliam shift his hold on her, preparing to carry her if necessary.

"Can you walk?" he asked quietly.

She nodded, though she wasn't sure it was true. But she wanted to leave this place on her feet, not in someone's arms. She'd earned that much.

They were led through the settlement to a large tree-dwelling, carved with symbols that probably marked it as important. Inside were separate rooms with real beds, fresh water, and broad windows that looked out over the settlement.

The moment they were alone, Briar's legs gave out completely. Eliam caught her, lifting her easily, carrying her to the bed.

"Are you going to tell me what happened?" he asked, his voice rough with suppressed emotion. "We heard you scream. Once. Then nothing for over an hour."

"I faced myself," she said simply. "The worst parts. The fears, the doubts. Everything I hated about what I'm becoming."

His hands stilled where they'd been checking her for injuries. "And?"

"And I accepted it. All of it. The darkness and the light." She pressed her hand to her chest, feeling both the warmth and the shadow resting there. "I've accepted that it's part of me now. That it doesn't dictate who I am."

He was quiet for a long moment, his hand covering hers over her chest.

"You're changing," he said finally.

"Yes."

"Into what?"

"I don't know yet." She met his dark eyes. "Does it matter?"

His hand moved to cup her face, thumb tracing her cheekbone. "No. You could become anything, and I would still—" He stopped, jaw clenching.

"Still what?" she asked, though exhaustion was making everything hazy.

"Rest," he said instead of answering. "The celebration starts at dusk and the Drak will be offended if their Shadow Walker doesn't attend."

She wanted to push, to make him finish what he'd been about to say. But sleep was already pulling her under, her body finally able to release the tension it had been holding.

The last thing she felt was his lips against her forehead, and words whispered too quietly for her to hear.

Chapter Thirty-Three

The Drak women who came for her didn't ask if she wanted their help. They simply arrived, carrying traditional garments and speaking in rapid bursts of their own language mixed with accented common.

"The Shadow Walker must be properly dressed," the eldest said, her scales a deep bronze that caught the lamplight. "You cannot celebrate in those rags."

Briar looked down at the practical clothes Veroc had given her for the trial. They were torn in places, stained with cave dirt and sweat, but calling them rags seemed harsh.

"I can dress myself—"

"Not in these, you can't." The younger one, scales bright green, held up what they'd brought.

The garments were nothing like the protective leather she'd worn into the cave. These were celebration clothes, and the Drak apparently celebrated with skin showing.

The top was essentially a wrapped binding of soft leather, dyed deep red, that would cover her breasts and not much else. Intricate beadwork decorated the edges, and small bones were woven throughout—honor markers, the bronze-scaled woman explained, for surviving the cave.

The skirt sat low on the hips, made of strips of leather and cloth that would move when she walked, showing flashes of leg with each step. More beadwork, more bones, and scales worked into the design.

"I can't wear this," Briar said, heat flooding her face.

"Why not?" The green-scaled woman looked genuinely confused. "It's good craftsmanship, it was specially made for you."

"It's very... revealing."

Both Drak women laughed, a sound between a chirp and a roar.

"This is a celebration," the bronze one said. "We celebrate survival, life, a body that still moves and breathes. Hiding the body is..." she searched for the word, "an insult to being alive."

They helped her dress despite her protests. The wrappings were more secure than they looked, everything staying in place despite the minimal coverage. They braided her hair, weaving in small bones and feathers—more honors, they explained. Survivors of the cave were marked so everyone knew what they'd accomplished.

Then came the paint.

"It's tradition," the green-scaled one said, producing pots of some sort of goop that looked like ash mixed with oil. "It represents what you faced and what you survived."

They painted symbols on her exposed skin—arms, stomach, back, legs. The paint was cool at first, then warmed, tingling slightly.

Sian was brought in next, already dressed in similar garments but in blue tones that complemented her water magic. She looked as uncomfortable as Briar felt, constantly trying to adjust the minimal coverage.

"This is..." Sian gestured at herself, at Briar, at the whole situation.

"I know."

"When they said celebration, I thought formal dinner. Maybe some speeches."

"Not being basically naked?"

Sian laughed, though it sounded slightly hysterical.

The bronze-scaled woman returned. "The men are ready. Come."

They were led through the settlement as full dark fell. Bonfires had been lit through-out the central area, massive ones that sent sparks spiraling into the night sky. The smoke smelled of herbs and wood, sweet but not cloying. Drums had started, a rhythm that seemed to sync with heartbeats, deep and primal.

The entire settlement had gathered, it seemed. Hundreds of Drak in their own celebration attire—leather and scales and exposed skin, bodies painted with symbols Briar couldn't read.

She saw their men before they saw her.

Eliam stood near one of the fires, dressed in Drak traditional clothing that left his chest bare except for crossed leather straps. His pants were leather, sitting low on his hips, and his skin had been painted with symbols that seemed to move in the firelight.

He looked dangerous and beautiful and completely out of place trying to maintain his usual cold control while essentially shirtless.

Arion was beside him, similarly dressed but in lighter colors. The paint on his skin seemed to capture and reflect his light, making him glow subtly. He was in conversation with Halian, who looked better than he had since Ferria's death, the celebration atmosphere working its magic even on grief.

Thaine stood apart, arms crossed, looking deeply uncomfortable in the minimal clothing but wearing it with the resignation of someone who'd given up fighting. Even Karse had changed into traditional garb, though he looked natural in it, comfortable in a way the others didn't.

Then Eliam saw her.

His expression shifted through several things quickly—surprise, hunger, something possessive and dark. His gaze tracked over the exposed skin, the paint, the bones in her hair marking her as someone who'd survived something significant.

She watched him take a step toward her, then stop, like he'd hit an invisible wall. His hands clenched at his sides.

Arion turned to see what had caught Eliam's attention, and his reaction was similar if more controlled. His light pulsed once, bright enough that several nearby Drak stepped back.

"Shadow Walker!" Mor'va's voice carried across the space. "Join me."

The crowd parted, creating a path to where the elder stood near the largest bonfire. Briar walked through, hyperaware of the eyes on her, of the way the skirt moved, of how much skin was exposed.

Mor'va held a carved horn, filled with a drink that smelled sweet and alcoholic.

"Here, you drink first," she said, loud enough for all to hear. "It is an honor, for surviving the cave."

Briar took the horn. The liquid inside was amber-colored, thick looking. She raised it to her lips and drank.

It burned going down, then spread warmth through her chest, her limbs. Not unpleasant, but strong. Immediately, colors seemed brighter, the fire more vivid, everything taking on a slight dreamlike quality.

"What is that?" she asked, trying not to make a face as she handed the horn back.

"It is a celebration drink," Mor'va said with obvious amusement. "Made from fermented fruit and dragon blood. Very mild."

"You call that mild?"

"For Drak." The elder's smile showed too many teeth. "For humans and fae... perhaps less mild."

The horn was being passed around now, everyone drinking. Briar saw Eliam take his share, then Arion, both of them still watching her with that intensity that made her skin warm beyond what the drink was doing.

"Now," Mor'va announced, "we dance!"

The drums increased in tempo, and Drak began moving. Not the formal, structured dancing Briar had seen at fae courts, but something rawer. Bodies moving to rhythm, individuals and pairs and groups, no set patterns, just movement and life and celebration of survival.

A Drak warrior approached her, male, young, scales a brilliant copper color.

"Would you honor me with a dance, shadow walker?" he asked, holding out a hand.

Before she could respond, Eliam stepped forward, shadows curling around his feet despite the brightness of the fires.

"No," he said flatly.

The warrior looked between them, but instead of backing down, he smiled. "The shadow walker can speak for herself, Forest Lord."

"I'd like to dance," Briar said, partly because the drums were making her body want to move, partly because Eliam's possessiveness sparked defiance in her.

She took the copper-scaled warrior's hand. His skin was warmer than human temperature, smooth where scales met flesh. He pulled her into the crowd of dancers before Eliam could object further.

The Drak way of dancing was nothing like the fae courts. No prescribed steps, no proper distance between bodies. The warrior's hands settled on her waist, guiding her into movement that followed the drums. Her body found the rhythm easily, the drink making everything feel liquid and natural.

"You honored our dead," the warrior said, leading her through a turn that made her skirt flare. "My uncle was among them."

"I'm sorry for your loss."

"No, you gave us closure. That matters." He spun her, and another Drak caught her, this one female with deep green scales.

"My turn with the shadow walker," she said, hands settling on Briar's hips.

The dancing became a blur of partners. Each Drak wanted a moment with her, to thank her, to celebrate her survival. Hands on her waist, her arms, her back. Bodies pressed close in the heat from the fires. The paint on her skin smeared and transferred, creating new patterns. The drink made everything feel intense and immediate—the heat of skin, the rhythm of drums, the smoke that made breathing feel thick.

Then familiar golden eyes. Karse caught her as she spun from another partner, his hands spanning her waist.

"Enjoying yourself?" he asked, and there was something lighter in his expression than she'd ever seen.

"The drink is strong," she said, having to focus on the words.

"For non-Drak, yes." He moved with her easily, naturally. This was his culture, his people. "You've given them hope. First time in decades."

"I just survived."

"You survived what none of them could." His hands shifted, pulling her closer as the drums intensified. "And you honored the dead. That matters here."

Someone called out in Drak, and Karse laughed, responding in the same language. Then other hands were pulling her away, another dancer claiming her. She caught a glimpse of Eliam through the crowd, his expression dark with frustration as he tried to move toward her but kept getting blocked by celebrating Drak.

Three more partners, each dance becoming more intimate as the celebration progressed. Bodies closer, hands bolder. The drink and drums and heat were making her skin hypersensitive. Every touch felt electric.

Then Eliam's hand closed around her wrist.

"Enough," he said, pulling her out of the current dancer's arms.

He didn't give her a chance to protest, pulling her against him fully. One hand splayed across her bare back, the other gripping her hip.

"Do you have any idea," he said against her ear, his voice rough, "what it's like watching them all touch you?"

She could feel his heartbeat against her chest, fast and hard. His skin was hot where it pressed against hers, the leather straps across his chest creating interesting texture. The paint on his skin had started to smear, and she could feel it transferring to her.

"It's just dancing," she managed.

"Nothing about this is just dancing." His hand moved up her back, fingers tracing her spine. "Look around."

She did. The celebration had shifted. Drak were paired off, pressed together, hands and mouths exploring. The dancing had become more intense and it made her face heat despite the drink.

"They celebrate being alive," Eliam said, his mouth close to her throat. "And you're practically naked, painted like a warrior, smelling like smoke and sweat and—"

Someone grabbed her arm, pulling her away from Eliam. A Drak warrior, laughing, saying something about the Forest Lord not monopolizing the shadow walker. Eliam's grip tightened for a moment, and she felt shadows gather, but then she was spinning away into another set of hands.

The celebration swirled around her. More partners, more heat, more skin. The drums were getting to her, making her body move without conscious thought. The drink made everything feel urgent and necessary.

Then Arion's light cut through the smoke.

He didn't grab her roughly like Eliam had. His hand found hers, fingers interlacing, and he drew her to him smoothly. His other hand settled at the small of her back, warm through the minimal fabric.

"You're flushed," he observed, though his own skin was gleaming with sweat in the firelight.

"It's hot," she said unnecessarily.

"Yes." His thumb stroked across her lower back, finding bare skin between the leather strips. "The drink affects humans more strongly."

"Mor'va mentioned that. After I drank it."

"Thoughtful of her." His tone was dry, but his eyes were focused on her with an intensity that had nothing to do with humor.

He moved with her to the drums, smoother than Eliam, more controlled. But his hands were just as possessive, keeping her close, his touch sending sparks across her hypersensitive skin. The paint on his chest was smearing where she pressed against him, creating patterns of light and shadow between them.

"You're covered in other people's paint," he observed, his hand tracing a smear across her shoulder.

"Everyone keeps touching—"

"I know." His grip tightened. "I've been watching."

The admission made heat bloom across her chest. Both of them watching her, wanting her, held back by the crowd and custom from claiming her.

His hand moved to her face, thumb brushing across her cheek. "You have no idea what you look like right now."

"Eliam said something similar."

His expression darkened at the mention of Eliam. "Of course he did."

A Drak tried to cut in, reaching for her, but Arion's light flared bright enough to make them step back. His usual control was slipping, affected by drink and drums and the press of bodies around them.

"Mine," he said, quiet enough that only she heard it.

The word sent heat through her that had nothing to do with the fires. His hand splayed across her back, pulling her flush against him. She could feel his heartbeat, as fast as Eliam's had been. Could feel the way his breathing had quickened.

"Arion—"

"Don't," he said roughly. "Just... dance with me."

They moved together, bodies aligned, the drums directing their movement. His hands were everywhere—her back, her hips, her arms. Not inappropriate, but possessive, claiming. The warmth in her chest was pulsing frantically, reaching for him.

Then shadows wrapped around her waist, pulling her backward.

She collided with Eliam's chest, his arm banding around her middle.

"My turn," he said to Arion, challenge clear in his voice.

"You already had your turn," Arion replied, his light sharpening.

"I wasn't finished."

"Too bad."

They stood there, Eliam holding her against him, Arion still close enough that she could feel his heat. The tension between them was electric, dangerous. Around them, the celebration continued, but several Drak had noticed the building confrontation and were watching with interest.

"Let her go," Arion said, his voice low, controlled but barely.

"No." Eliam's arm tightened around her.

"I'm not a possession you can fight over," Briar said, though her voice came out breathier than intended.

"No?" Eliam's mouth was against her ear. "Then why aren't you pulling away?"

She wasn't. She was standing there, caught between them, her body responding to both their proximity. The warmth in her chest was pulling in two directions at once, desperate and frantic.

"Because," she said, and the truth came out drink-loosened and necessary, "because I need to tell you both something Ferria told me. About what you really are."

Both men went still. The drums continued, the celebration swirled around them, but in their small bubble of space, everything stopped.

"What did she tell you?" Arion asked, stepping closer.

Eliam turned her in his arms so she could see both of them. Their faces in the firelight, so different but suddenly she could see it—the same bone structure, the same way of moving, the same intensity in their eyes despite the different colors.

The warmth in her chest pulsed once, hard, recognizing what she was about to reveal.

"You're the same person," she said. "Split in two."

The words settled between them, the heavy weight of an impossible truth. The drums continued their rhythm, the celebration swirled around them, but neither man moved.

"That's... impossible," Eliam said finally, his voice low. "Ferria was lying."

"The ritual," Briar continued, the drink making the words tumble out faster than she intended. "The night you made the bargain with my mother. He was trying to strip your power, but you interrupted it. The ritual didn't just fail... it backfired. It fractured you."

Arion's light flickered erratically. "Fractured?"

"Split your very being into two separate bodies." She looked between them, seeing their faces in the firelight.

"You're drunk," Eliam said, but his grip on her had gone rigid.

"The drink made it easier to tell you, but I'm not lying." She pressed her hand against her chest where the warmth pulsed. "This recognizes you both equally. Reaches for you both the same way. I thought I was broken, wanting two different men, but you're not different. You're the same person in two bodies."

Arion stepped back, his expression stricken. "I have memories. A past. I remember—"

"Do you?" Briar challenged. "Do you really remember your childhood? Your parents? Or do you just remember... existing, already grown, already knowing magic but not how you learned it?"

His silence was answer enough.

"This is insane," Eliam said, but she could see him thinking, processing. "We're cousins. We've always been—"

"Have you? When did you first meet? What was your relationship before that night?"

More silence. Around them, a particularly enthusiastic group of dancers nearly crashed into them, but Eliam's shadows lashed out, creating a barrier.

"The pull," Arion said quietly. "I've always felt pulled toward you." He was looking at Eliam now. "I thought it was just rivalry. Competition. But it's more than that."

"The way you mirror each other," Briar continued, placing one hand on Eliam's face and the other on Arion's. "The way your magic resonates on the same frequency. Shadow and light, two sides of the same power."

Eliam's hands had dropped from her waist. He was staring at Arion with an expression she'd never seen before—not quite horror, not quite recognition, but something between.

"When I'm near you," Eliam said slowly, "I feel... less like I'm missing something."

"Yes," Arion agreed. "Like a hollow space gets smaller."

"Ferria said Malus needs all three of us," Briar continued. "Both pieces of you and me as the catalyst. To force reunification. To restore you to what you were before the split."

"Reunification," Eliam repeated. "Becoming whole again."

"Becoming one person again," Arion corrected, and there was a hint of fear in his voice. "Which means one of us ceases to exist."

They stood there, the three of them, while the celebration raged around them. The firelight painted everything in orange and gold, and the drums seemed to sync with the frantic pulsing of the warmth in her chest.

"This is why," Arion said suddenly. "Why I was so drawn to you from the beginning." He was looking at Briar. "Not just attraction. Recognition. You carry a power that knew what I was, even when I didn't."

"The warmth has been trying to pull you together," Briar said. "Every time you're both near me, it goes wild. It wants you whole."

"But we don't know what that means," Eliam said, his voice sharp. "What happens to our consciousness? Our memories? Do we merge or does one dominate?"

"I don't know," Briar admitted. "Ferria didn't say. Maybe she didn't know."

The words hung there, the weight of everything unsaid pressing down on them. Eliam's face was a mask of controlled fury at the situation, at Malus, at the impossible choice. Arion looked shaken to his core, his light flickering erratically.

A wave of dancers crashed into them, drunk and laughing, jostling them together. Briar stumbled, and both men reached for her at the same time. Their hands met on her waist, overlapping, and the warmth in her chest erupted.

Golden light spilled from beneath her skin, visible even in the firelight. Where their hands touched each other and her, the connection flared to life—not just physical but something deeper. They all gasped at the same moment, feeling it.

The drums seemed to get louder, more insistent, pounding through their bodies. All around them, the celebration had reached its peak—bodies everywhere, intertwined, the air thick with smoke and desire and primal abandon.

The warmth was singing now, pulling them together with desperate need. Twenty-five years of carrying this power, and finally it had both halves close enough to touch.

Eliam's hands pulled her flush against him, but he was looking at Arion over her shoulder, and his expression held something she'd never seen before. Recognition. Understanding. Hunger not just for her but for completion.

Rather than retreat, Arion stepped closer, pressing against her back, and Briar found herself caught between them. The drums made thinking impossible. All she could focus on was the way their hands felt on her skin, their bodies pressed close, the warmth connecting all three in a circuit of need.

"We should—" someone started to say, but then Eliam's hips moved with the drums, pressing her back against Arion, who groaned softly. She could feel him hard against her lower back.

They began moving again, but barely, just their bodies finding rhythm together, no space between them.

"I can feel it," Eliam said as his hands spanned her bare waist, fingers spreading across her ribs, thumbs brushing the underside of her breasts.. "The pull. Not just to you anymore. To him too. Through you."

Arion's hands settled on her hips, holding her against him, and she could feel his arousal growing with each movement.

"Maybe..." Briar began but Eliam's mouth found her throat, teeth grazing her pulse, and the words died. His tongue traced the column of her neck, tasting the salt of her sweat mixed with ceremonial paint.

Behind her, Arion's hands moved up from her hips, sliding across her stomach. His fingers traced the painted symbols there, each touch sending sparks through her oversensitized skin. When his palm flattened against her belly, pressing her back more firmly against his arousal, she moaned.

The golden warmth in her chest wasn't just pulsing now, it was reaching out in tendrils, wrapping around both men, trying to bind them through her. Every point where their bodies touched felt electric.

Arion's hand slid up slipping beneath the minimal leather binding to cup her breast, thumb finding her nipple already hard and aching. His touch was gentle but possessive, and when he rolled the sensitive peak between his fingers, her knees nearly buckled.

"Here?" she gasped. "In the middle of—"

"Look around," Eliam commanded, his hand tangling in her hair to turn her head.

The celebration had descended into something primal. Drak couples and groups writhed together by the fires, hands and mouths exploring freely. The drums had taken on a deeper rhythm that seemed to bypass thought entirely, speaking directly to the body. This was what Mor'va had meant by celebrating life—pure, uninhibited expression of being alive.

"No one cares," Arion murmured against her ear, his other hand joining the first to cup both breasts. "This is what the celebration is for."

Eliam's mouth found hers, kissing her with a desperate hunger that had nothing to do with the wine and everything to do with the revelation of what he was. What *they* were.

She kissed him back just as desperately, her body on fire from their combined touch. When Arion's mouth found the side of her neck, sucking hard enough to leave a mark, she broke the kiss to cry out.

With a newfound sense of urgency, Eliam's fingers made quick work of the ties holding her top in place. The leather fell away, and then their hands were on her bare breasts, Eliam's from the front and Arion's reaching around. Four hands touching, teasing, making her writhe between them.

"Look at her," Eliam growled, his voice thick with desire as he watched Arion's hands move over her breasts. "So responsive. So perfect."

Arion's fingers pinched her nipples simultaneously, making her arch between them with a sharp gasp. The movement pressed her ass more firmly against his arousal, and he groaned against her neck.

The warmth in her chest was no longer just pulsing—it was singing, reaching out to wrap golden threads around all three of them. She could feel it trying to pull them closer, deeper, to merge them in ways that went beyond physical.

Eliam's hands slid down her sides, finding the ties of her skirt next. Once again the leather strips fell away, leaving her in nothing but the ceremonial paint and the two men's hands. She should have felt exposed, vulnerable, and she did, but she also didn't care.

Arion's hand slid down her stomach, fingers tracing the muscles that jumped under his touch. When he reached the apex of her thighs, finding her already wet and aching, they both groaned—as if they could both feel what he was feeling.

"The connection," Eliam said roughly, his forehead pressed to hers as Arion's fingers began moving in slow, teasing circles. "I can feel what he feels when he touches you."

"Both ways," Arion confirmed, his voice strained. "When you kiss her, I taste it."

The revelation sent a new wave of heat through her. They were connected through her, the warmth binding them together in ways none of them had understood. Every sensation was shared, amplified, reflected between them.

Eliam's mouth found her breast, tongue circling her nipple as Arion's fingers pressed inside her. She cried out, her hands grasping desperately at whatever she could reach—Eliam's hair, Arion's arm, anything to anchor herself.

Around them, the celebration continued its primal rhythm. The drums seemed to sync with her heartbeat, with the pulsing of the warmth that connected them. She could hear other sounds—moans, cries of pleasure, the celebration of life in its most basic form.

When Eliam's hand moved to join Arion's between her legs, she found her heart racing in anticipation. As he slowly eased his fingers inside of her, her hips rolled to meet his touch, her head falling back against Arion's shoulder He captured her mouth in a kiss that was all heat and demand.

His tongue swept past her lips, claiming and exploring, swallowing the sounds she was making. She could taste the fermented drink on him, sweet and strong, could feel his desperation in the way he consumed her mouth. His teeth caught her lower lip, tugging before soothing it with his tongue.

It was deep, possessive, his hand tangling in her hair to angle her head exactly how he wanted. Each stroke of his tongue matched the rhythm of their fingers below, deliberate and overwhelming. When she gasped for air, he barely let her breathe before claiming her mouth again, like he was trying to devour her very breath, to merge with her through the kiss alone. All the while his fingers continued to tease, the two of them working together instinctively, as if they could feel what the other was doing, adjusting their rhythm to drive her higher.

"I need—" she panted when Arion finally released his claim on her mouth. "I need more. Need you both."

The words had barely left her lips when Eliam lifted her effortlessly, shadows curling around her thighs to help support her weight. The position opened her completely to them both, and she felt exposed in the most delicious way, suspended between their bodies as the drums thundered around them.

"Hold onto me," Arion murmured against her ear, guiding her arms back around his neck.

She could feel them both hard against her—Arion's cock pressing insistently against her lower back while Eliam pressed himself between her spread thighs making her dizzy with want.

"Please," she whimpered, not caring that they were surrounded by other dancers, that anyone could see how wantonly she writhed between them. The Drak wine had stripped away her inhibitions, leaving only raw need.

Without a word, Eliam withdrew his fingers before positioning himself at her entrance. Arion's fingers traced down her spine, his touch leaving trails of starlight that made her shiver.

"Both of us," Eliam growled against her throat, not a question but not quite a statement.

"Yes," she breathed, the single word holding all her desperate need. The warmth in her chest flared so bright she could see it even with her eyes closed—golden threads wrapping around all three of them, pulling them together in ways that transcended the physical.

At her words, Eliam pushed inside her slowly, stretching her, filling her with a deliberate care that made her body tremble. Behind her, Arion's fingers moved lower, slick with her arousal as he prepared her carefully. The sensation was foreign but not unpleasant. When Arion pressed one finger inside her there, she tensed.

"Breathe," he murmured against her ear, his free hand stroking soothing patterns on her hip. "Let me make you feel good."

She forced herself to relax, focusing on the pleasure of Eliam moving slowly inside her, on the way their combined touch made the warmth in her chest pulse brighter. When Arion added a second finger, scissoring gently, the stretch burned but in a way that made her moan.

"That's it," Arion murmured against her ear as he replaced his fingers with the head of his cock, pressing gently but insistently. "Let us in. Let us have all of you."

"Together," Eliam said, his voice rough with restraint as he held still inside her. "Move together."

They did.

As Eliam withdrew slightly, Arion pressed forward, making her cry out. The initial burn gave way to an overwhelming fullness as Arion worked himself inside her inch by careful inch. She felt stretched beyond capacity, claimed in the most primal way possible.

Eliam groaned, his forehead pressed to hers. "I can feel—I can feel both sides. What you're feeling, what he's feeling—"

When they were both fully seated inside her, they paused. She could feel them both throbbing, could feel the way their breathing had synchronized. The warmth in her chest was no longer just pulsing—it was singing, a golden harmony that seemed to vibrate through all three of them.

"Move," she begged, rolling her hips experimentally. The motion made both men groan, their hands tightening on her.

They found a rhythm slowly, learning how to move together. When Eliam thrust forward, Arion pulled back. When Arion pressed deep, Eliam withdrew. The drums around them seemed to guide their movements, primal and deep.

Eliam's shadows wrapped around her breasts, teasing her nipples while his hands gripped her hips. Arion's light pulsed against her clit with steady pressure that made her buck between them. They moved together like they'd done this before, like their bodies knew each other through her.

"Look at me," Eliam commanded, and when she opened her eyes, his were pure black with desire. "I want to watch you come apart for us."

The pace increased, both men driving into her with a synchronized rhythm that spoke to their shared essence. She could feel the warmth spreading from her chest throughout her body, could see the golden threads growing brighter, pulling them closer together with each thrust.

Around them the Drak drums pounded relentlessly, their rhythm matched only by the frantic pounding of her heart. Briar couldn't tell where one man began and the other ended; they moved as one, their motions so perfectly in sync it was as if they'd rehearsed it a thousand times.

The connection between them only heightened the experience, every touch, every caress, every stroke amplified by the power of three. Each moan she gave was echoed back to her, intensifying her pleasure until she felt as if she were teetering on the edge of a cliff, the drop-off into oblivion dizzying and thrilling.

The world faded into nothingness, the celebration and drums and even the very air they breathed all but forgotten as they lost themselves in each other. They were the only three beings in existence, bound together by a force greater than any of them could ever hope to understand or control.

Ecstasy built within her, the warmth in her chest now a raging inferno, threatening to consume her whole. She clung to the feeling, to them, knowing that without this connection, without the anchor of their shared climax, she might fly apart.

"That's it," Eliam growled in her ear, his voice low and commanding, his thrusts driving her higher. "Come for us, Briar. Come with us."

"Yes," Arion gasped, his fingers digging into her hips as he pushed even deeper inside her. "Fall with us, Briar. Let go."

The call of their combined voices, the pull of their shared lust, was too much to resist. She arched, her head thrown back as her orgasm crashed over her in a wave of white-hot light. Their names tumbled from her lips in a breathless litany—Eliam, Arion, together, apart, it no longer mattered.

She felt them both follow suit, their moans mingling with hers as they filled her, their essence mingling with hers, their connection sealed in a way that went beyond the physical.

As they collapsed against each other, breathless and spent, Briar couldn't help but wonder what the future held for them. They were, after all, three halves of a whole, now bound by more than just circumstance or shared experiences. They were bound by the very fabric of existence itself.

Chapter Thirty-Four

B riar woke slowly, acutely aware of the warmth that surrounded her, of the arm draped across her waist, and a chest pressed against her back, rising and falling with a steady breathing that wasn't her own. For a moment she just existed in that space between sleep and waking, feeling protected and cherished.

Her eyes opened to amber light filtering through wooden walls. The Drak settlement. The celebration. Everything came back in pieces that didn't quite fit together yet.

Eliam asleep beside her, his face relaxed in a way she rarely saw when he was conscious. The paint from last night had smeared across his skin, dark lines broken and faded. His hair was a mess, and there was a mark on his throat that she had a vague memory of making. The sight of him made something warm bloom in her chest, affection and contentment mixing together.

That's when it dawned on her. If Eliam was next to her... then who was pressed against her back?

Arion.

Her heart lurched. She turned her head carefully, not wanting to wake either of them, to confirm what she already suspected. Arion was there, his honey blond hair falling across his face, one arm draped over her hip.

The events of the previous night crashed into her all at once.

The dancing. The drinks. The revelation about them being the same person split in two. The way the magic had pulled them together. The very public... everything that had happened after that.

Oh God.

They had done that. *She* had done that. In front of hundreds of Drak. With both of them. At the same time.

The memory was vivid enough to make her clench her thighs, but embarrassment quickly doused the heat that had begun blossoming. Everyone had seen. Everyone knew. The mortification was beyond anything she'd ever felt.

She needed to leave, to slip out before they woke up and she had to face what they'd done. She needed space to think, to process, to figure out how to look either of them in the eye ever again.

Briar started to ease herself forward, away from Arion's warmth, toward the edge of the sleeping platform.

Eliam's arm tightened around her immediately, pulling her back against him. His eyes were still closed but his voice was rough with sleep when he spoke.

"Where are you going?"

"I just—I need—" The words tangled in her throat.

His eyes opened, dark and focused despite having just woken. He studied her face with an intensity that made her want to look away. "Stay."

It was not a request. His arm remained wrapped around her waist, keeping her in place, and despite everything, she found she didn't actually want to pull away.

"Eliam, last night we—"

"I know what we did last night." His thumb traced small circles on her hip, the touch casual but possessive. "I was there."

Her face burned hotter. "Everyone saw."

"Yes."

"*Everyone.*"

"I'm aware." A smile was tugging at the corners of his mouth though he seemed to be fighting it. "You didn't seem to mind at the time."

"I was drunk," she said, though even as the words left her mouth she knew they were a weak defense. She hadn't been *that* inebriated. "That drink was—it affects humans more than—"

"You were tipsy," he corrected, his hand sliding up her side. "Not unconscious, nor unaware. You knew exactly what you were doing when you begged us to—"

"Don't." She pressed her hand against his mouth, mortification threatening to consume her entirely. "Please don't say it out loud."

He kissed her palm, his eyes glinting with dark satisfaction. When she pulled her hand away, his smile was pure smugness. "I had no idea you were such an exhibitionist."

"I'm not—I didn't—that's not—" She couldn't form a complete sentence, her face so hot she thought she might combust.

"The way you moaned when I—"

"Eliam, I swear—"

"And when Arion's hands were—"

She clapped her hand over his mouth again, harder this time. "Stop talking. Right now."

His shoulders shook with silent laughter, and she realized with horror that he was enjoying this. Actually taking pleasure in her embarrassment.

Behind her, Arion shifted. His arm tightening around her hip, pulling her back against him, and she felt him wake properly. His hand splayed across her stomach, fingers spreading wide.

"Good morning," he said softly.

The simple word carried too much weight. Good morning after what they'd done and earning what they were. The day they'd have to face everyone else with this knowledge.

"We should go," she said. "The others will be wondering—"

"The others are probably still sleeping off their own celebrations," Eliam said, but he was already pulling away, the loss of his warmth making her shiver.

They dressed in awkward silence, Briar's body protesting every movement—she was definitely sore, muscles aching in ways that made her blush remembering why. The traditional Drak clothing from the night before felt wrong in daylight, far too revealing. Briar wrapped herself in her cloak despite the warm morning, trying to cover as much painted skin as possible.

"We need to talk about what Ferria revealed," Arion said, adjusting the leather straps across his chest. "About what we are."

"Later," Eliam said curtly. "After we've dealt with getting to the seal."

"We can't just ignore—"

"I said later."

The sharpness in Eliam's tone made Arion's jaw clench, but he didn't argue further. The tension between them was different now—not the competitive edge of before, but something heavier. The knowledge of what they were to each other had changed everything and nothing.

Briar moved toward the entrance, needing to not be caught between them while they processed this impossible situation. The moment she stepped outside, she became aware of eyes on her.

Drak throughout the settlement were already engaged in their morning routines, and every single one seemed to look up when she exited from the dwelling. Some smiled knowingly, while others nodded respectfully, and a few of the younger ones whispered to each other in their own language. She caught the word "Shadow Walker" mixed in with terms she didn't understand.

They knew. Everyone knew what had happened at the celebration.

Groaning inwardly, Briar made her way quickly toward the housing she had shared with Sian, hoping to find her or literally anyone who could provide a distraction from the consequences of her wine-induced actions.

She finally found Sian at the communal water source, looking significantly worse for wear. Her friend's traditional garb was askew, paint smeared in ways that suggested her own celebration had been just as eventful.

"Don't," Sian said, not even looking up from where she was splashing water on her face. "Whatever you're about to say, just don't."

"I wasn't going to say anything."

"Good." Sian finally looked up, took in Briar's appearance and winced. "Though I will say, you're louder than you think."

Briar's face burned. "The drums were loud."

"Not *that* loud."

Before Briar could die of embarrassment completely, Mor'va appeared, looking far too composed for someone who'd presumably celebrated as hard as everyone else.

"Shadow Walker," she greeted, then looked past Briar to where Eliam and Arion were emerging from the dwelling. "Forest Lord. Star Prince." Her ancient eyes gleamed with knowing amusement. "I trust you found our celebration... educational?"

"Thank you for your hospitality," Arion said diplomatically.

Mor'va grinned. "The Drak believe in celebrating life fully. Connection, pleasure, the joining of bodies—these are sacred things. Especially when fate has conspired to bring together what was separated."

The weight of her words made all three of them go still.

"You knew?" Eliam's voice was dangerously quiet.

"I am old, Forest Lord. I have seen much." She studied them with those ancient eyes. "The resonance between you two has always been visible to those who know how to look. And now with the Shadow Walker connecting you..." She trailed off, then became businesslike. "Your companions are gathering in the main hall. Supplies have been prepared for your journey to the seal."

"You're helping us?" Briar asked, surprised.

"You survived the cave. You honored our dead. And more importantly," Mor'va's gaze moved between the three of them, "what comes next requires you all to reach the seal. The corrupted lands grow worse each day. Whatever must be done, it must be done soon."

She turned to go, then paused. "Veroc and a dozen additional warriors will escort you to the border of the seal's territory. Beyond that, you go alone. The magic there is too unstable for those without protection."

"What kind of protection?" Arion asked.

Mor'va looked at Briar. "The kind she carries. The kind that recognizes both shadow and light and can bridge what was broken." Her expression grew serious. "Be careful, Shadow Walker. The seal was made with sacrifice. It may demand the same to be maintained."

She left them standing there, the weight of her words settling over them like a shroud.

"We should find the others," Briar said, unable to bear the silence.

They made their way to the main hall, where they found Thaine, Halian, and Karse already assembled. Thaine looked them over with a hunter's assessment, taking in every detail of their appearance. His expression gave away nothing, but Briar thought she saw his mouth twitch slightly.

Halian looked hollow-eyed and grief-worn, barely acknowledging their arrival. The celebration had clearly not eased his pain over Ferria's death. If anything, he looked worse.

Karse lounged against a wall, somehow managing to appear completely unaffected despite having celebrated as hard as any Drak would have.

"Finally," he drawled. "Thought we'd have to send a search party. Though from the sounds of things, we would have known where to find you."

Briar wanted to sink into the floor.

"Enough," Thaine said sharply. "We have more important things to discuss." He looked directly at Eliam and Arion. "Is it true? What Briar said last night?"

"You heard?" Arion asked.

"Everyone heard. Drak celebrations echo, and profound revelations carry." Thaine's expression was grim. "Are you really one being split in two?"

Eliam and Arion exchanged glances.

"It seems so," Arion said finally.

"Well," Karse said after a moment of stunned silence, "that explains the sexual tension."

"This is serious," Thaine snapped. "If Malus knows this, if he planned this—"

"He knows," Briar interrupted. "His ritual backfired when Eliam put the piece of his essence inside of me. It caused him to split instead of stripping his powers."

"Then we're walking into a trap," Halian said, speaking for the first time. His voice was hoarse. "Going to the seal is exactly what he wants."

"Not going means the seal breaks anyway," Thaine pointed out. "It's already failing. You've seen the corruption spreading."

"So we're trapped either way," Sian summarized.

"Not trapped," Eliam said. "Challenged. Malus expects us to come. Fine. But he doesn't know we know about the fracture. That's an advantage."

"A small one," Karse noted. "Against someone who's had centuries to plan."

They were still arguing when Veroc arrived with the other Drak warriors, all armed and armored for travel. The morning light caught on their scaled armor, each piece overlapping like natural protection, purple and black in the shadows. The warriors moved with predatory grace despite the weight of their gear, their reptilian eyes scanning the gathering with professional assessment.

"The morning grows late," Veroc said, his ancient voice carrying the rumble of distant thunder. "If you're going to reach the seal's border by nightfall, we need to leave now."

There was a flurry of final preparations. Supplies were distributed from woven packs that looked deceptively small for what they contained. Weapons were checked with the careful attention of those who knew their lives would depend on them and armor was adjusted with practiced hands tightening straps and checking joints.

Briar found herself being handed a set of lighter traveling clothes by a young Drak female whose scales still held the brighter purple of youth.

"For the journey," the girl said shyly, her inner eyelids flickering nervously. "The ceremonial garb is not meant for travel."

Briar thanked her and changed quickly. The new garments were practical—soft leather that had been worked until it was supple as cloth, reinforced at the knees and elbows, with a dark tunic that would blend into forest shadows. The boots laced up to mid-calf, sturdy enough for rough terrain but flexible enough to run if needed.

When she emerged, she found Eliam waiting for her. He held out the star metal pendant, the chain catching the light like captured moonbeams, and she slipped it over her head. The weight of it settled against her chest, cold at first, then warming to her skin.

"Stay close when we travel," he said quietly. "The corruption will get worse as we approach the seal."

"I know."

He studied her face, something unreadable in his expression. "About last night—"

"We don't have to talk about it."

"We do." His hand rose to cup her face, thumb tracing her cheekbone. "Everything's different now. What we know, what we are to each other—"

"Eliam."

"I won't lose you." The words came out fierce, possessive. "Whatever happens at the seal, whatever Malus has planned, I won't let anything happen to you."

She wanted to point out that he might not have a choice, that if reunification happened, if Arion ceased to exist as a separate being, everything would change in ways none of them could predict. But Veroc was calling for them to move out, and there was no time for that conversation.

They left the Drak settlement as the sun reached its peak, their escort leading them back into the corrupted wilderness. Behind them, the safe haven of the settlement disappeared into the twisted trees, and ahead lay only uncertainty and the growing wrongness of lands touched by failing magic.

The seal waited, and with it, whatever trap Malus had set for them all.

The forest changed gradually at first.

The twisted trees grew thicker, their branches weaving overhead into an impenetrable canopy that blocked most of the afternoon light. What filtered through came down wrong, a sickly green that made everything look diseased. The warmth in Briar's chest recoiled from it, pulling tighter with each step deeper into the corrupted lands.

Veroc led them along paths that barely existed, sometimes having to hack through undergrowth that had grown wild and wrong. The vegetation here didn't follow natural patterns. Vines twisted upward in spirals, their thorns growing in directions that defied logic. Flowers bloomed and rotted in the span of heartbeats, their petals falling only to regrow in different colors, different shapes.

"Don't touch anything," Veroc said for the third time, his voice carrying the weight of experience. "The corruption responds to contact. Makes it worse."

Behind them, the other Drak warriors moved in formation, eyes constantly scanning the shadows. They'd been walking for hours, and with each mile, the wrongness intensified. The air tasted metallic now, coating the back of Briar's throat with something that made her want to gag.

"How much further?" Sian asked, her voice tight. She'd been quiet since they left, staying close to Halian who hadn't spoken at all.

"To the border? Another hour, maybe two." Veroc paused, studying a tree whose bark wept something dark and viscous. "The seal itself is beyond that. We don't go there."

"Why?" Thaine asked, though his tone suggested he already knew.

"Because those who do don't come back unchanged," Veroc said, his voice quiet. "Your fae magic won't work properly near the seal. The magic there is too old, too tangled. It recognizes nothing but what it was made to contain."

A branch cracked somewhere to their left. Everyone went still, weapons half-drawn, but nothing emerged from the shadows. The silence that followed felt worse than an attack would have.

They continued walking, the ground beneath their feet growing softer, spongier. It gave slightly with each step, as if the earth itself had begun to rot. Briar's boots squelched with each step, and she tried not to think about what might be seeping through the leather.

"Look," Thaine said quietly, pointing ahead.

A deer stood in their path. Or what had once been a deer. Its antlers had grown wild, branching and rebranching until they formed a crown of bone that should have been too heavy for any creature to carry. Its eyes were completely black, no whites visible, and when it opened its mouth, rows of teeth that belonged on a predator gleamed in the sick light.

It watched them for a long moment, head tilted at an angle that made Briar's neck ache in sympathy. Then it turned and walked into the undergrowth, moving wrong, its legs bending in too many places.

"The animals here," one of the younger Drak warriors said, his voice unsteady. "They're changing."

"Everything changes near the seal," Veroc said grimly. "The corruption seeps out, twists what it touches. Makes it into something else. Something that serves the creatures you locked away."

Arion moved closer to Briar, his light magic flickering weakly around them. It helped, a little, pushing back the worst of the oppressive atmosphere. But she could see the strain in his face, the effort it took to maintain even this small protection.

"You're exhausting yourself," she said quietly.

"I'm fine."

"You're not." She touched his arm, feeling the tremor in his muscles. "Save your strength. We'll need it."

He looked at her, something soft in his expression despite everything. His hand found hers, squeezing gently before letting go.

Ahead, Eliam had stopped, his palm pressed against a tree trunk. His face was drawn, shadows forming in his eyes. The forest that should have welcomed its king fought him at every turn, refusing to recognize him, refusing to yield.

"My lord?" Thaine asked, concern evident despite his attempts to hide it.

"The forest doesn't know me." The words came out hollow. "Or it knows me but won't acknowledge me. I can feel it pulling away, like it's waiting for something else. *Someone* else."

"Malus," Halian said, speaking for the first time in hours. His voice was rough. "It's already accepting him as king."

The implications of that settled over them like a shroud. If the forest itself had turned against Eliam, if it fully recognized and accepted Malus's claim, then they were walking through enemy territory with no escape routes.

A sound drifted through the trees—not quite laughter, not quite crying, something between the two that made everyone reach for weapons. It came from everywhere and nowhere, echoing wrong in the twisted space.

"Pixies," Veroc said, his hand on his blade. "But corrupted. They're scouting."

"For what?" Briar asked, though she already knew.

"Not what, who. Whoever controls this territory now." Veroc's expression was grim. "They'll report back. Tell them exactly where you are, how many travel with you, which direction you're heading."

"Then Malus knows," Eliam said flatly.

"He's known since you entered the corruption." Veroc started walking again, faster now. "The only question is whether he'll wait until we leave you at the border, or—"

The attack came without warning.

The ground erupted in a spray of rotted earth and bone. Something massive burst from beneath—not quite plant, not quite animal, a fusion of both that shouldn't exist. Tentacles of twisted wood shot toward them, each one tipped with thorns the length of daggers.

"Move!" Veroc roared, his blade already swinging.

The group scattered. Briar felt Eliam's hand grab her arm, pulling her sideways as a tentacle slammed into the ground where she'd been standing. The impact left a crater, the earth hissing and smoking where the corruption touched it.

Karse's fire roared to life, white-blue flames engulfing one of the tentacles. It recoiled, shrieking in that not-laughter-not-crying voice, but two more took its place, growing from the stump like a hydra of wood and rot.

"Don't cut them!" Veroc shouted, but it was too late. One of his warriors had severed a tentacle, and three more sprouted immediately, whipping toward him with renewed fury.

The thing rose higher from the ground, revealing more of its body—a trunk of fused bone and wood, wrapped in something that might have once been fur but now moved like it had a mind of its own. Eyes opened along its surface, dozens of them, all different sizes, all completely black like the deer's had been.

"What is that?" Sian gasped, water swirling around her in a defensive shield.

"Corruption," Veroc said simply. "Pure corruption."

The creature's tentacles swept toward them again, and this time they moved with purpose, with intelligence. They were being herded, Briar realized. Pushed together, grouped for easier capture.

"It's not trying to kill us," she gasped. "It's trying to trap us."

As if her words were a signal, the tentacles changed tactics. Instead of striking, they began to weave, creating walls of thorned wood around them, cutting off escape routes, forming a cage.

That's when she heard it. Footsteps. Measured, unhurried, approaching through the twisted trees. The pixies' not-laughter grew louder, more excited.

"He's here," Eliam said quietly, his hand finding hers. "Malus is here."

The footsteps stopped just beyond the wall of tentacles, and a familiar voice carried through, pleasant and warm as autumn sunshine.

"Well, well. How convenient to find you all together." Malus's tone held genuine pleasure. "Though I am disappointed. I expected you to get much closer to the seal before I had to intervene. This makes things almost too easy."

The tentacles parted like curtains, and Malus stepped through, dressed in his dark coat, looking perfectly at ease in the corrupted forest. Behind him came others—Forest Court guards, but wrong. Their eyes were solid black like the deer's, and when they moved, it was in perfect synchronization.

"Hello, dear one," Malus said, his eyes finding Briar immediately. "Did you miss me? Because I certainly missed you."

"Get behind me," Eliam said, pulling Briar back, but the movement triggered everything at once.

Veroc roared a battle cry in the Drak tongue, his blade igniting with flames as he charged. His warriors followed, meeting the corrupted Forest Court guards in a clash of steel and magic. The creature's tentacles thrashed wildly, no longer coordinated, responding to the sudden violence with violence of its own.

"Bring the girl to me," Malus commanded, his voice cutting through the chaos.

The corrupted guards moved toward Briar with that unnatural synchronization, but Karse's fire blazed between them, a wall of white-blue heat that made them stumble back.

"Run!" Arion shouted, his light magic flaring. "Get her out of here!"

The tentacle creature shrieked, its dozens of eyes focusing on different targets. One massive appendage swept through their group with devastating force. Briar felt Eliam's hand torn from hers as the impact sent her spinning. She hit the ground hard, mud and rot splashing across her face, filling her mouth with the taste of decay.

She pushed herself up, disoriented, ears ringing. Through the chaos she saw Eliam twenty feet away, Thaine pulling him behind an overturned log as tentacles slammed down where they'd been standing. How had she gotten so far from them?

A corrupted guard lunged at her. She scrambled backward on hands and knees, her palms sinking into the spongy ground. Karse's fire roared overhead, catching the guard and turning him to ash, but the heat and smoke blinded her. She stumbled to her feet, coughing, eyes streaming, and ran the only direction that seemed clear.

By the time her vision cleared, she'd lost all sense of direction. The battle sounds came from everywhere at once, echoing wrong through the twisted trees. She turned, trying to orient herself, to find her way back, but every path looked the same—dark, twisted, wrong.

Behind her, she heard Malus laugh, low and pleased. "Finally, some sport."

She ran.

Branches tore at her traveling clothes as she crashed through the undergrowth. The corrupted forest seemed to shift around her, paths appearing and disappearing, roots rising to trip her, thorns reaching for exposed skin. The warmth in her chest pulled desperately backward, toward where Eliam and Arion fought, but she couldn't stop, couldn't turn back.

She could hear him following. Not running, just walking. His footsteps were steady and patient, like he had all the time in the world and he knew exactly where she would go.

"Running through corrupted woods, dear one?" His voice carried impossibly well through the trees. "That's rather dangerous. So many things here that might hurt you. Better to come back. I promise to be gentle."

She ran harder, lungs burning, the metallic taste of corruption thick in her throat. A root caught her foot and she went down hard, palms scraping against bark that felt wrong, too soft, too warm, almost flesh-like.

When she pushed herself up, he was there.

He stood several feet away, not even breathing hard, looking at her with that mixture of amusement and satisfaction that made her stomach turn.

"Did you miss me?" he asked again, taking a step closer. "Because I've thought about you every day. The way you felt beneath me. The sounds you made."

She scrambled backward, but her back hit a tree—no, not a tree, one of the creature's tentacles, positioned perfectly to stop her retreat. She was trapped.

"There's nowhere to run." He closed the distance between them with casual grace. "Your defenders are busy. The Drak are falling. And you, dear one, are exactly where you're supposed to be."

His hand caught her chin, tilting her face up with deceptive gentleness. The autumn marks at her throat pulsed warm, reaching toward him like flowers toward sun.

"Such a long chase for such a small thing," he murmured, studying her face with the same attention he might give an interesting specimen. "Though I suppose you've grown more intriguing since our last encounter."

She jerked her head away, but his fingers tightened just enough to hold her still. Not painful—he rarely needed pain when control would suffice.

"Let go."

"No, I don't think I will." His thumb traced along her jaw, autumn magic seeping through the touch, making her limbs feel heavy. "Do you know what the most tedious part of ruling is? The constant need to appear reasonable. To pretend that violence is a last resort rather than the most efficient solution."

In the distance, the battle sounds were fading—less clashing, more screaming.

"But here, in these corrupted woods, with no one watching but the twisted trees?" His smile was almost fond. "I can be entirely honest about what I want."

"They'll come for me," she said, hating how her voice shook.

"Oh, undoubtedly. Your collection of would-be saviors is nothing if not persistent." He glanced back toward the battle sounds with mild interest. "Though I wonder how many will survive the enthusiasm of my new pets. The corruption makes them so... thorough."

He looked back at her, and his expression shifted to something almost regretful.

"I had hoped you'd come to me willingly, you know. After enough time, enough gentle pressure. But you're remarkably stubborn for someone so breakable." His grip shifted from her chin to her arm, fingers closing around her bicep with careful precision. "So we'll do this the crude way. Disappointing, really."

Without warning, he yanked her against him, his arm locked around her waist, half-carrying, half-dragging her back towards the fight. She fought, clawing at his arm, trying to dig her heels in, but he was fae-strong and she was just human, just tired, just small against his magic and will.

They emerged into the clearing where the battle had devolved into chaos. Several of Veroc's warriors were down, their blood staining the corrupted earth. The creature had wrapped tentacles around Halian, lifting him off the ground. Sian was trying to free him with water blades while dodging the corrupted guards.

Malus walked into the center of it all, dragging Briar with him, and simply stood there. Waiting.

It took only moments for the others to notice. Eliam turned first, thorns already sprouting from his hands, but Malus's arm had shifted to wrap around Briar's throat from behind, his forearm pressing against her windpipe with practiced precision.

"Careful," Malus said mildly. "I'd hate for my grip to tighten accidentally."

The pressure increased slightly, not enough to cut off air entirely, but enough that breathing became work. Black spots danced at the edges of her vision.

One by one, the others stopped fighting to stare. The corrupted guards stepped back in unison, weapons remaining at the ready. The creature's tentacles stilled, though they kept Halian suspended.

"Much better," Malus continued. "Now then, let's discuss terms. You're all going to lower your weapons and accompany me to the seal. Willingly. Cooperatively." He paused, his breath warm against Briar's ear. "Or I'll discover exactly how long a human can survive with a crushed windpipe. I'm genuinely curious—the texts are contradictory on the subject."

His arm tightened another fraction. Briar's hands came up instinctively, clawing at his sleeve, but she might as well have been trying to bend iron.

Eliam took a step forward, shadows gathering around him like storm clouds.

"Now, now," Malus chided, and his free hand came up to rest against Briar's throat, his thumb finding her pulse point. A single claw extended, just breaking the skin. A drop of blood welled and ran down her neck.

The scent hit the air, and Malus inhaled deeply, a soft sound of pleasure escaping him.

"Mm, I'd almost forgotten how exquisite you smell when you bleed," he murmured, his voice dropping to an intimate register. "Like copper and fear and that sweet humanity that makes you so... delectable." His thumb traced through the blood, spreading it. "I'm looking forward to tasting it again and discovering *every* flavor you have to offer."

The promise in his words made her stomach turn. She could see Eliam's entire body had gone rigid, his hands clenched so tight the thorns were drawing his own blood.

"Weapons down," Malus said pleasantly. "All of them. Now."

One by one, they complied. Karse's flames guttered out. Arion's light dimmed to nothing. Even Veroc and his surviving warriors lowered their blades.

"Excellent." Malus's hold on her throat loosened just enough to let her breathe properly. "Now we can all proceed to the seal like civilized beings. Or at least pretend to be."

Chapter Thirty-Five

T he forced march through the corrupted forest felt like walking through a nightmare that wouldn't end. Malus kept his arm around Briar's waist, half-sup-
porting, half-dragging her over the uneven ground. His touch was casual, proprietary,
fingers occasionally adjusting their grip in ways that made her skin crawl. Behind them,
the corrupted guards herded the others like cattle, their synchronized movements eerily
precise as they maintained formation.

"You know," Malus said, tone casual, as if they were taking a pleasant stroll through
the rose garden, "I really should thank you." Briar didn't respond, but that didn't stop
Malus from continuing anyway. "For taking care of Ferria."

Briar stiffened in his hold. Behind them, she heard Halian's sharp intake of breath.

"What?" The word tore from Halian's throat.

"Oh yes," Malus continued, easily navigating the uneven terrain and lifting Briar with disturbing ease when she stumbled. "She'd become quite the nuisance. All
that desperate pining, those constant demands." He laughed softly. "The poor thing
thought she'd finally have her precious Forest King, properly broken and collared for
her pleasure."

"You promised her—" Arion's voice was tight with barely controlled anger.

"I promised her many things." Malus's tone held genuine amusement. "She wanted
Eliam so badly she'd have done anything. Betrayed anyone. And she did, quite effectively."

Halian made a sound of pure rage behind them.

"But toward the end?" Malus sighed theatrically. "So tedious. Always whining about when she'd get her prize, demanding reassurances that I'd keep my word. I was trying to decide how to best remove her—" He squeezed Briar's waist in mock affection. "—but this clever little thing solved my problem for me."

"Misplaced as it was, she loved him," Halian spat, his voice breaking. "She spent centuries loving him, and you used that against her."

"Love." Malus tested the word like foreign wine. "Such a dramatic term for what was essentially obsession. She didn't love Eliam—she loved the idea of possessing him. Rather like a child coveting another's toy." His voice hardened slightly. "At least she died believing she'd won something. You're still breathing and already know you've lost everything."

That did it. Halian lunged forward with a wordless cry of rage, his hands reaching for Malus's throat. For a moment, just a moment, it seemed like his desperate fury might carry him through.

Malus didn't even slow his stride. His free hand made a negligent gesture, and autumn wind full of decay swept toward Halian, hitting him like a physical blow before he could close the distance. Where it touched, his skin grayed and cracked like old leather.

Halian screamed, dropping to his knees in the rotted undergrowth.

"Halian!" Sian tried to run forward, but the corrupted guards blocked her path, moving in that eerie synchronization.

"Now, now," Malus said mildly, the decay wind dissipating. "That was remarkably stupid, even for someone grieving."

Halian remained on his knees, the touched skin on his face and arms looking aged by decades. Not fatal, but painful—Briar could see it in the way tears streamed from his eyes. Sian managed to reach him, helping him struggle back to his feet.

"The fascinating thing about decay," Malus continued, returning to his conversational tone as they kept walking, "is that it can be controlled so precisely. A little ages the skin. A bit more withers muscle. Too much and things start to crumble entirely." He glanced back at Halian. "Would you like me to demonstrate further, or have we learned our lesson about unprovoked attacks?"

Halian said nothing, his head hanging forward, defeated.

"I thought so." Malus's attention returned to the path ahead. "Now, where were we? Ah yes, gratitude. You see, dear one," he said to Briar, "you've been remarkably helpful."

His fingers traced along her ribs, making her shudder. "Now you're going to help me understand exactly what my brother hid inside you."

"I won't help you with anything," Briar said through gritted teeth.

"Won't you?" His breath was warm against her ear. "We'll see. People are remarkably cooperative when properly motivated. And I have so many ways to motivate you."

His gaze swept over the others—Eliam rigid with suppressed rage, Arion's face carved from stone, Thaine favoring his injured leg, Karse's scales dulled with exhaustion, Sian supporting Halian as best she could.

"So many pressure points," Malus mused. "So many ways to make you *beg* to help me."

They crested a small rise, and through the twisted trees, Briar could see the corruption getting worse. The very air ahead shimmered with wrongness, like heat waves rising from tainted ground. In the distance, something that had once been a bird cried out, but the sound was all wrong, too many voices in one throat.

"We're getting close to the border," Veroc said carefully. He and his surviving warriors had been silent through the confrontation, but now the old Drak's voice carried warning. "Beyond that ridge, the corruption is absolute. We can go no further."

"How unfortunate," Malus said with false sympathy. "I suppose you'll have to abandon your new friends. Unless you'd like to test how well Drak scales hold up against pure Unseelie taint?"

Veroc's jaw clenched, but he said nothing.

They walked on, the sounds of the battle-torn forest fading behind them, replaced by something worse—the soft whisper of corruption spreading, the rustle of things that shouldn't exist, and underneath it all, a rhythmic pulsing like a massive heartbeat that Briar realized must be coming from the seal itself.

"Can you feel it?" Malus asked her softly. "The seal calling? It recognizes what you carry. What you are." His hand pressed flat against her stomach, and she felt the warmth in her chest recoil. "All that power my brother hid inside you, yearning to return to where it belongs. Or rather, to whom it belongs."

"You're a fool if you think you'll succeed," Eliam said, his voice so cold it made the corrupted air feel warm by comparison.

"Am I?" Malus glanced back at his brother with that pleasant smile that never reached his eyes. "We'll see. After all, power flows to those who hold it, not those who once claimed it. And right now..." His arm tightened around Briar. "I hold everything that matters."

The ridge appeared through the twisted trees like a natural boundary between horror and something worse. The corrupted forest they'd been walking through seemed almost healthy compared to what lay beyond.

Veroc stopped at the crest, his ancient face grim. "This is where we leave you."

The other Drak warriors shifted uneasily, their scales dulling with what Briar recognized as fear. Whatever lay beyond that ridge, even these ancient predators wanted no part of it.

"Such loyalty," Malus observed. "Abandoning your new allies at the first sign of real danger."

"We go where we can survive," Veroc said simply. "Beyond this point, the corruption doesn't just twist—it unmakes."

"How poetic." Malus's tone suggested he found it anything but. "Run along then. Wouldn't want to lose such... reliable allies."

Veroc's gaze found Briar, regret in his eyes. "Shadow Walker," he said formally. "May you find the strength you need."

Then he and his remaining warriors turned and disappeared back into the twisted forest, moving fast enough that it was clear they wanted distance between themselves and whatever came next.

"Alone at last," Malus said with satisfaction. "How cozy."

They crested the ridge, and Briar's breath caught in her throat.

The land beyond didn't follow any natural laws. Trees grew downward into the earth while their roots reached toward a sky that flickered between colors that shouldn't exist. The ground itself seemed uncertain, shifting between solid earth, viscous liquid, and something that felt like flesh. In the distance, shapes moved through the wrongness—things that had too many limbs or not enough, creatures that seemed to exist in several places at once.

And beyond it all, perhaps another hour's walk through this nightmare landscape, she could feel it—the seal. It pulled at the warmth in her chest with increasing insistence, like recognizing like.

"Beautiful, isn't it?" Malus said against her ear. "The Unseelie corruption in its purest form. This is what waits beneath every seal, pressing against the barriers, yearning to be free."

"It's an abomination," Thaine said, his voice rough with exhaustion and disgust.

"It's power," Malus corrected. "Raw, unlimited power that my ancestors were too frightened to harness. They chose to lock it away rather than learn to control it."

He started forward, pulling Briar with him. The moment they crossed the threshold, she felt it—the corruption trying to seep into her skin, to remake her into something else. The star metal pendant grew hot against her chest, and the warmth inside her contracted, building a barrier against the intrusion.

Behind them, the others followed reluctantly. She could hear Sian gagging at the smell—sweet rot mixed with metal and something organic that had no name. Karse's scales flickered with defensive heat, while Arion's light magic sputtered like a candle in poison wind.

Eliam walked in rigid silence, but she could see the way the corruption recoiled from him slightly, as if recognizing an enemy. Or perhaps recognizing what he'd once been, before the split, when he'd had the power to create seals like the one they approached.

"Tell me," Malus said conversationally as they picked their way through the unstable ground, "can you feel it calling to you? The piece my brother hid inside you?"

Briar didn't answer, but she didn't need to. The warmth was pulling harder now, almost painful in its insistence.

"It knows we're close," Malus continued. "It can sense the seal, the magic it was carved from. Part of the same whole, separated by time and my brother's fear."

A sound drifted through the corrupted air—laughter that wasn't quite human, wasn't quite anything. The pixies were back, but changed. She caught glimpses of them in the wrongness—faces that had too many eyes, wings that bent in impossible directions, mouths that opened wider than physics should allow.

"My pets have adapted well," Malus noted with satisfaction. "The corruption doesn't destroy everything. Some things it... improves."

"You're insane," Arion said flatly.

"Am I? I'm not the one who split himself in two rather than face his own nature." Malus's grip on Briar tightened as the ground beneath them shifted from solid to something softer. "I'm not the one who created a weakness that could be exploited."

They were deep in the corruption now. Reality itself seemed negotiable here. A tree to their left grew leaves, shed them, rotted, and regrew in the span of heartbeats. Water flowed upward in a stream of what appeared to be blood if blood could be that color.

And through it all, that rhythmic pulsing grew stronger. The seal's heartbeat, calling to the warmth in her chest with increasing urgency.

"Almost there," Malus said with anticipation. "Can you see it?"

Through the unnatural twilight, Briar could make out a clearing ahead. The trees, or what had been trees, formed a rough circle around an open space. Light emanated from within, but it was wrong somehow, shifting between colors that made her eyes water.

"The seal," Karse said, his voice laced with bitterness.

"The beginning of the end," Malus corrected with satisfaction. "Or perhaps the end of the beginning. Either way, everything changes now."

Briar stumbled as he pulled her forward, and with each step, the warmth in her chest burned hotter, fighting against his hold, reaching for something she couldn't see yet but could feel—ancient magic, old power, and beneath it all, the promise of destruction.

As they entered the clearing, Briar's knees nearly buckled at the sight before them.

The seal was nothing like she'd imagined. A massive circle of stone was set into the earth, carved with intricate patterns that seemed to move when she wasn't looking directly at them. Concentric rings within rings, each one inscribed with symbols that shifted constantly, as if her human mind couldn't quite process what they represented.

Around the perimeter stood ancient monoliths that should have been proud sentinels but now leaned at wrong angles, their surfaces cracked and weeping something dark. The glyphs that should have glowed with protective magic flickered weakly, like dying fireflies. Some had gone completely dark, their symbols eroded beyond recognition.

The air above the seal shimmered with sickly green light, and through it, Briar could see *things*. Shadows that moved independently of any source. Shapes that pressed against the barrier from below, testing, probing, searching for weakness.

"Magnificent," Malus breathed, genuine awe in his voice. "You can feel them, can't you? The Unseelie. Pressing against their prison, patient as stone, inevitable as time."

The corrupted guards spread out around the clearing's edge, taking positions. The twisted pixies chittered excitedly from the malformed trees, their too-many eyes reflecting the seal's poisoned light.

Malus finally released Briar, shoving her forward so she stumbled toward the seal's edge. The moment she got close, the warmth in her chest erupted in agony, pulling toward the ancient magic with such force she gasped.

"Yes," Malus said with satisfaction. "It recognizes the power my father used to make his little prison." He circled around her, studying her reaction.

"Don't," Eliam's voice cut through the clearing like a blade. "You don't know what you're playing with."

"Such skepticism, brother," Malus pulled a leather journal from his coat, its pages yellowed with age. "Our father's notes. His observations about the seal's construction. The power required to build it." He flipped through pages covered in cramped writing. "The power that could be reclaimed if one knew how."

"How? Those were destroyed," Eliam said, but his tone was laced with uncertainty.

"You thought they were destroyed. But I've always been better at keeping secrets than you, little brother." Malus set the journal on one of the tilted standing stones. "Now then, shall we begin?"

From another pocket, he produced items that made Briar's blood run cold. Bones that looked too human to be animal, a mixture of herbs that Briar recalled seeing in the gardens at Eliam's palace, and the blade he used the night he'd tried to drink her blood before the entire Forest Court.

"The traditional approach would be to simply break the seal," Malus explained as he began arranging the items in specific patterns. "But that would release everything at once. Chaotic and so very wasteful." He glanced at Briar. "No, what I need is a controlled breach. A careful extraction of power."

"Through her," Arion said, understanding dawning in his voice.

"Through her," Malus confirmed. "She's the perfect conduit, the magic will recognize her, flow through her, and with the right persuasion..." He smiled. "It will flow into me."

"That could kill her," Thaine protested.

"Possibly." Malus didn't sound particularly concerned. "But she's not just a human anymore, is she? She's become something greater, she's contained fae magic for her entire life."

He began drawing symbols on the ground around the seal's edge, using something that reminded Briar of chalk if chalk could leave marks that glowed with their own sickly light. The corrupted guards moved in response to some unspoken command, forcing the others to stand in specific positions around the circle.

"You here," Malus directed, pointing Eliam to a spot directly across from where Briar stood. "And you," to Arion, "there. Equal distance from both. A triangle of power—how poetic."

"We won't help you," Eliam said, refusing to move to his appointed area.

"Won't you?" Malus walked over to where Sian still supported Halian, whose face was still gray and cracked from the decay magic. Without warning, he pressed his palm against Halian's chest.

Halian screamed as autumn magic poured into him, aging him from within. His hair went white in seconds, skin pulling tight over bones that began to brittle.

"Stop!" Sian cried, trying to pull Halian away, but the corrupted guards held her back.

"I'll stop when they stand where I tell them," Malus said mildly, though his eyes never left Eliam. "Your choice, brother. Your pride, or their lives."

Eliam finally moved to the indicated position, his jaw clenched so tight Briar could hear his teeth grinding. Arion followed, light magic flickering weakly around him in futile protest.

Malus released Halian, who collapsed into Sian's arms, aged by decades but still breathing. Barely.

"Much better." Malus returned to his ritual preparations. "Now, according to father's notes, the seal responds to specific resonances. Blood of the makers, will of the breakers, and..." He looked at Briar. "A vessel capable of containing what's released."

He approached her with the ritual blade, and she tried to back away, but there was nowhere to go. The seal's edge was at her heels, and she could feel the wrongness beneath it, the things that waited below.

"Your blood first," he said, catching her wrist with inhuman speed. "Just a little. Enough to wake the seal's recognition."

She struggled to pull free, but Malus held fast without any sign of struggle. The blade bit into her palm, leaving a shallow gash of crimson. The pain was strange, lacking the sharp sting one would expect. Instead it felt hollow, as if it were draining something more than blood. Drops of crimson fell onto the seal's surface.

The reaction was immediate.

The symbols flared to life, not with healthy light but with that same sickly green glow. The ground trembled, and that rhythmic pulsing became audible—a heartbeat made of stone and ancient magic and contained horror.

Through the shimmering barrier, the shadows beneath pressed harder, sensing opportunity.

"Perfect," Malus breathed. "Now we can truly begin."

Malus began pulling more components from his coat—crystals that pulsed with their own sick light, empty vials, and a length of rope that seemed to be made of braided shadow.

"Now for the anchors," he said, moving to where Eliam stood rigid with suppressed rage. "Blood of the makers, brother. Our family line created this seal, your blood will help me unravel it."

He didn't wait for compliance. The blade flashed out, catching Eliam across the palm before he could react. Blood welled, darker than human crimson, almost black in the poisoned light. Malus caught it in one of the vials, the liquid inside immediately beginning to smoke.

"And the other half," Malus moved to Arion with the same swift efficiency, cutting his palm as well. Arion's blood was different—lighter, with an almost golden sheen. When it entered the second vial, the reaction was violent, the contents trying to escape the container.

"Interesting," Malus murmured. "Even your blood knows you're meant to be one. How it must pain you both, being so close to your other half yet unable to reunite."

He returned to the seal's edge, pouring the contents of both vials onto specific points in the carved symbols. Where the blood touched stone, the glyphs flared brighter, that sickly green deepening to something almost black.

The warmth in Briar's chest was burning now, pulling so hard toward the seal that she had to lock her knees to keep from falling forward.

"They know you're here," Malus said softly, standing behind her now. His hands settled on her shoulders, holding her in place when she tried to step back. "The Unseelie. They can sense what you carry. The power that could free them."

He wrapped the braided length of shadow around her wrist and Briar realized with mounting horror that it was hair.

Through the shimmering barrier, those shadows pressed harder. She could almost make out shapes now—faces that weren't quite faces, hands with too many fingers, wings that bent in impossible ways.

"Begin the chant," Malus commanded, moving to position himself in the very center of the seal. The corrupted guards started speaking in unison, their voices blending into something that scraped against reality itself. The twisted pixies joined from the trees, their chittering forming an unsettling harmony.

Malus stood at the seal's heart, arms raised, the ritual blade still gleaming with their mixed blood. The symbols beneath his feet pulsed in response to his presence, recognizing the Forest King's bloodline.

"Brothers of light and shadow," he intoned, his voice carrying over the chanting. "Split from wholeness, yearning for unity. Through the vessel that carries your essence, through the one who bore your fragment since birth, let power return to power."

The magic hit Briar like a physical blow.

She gasped as invisible forces seized the warmth in her chest, trying to pull it in two directions at once—toward Eliam, toward Arion, tearing at her from within. But instead of flowing outward, the magic reversed. She could feel it—Arion's light and Eliam's shadows being drawn *into* her, not from her.

"No," she gasped, dropping to her knees.

Power flooded through her, too much, too fast. Arion's light burned through her veins while Eliam's shadows froze them. The two magics met in her chest where the warmth resided, crashing together in violent opposition. She screamed, her back arching as golden and silver light erupted from her skin.

"What—" Malus's chant faltered. "This isn't—the flow is wrong. It should be coming through you to me, not—"

He strode toward her, his hand reaching for her chest where the magic concentrated. The moment his fingers made contact, he jerked back with a snarl. His palm was blistered, burned by the conflicting energies.

"Something's blocking it," he said, eyes narrowing. Then he saw it—the star metal pendant at her throat, glowing white-hot in response to the magical assault. "Of course. Arion's little gift."

He reached for it, but the moment his fingers touched the chain, the metal flared. The smell of burning flesh filled the air as he wrenched his hand back, his palm now a ruin of blackened skin.

"Star metal," he hissed. "Clever. But not clever enough."

He raised the ritual blade, intending to cut the chain, but that moment of distraction was all Arion needed.

Light erupted across the seal. Not the sickly glow of corruption, but pure, brilliant white light. Arion had broken from his position, crossing the distance in a burst of desperate speed. He slammed into Malus, sending them both sprawling across the carved stones.

"You won't touch her!" Arion snarled, light gathering in his palms.

They grappled on the seal's surface, Arion's light colliding with Malus's decay in bursts that left scorched patterns on the ancient stone. Malus caught Arion's wrist, twisting it backward until tendons strained. Arion drove his knee up, connecting with Malus's ribs, forcing him back a step. The chanting guards maintained their rhythm, voices rising and falling without pause.

Briar watched through vision that kept doubling and blurring. The magic continued to flow into her chest, hot and relentless. Her ribs felt too tight, as if her bones might crack from the pressure building inside them. Her heartbeat stuttered, racing too fast and then skipping beats entirely. Something vital was tearing, coming apart at the seams.

Arion landed a strike that sent Malus stumbling backward. Light gathered in his palms, building to devastating levels. He advanced, pressing his advantage.

Malus feinted left. Arion followed the movement, his guard shifting to block.

The ritual blade appeared in Malus's other hand. He'd been holding it low, hidden against his leg, waiting for the opening.

He drove it upward with brutal force.

The blade pierced through Arion's ribs, sinking deep into his chest.

Chapter Thirty-Six

T ime seemed to stop.

Arion's eyes went wide, looking down at the blade protruding from his ribs. Light began to leak from the wound. No blood, only pure radiance, his very essence escaping.

"No!" Briar's voice cracked across the clearing.

Another cry had echoed alongside hers and she looked to see Eliam on his hands and knees, clutching his chest as though he himself had been stabbed.

Arion stumbled back from Malus, his hand going to the blade. When he pulled it free, more light poured out, and Briar could feel it, his essence, flowing toward her with nowhere else to go.

He dropped to his knees beside her, one hand pressed to his chest, the other reaching for her face. She caught him when he tumbled forward, his body limp in her arms.

"I'm sorry," he whispered, light already fading from his eyes.

"No, no, not like this, it's not supposed to be like this," she gasped, gripping him tightly even as she felt his body beginning to fade in her arms.

"I'm not really..." he coughed. "I'm not leaving. Just... going home."

"Please," Briar begged, tears streaming from her eyes.

Arion smiled, closing his eyes. "I'll say it...because—" a groan escaped him, "—because he—he can't...I love you."

The magic rolled over her, not violent this time, but inevitable. Arion's essence, everything he was, flowed from his dying body into hers. The warmth in her chest recognized it, welcomed it, even as it burned through her.

And then she felt it, the pull toward Eliam. The two halves yearning to reunite after so long apart. The star metal pendant couldn't stop this, this natural flow of magic returning to where it belonged.

She could have fought it. Could have tried to contain it, to keep Arion's essence with her.

Instead, she let go.

The relief was immediate. The magic flowed through her like she was nothing more than a conduit, Arion's light streaming from her chest toward Eliam. She could feel every moment of it—memories that weren't hers, emotions she'd never experienced, the weight of centuries flowing through her in seconds.

It should have killed her. She could feel her body failing, her heart struggling under the strain, her bones feeling like they might shatter from containing so much power even temporarily.

But she didn't care. Arion was dying in front of her, and if reuniting him with Eliam was the last thing she did, then at least his death would have meaning.

Golden light erupted from her chest, arcing across the seal toward Eliam like lightning seeking ground. When it hit him, he gasped, doubling over as his other half returned home after centuries of separation.

Briar collapsed forward onto her hands, gasping. Copper filled her mouth. Blood ran warm from her nose, dripping onto the carved stone. Every nerve was on fire but she held onto consciousness through sheer will.

Arion's body was fading, becoming translucent as his essence completed its journey. His fingers twitched, reaching for her. His lips moved: "Remember me."

Then nothing. Empty air where he'd been.

"No!" Malus roared, autumn decay already pooling around his hands. "The power was supposed to come to *me*!"

Eliam straightened slowly from where he'd collapsed. The movement should have been labored, should have shown weakness after centuries of being fractured. Instead, he rose with fluid grace, his body humming with power that radiated outward in visible waves. The shadows beneath his feet spread across the stone, and where they touched, new growth erupted. Silver-edged thorns pushed through cracks in the ancient seal, gleaming with cold starlight.

His eyes burned with impossible patterns. Shadow and light swirled together in his irises, darkness and radiance fighting for dominance and somehow coexisting. When he spoke, his voice carried doubled harmonics, as if two people spoke in perfect unison.

"Hello, brother."

Malus raised his hands defensively, autumn decay gathering in poisonous clouds between his fingers. "You're still adjusting to being whole again. You can barely control it."

"Are you so sure?"

Eliam moved.

One moment he stood across the seal. The next he was there, directly in front of Malus, crossing the distance faster than Briar's eyes could track. His fist connected with Malus's jaw with enough force to send him stumbling backward. Thorned vines erupted from the seal beneath Malus's feet, forcing him to leap away or be impaled.

The chanting guards broke formation, scattering as the brothers collided again in the center of the seal. The ritual was forgotten. Whatever they'd been building dissolved into chaos.

Malus sent autumn wind howling across the clearing, leaves that aged flesh on contact, decay that withered everything it touched. Eliam dodged with speed and precision that hadn't existed before while striking with the same brutal efficiency he'd always possessed. Where Malus brought death, Eliam brought violent growth. Vines moved with purpose, thorns sought flesh with clear intent, and all of it gleamed with that silver-starlight edge that refused to succumb to decay.

"Impossible," Malus gasped, twisting sideways as silver-edged thorns whistled past his ear. One caught his cheek, tearing a line from temple to jaw that immediately welled crimson.

"I'm whole." Eliam's movements had changed—where before he'd been predictable, now he flowed between fighting styles. A brutal downward strike shifted mid-swing into a graceful arc that opened a gash across Malus's ribs. "For the first time in centuries, I'm whole."

Malus stumbled over a crack in the seal, his elegant coat now torn in a dozen places, blood seeping through autumn-gold fabric. He raised his hands, decay billowing out, but Eliam walked through it. The rot that should have aged him to dust slid off like water, repelled by silver light that danced just beneath his skin.

"You're finished," Eliam said, thorns erupting from the ground at Malus's feet, forcing him to leap back. More thorns, from the left, the right, above—a cage of silver-edged death closing in. "Surrender."

"Never." Malus spat blood, crimson stark against his pale face. His perfectly styled hair hung in sweat-soaked strands. "This is my court. My forest. You were just keeping it warm for me."

"Your court?" Eliam raised his hand, fingers splaying wide.

The air changed. Pressure built, the kind that comes before lightning strikes. Briar felt it in her bones—Eliam reaching for something ancient, something that had slept in roots and soil since before the courts existed. The deep magic. The forest's own will.

The clearing went silent. Not even breath disturbed the air.

Eliam's fingers curled, pulling at invisible threads. Veins stood out on his neck from the strain. A muscle in his jaw twitched, jumped, twitched again.

Nothing happened.

His hand trembled. Sweat beaded on his forehead despite the cold. He pulled harder, she could see it in the way his shoulders hunched, the way his other hand clenched into a fist so tight his knuckles went white.

The forest didn't answer.

"Oh no." Malus's laugh came out wet, breathless, but genuine delight lit his bloodied face. "Oh, this is perfect."

He straightened despite his injuries, autumn magic flowing back around him like a cloak. The decay that had seemed weak moments ago now pulsed with renewed strength.

"Did you really think," Malus said, taking a step forward, and now it was Eliam who stepped back, "that the forest would choose you? You, who abandoned it? Who left it kingless while you played at being the hero for a human?"

The trees around the clearing creaked, leaning toward Malus. Roots surfaced from the earth, reaching for him not as threats but as subjects greeting their king.

"The forest remembers who ruled it first," Malus continued, autumn wind picking up around him, lifting his bloodied coat like wings. "Who ruled it longest. Who never abandoned it for some misguided attempt at love."

Eliam tried again, both hands raised now, pulling so hard at the forest's magic that his whole body shook with effort.

Nothing. Worse than nothing. The forest actively resisted, pulling away from his call.

"This is delicious," Malus said, and with a gesture, the ground beneath Eliam's feet turned to rot. Eliam stumbled, his leg sinking into suddenly soft earth that reeked of decay. "The great Forest King, whole at last, rejected by his own domain."

"You see, brother?" Malus advanced now, autumn decay gathering strength with each step. The forest fed him power freely, eagerly, answering his call without hesitation. "You were always just a placeholder. A temporary king sitting on a throne that was never truly yours."

Leaves swirled around Malus, sharp with decay magic. They cut through the air toward Eliam, hitting him hard and sending him stumbling backward. More leaves followed, razor-sharp, cutting across his chest and arms. Blood bloomed through the tears in his clothing.

Briar watched through vision that kept blurring and clearing. Her body had gone numb in places, hot in others. She could taste copper constantly now, blood running from her nose down the back of her throat. The star metal pendant still hung cold and heavy, but something else stirred beneath it. That hollow space where the warmth had been, where Arion's essence had flowed through her on its way home.

She should have been dying, probably was dying. Her heart beat irregularly, sometimes racing, sometimes nearly stopping. Her breathing came in shallow gasps that never quite satisfied her lungs' demands. But her mind remained viciously, painfully aware.

Aware enough to feel something she shouldn't be able to feel.

The forest.

Not as words or thoughts, but as a presence, an awareness vast and ancient and patient. It pressed against her consciousness from all sides, neither welcoming nor hostile. Simply observing.

Briar didn't understand how she could feel it. Maybe the magic that had poured through her had opened something, or perhaps being this close to death meant existing partially in whatever space the forest's consciousness occupied.

It could have been that channeling Arion's essence back to Eliam had left her marked by forces far beyond human comprehension. It didn't matter why. What mattered was that she could feel the forest considering its options and deciding.

And it was choosing wrong.

Eliam crashed to the ground as Malus's magic caught him full force. Autumn decay spread across his skin where it made contact, aging flesh to leather, turning youth to advanced age in seconds. He gasped, trying to roll away, but roots erupted from beneath him and pinned him down.

"The forest knows who protected it," Malus said, standing over his brother. "Who fed it properly. Who understood that power requires sacrifice."

No.

The word formed in Briar's mind with perfect clarity. She remembered Eliam in his throne room, handling disputes between fae, remembered him punishing lords for crimes against the forest itself, for taking too much, for damaging the ancient places that could never be replaced.

She pushed those memories outward into the vast awareness surrounding her. Not with words, but with feeling, with the bone-deep certainty that Eliam had always served the forest first.

The forest listened.

She could feel its attention shift, focusing on her with intensity that made her remaining awareness fracture further. It examined the memories she offered, turning them over with the thoroughness of a being that measured time in centuries rather than seconds.

Malus had been strong. Had been brutal and efficient. Had ruled with an iron fist that demanded loyalty and fed on power without restraint.

But Eliam had been brutal too. Had executed without mercy, had ruled with cruelty that made even his own lords fear him. The difference was where that cruelty pointed. Every harsh judgment had protected the forest's balance, and each execution had been for crimes against the land itself. Every act of violence had served something larger than his own hunger for power.

The forest remembered. Remembered that Eliam's darkness had always bent toward preservation, even when it cost him, even when gentler rulers might have prospered more. Malus had sought to break the ancient seals, to release power that would consume everything. Eliam had fought to maintain what existed, to protect what could not be replaced, no matter how much blood it required.

The forest remembered that too.

Around the clearing, the trees began to shift. Slowly at first. Branches that had leaned toward Malus straightened. Roots that had risen to defend him sank back into the earth. The wind that had howled at his command fell still.

"What?" Malus spun, sensing the change. "No. How." His eyes scanned the clearing wildly before landing on Briar. "*You*. What are you doing?"

She couldn't have answered if she wanted to. Her lips wouldn't move. Her throat wouldn't work. But she held the forest's attention, and kept pushing the memories forward. Eliam protecting a grove of ancient oaks from a fae who had diverted a stream. Eliam punishing a sprite for poisoning the waters with iron in an act of retaliation.

The forest chose.

She felt the shift, magic prickled across her skin, slow at first then faster and with purpose. It flooded into Eliam, not the hesitant trickle he'd been getting before, but a massive surge that made the air itself crackle. The roots pinning him withered instantly and the decay aging his skin reversed, flesh returning to health in seconds. He rose to his feet, and this time when he called the thorns, they came eagerly.

Vines erupted all around Malus. Not weak and easily withered, but thick as a man's thigh and covered in thorns the length of daggers. They moved with clear purpose, driving Malus backward, forcing him into purely defensive movement.

"No!" Malus sent decay magic in all directions, but the forest absorbed it harmlessly. The earth itself seemed to reject his power now. "This is wrong! I am the rightful king!"

"The forest disagrees," Eliam said. His voice had returned to those doubled harmonics, but stronger now, backed by the full weight of the land itself.

Malus's eyes snapped back to Briar and she saw the calculation in his expression as he weighed his options.

Then he moved.

Not toward Eliam. Toward *her*.

Autumn decay gathered in his hands as he crossed the distance between them in three long strides. Briar tried to move, tried to roll away, but her body refused every command. Her arms wouldn't support her weight. Her legs wouldn't respond. She could only watch as he bore down on her, death pooling around his fingers.

All around them thorned vines erupted from every surface, desperate and wild, but they wouldn't reach in time. Malus was too close, moving too fast, his hand already reaching for her throat.

Strong hands grabbed her shoulders and yanked her backward just as Malus's hand would have closed around her neck.

Thaine.

"Got you," he gasped, his own breathing labored as he dragged her across the stone, pulling her behind one of the tilted standing stones. "Stay down."

Malus spun toward them, fury twisting his features. Briar could see her death in his eyes, could see that he would kill Thaine too just for interfering.

He moved towards them, but the forest moved faster.

Vines exploded from the seal directly beneath Malus. They didn't try to bind him or slow him. Instead their thorns pierced straight through his legs, his torso, before lifting him clean off the ground.

Malus screamed, his blood running down the vines in dark rivulets, dripping onto the carved stones. He clawed at the thorns impaling him, but more vines wrapped around his wrists, his arms, pulling them away from his body and holding them spread.

Eliam was there in the next breath, grabbing Malus by the throat, his fingers digging deep, nails drawing blood.

"You don't touch her," Eliam said, his voice resonating in a way that made the air itself vibrate. "You don't even look at her."

"The forest chose you because of her," Malus gasped, blood bubbling at his lips. The roots had punctured something vital. He was dying, and they both knew it. "She's your weakness, brother. Your fatal flaw."

"No." Eliam's grip tightened. "She's my strength."

More vines rose from the seal, wrapping around Malus's chest, replacing Eliam's hand at his neck. These were different from the roots impaling him. Thinner but covered in dozens of tiny razor sharp thorns that bit deep with each breath their victim tried to take. They coiled around his throat slowly, almost gently, but the thorns sank deeper with each loop.

Malus tried to speak, but the vines tightened. His eyes bulged. His face darkened from lack of air. He pulled desperately at the restraints, decay magic flickering weakly around his hands, but the forest absorbed it as quickly as he could produce it.

Briar watched through vision that kept narrowing and expanding. Part of her knew she should look away, that she should spare herself this final image, but she couldn't tear her eyes from Malus's face as the life drained from it.

His struggles grew weaker. His eyes, which had been wild with fury and desperation, began to glaze over with that particular emptiness that came only with death.

The vines squeezed tighter. Briar heard a crack. Bones giving way under the pressure. Malus's mouth opened in a soundless scream, but no air moved in or out. The thorns had closed his windpipe completely.

His body spasmed once, twice. Then went still.

The vines held him there for another long moment, thorns still embedded deep in his flesh, before they slowly began to lower his body to the ground. They laid him out almost reverently on the seal's carved surface, then withdrew, sliding back into the earth and leaving only the puncture wounds behind.

Malus's eyes stared sightlessly at the night sky. Blood still seeped from dozens of thorn wounds, pooling beneath him. His chest didn't rise. His heart didn't beat. The autumn decay that had surrounded him constantly, that essence of his power, had dissipated entirely.

Malus was dead.

Eliam stood over his brother's body for a long moment, his chest heaving. The doubled harmonics in his voice had faded, leaving only his own rough tones when he finally spoke.

"It's done."

The words should have carried triumph, relief, even regret, instead they fell empty in the sudden quiet, as empty as Malus's staring eyes.

Around them, the forest began to settle. The vines that had erupted during the fight sank back into the earth. The trees that had leaned and shifted returned to their natural positions. Even the wind, which had howled with Malus's fury, died to nothing more than a gentle breeze.

Briar tried to speak, to tell Eliam she was still conscious, still here. Her lips formed the shapes of words but no sound emerged. Her body had gone beyond exhaustion and that strange liminal space she'd been occupying grew darker at the edges, pulling her down despite her desperate attempt to remain aware.

Eliam took a step in her direction, then another. He paused, his body swaying, his hands rising to grip his head, fingers digging into his temples as if trying to hold something inside from breaking free. A sound escaped him, raw and pained.

Then his knees buckled.

He went down hard, catching himself on his hands before he could topple completely. His head bowed, shoulders heaving with the effort of simply remaining upright. The reunification, the battle, channeling the forest's full power—all of it had finally taken its toll.

She wanted to go to him, but the darkness kept pulling, and her body had nothing left to fight it with.

The last thing she saw before the blackness took her was Eliam on his hands and knees, trying and failing to reach her.

Then nothing.

Chapter Thirty-Seven

The bedchamber was too quiet.

Briar lay on top of the covers beside Eliam, watching the steady rise and fall of his chest. Three days. Three days since they'd returned from the seal, since Malus had died, since Arion had...

She pressed her hand to her chest where the warmth used to live, finding only hollow absence. Not painful, just empty. Like a tooth missing from her mouth that her tongue kept searching for.

Eliam looked peaceful in sleep. Younger. The harsh lines around his mouth had softened, and his white hair spread across the pillow in a way that made her fingers itch to touch it. But she kept her hands to herself, afraid that if she touched him, he'd disappear entirely.

The healers couldn't explain it. His body was whole, healthy. No injuries remained from the fight. The reunification had worked perfectly—too perfectly, one of them had muttered when they thought she wasn't listening. He should have woken by now.

Outside, the Forest Court continued without its king. Thaine held things together through sheer will and the threat of violence against anyone who suggested maybe they didn't need to wait for Eliam's return. The forest itself seemed to be holding its breath, waiting.

She'd woken in this same bed two days ago, her body screaming from what the magic had done to her. Thaine had been there, had explained how they'd carried both her and Eliam back from the seal. How the corruption was receding now that Malus was dead. How the seal itself remained cracked but stable, for now.

Karse had returned to his homeland, whatever debts he felt he owed now settled. Sian had taken temporary stewardship of the Star Court in Arion's absence—a difficult position, managing a court that had lost its lord in a way no one quite understood how to explain.

He hadn't mentioned Arion. Hadn't needed to.

The door opened quietly, and Thaine entered with a tray. The smell of food made her stomach turn.

"You need to eat," he said, setting it on the bedside table.

"I'm not hungry."

"I didn't ask if you were hungry." His tone was gentle despite the words. "You haven't eaten properly in days."

"He hasn't woken up."

"He will." Thaine moved to check Eliam's pulse, a ritual he'd performed every few hours. "His body just needs time to adjust. The reunification was traumatic."

"What if he doesn't—"

"He will."

The certainty in Thaine's voice should have been comforting. Instead, it just highlighted how uncertain everything else felt. The court without Malus's supporters—scattered or dead. The seal, cracked and weeping corruption. Arion, gone but not gone, existing now only as part of Eliam.

A sound from the bed made them both freeze.

Eliam's breathing had changed. His fingers twitched against the covers. His brow furrowed, and he made a soft sound of confusion or discomfort.

Relief flooded through Briar so intensely her knees went weak. She leaned forward, reaching for his hand. "Eliam?"

His eyes opened slowly, unfocused. He blinked several times, and his gaze found Thaine first.

"Thaine?" His voice was rough from disuse. "What are you doing here? Why are you in my chambers?"

"My lord," Thaine's relief was audible. "You've been unconscious for three days. How do you feel?"

"My head is pounding." Eliam started to sit up, wincing. "Three days? That's not—" His eyes landed on Briar for the first time.

She smiled, tears of relief already gathering. "You're awake."

His expression went cold. Not the controlled coldness she knew, the kind he used as armor. This was the flat disinterest of looking at a stranger. He looked from her to Thaine, confusion clear on his face.

"Who is this?" His tone was sharp, annoyed. "Can someone explain why there's a human in my bed?"

The words hit her like physical blows. She stared at him, waiting for the cruel joke to end, for his expression to crack into that smirk she knew so well.

It didn't.

"You don't..." Her voice came out small. "Eliam, it's me."

"I don't know you." He said it with such matter-of-fact certainty that her chest caved in. "Thaine, why is there a strange woman in my private chambers?"

This wasn't happening. This couldn't be happening. She reached for him, needing to touch him, to make him remember.

His hand shot out, slapping hers away with enough force to sting. He immediately shifted away from her on the bed, putting distance between them. The movement was instinctive, the way someone recoils from an unwanted stranger's touch.

"Don't touch me," he said coldly.

Her hand stayed suspended in the air where he'd struck it, her mind unable to process what was happening. Her heart hammered against her ribs, screaming denials her mouth couldn't form.

"My lord," Thaine said carefully, his huntsman's instincts recognizing something was very wrong. "What's the last thing you remember?"

Eliam's brow furrowed. "I was in the forest. Near the western border. There was..." He paused, concentrating. "Something about a disturbance. Report of an accident involving humans near the veil." His frown deepened. "Why can't I remember what happened next?"

Thaine's expression grew grim. "The night you went to investigate the humans. That was over two centuries ago."

"That's absurd." But uncertainty flickered across Eliam's face. He looked around his chambers, and Briar saw him notice small differences. Things that had changed. Her clothes draped over a chair. A glass of water on her side of the bed.

"You made a bargain," Briar said, her voice shaking. "With my mother, I was payment. Then you made a bargain with me for my sister's life."

He looked at her with complete incomprehension before grabbing hold of her wrist and holding it up, his grip so tight she had to bite her lip to keep from crying out. "If we'd made such a bargain, where are the marks? Where is the proof?"

Briar looked down at her arm, now devoid of the twisting vines that had once decorated it. They'd begun fading gradually, she had presumed it was because Malus had died, but now she wondered if perhaps it was because Eliam had simply forgotten making the bargain between Briar and the Forest King null and void.

When she could offer no explanation he released her and turned away. "Thaine, remove her."

"My lord—"

"My head feels like it's splitting open, and there's a strange woman in my bed making ridiculous claims." His voice rose, sharp with pain and irritation. "Remove her. Now."

Thaine's hand settled on Briar's shoulder, gentle but insistent. "Come on."

She couldn't move. Her body had locked up, every muscle rigid with shock. This wasn't real. Couldn't be real. After everything, after all they had been through, he didn't remember any of it.

He didn't remember *her*.

"Briar," Thaine said quietly. "We need to go. We'll figure this out."

She let him guide her from the bed, her movements mechanical. As they reached the door, she looked back. Eliam had already dismissed her, his hand pressed to his temple, eyes closed against the pain.

To him, she was nobody. A strange human who'd somehow ended up in his bed.

The door closed between them, and her legs gave out.

Thaine caught her before she hit the floor, his arms steady around her shoulders.

"Easy," he said quietly. "I've got you."

She couldn't stop shaking. Her teeth chattered despite the warmth of the corridor. Everything felt wrong, disconnected, like she was watching someone else's body fail.

"He doesn't know me." The words came out broken. "He looked right through me like I was nothing."

"Memory loss happens sometimes with magical trauma," Thaine said, but his voice lacked conviction. "The reunification was unprecedented. We don't know what effects—"

"He slapped my hand away." Her voice cracked. "Like I was some stranger trying to touch him. Like I disgusted him."

Thaine's jaw tightened. He bent and scooped her into his arms, carrying her toward her chambers. She didn't protest. Her body felt too heavy, too hollow, like all her bones had been replaced with glass that might shatter if she moved.

Her room was exactly as she'd left it days ago. The bed still unmade from when she'd rushed to Eliam's side after they'd returned. Her clothes scattered on the chair. Everything waiting for a person who no longer existed—the person who belonged to the Forest King.

Thaine set her gently on the bed. "Rest. I'll speak with the healers, see what can be done."

"What if nothing can be done?" The question escaped before she could stop it.

He paused at the door. "Then we figure out another way. You're still here. Still part of this court."

"I'm nobody to him."

"That's not true—"

"You saw his face." The tears finally came, hot and sudden. "I'm just some human who was in his bed. Less than nobody. An annoyance."

Thaine's expression was grim. "Rest. We'll figure this out."

The door closed with a soft click.

Briar curled onto her side, pulling her knees to her chest. Through the wall, she could hear movement—Eliam's footsteps as he moved around his chambers. So close. Close enough that if she pressed her hand to the wall, only stone and wood would separate them.

But the real distance was insurmountable. Six months erased. Every touch, every word, every moment gone like they'd never existed.

The tears came harder. She pressed her face into the pillow to muffle the sobs, but they tore from her chest anyway. Raw, ugly sounds that hurt her throat. Her body shook with the force of them until her ribs ached, until her head pounded, until she had nothing left.

Then she just lay there, hollow and spent, watching the light change.

The sun crept across the floor, marking hours she couldn't feel. Orange to red to purple to gone. The room fell into darkness, and she didn't move to light a candle. The dark felt appropriate.

Through the wall, she heard Eliam's door open. Voices—his and Thaine's. She couldn't make out words, just tones. Eliam sounded irritated. Impatient. The voice of a king dealing with tedious matters he didn't understand.

Was she a tedious matter now?

Her chest ached where the warmth used to live. Not because it was gone—that absence she'd grown used to. But because it was so close, just beyond the wall, inside someone who didn't want her anymore. Who didn't even know to want her.

The door to her room opened quietly. She didn't look up.

"Oh, child." Síocháin's voice, those strange musical tones. "Thaine told me."

The bed dipped as the fae woman sat beside her. Those impossible fingers smoothed her tangled hair back from her face.

"He doesn't remember anything," Briar said into the pillow. "Not the bargain. Not the marking. Not—" Her voice broke. "Not any of it."

"The mind is a strange thing," Síocháin said, continuing to stroke her hair. "Especially when magic tears it apart and puts it back together. The reunification saved his life, but perhaps it cost him something else."

"Everything. It cost him everything."

"No. It cost you everything. He doesn't know what he's lost."

The distinction made it worse. Briar turned her face deeper into the pillow, fresh tears coming though she'd thought she had none left.

"You must be strong," Síocháin said gently. "The court needs—"

"I can't." The words came out muffled but firm. "I can't be strong anymore. I've been strong through everything. Through the bargain, through the hunt, through Malus, through watching Arion die. I can't."

Síocháin was quiet for a long moment. Her fingers never stopped their gentle motion through Briar's hair.

"Then don't," she said finally. "Tonight, you grieve. Tomorrow, we see what comes."

"What if he never remembers?"

"Then you decide if you can live with that. If you can stay here, seeing him every day, being nothing to him. Or if you leave."

Leave. The word sat heavy in the darkness. Leave the Forest Court. Leave Eliam. Go back to the human world where she belonged.

"My sister," Briar said suddenly, remembering. "The bargain. If he doesn't remember it, is it still valid? Is Allegra still healed?"

"Magic doesn't require memory to function. The bargain was made. The price was paid. Your sister remains whole."

Small comfort, but comfort nonetheless. At least her sacrifice hadn't been entirely erased.

Through the wall, she heard Eliam's footsteps again. Pacing. He'd always paced when something bothered him, though he probably didn't remember that about himself either.

"Is everything lost?" Briar asked into the darkness.

Síocháin's fingers stilled in her hair. "I don't know, child. I truly don't know."

The honesty was worse than false comfort would have been. Briar closed her eyes, but sleep wouldn't come. She just lay there, listening to the king she loved pace in the room next door, a stranger wearing the face of someone who'd once wanted her.

The hours stretched toward dawn, and still she didn't sleep. She just existed, suspended between what was and what could never be again.

Day flowed into day and Briar found herself wandering halls that had once felt alien and now felt empty of anything but pain and sorrow. She wasn't sure how she ended up there, but the conservatory was exactly as she remembered.

Glass walls reached toward a winter sky, trapping warmth that had no right to exist in this season. The fountain still bubbled its too-dark water. The vines still reached for anyone who passed, desperate and hungry. And the roses—the roses still grew on the pillar, black-thorned and beautiful.

Briar stood where she'd stood months ago, staring at the flowers that had drunk her blood that first day. Her hand ghosted over her palm where the scars had long since faded. Such a small beginning to everything that followed.

This was for the best. His memory loss was a blessing, a chance for her to leave without the messy pain of rejection. He didn't remember marking her, claiming her, wanting her. Didn't remember the way he'd said her name like ownership and promise combined. It was cleaner this way. Kinder, even.

Her heart disagreed violently.

She reached toward one of the roses, careful now in a way she hadn't been then. The thorns were sharp as ever, gleaming with that hungry intelligence. One pricked her finger despite her caution, and she watched the blood well up, remembering how fascinated he'd been by the sight.

Footsteps echoed on the glass floor. That particular measured pace—not hurried but purposeful and predatory. She'd heard it so many times, but never directed at her like this. Not since those first days.

"What is a human doing in my conservatory?"

She turned slowly, her bleeding finger curling into her palm. He stood in the doorway, blocking the exit without seeming to. He wore black, as always, but there was something different about how he carried himself. He was colder and more distant. The way he'd been before she'd started mattering.

"I needed air," she said.

"The gardens are full of air. Yet you chose to enter a private space." He stepped closer, and her body remembered this—the way he moved when he was about to be deliberately cruel. "Wandering about as though you have some right to be here. As though you belong."

"I *do* belong here." The words came out desperate. "You brought me here months ago. You taught me about your world, about the roses, about—"

"Stop." The word cut through her rambling. He was closer now, close enough that she could feel the heat emanating from him. "I don't know what delusion you're nursing, but I've never brought a human here, let alone taught one anything."

"You did. You gave me a rose and it drank my blood and you said everything here has a price, especially gifts."

His eyes narrowed. Something flickered in them—not recognition but something worse. Interest. The kind of interest a cat shows in a mouse that's behaving strangely.

"You're very familiar with my habits for someone I don't know." His voice dropped to that dangerous softness she knew too well. "Tell me, little human, why do you think you know me?"

"Because you marked me." Her voice cracked. "Because you claimed me in front of your entire court. Because you—"

He moved fast, backing her against the pillar. The roses rustled, eager, remembering her blood.

"Careful," he said, and his breath ghosted across her face. "Lying about a fae lord is dangerous. Claiming intimacy where none exists is... unwise."

"I'm not lying."

"No?" His hand came up, fingers wrapping around her throat, feeling her pulse race. "Then why does my mind not know you? Why does my magic not recognize you?"

Tears burned her eyes. "I don't know."

He studied her face with that clinical curiosity that used to precede either cruelty or unexpected gentleness. Now it was just cold assessment. His thumb traced along her jaw, and her traitorous body responded, remembering this touch even if he didn't.

"Interesting," he murmured. "You react as though you know me. Your body expects my touch."

"Because you've touched me a hundred times."

"Have I?" His head tilted, predatory interest sharpening. "Then you won't mind if I test that claim."

Before she could respond, his mouth was on hers.

It was nothing like before. No careful control, no possessive tenderness, no dark affection. This was meant to prove a point, to frighten her, to show her what happened when humans overstepped. His kiss was cruel, invasive, taking without giving.

But his body betrayed him. She felt the moment he registered how perfectly she fit against him, how her mouth opened under his without hesitation, how she knew exactly how he liked to be kissed. He made a sound—confusion, frustration, want he didn't understand—and pressed closer.

That's when she shoved him.

Her palms hit his chest and pushed hard, and he actually stepped back. The old Eliam would never have allowed it, would have grabbed her wrists and held her in place. But this Eliam let her push him away, and somehow that was worse.

"There," he said, his breathing slightly uneven. "You see? You know you don't belong here. Your body knows I'm a threat."

"You're not a threat. You're just lost."

"I'm exactly where I've always been." But there was something in his expression—a flicker of uncertainty, of frustration at his own reaction to her. "You're the one who's lost. A human with delusions of importance."

"Then why did kissing me affect you?"

His jaw clenched. "It didn't."

"Liar."

The temperature dropped so fast frost formed on the glass walls. "Leave."

"Eliam—"

"Leave before I decide to stop being generous about your trespass." His voice was deadly quiet. "Whatever game you're playing, whatever you think you're owed, it ends now."

She stood frozen, her lips still burning from his cruel kiss, watching him walk away. At the door, he paused without turning.

"And little human? Don't come here again. The roses remember blood, and they're always hungry."

Then he was gone, leaving her alone with the hungry flowers and the shattering of her heart.

Chapter Thirty-Eight

T he night stretched endless and hollow.

Briar lay on her bed, staring at the ceiling, counting each sound from the room next door. Eliam's footsteps pacing—seven steps, turn, seven steps, turn. The scrape of a chair. The creak of his bed when he finally lay down. Every sound proof of how close he was and how utterly unreachable he'd become.

Her lips still ached from his kiss. She touched them with trembling fingers, feeling the slight swelling where he'd been deliberately rough. Her body remembered even if he didn't—the way she'd melted into him for that brief moment before reality crashed back. The way he'd made that confused sound, caught between want and rejection.

She pressed her palm flat against the wall that separated them. The stone was cold, solid, real. On the other side, he was probably sleeping peacefully, unburdened by memories of her. No dreams of gardens or moonlight or the way she'd gasped his name. Just blissful, empty sleep.

Her chest hitched with a sob she wouldn't let escape. She'd cried enough. Been weak enough. But the pain kept building, wave after wave of it, until she couldn't breathe properly. Her throat burned with suppressed sounds. Her eyes burned with tears that wouldn't stop coming no matter how many times she wiped them away.

She touched her neck where the marks used to be. The skin was smooth now, unmarked, ordinary. As if he'd never claimed her at all. Her fingers searched for any trace, any raised line or roughness that would prove it had been real. Nothing. Just soft human skin that would never bear his thorns again.

The bargain was complete. Allegra was healed. The bond was gone.

The thought kept circling through her mind as the hours crawled toward dawn. She had no reason to stay. No claim on him. No place here.

By the time pale light crept through her window, she knew what she had to do.

She found Thaine in the weapons hall, running a whetstone along a blade with mechanical precision. The scrape of metal on stone stopped when she entered. He looked up, and his expression crumbled slightly before he caught himself.

"You're leaving." Not a question.

"The bargain is complete. The bond is gone." The words came out steady though her chest felt like it was caving in. "I want to leave on my own terms."

"Briar—"

"Don't." Her voice cracked. She pressed her hand to her mouth, fighting for control. After a moment, she tried again. "He kissed me yesterday to prove a point. To show me I don't belong here. And he's right. I don't."

"He doesn't know what he's doing. If we just give him time—"

"Time for what?" The words burst out, too loud in the quiet hall. "Time to maybe remember? To watch him look through me every day? Time to see him find someone else because he doesn't know I ever existed?"

She sank onto a bench, her whole body shaking. Thaine crossed to her, crouched in front of her, his usual stoicism cracking.

"I can't do this anymore," she whispered. "Every time I see him, it breaks me a little more. He's right there, Thaine. Right there. And he doesn't know me. Doesn't want to know me. I need to leave before there's nothing left of me to save."

"Where will you go?"

"Back to my life. My family. My world where things make sense."

"You belong here too."

"No." She met his eyes, and she saw him flinch at whatever was in hers. "I belonged to him. Without that, I'm just a human in a world that wants to eat me. I want to go home. Please."

Thaine's jaw worked. She could see him fighting for arguments, for reasons to make her stay. Finally, his shoulders dropped.

"When?"

"Now. Before I lose my nerve. Before he wakes up and I have to see him look through me again."

He stood slowly, like his bones hurt. "The veil is thin near the western border. I can take you through."

The walk through the castle was agony. Every corner held a memory. Here, where he'd pressed her against the door after the first dinner. The dining hall where he'd fed her from his own hand. The corridor that led to gardens she'd never see again.

At his door, she stopped.

Her feet wouldn't move past it. Her hand rose without permission, palm flat against the wood. On the other side, she could hear him stirring. Waking. In moments he'd rise, dress in his dark clothes, and go about his day without a single thought of her.

"Please," she whispered to the door, to him, to any power that might be listening. "Please remember."

She waited, just for a moment. Just to torture herself with the possibility that it might open, that he might remember, that this might not be the end.

The door stayed closed.

Thaine's hand settled on her shoulder, gentle but insistent. She let him guide her away, each step feeling like tearing off pieces of herself and leaving them behind.

The forest paths opened reluctantly for Thaine. The journey felt both endless and far too quick, her body moving while her heart screamed to turn back, to try one more time, to fight harder. But she was so tired of fighting, so tired of being strong.

Before she knew it, they were at the veil, that shimmer in the air that separated worlds.

"Your car is just beyond," Thaine said quietly.

She could see it through the shimmer. Her dusty, ordinary car in an ordinary parking lot in an ordinary world where magic didn't exist and neither did Forest Kings who forgot the women they'd claimed.

"Thaine." Her voice broke completely. "What if he never remembers?"

"Then he's lost something precious." His voice was rough. "And he'll never know it."

That broke her. The tears came hard and fast, her shoulders shaking with the force of them. She covered her face with her hands, trying to muffle the sounds, but they tore from her anyway.

"I have to go," she gasped between sobs. "If I don't go now, I never will."

"I know."

She stepped toward the veil, then stopped. "Tell him—" She stopped. Tell him what? That she loved him? That she'd chosen him even when he'd been cruel? That losing him like this was worse than if he'd died? "Don't tell him anything."

She stepped through.

The transition was jarring, as everything magical, everything otherworldly, everything that had made her feel like she might be more than ordinary, fell away. She stood in a cracked parking lot beside a car covered in two weeks of dust and bird droppings, wearing clothes that smelled of the fae realm but were already losing that scent in the mundane air.

The car door handle was cold under her fingers.

She got in and turned the key. Nothing. The engine clicked but wouldn't catch. Of course. Two weeks of cold had killed the battery. She turned the key again, and again, each failed attempt feeling like another small cruelty.

"Please," she whispered to the dead engine. "Please, just work."

Still nothing.

She folded forward, her forehead hitting the steering wheel, and screamed. The sound filled the car, raw and broken and terrible. She screamed until her throat burned, until her voice cracked, until there was nothing left but harsh breathing and the taste of copper in her mouth.

The engine suddenly roared to life, magic giving her this one last gift.

Through blurred vision, she saw Thaine's hand lowering in the space between worlds. Then he was gone. The shimmer was gone. There was just trees and sky and the normal world that didn't know she'd been gone for months, that didn't care that her heart was shattered, that would expect her to just continue as if nothing had happened.

She put the car in drive, but her vision was too blurred with tears to see. She had to pull over after barely making it out of the parking lot, sobbing so hard she couldn't breathe. Her chest hurt. Everything hurt. She beat her fists against the steering wheel until her hands ached, needing the physical pain to match what was tearing through her chest.

A couple walked by, glancing at the woman having a breakdown in her car, then quickly looking away. The normal world, where people politely ignored visible grief.

Briar drove home through tears that wouldn't stop, taking wrong turns because she could barely see, having to pull over twice more when the sobs made it impossible to continue. By the time she reached her house, she had nothing left. No tears. No voice. No energy.

Just an emptiness that she was convinced would never be filled.

She sat in the car for a long moment, staring at her ordinary house in her ordinary world, trying to remember how to be ordinary again. Trying to forget the feeling of thorns and shadow and a possessive voice whispering her name in the darkness.

The keys were heavy in her hand. Real. Cold metal with worn edges from years of use. She turned them over once, twice, then finally climbed out. Each step toward the house felt heavier than the last, her feet reluctant to carry her back to this life. What would she say when Allegra asked where she'd been? How could she explain the things she'd witnessed, experienced, lost?

She couldn't.

Briar climbed the steps to the porch and stopped. She stared hard at the peeling paint on the door frame, at the doorbell that David had promised to fix a lifetime ago, and the welcome mat that said "Home Sweet Home" in faded cursive.

Everything was exactly as she'd left it months ago, no, two weeks ago—time was a broken thing now, fractured between worlds—but everything about it felt distant. It was too small, too bright, too simple. As if she were seeing it through different eyes, eyes that had seen impossible things and could never quite focus on the mundane again.

She still had her key but using it felt wrong, so she knocked instead, the sound sharp in the quiet afternoon.

Footsteps approached, quick and eager. The door flew open and Allegra stood there, vibrantly alive, color in her cheeks and a glow about her that had nearly been snuffed out. The sight of her sister's health should have filled Briar with joy. Instead, she felt nothing. A hollow acknowledgement that the bargain had worked.

"Oh my God, finally!" Allegra practically shrieked, throwing her arms around Briar. "Mom said you went on some last-minute trip but that's so not like you and you didn't even text and—" She pulled back, eyes narrowing. "You didn't bring me anything."

"What?"

"From your trip. Two weeks and you didn't bring me back anything? Not even like, airport chocolate?"

Briar stared at her sister. Airport chocolate. As if she'd been to Europe or Vegas or somewhere that sold souvenirs instead of bleeding on ancient stones while magic tore through her body.

"I... forgot."

"You forgot." Allegra stepped back, arms crossed. "You disappear for two weeks without saying goodbye, don't even *call*. Mom acts all weird and secretive about where you went, and you just *forgot* to bring me something?"

Their mother appeared in the hallway behind Allegra, and the temperature seemed to drop. She looked older, grayer, but her eyes were sharp and alert and afraid.

"Briar." Not a greeting, but a statement. An assessment.

"Mom."

"Allegra, why don't you go put the kettle on? Your sister probably wants tea."

"She probably wants to explain where she's been," Allegra muttered, but she headed toward the kitchen.

The moment she was gone, their mother stepped forward, voice dropping to a whisper. "What happened? How are you here?"

"He let me go."

"Let you go?" Her mother's eyes darted toward the door, as if expecting to see fae warriors stalking down the suburban street. "Or did you escape? Are they going to come looking for you?"

Briar fought the urge to frown. Not 'are you okay?' Not 'I'm so glad you're safe.' Just immediate fear about what Briar's presence might bring. If she had ever doubted her mother's priorities, they were devastatingly clear now.

"He doesn't remember me," Briar said at last, fighting to keep her voice even. "The bargain is complete. Allegra is healed. I'm free to go."

"He doesn't—how is that possible?"

"Does it matter?"

Her mother's hand went to her throat, a nervous gesture Briar recognized from childhood. "If he doesn't remember the bargain, will it hold? Will Allegra stay healthy?"

Of course. Even now, the only concern was whether Allegra would stay healed. Not what it had cost Briar. Not what she'd endured.

"Magic doesn't require memory," Briar said, repeating Síocháin's words. "The bargain stands."

Relief flooded her mother's face, followed immediately by suspicion. "Then why would he let you go? What aren't you telling me?"

"Mom!" Allegra called from the kitchen. "The kettle's whistling!"

They moved to the kitchen, the familiar space feeling like a stage set and she didn't know the part she was meant to play. The white cabinets and cheerful yellow walls belonged to a different life. Briar sat at the table where she'd eaten thousands of meals, her hands flat on the surface, trying to ground herself.

Allegra poured tea, chattering about her classes, her friends, how she'd joined theatre club and would Briar come to her first performance. "It's Peter Pan, I'm playing Wendy," she said.

"I'll try," Briar replied, unwilling to make any more promises she wouldn't be able to keep.

"So where did you go?" Allegra asked, sliding a mug toward Briar. "Mom just said you needed to take a trip."

Briar looked at their mother. "That's what you told her? That I went on a trip? What were you planning to say when I never came back?"

Allegra's eyes widened, looking between them.

"What do you mean, never came back?"

"Nothing," their mother said quickly. "Briar's being dramatic."

Briar gripped her mug so tightly her knuckles had gone white.

"I was going to cross that bridge when I came to it," June continued, not looking at either daughter. "I didn't expect... I thought..."

"You believed I was gone forever." Briar's voice was hollow. "You made peace with that. Were you going to tell her I died or that I just abandoned you both?"

"Okay, what is happening right now?" Allegra set down her mug hard enough to slosh tea. "What are you talking about?"

"Nothing," their mother said again, but her hands were shaking. "Briar just... had some difficulties. While she was gone."

Difficulties. Briar almost laughed. She'd been marked by thorns, hunted through forests, kissed by someone who forgot her entirely, watched someone die in her arms. Difficulties.

"What really happened, Bri? You look terrible," Allegra said, studying Briar's face. "Have you been eating? You've lost weight."

"I'm fine."

"You're not fine. You're being weird. More weird than usual."

"Allegra," their mother warned.

"What? She disappears for two weeks, comes back looking like a ghost, and you're both talking in code about never coming back and bridges and—" She stopped, frustration clear on her face. "Why won't anyone ever tell me anything? You guys always do this! I'm not a baby anymore."

Their mother looked away. Briar couldn't find words that would make sense. How did she explain the truth when the truth sounded like an impossible lie?

"Is this about money?" Allegra asked suddenly. "Because of my hospital stuff?"

The guess was so far from the truth but so close to the heart of it that Briar almost laughed. Yes, it had been about the medical bills, in a way. About the cost of keeping Allegra alive.

"It's complicated," Briar said softly.

"You always say that." Allegra's bottom lip jutted out in a pout, a childhood habit she hadn't quite outgrown. "Everything's always complicated and I'm always too young to understand."

Briar looked at her sister, healthy, alive, oblivious, and then at her mother, guilty, frightened, already calculating dangers. The kitchen suddenly felt too small, too full of everything she couldn't explain and they wouldn't understand.

"I'm moving out," she said.

Both of them stared.

"What?" Allegra asked.

"I need my own space. Time to figure things out."

"Figure what out? You just got back from wherever—" Allegra started to protest.

"I just—I can't be here." The words came out harder than intended.

"Briar," her mother started, reaching across the table.

Briar pulled back. The gesture was small but her mother's hand froze midair, then slowly withdrew.

"Is this because of where you went?" her mother asked carefully. "Did something happen that might bring... trouble?"

There it was again. The fear. Not for Briar but *of* her and what she might bring to their doorstep.

"No trouble," Briar said, standing. The chair scraped against linoleum, too loud. "I'm not a danger to you. I'm just... I'm done."

"Done?" Allegra stood too. "Done with what? With us?"

"With being the one who fixes everything." The words tumbled out before Briar could stop them. "With being the one who handles it, who takes care of it, who pays the price."

"What price? Bri, you're scaring me."

She was scaring herself. The emotions were still too raw, too visible. She needed to leave before she said something that couldn't be taken back. Before she screamed that Allegra's miracle cure had cost everything, that their mother had traded her away like currency.

"I'll get my things later," she said, moving toward the door.

"You can't just leave!" Allegra followed her. The hurt and confusion in her sister's voice gave Briar pause. "You just got home!"

She took a deep breath, hand resting on the door knob. "I'm sorry, Ally-cat. This isn't home anymore."

"So you're abandoning us," her mother said quietly. June hadn't moved from the table, her hands wrapped around her tea mug like it might protect her. "After every-thing."

After everything. After years of sacrifice. After working multiple jobs to help cover costs when June had been unable to work her own job. After giving up college, her youth, her dreams. After being traded to a fae lord and forgotten entirely.

What more did her mother want?

"I saved her," Briar said, hand tightening on the door handle. "The debt is paid. Whatever happens now, you'll have to handle yourselves."

She left before they could respond, closing the door on Allegra's confused protests and her mother's calculating silence. She walked toward her car, keys already in her hand, needing to leave before she broke completely.

"Bri, wait!"

Footsteps slapped on concrete behind her. Before Briar could turn, Allegra crashed into her, thin arms wrapping around her waist from behind.

"Don't go," Allegra said into her back, voice muffled by Briar's coat. "I don't under-stand what's happening but please don't go."

Briar's composure cracked. She turned in her sister's arms and hugged her properly, tightly, the way she had when Allegra was small and crawled into her bed at night because she was scared of thunderstorms. The memory made Briar's chest ache.

"I love you," Allegra said, voice muffled against shoulder. "Whatever's wrong, whatever happened on your trip or wherever you really went, I love you. You're my sister and I love you."

The tears came then, hot and sudden. Briar held her sister tighter, memorizing this, the simple pure love of a child who didn't understand and loved anyway.

"I love you too," Briar whispered into Allegra's hair. "So much. More than you'll ever know."

"Then why are you leaving?"

"Because I need to figure some things out. Adult things. Complicated things."

"I hate when you say that."

"I know." Briar pulled back enough to see Allegra's face, those bright eyes that held no trace of illness now. "But this isn't about you, okay? You didn't do anything wrong. I just...this is about me needing space. It doesn't mean I don't love you."

"Will you visit?"

"Of course."

"Promise?"

Briar couldn't promise. She didn't know if she could keep coming back to this house, seeing the life she'd saved while mourning the one she'd lost. But Allegra was looking at her with such hope, such desperate need.

"I'll try," she said instead. "I'll really try."

Allegra hugged her once more, fierce and quick, then stepped back. "Okay. But I'm texting you every day and you better answer."

"Deal."

Briar climbed into her car and started the engine. In the side mirror she could see where Allegra stood on the sidewalk, shivering in just her sweater. Briar waited a moment, but Allegra didn't go inside. She stayed there, watching, as Briar pulled away from the curb.

She glanced in the rearview mirror and saw her sister wave. After a moment, Briar waved back, trying to match her sister's enthusiasm, but coming up short.

Briar drove through town without thinking, muscle memory guiding her through turns while her mind stayed carefully blank. The streets blurred together, familiar landmarks she didn't want to recognize, memories she didn't want to acknowledge.

Then she saw the sign.

Sea Breeze Motel. The same faded turquoise paint. The same flickering neon with the "e" in Breeze dark. The same cracked asphalt parking lot.

If she had known she would end up back here, she might never have left to begin with.

Her hands turned the wheel without her permission.

The parking lot was nearly empty. Just a beat-up sedan and a motorcycle that had seen better days. No forest. No vines breaking through concrete. No impossible trees older than memory. Just an ugly motel that rented by the hour and didn't ask questions.

She sat in her car for a long moment, engine running, staring at the office door. The same door she'd burst through while running from Thaine. The same window where she'd seen the clerk wrapped in roots and white flowers, dreaming terrible dreams.

Her hand was on the gear shift to reverse when something made her turn off the engine instead.

The office smelled exactly the same—mildew and air freshener that didn't quite cover the underlying rot. But the clerk was different. Younger, maybe twenty, with gauged ears and tattoos creeping up his neck. He didn't look up from his phone when she entered.

"Forty-nine plus tax."

The same price. The same bored tone. Different voice.

"Room 23," she said.

That made him look up, a flicker of annoyance crossing his face. "I got eighteen available. Take your pick."

"I want 23."

He stared at her for a moment, then shrugged. "Whatever. Forty-nine plus tax."

She paid cash. The same amount she'd paid that night when she thought she was being clever, thought she could outsmart a bargain made with something ancient. The register looked the same. Even the pen was the same cheap Bic, though the ink was blue now instead of black.

Room 23 was at the far end, exactly where it had been. The key stuck in the lock the same way. The door opened with the same protesting creak.

Everything was identical. The water-stained ceiling. The carpet that felt damp even when it wasn't. The bedspread with its pattern of faded seahorses that had probably been cheerful once. The bathroom door that didn't quite close properly.

Briar stood in the doorway, unable to move forward. What felt like a lifetime ago, this room had been transformed into something impossible, had been claimed by forest and fury. But looking at it now, it was just a room. Ugly and sad and utterly mundane.

She made herself walk to the bathroom. The tiles were intact, grout stained but unbroken. No sign that massive roots had burst through, splitting ceramic and porcelain. She touched the spot where the toilet had cracked, where water had sprayed everywhere before being absorbed by spreading moss.

Nothing.

Just old caulk and rust stains.

The window she'd smashed through was whole, not even a crack in the glass. She pressed her palm against it, half-expecting it to shatter at her touch, for vines to grab her wrist, for Thaine's mocking voice to tell her she was predictable.

Silence.

She sat on the bed in the exact spot where she'd woken to find her mark burning, the forest coming to claim her. The mattress sagged the same way. The springs creaked with the same tired protest. But no moss grew across the floor and no roots split the walls. No voice from everywhere and nowhere told her she was caught.

Fingers traced the place where the mark had been, pressing hard enough to hurt, trying to find some evidence that it had been real.

Nothing.

The room felt bigger than she remembered. Or maybe she felt smaller. Hollow. Like something essential had been scooped out and she was just the shell that remained, going through motions that looked like living.

Outside, cars passed on the highway. Real cars with real people living real lives. Inside, she sat in a room that had once been transformed into something impossible, looking for proof that any of it had happened.

Her phone buzzed. Allegra again.

Mom says you need space but are you okay? Love you

She stared at the message. Love you. So simple and uncomplicated. From someone who would never know what that love had cost.

Love you too. I'm okay.

The lie came easily. Everything was a lie now. She was okay. She was fine. She was handling things. She was moving forward. All lies told to make others comfortable while she sat in a cheap motel room, looking for evidence of magic in a world that had none.

She lay back on the bed, stared at the ceiling where the stains made the same pattern as before and listened as the heater made the same rattling wheeze. Everything was exactly as it had been, as if the forest had never come, as if she'd never been marked, claimed, and then forgotten.

As if none of it had ever been real at all.

The sun set eventually, darkness filling the room. She didn't turn on the lights. Just lay there in the dark, in the same room where she'd been captured, now capturing herself in a different kind of prison. One made of memory and loss and the terrible possibility that she was the only one who remembered any of it had happened.

Tomorrow she'd find an apartment, maybe enroll in school, try to build some kind of life.

But tonight?

Tonight she lay in Room 23 of the Sea Breeze Motel, pressing her unmarked wrist to her chest where warmth no longer lived, and tried to convince herself that forgetting would be a mercy.

She failed.

Chapter Thirty-Nine

One Month Later

The alarm buzzed at 5:30 PM, pulling Briar from the restless half-sleep she'd fallen into after her morning shift at the hospital. She silenced it immediately, already regretting the twenty-minute nap. Sleep brought dreams, and dreams brought memories of places that couldn't exist.

Her studio apartment was aggressively normal. White walls covered in cheap prints of abstract art—nothing that could remind her of enchanted forests or midnight gardens. IKEA furniture in bright yellows and blues that had no equivalent in the fae realm. Every lamp she owned stayed on until she left, keeping shadows at bay.

She rolled out of bed and pulled on her scrubs—navy blue, practical, forgettable. The community college's nursing program had been happy to accept her despite the gap in her transcripts. She'd told them family medical emergency. Close enough to true that the lie came easily.

Her reflection in the bathroom mirror looked functional. Concealer hiding the dark circles that had become permanent residents under her eyes. Her face thinner than it used to be, cheekbones sharp enough to cut. She'd dropped fifteen pounds in a month without trying. Food tasted like ash most days.

Her phone buzzed. Allegra.

Mom's making your favorite tonight. Come over after class?

Briar stared at the message. Her sister had been texting more lately, worried about Briar's sudden distance. Allegra was thriving—healthy, energetic, full of life. Everything the bargain had promised. Everything Briar had paid for with a price no one else remembered.

Can't tonight. Big test tomorrow.

The lie came automatically. There was no test, but she couldn't sit across from Allegra and pretend everything was fine. They thought she'd had some kind of breakdown and moved out. Let them think that. It was easier than the truth they'd never believe.

She packed her backpack with mechanical precision. Anatomy textbook. Laptop. Notebooks filled with meticulous notes she took to keep her hands busy and mind occupied. A protein bar she wouldn't eat. Her hand hovered over her keys, and she caught herself looking toward the corner where shadows pooled despite the aggressive lighting.

Nothing there. Never anything there. Just her broken mind playing tricks.

The walk to the bus stop was routine now. Seven minutes through suburban streets where normal people lived normal lives. A woman walked her dog. Kids played in a yard despite the cold. Everyone bundled in winter coats that were just fabric and insulation, nothing magical about them.

She told herself she took the bus because parking downtown was expensive and difficult, but the truth was simpler—she felt less alone. On the bus, strangers surrounded her without demanding anything. No questions about the shadows under her eyes or why her hands sometimes shook. Just bodies and noise and the mundane rhythm of stops and starts that let her exist without explaining herself.

Briar sat behind two girls from her program.

"Did you see Brady's Instagram from that party?"

"Oh my god, yes. He was so wasted."

"I heard he hooked up with Maria."

"No way! Isn't she dating—"

Briar pressed her forehead against the cold window, letting their chatter wash over her. Normal drama. Normal problems. She tried to remember caring about such things, but it felt like remembering a different person. Someone who hadn't been marked by thorns, hadn't watched light die in silver eyes, hadn't been kissed by someone who didn't know her.

Her hand rose to her throat, fingers searching for marks that were never there. She jerked it back down, but not before catching an elderly woman watching her with concern.

The community college's medical building was overcrowded and underfunded, fluorescent lights harsh enough to eliminate any shadows. She took her usual seat in the back corner of the lecture hall, opened her notebook to a fresh page, and tried to care about the circulatory system.

"The heart has four chambers," Professor Martinez began, pulling up a diagram. "Two atria, two ventricles. Blood flows in, blood flows out. The average heart beats 100,000 times per day."

Briar wrote it all down, every word, keeping her hands busy. But her mind drifted.

Did fae hearts work the same way? When Eliam had let her feel his heartbeat that night in the garden, it had seemed slower than human normal. When Arion died, had his heart stopped first, or did the light just fade all at once?

"Miss Washington?"

She jerked back to attention. The professor was looking at her expectantly. The entire class had turned to stare.

"I asked if you could explain the difference between oxygenated and deoxygenated blood flow."

"Right. Yes." She forced her brain to work. "Oxygenated blood flows from the lungs to the left atrium, then to the left ventricle, then out through the aorta to the body. Deoxygenated blood returns through the vena cava to the right atrium, then right ventricle, then to the lungs via the pulmonary artery."

"Correct." The professor moved on, but a few classmates still stared. She never volunteered answers, never joined study groups, never stayed after class. The ghost girl who knew all the material but never seemed present.

Three hours of pretending to care about things that didn't matter. Three hours of fighting not to think about what time it would be in the Forest Court. Whether Eliam had found someone else to occupy his bed. Whether he ever had strange dreams about a human woman he didn't remember.

By the time class ended, full dark had fallen. Winter came early and harsh this year, or maybe cold just felt different now. She waited for the bus with other students complaining about the exam next week, about their clinical rotations, about normal things that should matter.

The ride home was quieter, fewer passengers at this hour. She let herself close her eyes, just for a moment, and immediately saw silver-touched shadows behind her lids. Her eyes snapped open.

Her apartment building's security light was broken, leaving the entrance darker than usual. She climbed the three flights to her floor, keys already in hand, moving quickly through the pools of shadow that gathered in the stairwell corners.

Her apartment was as she'd left it—every light still on, no shadows allowed. She dropped her backpack by the door and moved through her nightly routine. Protein shake she'd force herself to drink. Shower hot enough to hurt. Meditation app that never worked. Textbook reading that might hold her attention for twenty minutes if she was lucky.

She stood at her door in pajamas and a coat, ready to take out the trash. Her hand was on the doorknob when she hesitated.

The lights were all on, but darkness still gathered in corners, under furniture, behind doors. Darkness that felt heavier lately, more present. More watchful.

She glanced over her shoulder toward the living room. The shadows in the corner by the bookshelf seemed deeper despite the aggressive lighting. For just a moment, she could swear they had shape, substance, intent.

But when she blinked, it was just a shadow. Just her broken mind trying to make the ordinary world magical again. Trying to pretend she hadn't left everything that mattered in a realm she could never return to.

She pulled the door closed behind her, the lock clicking with finality.

Inside the empty apartment, the shadows in the corner shifted and solidified. A figure stood where darkness had pooled, watching the door she'd just walked through. Patient. Silent.

Waiting.

Content Warnings

- Dubious consent situations

- Captivity and imprisonment

- Sexual Assault (Not the MMC)

- Coercion

- Violence

- Emotional abuse

- Blood and gore

- Forced bargains/loss of autonomy

- Morally gray characters who commit questionable acts

- Dark romance with toxic relationship dynamics that evolve

About the Author

A velley Greer is a romance and fantasy author who firmly believes that the best stories happen when magic gets messy and love gets complicated.

Growing up devouring the works of Robin Hobb, Tad Williams, Madeleine L'Engle, and Philip Pullman, Avelley learned early that the most compelling tales live in the grey areas—where heroes make terrible decisions, villains have excellent points, and nobody's moral compass points quite north.

When not conjuring up new ways to torment beloved characters (before giving them their hard-won happily-ever-afters, of course), Avelley can be found:

- Ugly-crying over the latest K-drama plot twist

- Defending unpopular BTS theories with the passion of a thousand suns

- Playing survival horror games while all four cats—Oliver, Hobi, Rosie, and Nova—judge from various perches

- Watching horror movies through strategically placed fingers

Avelley writes for readers who appreciate their fantasy with sharp edges, their romance with real stakes, and their happy endings earned through blood, sweat, and maybe a few supernatural tears. She's particularly drawn to stories featuring morally grey characters, unconventional magic systems, and relationships that challenge everything we think we know about love.

Currently plotting her next novel while surrounded by too many notebooks, an unreasonable amount of purple pens, and at least one cat who's definitely plotting world domination.

Follow Me

Want to stay up to date on the upcoming releases, sneak peaks, and other bookish related content?

Mailing List – subscribepage.io/m96ZTx
Instagram – https://www.instagram.com/avelley_greer/
Tiktok – https://www.tiktok.com/@authoravelleygreer

Want More...?

A KISS SO CRUEL

Book One of the Fractured Crown Trilogy

RACING RUIN

A Dark Contemporary Romance

Available on Barnes & Noble, Amazon & Kindle Unlimited